The Beauty Chorus

'Take three girls, with one thing in common – flying. Add a war and a smattering of romantic interest, and you have the recipe for a great read... *The Beauty Chorus* is a story of love and adventure, of loss and pain, and heroism. I can already see the movie.'
Daily Mail

'Drawn from the home front diaries of the second world war, this time in Britain, is Kate Lord Brown's rip-roaring *The Beauty Chorus*... Dazzling debutante Evie Chase pitches in and jumps into the cockpit to fuel a novel that covers the popular literary terrain of tragedy, romance and fortitude... The book soars as if it has a pair of Merlin engines strapped to its covers... a dramatic bird's eye view.'
Spectator

'An authentic and moving novel about the women who flew Spitfires (and other planes) during the war. three girls from different backgrounds find romance, confront loss and forge friendships.'
The Lady

Kate Lord Brown has worked as an art
consultant, curating collections for palaces
and embassies in Europe and the Middle East.
She was a finalist in ITV's The People's Author
competition in 2009. Visit her website at
www.katelordbrown.com.

The Beauty Chorus

KATE LORD BROWN

CORVUS

First published in hardback in Great Britain in 2011
by Corvus, an imprint of Atlantic Books.

This edition first published in paperback in Great Britain in 2012 by Corvus.

987654321

A CIP catalogue record for this book is available from
the British Library.

ISBN: 978-1-84887-872-3 (paperback)
ISBN: 978-0-85789-425-0 (eBook)

Printed in Great Britain by Clays Ltd, St Ives plc

Corvus
An imprint of Atlantic Books Ltd
Ormond House
26-27 Boswell Street
London WC1N 3JZ

For GB, CB & GB

Oh! I have slipped the surly bonds of Earth
And danced the skies on laughter-silvered wings;
Sunward I've climbed, and joined the tumbling mirth
Of sun-split clouds — and done a hundred things
You have not dreamed of — wheeled and soared and swung
High in the sunlit silence. Hov'ring there,
I've chased the shouting wind along, and flung
My eager craft through footless halls of air...
Up, up the long, delirious, burning blue
I've topped the wind-swept heights with easy grace
Where never lark nor even eagle flew —
And, while with silent lifting mind I've trod
The high untrespassed sanctity of space,
Put out my hand, and touched the face of God.

'High Flight' by John Gillespie Magee, Jr,
Spitfire pilot, No 412 Fighter Squadron RCAF.
Killed 11 December 1941, aged 19.

Squires Gate, 11.39 a.m., Sunday 5th January, 1941

I have four and a half hours to live. I am leaning against the wing of the yellow-bellied Airspeed Oxford, smoking contentedly while the ground crew chaps run their final checks. The freezing rain hisses as it hits the glowing coal of my cigarette, drums softly on the tin roof of the hangar. Call me Johnnie, by the way. Everyone does.

There is no changing fate, but when I look back at my last moments on earth I want to rush through the molecules of my body and shake off my reverie: I want to yell 'Wake up, you silly bugger, make the most of this! This is the last time you will feel the rain on your face, the ground beneath your feet.' But I didn't believe in premonitions and guardian angels so I doubt I would sense anything. Now I know better.

The flight to the RAF base at Kidlington in Oxfordshire should have been simple enough – ninety minutes at most. What I did with my last hours is a mystery. The journey is a government secret still. Maybe I'll tell you why I died 100 miles off course, maybe I won't. Why don't you make up your own mind?

WINTER

1

'Ten, nine, eight ...' Swing music and laughter from the party drifted out through the open door to Evie. As she walked down the long moonlit driveway to her father's house, snowflakes caught on her eyelashes. Her footsteps on the frozen gravel fell into time with the big-band tune bubbling into the chill midnight air and she sang under her breath: 'How High the Moon ...' The Bentleys and Rolls Royces parked along the drive had a light coating of snow on them already, and in spite of her white fur coat she shivered with cold, her feet frozen in her silver evening shoes.

'Miss Evelyn!' The butler stepped forward to catch her mink coat as it slipped from her shoulders. As the staff door swung closed, Evie caught sight of the grey-uniformed chauffeurs smoking and chatting, one with the pink-cheeked housemaid on his knee sipping Guinness. 'Your father has been asking for you,' the butler said as she shook the snow from her glossy dark hair.

'Has he, Ross?' She smoothed her pale silver satin Schiaparelli gown, and raised her chin defiantly as a cheer went up.

'1941!' Leo 'Lucky' Chase cried out, one arm raising a glass of champagne, the other clutching Virginia, his latest wife.

'I'm amazed he even noticed I'd gone.' Evie nodded her thanks to Ross. She touched up her red lipstick in the hall mirror then twisted her shoulder to adjust the long rope of diamonds that fell from her throat to the deep curved back of the dress. She glanced down at the hem of her gown and noticed for the first time how wet it was from trudging through the snow. 'In for a penny ...' she murmured.

Instead of going in to the party, Evie walked on across the marble hall. Heads turned as she passed, the silver dress rippling over her curves like mercury. She flung open the terrace windows and slipped off her shoes, swinging them nonchalantly in one hand. She dropped them at the edge of the steaming, heated pool. Leo liked it to be warm all year. A crowd gathered on the terrace as Evie executed a perfect dive, her body streaking underwater like a silver fish before surfacing at the other end. A cheer greeted her as she stepped elegantly up from the pool, squeezing the water from her hair.

'Evie! You're bonkers!' A young officer in uniform planted a kiss on her cheek and draped a blanket around her shoulders. 'Happy New Year!'

'Hello, Peter.' She slipped her arm through his.

'Come on, let's get you inside before you catch your death.'

He led her around the packed dance floor to the bar. People smiled indulgently as she passed – you could always count on Evie to make an entrance.

'Where have you been all night?'

A drunken girl in a pale blue bias-cut gown giggled as Peter handed Evie a brandy.

'I went to see Mary, Charles's mother.'

Evie put the glass on the mantelpiece and warmed her toes by the fire. Somehow she managed to make even a blanket look like an elegant wrap.

'How is she?' The smile fell from Peter's face as Evie pursed her lips and shrugged. 'Jolly decent of you to go out tonight.'

'I didn't like to think of her alone. She looked so awfully sad on Boxing Day.'

'Of all of us, I thought Charlie would make it through,' Peter said quietly. 'He was so full of life. I'll never forget the two of you bombing down that black run in Chamonix. You were determined to beat him.'

Evie shook her head. 'He was like a brother to me. You never can tell which one of us is going to get bumped off next.'

'Evie!' Leo cut through the crowd towards her. He barely cleared five feet, but he was a dynamo of a man and whenever he bore down on her Evie pictured a missile skimming through water. Without her heels their gazes locked, eye to eye. He eyed her wet, clinging dress with exasperation.

She held up a hand. 'Before you start, I went to see Mary.'

Nonplussed, he thought quickly. 'She's only in the next village. What took so long?'

'I ran out of petrol.'

'Not again! How many times have I told you?'

'Daddy, I can't get used to this rationing … I thought I had enough left.'

'You can't drive on fumes! Especially not at the speed you drive. Where's the Aston?'

'On the verge between here and White Waltham.'

He frowned. 'I'll send Cullen in the morning.'

'Sorry, Daddy.' Evie bit her lip.

'What am I going to do with you?' As Leo embraced her, Evie saw the scowl on Virginia's face and raised a triumphant eyebrow.

'Happy New Year.' She planted a quick kiss on his cheek before he bustled back into the party. Her father's cocksure, springing step reminded her of a Jack Russell out on the razzle, up to no good.

'I don't know how you do it.' Peter shook his head.

Evie watched her father in his element, surrounded by friends and hangers-on, and that old familiar loneliness crept in. 'Years of practice. So,' she said briskly, 'what have I missed?'

'It's been marvellous!' the drunken girl trilled. 'Lucky always throws the most wonderful parties. Tonight you'd never know there was a war on!' A young soldier grabbed her hand and pulled her onto the dance floor as the big band struck up 'In the Mood'.

Evie shook her head. 'Silly girl.'

'Come on old thing!' Peter laughed. 'You're only twenty yourself! Have some fun.'

She shook her head. 'No. I'm tired of ...' She waved her hand. 'All this. Talking to Mary tonight, I felt I must do something. Even the Countess of Wharncliffe is running a bomb factory, and I heard the Duchess of Norfolk is breeding rabbits.'

'What do you know about bombs and rabbits?'

'Nothing, but I could learn.' Evie frowned.

Peter tilted his head, gently took her in his arms. 'Don't be blue. Charlie ...' He sighed. 'It's just awful bad luck, but if we let every death get to us, we'll never win this bloody war. We've got to be strong.' His voice shook slightly. 'Besides which, this is my last night of freedom, and I at least deserve to have some fun.'

'I'm sorry, Peter.' Evie shivered as she pulled the blanket around her. 'I'd forgotten. When are you leaving?'

'I have to be at Debden first thing.'

'When I see all you chaps going off to fly, I wish—'

'You're a more natural pilot than I'll ever be!' Peter cut in. His gaze settled on a table of men in uniform on the other side of the dance floor. 'Are you serious?'

'About what?'

'Doing something useful.'

'Absolutely!'

'Come on then.' He took her arm and steered her through the crowd, stopping at the table. 'Excuse me, sir.' He leant down to talk to the distinguished-looking grey-haired officer smoking a pipe. 'Squadron Leader Peter Taylor.'

The officer stood and shook his hand. 'Pleased to meet you.' He turned to Evie. 'And this lovely young lady is Miss Chase, if I am not mistaken?' He kissed her hand.

'Evie, this is Captain Eric Bailey.'

'But you can call me Badger, everyone does.' He smiled as he smoothed the white streak in his hair. 'At least behind my back.'

'Miss Chase is a pilot, sir,' Peter said.

Bailey eyed her wet dress. 'Really? I'd have had you down as a sailor.'

'Most amusing, sir.'

'How many hours have you got?' Bailey sucked at his pipe.

'Oh, not—' Evie's eyes opened wide.

'She's a very good pilot,' Peter interrupted. Turning to Evie he said pointedly, 'Captain Bailey helps run the Air Transport Auxiliary at White Waltham.'

'The ferry pilots?' She held Peter's gaze. He nodded.

'What have you flown?' Bailey folded his arms.

'Tiger Moths mainly.' She tried to sound confident. *Tiger Moths only*, she thought, *and a couple of hundred hours at that.*

'Well, Miss Chase, we need good pilots. Why don't you come over to White Waltham one morning and see what you think?'

'Really?'

'It's not what you're used to. But we need all the chaps ...' he corrected himself, 'and gals we can get our hands on. In fact, we have some new recruits arriving tomorrow. Why don't you join them, come along for a test flight and see what you think? Ask for Commander Pauline Gower.' He shook their hands and rejoined his table.

'Why didn't Daddy tell me he was going to be here?' she said to Peter as they stepped onto the dance floor.

Peter laughed as he swung her around to the music. 'Probably because he knew you'd jump at the chance of signing up.'

In the early hours, as dawn broke over the frozen fields and cars negotiated their way up the driveway, thin beams of blacked-out headlights guiding the way, Evie and Peter stood in the porch. He tucked his cap under his arm. 'Well, old girl, here we are again.' He forced a smile. 'I'll see you in the spring, if I'm lucky.'

She screwed her eyes tight shut as she embraced him. 'Silly boy, of course you will.'

His lips brushed her hairline. 'You remember our promise? If you're not married by your twenty-first ...'

Evie laughed as she stepped back. 'Oh, Peter, we were just children.' She saw the pain in his eyes, and pulled her fur coat close around her. 'You're serious, aren't you?' she said, as Leo and Virginia showed the last guests to their cars.

'I adore you, Evie, I always have.' He took her hand. 'No, don't say anything, please. I know we had fun, deb's delight and all that, but you mean more than that to me. I just wanted you to know, that's all, in case—'

'Don't.' She touched his lips. 'I'll see you in the spring.'

'Are you off now, Peter?' As Leo strode over, they moved apart.

'Yes, sir. Thank you for a marvellous send-off.'

'You be safe now.' Leo shook his hand. 'Go give Jerry what for!'

'Good luck, Evie.' Peter turned towards her as he walked away, his footsteps crunching along the dark driveway. 'You will write and let me know how you get on tomorrow?' he called.

'What are you doing tomorrow?' Leo slipped his arm around Virginia's waist.

'I've a test flight with the ATA at White Waltham.' Evie waited for the explosion.

'Over my dead body!'

'Daddy, I'm twenty years old, you can't stop me.'

'If you go I'll cut off your allowance.'

As Ross closed the heavy wooden door behind them, he coughed discreetly. 'Will that be all, sir?'

'Yes thank you, Ross,' Leo said. 'The Aston's stranded on the White Waltham road. Would you ask Cullen to pick it up in the morning?'

'Yes, sir.'

The moment the kitchen door swung closed, Leo turned on his daughter. 'Right. What's all this nonsense?' The colour rose in his cheeks. 'What do you think you're going to do? Deliver planes around the country in all weathers, with no guns?'

'I think it's a marvellous idea.' Virginia folded her arms.

'What?' Leo and Evie said simultaneously.

'Lucky, darling, Evie's been saying for months she wants to do something to help the war effort, and she does love to fly.'

'No!' Leo clenched his fists. 'I'm not having it. We'll talk about this in the morning.'

Virginia calmly reached for a cigarette from the silver box on the hall table as he stormed upstairs. 'I'll talk to him.' She leant against the table as she exhaled a plume of blue smoke.

'Why are you being so reasonable about this?' Evie said.

'Why do you think? I want you out of our house.'

Evie's temper flared. 'Your house? Since when? This is my father's house, I have every right—'

'Oh, Evie, of course you do.' Virginia's voice was sweet, cajoling. With Evie, she often felt like she was talking to a petulant toddler. At least once a day Virginia found herself clinging, white-knuckled, to her patience. She smiled sweetly as she counted to ten. 'But think of your father. You know how hard he's been working, how tired he is—'

'Tired? Daddy? What rot.' Evie shook her head as she laughed.

'You're always gadding around here with your friends, you won't have noticed.' Virginia smiled sweetly. 'It would be so much better for your father to have some peace and quiet for a change. Quite frankly, you want to fly, and I want you to fly the nest.' She flapped her hands. 'Do we have a deal?'

'Where do the ATA girls stay anyway?' Evie bit the inside of her cheek.

'Oh, I don't know.' Virginia stifled a yawn. 'No doubt there are some ghastly barracks or something. It will do you good to rough it for a change.' Her eyes glinted as Evie headed towards the stairs. 'I bet you won't last a day.'

On the first step, Evie paused and turned, the light of the chandelier catching on the rope of diamonds at her throat. She walked back towards her stepmother. 'You want to bet?'

'What's the wager?'

'If I win,' she said, 'if I don't get bumped off before this horrible war is over, you leave.'

Virginia gazed down at her, an amused smile twitching on her lips. 'And if I win? If you give up?'

'Then I'll move out anyway, join the Red Cross in town or something.'

'You have a deal,' she said as she stubbed out her cigarette. 'Not that I can imagine you folding bandages for a moment.' She clicked her fingers. 'The diamonds, please.'

'These were my mother's!'

'If Leo's going to cut you off I don't want them ending up at some dreadful pawn shop.'

'I don't want the diamonds, or the money. You're welcome to them.' Evie yanked off the jewels and thrust them into Virginia's waiting hand. She watched as her stepmother looped the glittering necklace around her wrist and held it to the light. As the diamonds gleamed coldly against her skin, Virginia wondered if it had all been worth it. Once, jewels, money had been all she had ever wanted. Now they were all she had. It seemed to her that her life as Mrs Leo Chase was like a clock slowly winding down. These days he came home at night less and less. Even her attempts to make him jealous went unnoticed now. She had tried with Lucky, she *really* had – and with Evie for that matter. She saw the angry defiance in Evie's face and wondered whether she had ever really given her a chance.

Virginia pressed her lips into a tight smile and patted Evie's cheek slowly – once, twice. 'Now, run along. You'll need a good night's sleep.' She watched as Evie turned on her heel and stalked up the stairs. 'Sweet dreams,' she called, her smile fading as she turned out the lights.

2

Stella had been making bread in the cramped kitchen of her aunt's flat when the siren went off. She hadn't noticed, just went on pounding the dough again and again, tears running silently down her cheeks. Her aunt had taken her gently by the arm, led her out onto Oxford Street, where people scurried, hunch-shouldered, heads down beneath the sweeping searchlights, to the shelters.

In the crush of bodies, they were separated. Stella found herself swept along in the darkness, down makeshift steps to a crowded chamber where people were already settling down for the night. She squeezed onto a bench and closed her eyes, hoping no one would talk to her as she tried to calm the panic rising in her. In spite of the cold, her hands were clammy with sweat.

For hours she sat feigning sleep as the bombardment continued, willing the claustrophobia to subside. The cry of a baby finally roused her, and her eyes flickered open, focusing on the little group of cradles beneath a forlorn Christmas tree decked with pink lights.

'Hush,' the woman sitting beside Stella cooed, tucking one of the babies in. She glanced at Stella. 'You're new aren't you, dear? Haven't seen you in our shelter before.' As she settled back and shook out her knitting, a powdery scent of violets and stale sweat escaped the tight embrace of her tweed coat.

Stella blinked. 'Yes, yes I am.' At the sound of her voice, so unlike theirs, several people looked up. Cut-glass, that's what they called it around there.

'Visiting family?' the woman probed, needles flashing in the light of the paraffin lamp.

She nodded. 'My aunt—' At the sound of another bomb overhead she broke off. Those awake held their breath, mentally tracing the path of the bomber, the rat-tat-tat of the anti-aircraft guns. The breath caught in Stella's throat, she gagged slightly.

'Oh I know,' the woman whispered. 'You get used to it. I've complained to the warden about the stink down here. Oxford Street, I ask you, and here we are living like rats with the chemical closets overflowing.' A muffled moan came from the furthest bunk and she tutted again. 'Those two should get themselves off to the courting shelter. Don't want that sort of goings-on in here.'

As the bomb exploded, everyone exhaled. Not them this time. A muffled cheer filtered through from the next-door shelter and Stella heard a Glenn Miller record strike up.

'Your aunt you say?'

'Sorry?' She pulled her attention back to the woman's tired, puffy face. 'Yes.' She ran a hand through the waves of her blonde, newly bobbed hair. There was a bruise on her forehead. In the confusion as the warden ushered her into the shelter, she hadn't ducked low enough for the door, had banged her head on the way in. 'I'm staying the night with Dorothy, Dorothy Blower.'

'Well you picked a good one!' A man laughed from the shadows. 'Worst so far. The last few nights it's been like the Great Fire all over again.'

'You're Dot's niece? Fancy that,' the woman said. 'We're in the flats opposite. Where is she? Surely she's not at home in the middle of all this?'

'No, I lost her on the street. It was all such a rush.'

The woman laughed indulgently. 'She'll be fine, don't you worry. Dot likes the shelter down the road a bit – you know how she likes her cards.'

Stella didn't know that. She had only met her a few hours before. She jumped as another bomb exploded. Dust motes drifted down from the ceiling, hissing in the flame of the paraffin lamp.

'Not used to this are you?'

'No.' Stella instinctively looked up as the baby whimpered again. She longed to hold the child, just for a moment, to feel the weight of him in her arms, the warm, soft skin.

'Hush.' The woman reached over, smoothed the baby's blanket.

'Is he yours?' Stella asked.

'This little one?' The woman shook her head. 'His dad was killed at Dunkirk, and his mum …' Her eyes clouded for a moment. 'Well, that last raid got her. Bless her, she was only nineteen. Worked in the munitions factory with me. I'll look out for him until her family turn up from Kent.' She carried on knitting. 'Do you have children?'

'Yes, a boy.' Stella folded her arms across her stomach.

'Is he with your aunt?'

'No, I—' The tears caught her suddenly.

'There, there love.' The woman's knitting slipped softly to her lap as she put her arm around Stella. 'Let it out. A little cry is good for us all now and then. There's not a woman here who hasn't lost someone.'

Stella pulled a handkerchief from the pocket of her coat. Her fingertip brushed the letter folded carefully there.

'How did he …?'

'Oh no, he's alive still.' Stella wiped at her eyes, quietly blew her nose. 'I'm so terribly sorry,' she said, quickly recovering herself. 'I do feel silly, and in front of a perfect stranger. Please excuse me.'

They heard the staccato crack of gunshots as planes flew overhead. 'We're all friends now,' the woman said. 'I'm Eileen by the way.'

'Thank you, Eileen. I'm Stella, Stella Grainger.'

'So where is he, your little lad?'

'David?' Even the sound of his name was music to her. She wanted to say it again, *David, David, David*, to somehow conjure him back to her. 'He's in Ireland, with my husband's mother. I just … I just left him there.'

Eileen heard the pain in her voice. She patted her hand. 'I'm sure he'll be safe there, love.' She sighed. 'How old is he?'

'Six months.'

'Is that all? Oh, it's hard isn't it—' Eileen broke off as the sleeping man at her side let out a snore. 'Shut up, Jack.' As she elbowed him, he snorted. 'You'll wake everyone up.'

She turned back to Stella. 'Not that it's anything I haven't put up with for thirty years. Look at him with his false teeth hanging out. Put them in, Jack! Nobody wants to be seeing that!'

The man raised his hand to his lips and adjusted his teeth, flashing Stella an even, yellow smile before turning and settling back to sleep.

'So where's your husband, is he fighting?'

Stella didn't answer. *Careless talk costs lives*, she thought.

The lamp guttered and went out. 'Oh, ruddy hell, not again.' Eileen fumbled with her bag as she put her knitting away.

Someone coughed, hacking, waking in the shelter. From the sliver of light around the entrance, Stella guessed it must be sometime towards dawn.

'So where is he? Your husband?' Eileen tried again.

'I lost him,' Stella said curtly.

'Oh love, I am sorry.' Eileen felt for her hand in the darkness, squeezed her fingers.

In the corner, the Christmas lights washed the faces of the sleeping babies pink. From the nearest cradle, a pair of small arms stretched up and a high, keening wail began.

'Hush. There, there.' Eileen picked him up. 'You miss your mum, don't you?'

Stella felt the old familiar tightening in her chest as the baby cried, the tingling pinpricks. 'How old is he?' she asked quietly.

'I don't know.' Eileen settled beside her, the baby in her arms. 'Two, three months perhaps?' The baby cried out as he pushed away the teat of the glass bottle she tried to coax into his mouth.

'Poor little mite. Don't like the bottle do you? But you'll have to eat, you're wasting away.'

'David never wanted a bottle.' Stella turned the gold band on her finger slowly. She thought of the milk she had been throwing away since she'd left Ireland. She wondered whether he too cried out for her at night. It had seemed almost criminal at a time when everyone was making do, pouring her milk away, a little less each day. The tightness in her chest became unbearable. She felt Eileen watching her.

'Were you feeding him?'

'Yes.'

Eileen looked at the anguished face of the baby. 'Could you? I wouldn't ask but ...'

Stella recoiled. 'No! I couldn't possibly.'

As Stella shrunk back in her place, Eileen turned to her. 'He'll die soon,' she whispered. 'I've seen this too often lately.'

Stella inhaled sharply as a wave of anxiety washed over her. 'I can't, I just can't.'

'Your baby is safe.' Eileen shoved the child into her arms. 'You're here for a reason tonight, I'm sure of it.' Stella instinctively held the child closer, supported his head. 'We all have to do what we can.'

Stella nodded silently, unbuttoned her heavy overcoat with trembling fingers. She glanced self-consciously around, but everyone had averted their eyes. As she loosened her shirt, the dawn air penetrated her thin silk camisole, felt cool against her skin. She shifted the child in her arms, cooed softly to him. She was so used to David's plump arms, his soft, heavy body. This child was smaller, his shoulder blades like angular wings beneath his knitted blanket. As she held him against her body, she felt him relax, sobs turning to snuffles, then silence as he began to feed, a small fist clutching at her shirt.

'There now,' Eileen said approvingly. 'When I was in hospital with my last, I had so much milk I fed half the babies on the ward.' She pulled the blanket closer around him.

Stella sensed the woman on the bunk opposite watching her, and looked over.

'Good for you, love,' the woman said. 'Anything we can do to help these poor wee children ...' Her voice trailed off. 'Where is your lad Eileen?'

'I don't know.' She smoothed her creased skirt. 'He's on the Lancasters,' she said to Stella. She took a deep breath, sat upright. 'Still, at least Annie's nearby. She's driving ambulances.'

'What about you, love?' the other woman asked Stella.

She hesitated. 'I'm a pilot.'

'No!' Eileen's face lit up.

'I'm joining the Air Transport Auxiliary.' She felt the baby break away from her breast and she lifted him to her shoulder, rubbing his narrow back.

'But women can't fly planes can they?' the woman asked.

'Of course they can!' Eileen folded her arms. 'What about that Amy Johnson?'

'She's one of our ATA girls,' Stella said proudly. The baby burped, pushed back against her collarbone, searching hungrily now.

'There's a good lad!' Eileen laughed.

'We've just arrived from Singapore. I heard the ATA were taking women pilots, and I wanted to do my bit. Now David is safely in Ireland, I'm joining up tomorrow... today,' she corrected herself. She felt Eileen watching her and looked up.

'Your husband would be proud,' she said.

Would he? Stella wondered. Or would Richard think she was a fool to risk her own life and leave their child motherless like the baby in her arms. The truth was, she no longer cared if she lived or died now she had lost him. For months it had felt like she was looking at the world from beneath deep water – everything was muffled, blank, deadened. When she slept, fitfully, she always hoped tomorrow would be the day she would wake and feel like her old self, but she never did. She woke exhausted, and would lie listening to David's pitiful cries, not knowing how she could drag herself from bed and survive another day. Each time she admitted this to herself she was overcome with guilt. David still needed her – or did he? Perhaps he would be safer and happier on the farm with dear, dependable Sarah and George. That's what she had told herself a thousand times – that he was better off without her.

From outside, the wail of the 'all clear' siren cut through the dank cold air, and people began to stir. In a lifetime spent overseas, she had always longed to visit England, always imagined she would feel at home. But everything was alien to her. Today was the first day of her new life. She had shed her skins. She was not a wife, not a mother any more. Who was she? Was this country that she had never set foot in before meant to be her homeland, with its blacked-out windows and sinister balloon-filled skies? Stella scanned the faces of the grey-skinned people in their greasy coats as they crowded towards the door and felt more alone than she had in her entire life.

She had no idea how many people trailed past as she stroked the baby's fragile skull, her fingertips tracing the soft down of his hair. She imagined the thousands of men, women and children stirring across London in Tube stations and basements, emerging to face another uncertain day. Sated, the baby finally released his grip on her blouse and fell back into a deep, relieved sleep. His tiny fingers extended, waved liked the fronds of a sea anemone. She looked down at his face – perfect, unblemished. 'Sleep well, sunny Jim,' she whispered as she handed him to Eileen.

She stood, stretched out the cold and ache of her limbs and buttoned her coat.

Eileen caught at her fingers. 'Thank you, love, you might just have saved this little lad's life.' Wordlessly, Stella squeezed her hand.

Pale winter sun rose over London. Stella scrambled from the shelter, shielding her eyes. Oxford Street was deserted, silent, its pavements glistening, encrusted with shattered glass like diamonds. Fragments crunched beneath her shoes, the mournful 'all clear' siren rising and falling in a wave across the frozen air From the centre of the road Stella scanned the grey figures emerging like ghosts from a tomb. Then she saw her.

'Auntie!'

Dorothy looked over, ran to her. 'I thought I'd lost you.' They held tight to one another as weary figures drifted by.

'I was just down the road.'

'Come home now, love, let me make you some breakfast.'

Stella slipped her hand into her coat pocket. The letter with her instructions was still there. Home. Where was home now? Richard was her home, her place in the world, and that had gone now. 'I can't. Please don't let's argue again.'

'But you've only just arrived, and you're the last! Your brother. My Nigel.' Fear and sadness clouded her face. 'This wretched war. We've lost everyone we loved.'

'That's why I have to go.'

'I can't bear it.' She hung her head. 'Not you too. You're so young.'

'I'm old enough, and the ATA needs all the pilots it can get.' A defiant, uncertain smile flickered across her lips. She glanced at her watch. 'The morning train ... I must go.' Dorothy nodded silently, fighting her tears. 'Take care, Auntie,' Stella whispered as she kissed her. The scent of violets lingered as she walked away. Stella turned back, her face bright in the morning sun, and waved. 'I'll be home soon!'

3

Megan cycled along the coast path above Barafundle Bay, the wind whipping her dark curls, the dogs racing joyfully behind her. Her battered brown leather sheepskin flying jacket was zipped up to her chin, but she was still freezing. Her face and hands were pinched by the cold air as it skimmed across the dunes and cliffs from the glittering sea below. Gulls wheeled in the clear Pembrokeshire sky, a rosy sun rising on the horizon. At the hangar on the far side of the airfield she swung her right leg over the bike, freewheeling to a standstill by the main door.

'Come on boys! Rex!' she called. The old collie perked up his ears, left the rabbit warren he was nosing around and raced towards her. Megan heaved open the door and dawn light flooded the dark interior of the hangar. Her breath hung in a cloud on the freezing air. It was as if the Tiger Moth was waiting for her, and as she walked by she touched the wing as if she were greeting an old friend. She sprang up into the cockpit and sighed contentedly. She lost herself running through procedures, closed her eyes as she handled the controls, imagined soaring out over the sea. By the time the dogs barked, the sun was high in the sky.

'I thought I'd find you here.' Rhodri strode through the open door. 'What are you doing, love?'

'Oh you made me jump, Da!' It felt strange to smile. Since the news about Huw there had been no laughter in the house. 'I'm just practising. It's been so long since I've flown.'

'You'll be the best pilot there.' Rhodri smiled up at her. 'The ATA are lucky to have you.' He offered her his hand as she jumped down. 'Some lads from the RAF are coming to pick this old girl up in the next couple of days. I think they're taking her up to the base at Angle.'

'They'd better take good care of her.' Megan patted the wing. She was the same height as her father, and she had his dark curls, though his were streaked with grey now.

'Come on, love, your mother's got lunch waiting, and your cousins have come over from Tenby.'

Megan bridled. 'What are they doing here?' She stooped to pick up her bike, and wheeled it beside her father as they crossed the old airfield.

'Don't be like that,' he said gently. 'Without your brother, God rest him, there's no one to take on the farm and airfield after the war. They are family—'

'No!' Her temper flared. 'The airfield was Huw's, and mine.' She fought the wave of nausea as she thought of her brother, the way he had teased her on his last leave, tickling her until she was breathless with laughter, pinned to the cool summer grass on the lawn. Whenever they got together it was as if they were small children again. Now he was gone. 'What do the Davies cousins know about flying? Nothing!'

'They know about business, love. How can you manage all this and the farm on your own?' Rhodri said tenderly. 'Your ma and I aren't getting any younger.'

Megan glanced at him. It was true. They had married late, and Nia was forty when she had Megan. Since receiving the news that Huw was missing, presumed killed on a bombing raid, it was as if they had aged ten years overnight. Her father's kind, dark eyes were red-rimmed, with fresh wrinkles circling them.

'They know about money,' she said bitterly. 'They couldn't care less about whether the airfield reopens after the war. They're just after the farm. This is our family business, and I'll run it alone if I have to.'

'It's too much,' he said as they entered the farmyard, chickens scattering ahead of them. 'You've not got enough experience flying, or with the business, love.'

'But I will have! I'm going to be flying all sorts of planes, Da.' She looked up as a young man in shirtsleeves stepped out of the milking parlour. He stooped to the well and pumped water into a cast-iron pail. 'I've got Bill, too. He'll help me with the animals.'

Rhodri sighed and put his hands in his pockets. 'After you've done the cows can you take Rex up to the barns and check the sheep, Bill?'

The boy glanced up, swept his dark hair away from his face. Megan blushed. The first time she had seen him, last summer, he was fly-fishing in the stream down in the valley. She had thought he looked like Errol Flynn. 'Yes, Mr Jones. Hello, Megan.'

'Bill.' She lowered her eyes as he smiled at her.

Rhodri caught the exchange. 'Come on.' He took her arm. 'They're waiting.' As they took their boots off in the porch, he frowned. 'You're not to spend so much time with him.'

'What do you mean?' Megan couldn't look at her father.

'He's a good lad ...'

'But not good enough for me? Is that what you mean?' She flashed him a quick, angry look.

'He's a hard worker, but ...' He brushed a strand of hair from his daughter's face. 'You're young, Megan, and he was working in the fairgrounds when he came here.'

Megan thought of the silvery scars on Bill's face, reminders of the bare-knuckle fights and baying crowds. She could never reconcile his gentleness, the way he could calm any animal, or his stillness when she read to him, with his brutal past.

'I've been helping him with his reading and writing, that's all,' she said defensively.

Rhodri tilted his head. 'Megan, I can see the way you look at one another. I was young once too, you know.' Megan gazed over her father's shoulder as Bill strode up the hill, the dogs bounding along behind him. 'Perhaps it's a good thing you'll be away for a while.'

'Ma doesn't think so.'

'Leave your ma to me.' Rhodri put his arm around her. 'She's just worried she'll lose you too. I think it will be good for you to get on and do something, meet some new people. Perhaps it will help.'

He opened the door to the kitchen and a warm draught carrying the scent of roast beef met them. Nia was at the range, making gravy from the scrapings of the roasting pan. Megan's two cousins sat at the table, napkins already tucked into the necks of their shirts. They reminded her of the photographs of crocodiles she had seen, the way their eyes swivelled hungrily towards her.

'Hello, Megan,' the plump one said. His fingers were laced over his pot belly. His skinny brother carried on chewing the end of his pipe, adjusting his wire-rimmed spectacles to get a better look at her. She lifted her chin in silent greeting.

'Now then Megan, wash your hands, love. Lunch is ready.' Her mother placed a dark, glistening joint of beef in front of Rhodri. As he sharpened the carving knife on the steel with a swish, swish, swish, Megan scrubbed her hands in the kitchen sink, sensing her cousins' eyes as keenly as a knife blade between her shoulders. She turned as she dried her hands on a clean linen towel, defiantly holding their gaze.

'So you're off tomorrow are you, Megan?' the fat one asked, his attention distracted by the thick slices of beef Rhodri was carving from the steaming joint. Megan helped her mother carry bowls of vegetables to the table, carrots and potatoes, all from their own garden.

'Megan.' Her mother nudged her.

'Yes I am.' She sat opposite the cousins, and folded her arms.

'We were just saying to your mother we'd be glad to help out more on the farm now Huw and you are gone.'

'I'm not "gone".' Megan leant forward.

'Arms off the table, love,' Nia said as she sat beside her.

'Ma,' Megan whispered out of the corner of her mouth, 'I'm not a child any more.'

'Let's say grace.' Nia took her hand. Rhodri lay down the knives and took Megan's other hand. 'Dear Lord.' Nia closed her eyes. When Megan peeked she saw both cousins staring straight at her. 'Thank you for our food and family. We ask you to look after our son Huw, and take care of our daughter Megan when she is in London.' Nia said 'Lon-don' with such distaste it was as if Megan were travelling to Sodom and Gomorrah. 'Amen.'

'It's not London, Ma,' Megan said. 'It's Maidenhead I'm going to.'

'Close enough.' Nia looked at her lap as she shook out her napkin. Her brow furrowed. 'Oh, when I think of those bombs ...'

The grandfather clock by the settle ticked away the minutes as plates were passed to and fro and awkward small talk was made. The wind rattled the kitchen door on the latch. Megan stared sullenly at the chipped gilt edge of the vegetable bowl as she chewed her beef, wondering when the cousins would make their move.

'How's business in town?' Rhodri asked, as the fat one pushed back his empty plate.

'Mustn't grumble,' he said as he untucked his napkin from the greasy collar of his shirt. 'Things are hard for people, but you can always find a bit extra for your best customers, if you know what I mean.' He nudged his brother, their laughter dying away as they realised Rhodri and Nia weren't laughing with them. 'How about the farm now? Are you coping?'

Megan fiddled with the crocheted tablecloth, twisting a loop of thread tight around her fingertip, cutting off the blood.

'We're fine,' Rhodri said. 'Bill's a good lad.'

'Is he now?' The thin one spoke up. 'I'd watch him if I was you. No one knows who his family is, he just blew in with the fair didn't he?'

'What do you know about anything?' Megan leapt to her feet. 'Come on. Why don't you just get on and say what you've really come for?'

'Megan!' Her mother grasped her arm. 'I'm sorry, she's still upset about Huw. We all are.' She blinked quickly, looked down at her lap.

'I can talk for myself—'

'That's enough!' Rhodri thumped his fist on the table, and the colour drained from Megan's face. Her father never raised his voice. 'You're upsetting your mother.'

Angry tears stung her eyes. 'Well it's just as well I'm leaving tomorrow, isn't it? But I tell you one thing.' She jabbed her finger at the cousins. 'I'm coming back. This is my family's farm and I will run the airfield after the war.'

'But there's no call for it round here.' The fat one turned to Rhodri, ignoring her. 'Think about it. If you plough up the airstrip, how much more money you could make with—'

'No!' Megan cried. 'Don't do it, Da.' She wiped away a burning tear from her cheek. 'It's mine, and yours, and Huw—'

'Huw's dead, love,' her father said softly.

'It was Huw's dream.' Megan pushed back her chair, the legs scraping on the flagstones. 'No one is going to take that away.' She turned on her heel and flung open the kitchen door, the latch rattling as it slammed shut after her.

Rhodri stood up slowly and patted Nia's stooped shoulder as he passed. It was getting dark now and with a taper he lit the gas lamp over the table. The warm light illuminated the cousins' expectant faces.

'I'm sorry. She's young.' He ran a hand through his hair as he sat down again.

'Which is why she needs our guidance,' the thin one wheedled.

Rhodri thought to himself how he had never seen twins so unlike one another. His sister had died giving birth to them. For that he had never quite forgiven them.

'Rhodri, we're family. Are we not doing a good job of running Father's butchers? Just think what we can do with this.'

Megan's father studied their faces closely – pockmarked, blotchy from too much ale. He was a strict Methodist himself, and he disliked what he had heard about them around the village.

'No.' He shook his head as he took Nia's hand. 'Megan is right. The airfield was Huw's dream. I have to at least give her a chance.'

Megan ran, unseeing, into the grey afternoon, snow eddying around her as she pounded up the steep hill, her boots slipping in the frozen ruts of the sheep track. She didn't know where she was running to, but something was drawing her up towards the winter barns. Against the leaden sky, the open barn door glowed invitingly, golden lamplight spilling out. As she drew closer, Bill stepped out, Rex following.

'Megan?'

'Bill, oh Bill.' She ran into his arms, buried her head in the rough knit of his thick sweater. She felt safe there, as he held her, and she gave in to her tears.

'Hush now,' he murmured, stroking her head. 'What's the matter?'

'Those horrible, horrible men.' She balled her fist against Bill's chest. 'They want to take all this away from me, from us.'

She sensed Bill stop breathing for a moment, and realised what she had let slip. Warily, she raised her eyes to his.

'Do you mean that?' he asked. 'You're going away, I thought ...'

Megan blinked, brushed away the tears that had soaked her lashes into dark points. 'I'll come back though, Bill.'

He cupped her cold cheek in his hand, and kissed her, crushing her lips to his. Megan's eyes flew open in surprise. She had kissed a few of the lads in the shadows of the village hall at dances, but nothing like this. Bill was a man, his face rough with stubble, and his dark moustache tickled her nose. She couldn't help laughing.

'What is it?' He stepped back, panting slightly.

'Nothing!' She giggled. 'It's just I've never—' But it was too late, Bill stormed back inside the barn. She ran after him, pulled at his sleeve. 'Wait! I'm sorry, Bill.'

In here it was warm, with soft hay underfoot, and the gentle shift of the sheep's solid bodies in their stall. Snow fell silently beyond the door. When she saw the wounded look on his face, she stepped closer to him, traced the silver scars on his cheek with her fingertips.

'I don't understand. Why are you so cross?'

'You laughed at me.'

He tried to turn away from her, but she stopped him, took his face in her hands. His jawbone was hard against the palm of her hand as she kissed him again.

'There,' she murmured. 'You took me by surprise, that's all, Bill.'

'I'll not have anyone laughing at me. Not even you.'

Megan remembered the stories he had confided in her, how he had struggled at school, how tough it had been in the fairgrounds. Bill was proud, and she had hurt his feelings. She reached up and wrapped her arms around him, held him close.

He rested his head against hers. 'I'm sorry. It's just I've wanted to kiss you for so long.'

'And what do I do? Burst out laughing,' she said. 'I've never been kissed like that before, that's all.'

'Never?' Bill smiled shyly. 'I thought I'd lost my chance.'

'Because I'm leaving tomorrow? I'll come back, I said so.'

'Will you?' Bill took her hand in his, pressed her fingers to his lips. 'You won't forget?'

'Forget you? This place?' She smiled. 'This is my home, Bill. My heart is here with you.' She cocked her head playfully. 'What about you then? How do I know the minute I'm off you won't be down the village with Bronwen Maddocks? She's had her eye on you for ages.'

Bill laughed as he hugged her, lifting her clear off the ground. 'Don't you be thinking about Bronwen Maddocks. Just get yourself home in one piece, alright?' He gazed into her eyes as he set her down. 'I love you, Megan. I'll be waiting right here for you.'

Squires Gate, 11.40 a.m.

I flew with the forgotten pilots, the 'Ancient and Tattered Airforce' of one-armed veterans and adventurers, and the beauty chorus of debutantes and pink-cheeked Oxbridge graduates. We had conjurors, strippers, joyriders and decorated heroes in our ranks.

I was just a jobbing ferry pilot, but it would have been different if they had asked me to run the show. Why they chose Pauline over me I don't know. While she flew joyriders, I flew single-handed around the world with just an evening dress and a tennis racket in my luggage. I pitched up in deserts where I fended off sheikhs with ju-jitsu, and mended my plane's wings with sticking plasters. Actually, I do know why they chose her. The English are snobbish about celebrity. They did not like the trace of Hull in my accent, in spite of all the elocution lessons, nor that cod and herring bought me my wings. They did not like that I commanded headlines, dined with Roosevelt and Chaplin. How else was I supposed to fly, but earn my way? I have paid my dues. I was a secretary. I was a teacher. I always wanted more.

I feel guilty sometimes. I made flying glamorous, encouraged girls to see it all as a great adventure. Pauline said 'all women should fly', but by the end of the war one in seven of my ATA sisters were dead, and I was among the first to go.

Perhaps that is why they chose her. Pauline was a safe, established pair of hands. It was easy to imagine her charging down a hockey field. She ensured that we earned more than the RAF fighter pilots, and eventually the same as our male ATA colleagues, another first. No glass ceilings for us girls – the sky had no limits. Not everyone was happy about this – there was sugar in our fuel tanks, vital tools and parts often went missing. But Pauline knew the secret of getting ahead. She orchestrated a quiet revolution. Get in, get your head down and do better than expected without making a fuss.

Perhaps you've heard of me? On Civvy Street everyone knew my name. In the fug of a pub's back room you'd often hear someone strumming out the song on a banjo: 'Amy, wonderful Amy, how can you blame me for loving you?' Or maybe you've seen the film They Flew Alone? I used to love the cinema. Frankly you couldn't make me up – no one would believe you. It amused me, sliding into an empty seat beside Pauline at the premiere in Leicester Square, my spirit unnoticed as they celebrated my memory on screen. How strange to see your life, your loves and losses, played out in black and white, the image of 'me' and 'Jim' flickering on a grand scale. We pranged a lot of planes between us, in truth, but no one seemed to mind.

In black and white what you cannot smell is the cocktail of doped canvas, fuel and engine oil, of sweat and adrenalin. You cannot feel the wind, hear it whistling in the wire braces as the wings sing, or taste the salt of our kiss in the blazing Australian sun. We were the 'Flying Sweethearts'. I wonder what Jim thought of it, when he watched the film. Did he feel regret, mourn my loss again? I hope so. I broke records, but that man broke my heart.

'Marry me.' He reached across the crisp white tablecloth in Quaglino's and took my hand, the sleeve of his dapper double-breasted suit riding up over his tanned wrist. I could tell he was shot up, on his second White Lady of the day. Close to, his breath smelt of booze. It often did, but he was mine, and I loved him.

'You're mad!' I laughed, my heart racing.

'We make a good team, Amy.'

I was what used to be called a handsome woman. The truth is he made me feel as beautiful as my publicity shots, the ones that showed my long arched eyebrows darkened with kohl, my strong features softened cleverly by the lens. For him I had my teeth fixed, learnt to elongate my vowels. I healed my broken heart by flying, just as I did when Irene killed herself. I lost my little sister, but I have found a sisterhood among the girls here. While other women wept secretly in dark wartime cinemas, we took our passions and bereavements, our anger and frustration, and gave them wings.

The girls talked excitedly of how I 'just mucked in' at the airbases, but what else do you do in these circumstances? There were three stooges when I passed through White Waltham for the last time, waiting to go in for their briefing with Pauline. When they saw me in the Ops Corridor, their chatter stopped. They looked like the three wise monkeys sitting on the cane-backed chairs. One dark and small, muffled against the cold in a mink coat, diamonds glittering in her ears. The girl next to her was practically a child, bright eyed and fresh cheeked. Her mouth actually fell open when she saw me. Finally a cool blonde – when she smiled, her eyes remained closed, like a blacked-out house. Like mine. She has lost someone close, *I thought,* she is the walking wounded.

'Miss Johnson!' The young one leapt up keen as mustard, dark curls bouncing as she reached out her hand. 'Oh! How marvellous to see you! We were just saying, you're the reason we are all here.'

'Thank you.' I smiled cordially. 'Do call me Johnnie, everyone does.' God they looked young, and untested. That will change, I thought; they will age years in only a few months. We all found ways of coping with the waiting and the stress – some drank, but knitting did it for me. No wonder that the black, secret nights of love, lust and gaiety became the counterpoint of our dangerous, solitary days. This is why the girls danced all night to Fat Tim at the 400 Club. Why they lost themselves in the beat and swing of the big bands, the heat of the dance floor and the comfort of a stranger's arms. As they say, the generous heart gives in wartime.

It beats faster, reminds you that you are still alive when death is all around you.

It is no wonder that, before we take off, most pilots withdraw, go silently into our own worlds. Some of the women hammed it up, had a fit of the feminine vapours, trailing the contents of their handbags as they went to their planes. 'Oh my dear, I can't possibly fly today, I have the most awful headache.' Male officers swooping after them, picking up handkerchiefs, escorting them to their aircraft. Sometimes I think seeing a young slip of a girl step out of a huge plane is still many men's worst fear. I never had any flak from the boys, but I know some had. The thing is if you looked closely at these powder-puff girls, once they were in the cockpit they were as focused as the rest of us. They had the look of an oiled prize-fighter dancing through the crowds to the ring.

As I go back to my last flight, this is where I am now, in my own world. The smoke as I exhale is invisible against the luminous milky sky, drizzle soft and cold on my cheeks, sound muffled. I clamber into the high, glazed cockpit, run through my final checks, the metal and the glass dials cold beneath my fingertips. It takes me a moment to realise one of the refuellers is hovering shyly by the door, a piece of paper in his oil-blackened hand.

'Is everything alright?'

'Yes, I'm sorry to disturb you, Miss.' The lad is blushing furiously, can hardly look at my face. 'Could I have your autograph for my daughter? She's a big fan.'

'Of course, jump in.'

He swings in to the office – you get used to flying alone but it's good to have some company in the cockpit for a while. I switch my cigarette to my other hand, and take the pen and paper from him. 'What's her name?'

'Elizabeth.'

He's beaming with relief. Maybe he thought I'd bite his head off.

'How old is she?' I lean against the charts, write 'To Elizabeth, with love, Amy Johnson.'

'She's only ten, but she wants to be a pilot just like you when she grows up.'

'Good for her.' I hand him the autograph.

'Thank you, Miss.' It's as if I've handed him a cheque for a million pounds. 'She'll be cock-a-hoop when I get home.' He backs out, smiling broadly.

'Hold on.' I root around in my pigskin flight bag. I pull out an enamel brooch with wings, and offer it to him. 'For Elizabeth. Tell her there's no better career for a young woman.'

4

Evie raced along the tree-lined Bath Road, across Maidenhead Thicket, with the Aston pushing 85 mph. It was a short fifteen-minute hop from her father's house, but as usual she had slept through her alarm and she was late. She looped around the village green, past the inn and on to Cherry Garden Lane. In spite of the bitter cold, she had the roof down, and as the fresh air gradually revived her she began to come up with a plan. If she liked the look of the job, why rough it in digs when there were all those empty bedrooms at home? *The best of both worlds*, she thought. *Fly all day and a few home comforts at night.*

After a mile, she spotted the airfield. She steered the Aston Martin 15/98 around in front of the offices and pulled to a halt. People were piling out of ATA coaches and walking briskly through the mist to an assortment of small wooden huts around the perimeter of the airfield. Her gaze followed a black-and-white-chequered van as it rumbled past the anti-aircraft guns at the centre. As she watched, an Anson taxi plane touched down nearby, and she heard the airscrews slow and stop.

Evie untied her Hermès headscarf and tossed it onto the passenger seat. *Well at least Daddy was joking about the HQ being a wooden hut on the runway*, she thought as she scanned the offices. A long two-storey building led to a curved office wing and a small terrace overlooking the airfield. But this was not what she had imagined at all. Where were the elegant white Art Deco buildings? The dashing men in uniform?

She heard a tannoy system crackle into life. 'Hello, hello. Will the following pilots go to Anson 9972 ...' As she watched, several people carrying parachutes trooped through the mist and fumes to the waiting plane.

'Are you lost?' An airman strolled towards her out of the sun. His cap was tilted over his eyes, and as he raised his face Evie tried not to stare at the white dressing covering his left cheek. He was smoking, his left hand tucked into the pocket of his great coat. She sensed his lean strength – but there was something about the careful way he carried himself that seemed awkward. It was as if every step was an effort. His eyes travelled slowly upwards, taking in her high heels and mink coat. 'The Café de Paris is about fifty miles that way.' He indicated the Maidenhead Road with a nod of his head as he ground the cigarette beneath his boot.

'Do I look like I'm lost?' Evie put her hands on her hips. She was nervous, and, frankly, this man wasn't helping.

'Oh no, all the chaps are wearing mink this season.' He stepped closer, tipped his cap backwards. Now she could see his clear blue eyes she was even more unsettled. 'You certainly don't look like you belong here. Are you visiting one of the men?'

'You think I'm a camp-follower?' she said, trying to sound brave, and worldly.

'We get a lot of girls hanging around the bases.' He began to walk away, but Evie followed him.

'I'll have you know I'm a pilot, and a damn good one.' She had to half run to keep up with him. 'Is this the ATA headquarters?'

'Yes, why?'

'I just expected something more.'

'In the old days all they had was a shed at the east end by the de Havilland hangar.'

'Daddy wasn't joking then,' she said as he pushed open the door for her. 'Would you kindly show me the way to the

Recruitment Office?' To her annoyance he began to laugh.

'What's so funny?' The dark-haired officer striding down the Ops Corridor did a double take when he saw Evie.

'Nothing.' Beau took off his cap and ran a hand through his blond hair. 'Just another Daddy's girl turned up to give this ferrying lark a go.' When she saw the burn on his left arm, she recoiled, realising too late that the man had seen the shock on her face. His face hardened. 'Looks like Pauline's scraping the bottom of the barrel, old boy.' He turned on his heel and marched off towards the mess.

'I see you've met Beau.' The other officer offered her his hand.

'Why is he called that?'

'Because he is ... or he was, so handsome. Our Wing Commander Beaufort managed to get his Spit home after the Battle of Britain, but it was on fire by the time it hit the deck. If the ground crew hadn't dragged him out so quickly ...' The officer shook his head. 'It's only been a few months, he's doing well considering. Until they say he's fit for combat he's giving us a hand here.'

'Well, I've never met such a rude man in my whole life,' Evie said indignantly. 'I wonder if you can help me. I have an appointment with the Recruitment Office. I'm Evelyn Chase.'

'Welcome to White Waltham, Miss Chase,' he said with a smile. As he guided her towards the office, his hand pressed against the small of her back. 'I can assure you not all of us are as prickly as Beau. I'm Edward Parker, Operations Officer, but everyone calls me Teddy.' The corridor was heaving with office staff and pilots. Some were in uniform, but most wore an odd assortment of civilian flying gear.

'This all seems a bit ...'

'Rough and ready? It's an unofficial ATA motto – get going and get comfortable later. Most of the chaps have been working so hard they haven't had a chance to get their uniforms yet.' He pointed at a man in a grubby-looking mackintosh. 'See that chap? He's still wearing the clothes he was wearing when he came for interview. He's been flying non-stop ever since.'

Evie glanced outside as the door blew open. 'What are all the funny little huts on the airfield?'

'There's all sorts out there – stores, engineers, you name it. We call it the Chinese Village. As the organisation is expanding so quickly we need offices pronto.' Teddy rubbed his hands together. 'Well you picked a chilly day for your test. Good weather for camping, eh?' He caught the eye of a pretty girl walking past carrying a pile of paperwork. 'Mikki, can you show Miss Chase where she should be?'

'Yes, sir.' She ticked Evie's name on a list. 'Follow me, Miss.' She led Evie along a corridor lined with a long, polished wooden shelf where groups of pilots were checking their orders for the day. 'You've caught us at a busy moment. The chits have just come out,' she said over her shoulder as they pushed through the crowd.

'What do you do?'

'Me? I try and keep this lot in order. I take care of admin, paperwork, anything that needs doing. There you are.' She indicated an empty Windsor chair next to a couple of girls. 'Perhaps you'd start filling out your application forms while you're waiting?'

'Morning, ladies.' Teddy winked at the girls already waiting as he sauntered past. 'If you need anything,' he said, gazing at the row of neat, stockinged ankles, 'anything at all, my office is just up the corridor.'

'He's a bit much, isn't he?' Stella said under her breath as he walked away. She scanned the paperwork. 'Next of kin? That's ominous.'

'I don't know, he seems friendly enough,' Megan chipped in.

'Are you from Wales?' Evie asked her.

'Oh God, is it the accent?' Megan blushed. 'Everyone here talks so beautifully.' As the girls introduced themselves, her eyes opened wide. 'No!' She grabbed Stella's arm. 'You know who that is, don't you? It's Amy Johnson, isn't it? Miss Johnson! Miss Johnson!' She leapt to her feet, her new shoes skittering on the lino.

'Do you think she's always this enthusiastic?' Evie sighed. She was still feeling nervous but tried not to show it.

Stella laughed, stretched out her legs. She was still aching from the night in the shelter and the slow, cold train ride down. 'She's just a kid.' She eyed Evie curiously. 'So what are you doing here?'

'I'm beginning to wonder myself.' Evie tucked her coat around her as Amy Johnson strolled over.

'Are you waiting to see Pauline?' Amy asked.

'What's she like?' Megan gazed at her, awestruck. 'I'm that nervous.'

'Pauline's a doll, you'll see,' Amy said kindly. 'I'm based down at Hatfield with her. I just stopped off to see my dog, Christopher, before my next flight.'

'Is Hatfield a good pool?' Evie asked. She wanted to make sure she was posted to the best base.

'If you liked boarding school you'll be in your element.' Amy smiled. 'Perhaps they'll let you stay here. I heard a rumour they need more pilots.'

'Hello, Amy,' Frankie Francis said as he strolled by, his parachute slung over one shoulder.

'Who's that?' Megan's eyes were on stalks.

'Frankie?' Amy laughed. 'All the girls love Frankie, but I'd concentrate on flying for now if I was you.' She picked up her flight bag. 'Best of luck.'

Commander Pauline Gower had seen all sorts of girls come through here. Frankly, she didn't care about their personal motives as long as they were good pilots. She leant back in her chair and screwed the cap on her fountain pen, placing it on the leather-topped desk in front of her. Her wide mouth broke into a reassuring smile.

'So, girls, what brings you to the ATA?'

For a moment there was silence. Megan looked expectantly at the older women. 'I want to do my bit for the war. I want to fly,' she spoke up finally.

'We all do,' Stella said firmly.

'And what about you?' Pauline patted the neat dark waves of her hair as she glanced at her notes. 'Evelyn Chase. Are you Lucky's daughter?'

'Yes, Commander.' Evie met her gaze steadily.

'He's a friend of my father's,' she said. 'What's he doing now?'

'Daddy's working with the Air Ministry in London. I don't think he likes being stuck behind a mahogany Spitfire.'

'Still driving too fast?'

Evie laughed. She liked Pauline already. 'Yes. Daddy likes everything fast,' she said to the girls. 'Cars, women ...' When she turned to Pauline she could see she had overstepped the mark, and blushed.

'Your hours are a bit low.' Pauline frowned as she scanned Evie's application. 'We need at least two hundred, ideally more.'

'But I'm a good pilot,' she countered. 'I would have had more hours but I had to pay for them myself. I taught French,' she said to Stella. 'Daddy didn't want me to fly so he wouldn't cough up for the lessons, and then the war came, and I had to stop just before I got my instrument rating.' Evie thought of the endless nights she had spent studying the flight manuals, the long hours she had put in teaching herself far more than she needed to know since she had been grounded. She was desperate to get in the air again.

Pauline laughed lightly. 'I taught violin to pay for my lessons.' She scanned Evie's application. 'Where did you train?'

'I learnt at Stag Lane.'

'With Captain Baker?'

'No, he left in '34 before I—'

'Shame.' Pauline weighed the girls up. She had taken the measure of them quickly. Her clear, bright eyes were fizzing with concealed humour as she looked at Evie, Stella and Megan in turn. *Adventure, revenge, experience,* she thought to herself. Her gaze turned to Evie. 'You obviously have friends in high places. Most girls wouldn't have made it through the door.'

'Let me do the test flight. Then, if I'm no good I won't bother you again.'

'Right.' Pauline pushed her chair back and handed each of the girls a typed sheet of paper. 'Take these out to the airstrip. Mrs Grainger, you will go first, then Miss Jones, and finally Miss Chase. Each of you will do your flight test in turn. If all goes well you'll be brought back for a final chat with the Chief Flying Instructor, and then we can sort out the paperwork. Good luck.'

Stella and Evie sat outside the Recruitment Office waiting for Megan to do her circuits.

'Do you think you've passed?' Evie asked, her foot tapping impatiently.

Stella shrugged, and shook her head as Evie offered her a Players cigarette from a tortoiseshell case. 'No thanks, I don't smoke.'

'Really? I thought everyone did.'

'I used to. Richard, my husband, he didn't like to see women smoking.'

Evie clicked at her gold lighter. 'Damn, must be out of fuel. I'm just going to cadge a light from someone.'

She walked along the Ops Corridor to the mess, past offices piled high with files and charts. Several pilots were waiting for their aircraft to be called, playing bridge, reading *The Times*, listening to the radio. She spotted Teddy chatting with some of the men by the canteen.

'Excuse me, do any of you have a light?'

'Of course, Miss Chase.' Teddy pulled a black Zippo from his trouser pocket, and the lighter flared. 'Sorry,' he said, laughing as she recoiled. 'We chaps tend to use petrol in them. Won it off one of the Yanks in a game of cards.'

'You'll have someone's eyebrows off with that, sir,' the tea lady said as she poured cups of steaming tea for them from the urn.

'Don't you worry, Jean,' Teddy said. 'Can I tempt you?' He offered Evie a cup.

'No thank you.' As she took a drag of her cigarette, her hand shook.

'Nervous?'

'No,' she said firmly. 'Once I'm in the air, it will be fine.'

'I'll tell you a secret.' Teddy leant closer. 'We're all a little nervous every time we go up.' The men around him eyed her curiously. 'These are First Officers Doyle and Stent.'

'Pleasure to meet you,' she said. 'So if I pass, I'll be flying under you?'

'Under, on top, we're all very friendly round here.' Doyle's eyes glinted.

Teddy shot him a warning glare. 'What FO Doyle means is we work as a team here. We're all civilians, apart from the RAF chaps they sometimes second over to us.' He took a sip of his tea. 'Some of us were in the forces, but can't fly now for one reason or another.' He tapped at his leg. 'No wonder they call us the Ancient and Tattered.'

'Miss Chase?' A young orderly marched into the mess.

'Yes?' She looked up.

'Miss, the instructor has been waiting for you. If I were you I wouldn't keep him hanging around any longer.'

Evie ran out onto the airfield, wishing she had worn flat shoes as her heels sank into the grass. On the runway, an RAF yellow Tiger Moth stood waiting, and her heart began to beat faster, stronger, as the familiar smell of doped canvas mixed with petrol and oil reached her. At least it was a plane she had flown before. On the other side of the fuselage she could see a pair of legs.

'I'm terribly sorry,' she called out as she stumbled around. 'I ...' Her mouth dropped as Beau turned to her. 'Oh no. You ...'

'Yes, me. We haven't been formally introduced, Miss Chase. Wing Commander Beaufort, scheduled to do your flight test,' he said as he checked his watch, 'five minutes ago.'

Evie gave him her most winning smile. 'Can't we bend the rules?'

'It's too late.' He slammed his clipboard shut.

'What do you mean it's too late?'

'I'm not flying with some chit of a girl who can't even be bothered to turn up for her test on time.'

As he strode away, Evie chased after him. 'Now just hold on a minute! I'm a damn good pilot.'

'So you said. It's bad enough they've dragged me in today to check new pilots.' His pace slowed as they reached the offices. 'Margaret Cunnison is up to her eyes testing recruits. It seems they're short of pilots.' He held the door open for her, but instead of walking inside she squared up to him. 'But not short enough.'

Evie stretched herself up to her full five foot two inches. 'I'm not leaving here until you give me a test flight.'

Beau sighed wearily. 'Why don't you save us all some time and just go home and count your diamonds, Miss Chase?' He unzipped his black leather flying jacket as they walked into the offices. Evie could see Stella and Megan signing paperwork with Pauline and the Chief Flying Instructor. Megan gave her the thumbs up.

Evie's first reaction was to slap him, hard, but she restrained herself. How dare he speak to her like that? 'You, sir, may be an officer but you're no gentleman.'

Beau frowned, but a faint smile flickered on his lips as he turned away. As she watched him stride up the corridor, she realised he was her only chance. She ran after him. 'Wait, please.' She caught at Beau's sleeve. 'You have to at least let me try.'

'I don't *have* to do anything.'

'Actually, old boy, I think you'll find you do,' Teddy said smoothly as he appeared at his side, Doyle and Stent close behind.

Beau ignored him. 'We need pilots we can rely on,' he said to Evie.

'But Miss Chase was with me, Beau.' Teddy's voice was sibilant, threatening. 'I was briefing her about her role at the ATA.'

'What role? She hasn't got a role.'

'Yet.'

Evie watched the exchange, her heart racing. 'Test her yourself if you're that keen.' Beau tried to barge past the men, but Stent stopped him. 'Oh, I forgot, of course you can't—'

'What a horrid thing to say!' Evie cut in, thinking of Teddy's injured leg. Beau looked at her curiously.

'I'd remind you who you are talking to, sir,' Teddy warned him. 'You will fly with whomever we ruddy well tell you to.'

Beau glared at Teddy. 'Right, Miss Chase,' he said. 'You think you can fly? Come on then.'

'Good luck.' Teddy winked as she followed Beau out onto the airstrip.

'Pretty girl,' Doyle said as they watched her walk outside.

'Isn't she. You know who her father is?' Teddy slipped his hand in his pocket. 'Lucky Chase, the jockey. The grandfather made a fortune in steel. They have more money than they know what to do with.'

'Do you think she can fly?'

'Let's hope so. The more pretty girls around here the merrier.'

Beau pulled on his leather flying helmet. 'What happened, Miss Chase, did you tire of horses? Most little girls simply move on to boys rather than airplanes.' He glanced down at her shoes. 'You're not flying in those heels.'

'I thought it was just an interview this morning. I hadn't realised you'd actually want me to fly.'

Beau exhaled. 'That is generally what a flight test involves.'

'I can fly barefoot,' Evie said as she kicked off her heels.

'Perhaps you can, Miss Chase, but you're certainly not going to with me in the back seat.' He tossed his clipboard onto a bench. 'Wait here.' He reappeared a few moments later and handed her a pair of boots. 'These should fit you.'

'Thank you,' Evie said.

Beau strode ahead to the aircraft and Evie quickly slipped her cold feet into the boots, before racing after him. Beau indicated she should take the front seat. Without her heels Evie had to look up at him. 'You seem rather taller now.'

'Haven't you heard, Miss Chase? With flying, the chap who has height wins the battle.'

'We'll see.' She had to hitch up her narrow skirt to climb into the cockpit, and she caught him watching her legs. 'You know, a girl never tires of horses; they are much more reliable than men.' She adjusted the Gosport communications tube as he slid into the back seat. 'And a lot more fun,' she said under her breath. Pulling her mink coat up around her chin, she looked around the high-sided cockpit and felt the old, familiar calm descend on her as she checked the control panel.

Beau's voice reached her through the speaker tube. 'Contact.'

Evie craned her neck trying to listen to him as the ground crew swung the propeller and the Gypsy engine roared into life. The crew pulled the chocks away, and at her touch she felt the plane begin to move.

'Right,' he called. 'Climb to 2000 feet, turn left, turn right – first with a gentle turn then with a steep bank. Then a forced landing.'

'Is that all?' Evie called back to him as she steered the plane into the wind. They raced across the bumpy grass strip, the entire plane rattling and vibrating. Her heart was thundering with a mix of excitement and nerves. *Come on, Evie*, she thought to herself as they gathered speed. *You can show him. Pull back on the stick gently ...* Then they were airborne, and all sense of speed vanished. She had to stop herself shouting out 'Yes!' with the sheer joy of being in the air again. The wire braces of the plane sang as she gained height to 2000 feet, the fields and lanes beneath them slipping away to a patchwork of frosted greens. The drumming engine, the clean air were intoxicating – she hadn't felt this alive in months.

'When you're ready,' Beau called through to her.

'Gosh, yes, sorry.' Evie banked the aircraft to the left. She wished she could fly on forever.

Too soon, she successfully completed her turns and had to head back into the circuit for a forced landing. *Right old girl*, she thought, *into the wind, 40 mph, glide her in ...* She held her breath as she slammed the old Moth in hard on the runway.

'Good God, woman, I said forced landing, not crash landing,'

Beau yelled from the back seat as she taxied to a halt. He leapt out, wincing slightly.

'So?' Evie pulled off her flying cap, shook out her glossy hair. She was breathless, exhilarated. He offered her his hand as she jumped down to the ground. 'How did I do, Beau?'

His face spun sharply to hers. 'What did you call me?'

Evie felt a sense of sickening dread. Now he was sure to fail her. Awkwardly she realised she was still holding his hand, and she let it fall. 'I'm sorry, I thought everyone called you ...'

'It hardly seems appropriate any more.' He gestured at the dressing on his face.

'Nonsense,' she said firmly. 'You're still a very handsome man.'

Beau made a couple of notes and signed off the test sheet. 'I'm immune to flattery, and it's too late to make any difference.'

Evie put her hands on her hips. 'If you think for one moment I'd try and flirt my way in to this job ...'

Beau held her gaze as he tucked his clipboard under his arm. 'My name is Wing Commander Beaufort, but as a cadet you can call me sir.'

Beau walked to CFI MacMillan's office and handed him the clipboard.

'Thank you, Wing Commander,' MacMillan said.

Without a word, Beau strode past Evie in the corridor.

'Cocky bugger,' she said under her breath as she watched him leave.

MacMillan burst out laughing as he read the notes. 'Miss Chase? Do come in. I'm pleased to tell you that you've passed.'

'I have?' Evie said incredulously.

'Very well as it happens.' He indicated that she should sit, and Evie pulled up a chair. 'Highly strung, temperamental, Miss Chase could be a fighter pilot,' he read aloud. MacMillan tossed the notes onto the desk. 'Congratulations. In spite of your hours, you're clearly a natural pilot. Some people are born to fly.'

'Thank you.' Evie couldn't stop beaming. 'I've done a lot of work, taught myself about instruments.'

'Well you won't be needing that with the ATA,' he said briskly. 'Now, here's all the information about your appointment.' He handed her a sheaf of papers. 'You'll be based here for your elementary training as a cadet. If all goes well, you'll start out as a Third Officer ferrying Class 1 single-engine light planes to our squadrons; Magisters, Moths and so on.'

'It's incredibly exciting! What about the Spitfire?'

'Let's walk before we run shall we?' He hesitated. 'This is a job many men and women would love to do, Miss Chase, but remember what you are taking on. I need you to be cool, calm and collected at all times – a little adrenalin is good, but I've seen too many pilots lost thanks to a combination of excitement and lack of experience. I've also seen chaps with thousands of hours cock up because they think they know it all and won't listen to instructions. What I expect from my pilots is hard work, enthusiasm and a love of flying. We have some first class pilots based here, and you can learn a lot from them. Talk to Joan Hughes – she'll show you the ropes. She's been with us a year now.'

'Thank you, I'll try and find her.'

'Now, if you follow Mikki you'll be given a numbered flight authorisation card and chits for your uniform. As a cadet you'll have a single half stripe.'

'Oh.' Evie longingly eyed the numerous braid stripes adorning his shoulders.

'Mikki will also sort out your medical and give you the address of your billet.'

'My billet? No, that won't be necessary, I plan to live at home.'

'Miss Chase, we are a small operation here. At first, it would do you well to muck in a bit, prove to the girls you're one of the team.'

Evie frowned, but she understood what he was talking about. 'Yes, sir.'

'This is the address where you will be billeted. The other new girls have gone over already. It's a pretty little estate cottage, and we have several pilots staying close by.' He paused, eyed Evie's mink coat and muddy high heels. 'But it might be rather more basic than you are used to.'

Still smarting from the indignity of the medical Doc Barbour had subjected her to, Evie went to the mess for a restorative cup of tea. Jean the tea lady looked up from wiping the counter.

'Yes, love, what'll it be?'

'I don't suppose you've got anything stronger than orangeade hidden back there?' Evie leant against the counter with her arms folded protectively across her chest.

'Now, you'll get me in trouble!' Jean tossed her head back as she laughed. 'You're new aren't you?'

Evie introduced herself as Jean poured the tea. 'I've just had my medical.' She cupped her hands around the tea to warm up.

Jean clucked her tongue. 'What you want is a spot of brandy in that then.' She folded her arms over her ample bosom and leant closer to Evie. 'Don't take it personal, love. Men, women, old Doc Barbour gets them all in their birthday suits. They say,' she whispered, 'he likes them blue movies too.' She leant back, pursed her lips disapprovingly and patted her turban.

'He had the cheek to say I'm too short for the ATA.' Evie bit her lip. 'Still, he passed me anyway.'

'Well, you're through the worst of it now, Miss. Welcome on board.'

Evie frowned. She hoped Jean was right, but she had a feeling this was just the beginning.

5

'Damn it, where is this place?' Evie said as the Aston crawled along Cox Green Lane. In the failing light and the thin beams from her blacked-out headlights she could see no sign of the farm. As she passed the same cottage for a second time, she spotted a chink of light coming from a tear in the blackout curtains on the ground floor, and she pulled to a halt to ask directions.

Evie shivered as she clambered out of the car, her shoes sliding on the frozen road. 'Beehive Cottage.' She read the name on the gate as she walked gingerly up to the front door. Deep scratches gouged the wood and she hesitated before ringing the bell. As it rang, a wild growl and the sound of frantic claws greeted her from behind the door. She could have sworn she heard a monkey too.

'Get down, Spot!' she heard a deep male voice call out. She stepped back uncertainly as the bolt on the door slid. An attractive man still in his uniform popped his head around the corner. 'Can I help you?'

Evie's eyes widened in horror at the sound of a low, threatening yowl. 'I hope I'm not interrupting?'

'No, no, not at all.' He disappeared again. 'I told you, Spot, if you start playing up again, I'll—'

'I'm awfully sorry to disturb you.' Evie started edging her way back down the path, but froze as the front door swung open.

'What on earth?' she cried, as a cheetah appeared at his side.

'Don't worry about this chap.' The man affectionately patted his head. 'This is Spot.'

Evie moved closer. 'May I?'

'Oh yes, he loves a good ear rub, don't you, Spot?'

'He's beautiful.' She laughed delightedly as he leant into her hand, the fur on the tight, strong skull soft against her fingertips.

'He's a very naughty boy, that's what he is. Knocked the Hatchard's Dairy boy clean off his pony today, didn't you, Spot?'

'Are you a pilot?' Evie asked.

'Yes. I'm Harben. Everyone calls me Bill.' He offered her his hand. 'I've just joined the ATA myself.'

'Oh, well, you'll appreciate this.' He unhooked a framed photo from the wall. 'Here's Spot with Pop d'Erlanger.'

'Friends in high places?' Evie handed the photo back. 'I'm trying to find my billet. Is there a farm near here?'

'Yes, you missed the turning about quarter of a mile back. It's not marked now they've taken all the signposts down.'

'Ah.' Evie nodded. 'That explains it.'

'Head down Highfield Lane, there's a stile just opposite the turning,' he called after her. 'Can't miss it!'

'Wouldn't bet on it.'

'Toodle-oo.' He waved, and the lane fell into darkness as he closed the door.

The Aston bumped along a rutted farm track, the headlights weakly illuminating an overgrown path. If the farmer himself hadn't told her the cottage was down here, Evie would have thought she was driving into the middle of nowhere. Then, up ahead, she saw a sliver of light around the door of an old stone house with blackout blinds and criss-crossed tape on the downstairs windows. She parked up outside and knocked on the door. She could hear a radio playing somewhere in the house and when no one answered she pushed the door open.

'Hello?' she called. The smell of musty air made her screw up her nose. It was also bitterly cold, though someone had lit the wood-burning stove in the hearth. Boards creaked upstairs, so, feeling her way in the weak light shed by the bare bulb that hung from the centre of the living room, she trod carefully up the staircase. 'Hello?' she called again.

Stella popped her head around the door. 'Oh, well done! We were just saying we hoped you'd get in too. What do you think of this place?'

'Bit cronky isn't it?'

'Oh I think it's just lovely!' Megan skipped out onto the landing. 'I'm so excited, I've never been away from home before, and look at this place! We're going to have so much fun.'

Evie looked doubtful as she ran her finger through the dust on the banister, and wondered if she could persuade Leo's housekeeper to give it the once-over.

'Don't worry about that,' Stella said. 'We'll get this place shipshape in no time.'

'Where's my room?' Evie asked.

Stella pointed to the end of the corridor. 'Sorry, we bagged the two doubles.'

'Well, you were here first.' She shrugged. As she pushed open the door and flicked on the light, something scuttled across the floor. Evie screamed.

'What is it?' Megan raced to her side.

'It was a rat! An enormous rat, and it's under my bed!'

Megan squatted down. She could see a small brown mouse nosing its way into a hole in the skirting board. 'It's alright, it's gone. Have you never seen a mouse before?' She laughed as Evie shook her head. 'Well it's a good sign. If we've got mice, then there aren't any rats. The mice always move out once they move in.'

Evie took a step forward into the tiny single room, and sat on the bed. The old mattress protested, bed frame squeaking, and she winced as springs dug into her bottom. She took a speculative bounce.

'Listen, I'm going up to the farm to get some milk,' Megan said. 'Maybe they've got a cat they can loan us for a bit.'

'I'll give you a lift.' Evie pulled her coat around her.

'Aren't you staying?' Megan looked disappointed.

'I haven't got my things with me.'

'Oh, right. Does your family live close by then?'

'My father has a house the other side of Maidenhead.'

'And your mother?'

'Stepmother. My real mother left shortly after I was born.'

'You poor thing. I don't know what I'd do without my ma.' Megan squeezed her arm. 'Gosh, that coat feels amazing!'

'Mink.' Evie regarded it vaguely.

'You must be loaded!'

Evie thought for a moment. 'Yes, I suppose I am. Or I was.'

After dropping Megan at the farm, Evie sped back along the dark winter lanes to her father's house, moonlight gleaming on the elegant wheel arches of the car. The camouflage paintwork Leo had insisted on as a precaution left the house just visible in the half light as she pulled into the long driveway. For the first time, she looked at everything Leo had achieved with the eyes of a stranger. *Loaded*, she thought.

She rang the bell, and the butler soon answered.

'Hello, Ross, is Daddy at home?'

'No, Miss Evelyn, he's working late in London tonight.' He caught her mink as she shrugged it from her shoulders.

Working late, she thought to herself. She knew what that meant. He was probably in the 400 Club with some girlfriend. Last time she had been to the 400, the maître d' had diplomatically warned her that Leo was there somewhere. Everyone seemed surprised that she took her father's girlfriends in her stride. It was Virginia she couldn't stand. Just at that moment, her stepmother strode through from the living room, her silk palazzo pants rippling as she moved, a long rope of pearls swinging from her neck.

'What are you doing here?' she demanded. 'You're not staying?'

'Why on earth would I want to be here with you,' Evie said, 'when I can be having a super time in the most delightful little cottage with the other pilots?'

'Men?'

'No, not men. Typical you to think of sex.' Evie started upstairs. 'I've just come to get my clothes.'

'So you're going ahead with it? Leo's furious. I tried to calm him down, but he's quite beside himself you know. What shall I tell your father?'

'Tell him they said I was born to fly,' she called over her shoulder.

'Château Lafite 1926?' Stella turned the label of the wine bottle to the light. 'This looks expensive.' As she replaced it on the coffee table, the flames illuminated the glass.

'Daddy won't miss it.' Evie was still smarting from her run-in with Virginia and she chewed angrily at her lip. She hoped her father would come round to the idea. She stretched her stockinged feet towards the fire and took a sip of the deep red wine. 'It was a good year, apparently, not that I know much about these things. He laid down a few cases for my twenty-first. I'm just celebrating a bit early. We deserve it after the day we've had.' On the kitchen counter next to the remains of the bread and cheese they had bought from the farmer, there were several other bottles liberated from the Chase cellars. 'Sure I can't tempt you?' she asked Megan.

'No thanks. Methodist, you know,' she said smiling. 'Puss, puss.' Megan was curled up on the hearth rug, tempting a cross-looking one-eyed ginger tom with a piece of cheese. As her hand edged closer, he hooked it out of her fingers, catching her with his claws. 'Ow!' She sucked the blood from her fingertip. The cat hissed and retreated into a dark corner. 'He's not very friendly is he?'

'What were you expecting? Some darling little kitten with a ribbon around its neck to go with the heavenly cottage?' Stella said drily.

'I think we should call him Stalin,' Evie said. 'He's red, and he's clearly a bit of a dictator.'

'Well, as long as he keeps the mice out I don't care what he's called,' Megan said. 'Stalin it is. I'll get hold of some fish heads for him in the morning.'

'Talking of which, we should sort out who's doing what around here. What are you good at?' Stella asked Evie. 'You look like shopping might be your forte.'

Evie frowned, then realised Stella was teasing her. 'As it happens, it is a strength. Why don't I take care of the groceries and cooking?' She picked up a dusty copy of *Wartime Cookery* from the table and flicked through the pages. 'What do you fancy girls ... tripe and liver hotpot?'

'Tripe? Yuck.' Stella screwed up her face.

'Maybe not.' Evie turned the page. 'Meat and macaroni pie? Pea soup?'

'That's more like it.' Stella sipped her wine. 'We'll give you our ration books in the morning. If Evie's taking care of the cordon bleu, why don't I see to the housework and laundry?' She glanced around the cold and dusty room. The dirt made her anxious. It was as if she could taste the shelter in her mouth again. She took another sip of wine.

'And I can do the garden!' Megan's face lit up. 'There's a smashing little veg patch out back. Come March I can do us some beans, sprouts, leeks—'

'Digging for victory?' Evie stood and stretched, handing Stella a ball of wool that had dropped to the floor. 'What are you knitting?'

It took Stella a moment to realise Evie was talking to her. 'Oh, it's a little jacket for my son, David.'

'You have a baby?' Evie looked up, surprised.

'He's six months old.' Stella carried on knitting as she talked.

'Where is he?'

'With my husband's parents in Ireland. I thought it would be safer.'

'Safer? How on earth can you bear to be parted from him?'

Stella flushed, the colour rising in her cheeks. 'One does what one has to do.'

'Is your husband fighting?'

'Richard ...' Stella hesitated. 'We were in Singapore.'

'No! How amazing!' Megan perched on the arm of Stella's chair. 'What's it like?'

Stella thought of the colour, the tropical warmth. 'It's beautiful. I was born in India, but I grew up there. Richard was an airman ...'

'Was?' Evie picked up on her tone.

Stella nodded mutely.

'I'm so sorry,' she said quietly. 'You must miss your baby too.'

Stella held up the matinee jacket. 'Me, and every other mother in the country. You know, I had to sew his name into all his little clothes on the boat on the way over. That's what they tell you to do in the leaflet about evacuating children. "If you have made private arrangements, send them away immediately." They make it sound so simple, like you're returning a dress that doesn't quite fit, or a library book.' Her eyes fell.

'It must be hard,' Megan said kindly.

'They never tell you that, about having a child.' Stella blinked. 'When you're apart it's like a piece of you is missing. I shouldn't think that changes if your child is six months or sixteen. You lose your completeness.' She took a deep breath. 'I keep thinking I've forgotten something important, left something vital somewhere.' She ran her hand through her hair. 'Gosh, sorry. Look at me rabbiting on.' She forced a smile. 'It's not like me at all. Must be the wine.' Stella glanced at Evie. 'Thank you. I haven't relaxed like this for a long time.'

'Pleasure. I think we're all feeling a bit keyed-up,' Evie said. 'Tired, nervous ...'

'Excited!' Megan added.

Stella looked uncertainly at her. 'I am rather tired. I think I'll turn in. What's the plan for the next few days?'

'Let's get settled in here, then first thing Monday why don't we go to Austin Reed, to get our uniforms measured up.' Evie drained the last of her glass and handed it to Megan. 'Thanks. I'm not having this nonsense about being too busy to get your uniform sorted out. Looking the part is the whole bally point as far as I'm concerned. I'll drive us up to town if you like.' Her eyes scanned the room. 'Perhaps we can borrow a few things from Daddy's flat in Chelsea to cheer this place up.'

Megan went through to the kitchen and rinsed the glasses in the old Belfast sink. 'Won't he mind?'

'*He* won't. My stepmother will be livid, but that's half the fun,' she said.

Evie couldn't sleep that night. Moonlight gleamed around the ill-fitting blackout curtains, and she lay shivering under the eiderdown, clutching two hot water bottles. She was dying for a wee but couldn't face negotiating the dark, cold path to the outside loo. As she tossed and turned, trying to find a position that didn't have a spring sticking into her, she thought longingly of her bed at home, the plump goose-down pillows and crisp cotton sheets. Every scratch of tiny claws jolted her fully awake. She closed her eyes, tried running through the procedures for take-off, hoping she would finally drift off. She couldn't believe how noisy the countryside was. Outside she could hear an owl hooting, and the shriek of a fox.

'Hush little baby, don't you cry …' The song drifted to her from the landing, and her eyes flickered open in irritation.

'For heaven's sake, now what? Is this place haunted too?' she muttered under her breath, wrapping the blanket around her as she sat up. The song continued, and she heard Megan's door open. Evie popped her head out. 'What is it?'

Megan yawned sleepily. 'Don't know.'

They crept down the corridor to Stella's room, and slowly pushed her door open. A sliver of moonlight illuminated the spot where Stella sat in the rocking chair, swaying backwards and forwards, her arms cradling empty space. There was a gentleness to her face Evie hadn't seen before.

'Do you think she can see us?' Megan whispered.

'No.' Evie shivered, tucking the blanket around her neck. 'She's sleepwalking.'

'What's she doing?'

'What do you think, silly? She's singing to her baby.'

'Let's try and get her back into bed.' Megan took a step forward, and as the board creaked, Stella jerked awake.

'Oh!' Her hands flew to her face in shock.

'Megan ...' Evie muttered. 'You're not supposed to wake sleepwalkers.'

'Why not?'

'I don't know. It's dangerous they say.' She stepped into the room. 'Are you alright, Stella?'

'Yes, I ...' She looked around her, confused. 'What am I doing here?'

'You were singing.'

'Singing? You must think I'm mad.' Her face regained its usual cool composure. 'I haven't been sleeping well for a while, but I don't normally ...' Her mouth twisted, and she balled her fists in her eyes. 'He was here, with me.' Her shoulders shook as she started to cry. 'It was so real, I could smell him.'

'David?' Evie asked gently. She put her arms around Stella, held her close until the sobbing subsided.

'I am sorry. It's just ... I miss him.' Stella wiped at her cheeks with a shaking hand. 'I don't know if I've done the right thing. I do hope he's alright. Richard's parents seem lovely, but it's not the same. He's so little still.' Her stomach clutched with anxiety. 'I keep telling myself that he's better off without me.'

'Nonsense!' Megan said brightly. 'Every baby needs his ma.'

Evie dug her in the ribs as Stella broke down again. 'What Megan means is that you're being very brave,' she said kindly. 'No one knows which way this war will go, and you're just trying to do your best.'

'That's all one can do, isn't it?' Stella's fingers trembled as she touched the back of her hand to her cheek. 'It's funny, when he was born, I used to ... I used to worry so. You think babies are these tough, bonny little creatures but a newborn is such a funny little thing, so fragile.' She bit her lip. 'I used to have these horrible, anxious thoughts, imagined him falling onto the tiled floor at home.'

'I think all new mothers go through that,' Evie said.

Stella shook her head. 'Everyone said to me "Oh, you are coping well!" but what they didn't see was that behind closed doors I was in pieces. I couldn't sleep, I was obsessed by housework ...'

'At least that will be useful here!' Megan's laugh tailed away uncomfortably.

'Was there no one you could talk to?' Evie asked. 'What about your mother?'

'She just laughed and told me to pull myself together. "Have a drink, darling!" That's what she said.' She frowned. 'I thought if I told my doctor how I was feeling, they would take David away from me.'

'You poor thing.' Evie squeezed her shoulder. 'Are you sure you're up to all this?'

'Yes, quite sure.' Stella pulled her dressing gown closer around her. 'Flying is the one thing I'm still sure I'm good at. That's why I applied to the ATA. I do so want to do something useful, to do something right.'

'It might take your mind off all that,' Megan said.

'I hope so.' Stella forced a smile. 'I do worry though. What if David doesn't know me when I visit?'

'He'll know you,' Evie said. 'I didn't see my mother ... my real mother for years.'

'Is she still alive?'

Evie nodded. 'She's in America now. New family, new children, haven't seen her for yonks.' She hoped she sounded blasé. She hoped no one could tell how much it still hurt to talk about her.

'How sad.'

'Oh, I don't know, you have to get on with these things, don't you? I mean, she came to see me, to say goodbye, just before she flew to New York. She didn't just disappear.' Evie's face fell. 'I think she'd be proud I'm doing this, unlike Daddy. She always loved flying.'

'Was she a pilot?'

'Yes, one of the first women to get her licence. That's why when an old boyfriend suggested I start taking lessons I jumped at the idea. Daddy loved her spirit of adventure.' Evie paused. 'But it's funny, he's never liked me flying.'

Stella thought for a moment. 'Maybe your mother was too adventurous for him. Perhaps he's afraid of losing you too.'

'I don't know how anyone could leave their child …' Megan began. She stopped short as she realised what she had said. 'Sorry, Stella, I didn't mean you. There's a war on, it's different. I was talking about Evie's ma.'

Evie saw Stella's brow furrow as she looked at Megan. 'Ingrid had her reasons, I'm sure. Maybe she just wasn't cut out to be a mother so young.' She smiled as she thought of the last time she had seen her. 'She was terribly young, and very beautiful. I remember this car turning up one Christmas when I was about ten. This slim, elegant woman stepped out, holding the loveliest doll you've ever seen. It had a beautiful china face and dark wavy hair like mine.' Evie stretched and walked to the window. 'I knew it was Ingrid, my real mother, immediately. I ran out to her through the snow, and she leant down and held me so tight …' She hung her head. 'Then Daddy and Virginia appeared. He was thrilled – I don't think he's ever really gotten over losing her – but Virginia flew into a rage. They had just become engaged and I think she thought Mummy was there to try and put a stop to it.' Evie pulled aside the blackout curtain and traced a circle in the frozen condensation on the window. 'That night, when Nanny came in to tuck me up after my bath, the doll was lying on my bed. I was so excited to show her what Mummy had given me, I grabbed it, and ran towards her. I tripped on the rug, and dropped it. When I turned it over, the face was smashed in.' Evie hesitated, her fingertip resting against the cold glass. 'I ran to Virginia, begged her to help me mend the doll before Daddy saw. She refused. She said, "Let that be a lesson to you to look after your things". Daddy was furious with me.' Evie's voice grew quiet. 'I never understood why. He was in such a rage. When Nanny stood up for me, tried to explain it was an accident, Virginia managed to convince Daddy she was a bad influence on me. She had her sacked.'

'Over a doll?' Stella said.

'She said she was insubordinate. I think she'd just been waiting for her chance,' Evie bit her lip. 'With Nanny gone, I was packed off to boarding school. It's what Virginia had wanted all along. She had Daddy to herself, and I never saw my mother again.'

The sound of blubbing from the doorway interrupted her story. 'Oh, you poor thing. I miss my ma too,' Megan said as she sobbed.

'Good grief, look at the state of us.' Stella laughed, wiping her eyes. 'Come on, why don't we all bunk down in here for the night? The bed's huge and this place is ruddy freezing.'

The girls clambered in together, piling all the bedding in the house on top of them. Megan fell asleep within minutes, and Evie felt the steady rise and fall of her back against her arm.

'I still can't feel my toes,' Stella whispered.

'Neither can I.' Evie stared up at the dark ceiling. 'I'm not sure I can hack this place. It can't get any worse than this, can it?'

Stella yawned as she rolled over to face Evie. 'We'll be fine. We've got each other now.'

'The Three Musketeers?' Evie laughed quietly.

'All for one ...' Stella said sleepily. 'You know what the boys call the female pilots, don't you? The beauty chorus.'

'Cheeky devils,' Evie murmured, her eyes drooping as sleep embraced her. 'Just you wait. We'll show them what we can do.'

6

It was still dark when they left the cottage, the windows of the car misty with their breath. Evie rubbed wearily at her eyes. She had slept badly since moving in, and this morning had woken early after fitful dreams of her mother. She wondered if Ingrid missed her, as Stella missed her child. She glanced vaguely at Megan as she chattered excitedly in the passenger seat about the car, her first trip to London, their new uniforms.

Stella was curled up on the back seat, watching the hazy landscape appear in the dawn light. She had not been back to London since her night in the shelter, and she thought uneasily of the orphaned baby, wondering whether he was alive still. As country roads gave way to gloomy city streets she sensed the brooding, turbulent energy of the capital.

Evie swung the Aston confidently along back routes parallel to Regent Street and they parked a couple of streets from the tailors. As they walked past bombed-out buildings, empty playgrounds, Stella's palms were damp, her breath shallow. Her vision blurred, and she leant against a shop doorway as a wave of faintness swept over her.

'Can you hold on a minute?' Megan ducked into a newsagent's.

Stella looked down at her feet. A pink bus ticket lay on the ground, 'Careless Talk Costs Lives' printed on the reverse.

'Are you alright?' Evie asked.

Stella glanced at her. 'Yes, I'm perfectly fine. A little tired after last night, that's all.' She turned away, took several deep breaths. 'It's like the Pied Piper has been here,' she said. 'No children, no laughter—'

There was a sudden explosion, then silence, like the city holding its breath. Then came a sound like the crashing of waves on rocks. Stella's head jerked up as the facade of a building on a nearby side street crumbled.

Megan reappeared clutching a trade-card album. 'Wow! Look at that!' They stopped to watch the dust settle, but the crowd milled on around them. 'It's like a doll's house,' she said. Abandoned rooms were laid bare, wardrobes, tables laid for supper, unmade beds suddenly open to the air.

'I can't believe what they say about the bombs,' Stella said, a knot of anxiety tightening in her stomach, 'that brick walls ripple, glass bulges – it's like everything that is solid doesn't seem real any more.' She coughed, the smell of burnt brick and damp sandbags filling her lungs. As they walked on she noticed everything was covered in grey dust. The faces of the people walking towards her were like masks.

'Isn't it stunning?' Evie looked up to the sky as a plane droned over. 'There's so little traffic now, you can walk everywhere.'

'Stunning?' Stella shot her an incredulous look.

'It's so open now.' She gestured along Regent Street. 'You can really see all these lovely old Nash buildings properly. The city will bounce back, you'll see. It will take more than Hitler to knock these streets for six ... Ah, here's Austin Reed.'

As she pushed open the heavy polished door, a brass bell on the storefront rang. A tailor stepped forward to welcome them. 'Good morning, ladies, how may I help you?'

'Commander Gower has sent us to be fitted for our ATA uniforms.' Evie placed her gloves and handbag on the glass counter as she handed him their chits.

A panicked look came into his eyes. 'Do you have an appointment?'

'Well, no.' Evie hesitated. 'But it's imperative our uniforms are made up immediately.' Megan glanced at her, impressed.

'All our ladies are on their break. Perhaps you could come back later?'

'No, I'm sorry, that's quite impossible.' Evie stroked a bolt of blue wool on the counter. 'We're expected back at HQ this afternoon.'

'Mr Green?' the tailor called over his shoulder. From the back room, a short-sighted man in shirtsleeves and waistcoat with a measuring tape around his neck appeared. 'These young ladies are here to be fitted for their uniforms. I'll take down the measurements.' He made a dive for the order book before his colleague had a chance.

Mr Green nervously fingered his measuring tape. 'Which of you ladies would like to go first?'

'You go ahead.' Stella ushered Megan forwards and sat down beside Evie on the cane chairs. 'Mr Green looks absolutely terrified,' she whispered as he gingerly took Megan's measurements.

'And chest, Mr Green?' His colleague appeared to be laughing quietly to himself.

The tailor winced, flung the tape measure out, and decorously turned his head away as he lassoed Megan.

By the time the girls clambered back into the car, they were helpless with laughter. 'Do you think the uniforms will fit?' Megan caught her breath. 'Poor man, the look on his face!'

'We can always get them taken in,' Evie said. 'I heard a couple of the girls went to the men's tailor in Maidenhead and their trousers came up two sizes too big.'

'I can see why, the inside leg was the funniest – he should have just asked me to hold the tape for him,' Stella said. Her nerves had settled now, their laughter had taken the edge off her anxiety.

'You'd think they'd never seen a woman before!' Megan agreed.

'I can't wait to get our uniforms.' Evie glanced over her shoulder and pulled out into the traffic. 'Even *Tatler* said uniform is the look of the season, and ours is gorgeous – the dark blue with gold braid is so smart.'

Evie had always loved driving. It was a passion she shared with Leo – that and horses. As soon as her legs were long enough to reach the pedals, he had let her drive any of his cars, propped up on cushions so that she could see over the steering wheel. She had spent hours at racetracks with him over the years, caught up in the adrenalin of watching horses or cars whizz round. From him, she learnt to love speed. *And what did I learn from Ingrid? Sometimes I wonder if she wouldn't walk straight past me in the street.* Evie pushed the uncomfortable thoughts of her mother away, imagined closing a door in her mind. Up ahead she saw a queue of people snaking around a street corner. 'I say, are you hungry?'

'Famished,' Megan said. She had heard Evie say the word last night and was trying out a new vocabulary.

'I've always wanted to try one of those British Restaurants. Meat, dessert and tea all for a shilling. What do you say? We've got time for a quick bite, then we'll stop off to loot the flat in Chelsea on the way home.' She pulled over and the girls jumped out. The queue was long but moved surprisingly quickly. The restaurant was bright and clean inside, its noisy tables filled with servicemen and office workers.

'I'll say one thing for the British,' Stella remarked as they sat down with plates of piping hot food. 'They're efficient, and they certainly know how to queue properly.' She raised her cup of tea. 'Well, here's to the ATA and here's to us.'

'The Always Terrified Airwomen?' Evie said drolly. 'I think I prefer "the beauty chorus".'

'Rather that than "Ancient and Tattered".' Stella held Evie's gaze as Megan enthusiastically tucked into her roast beef. 'Do you think we'll cope?'

'Of course we will.' Evie raised her chin. 'We'll be running the bally show by spring.'

The girls raced back from London with the roof down. Beside Megan on the back seat there was a table lamp with an oyster silk shade, and a tangled assortment of cushions, drapes and crockery.

'I could get used to this,' Megan called through the wind.

'Make the most of it,' Evie said as she turned onto the White Waltham road. 'We'll have to watch our petrol rations from now on. I'm thinking of getting something smaller for the time being.'

'I can't picture you on a bicycle,' Stella said.

'Why not? Jolly good exercise too when you think we'll be sitting on our bottoms ferrying planes all day. I saw some of the girls doing exercises in the mess yesterday too. Perhaps we could get a little class going.'

Evie pulled up outside the offices, letting the car tick over for a minute before turning off the engine. A Spitfire was just landing, and she looked longingly at it. 'I'm going to fly those one day,' she said firmly.

As the ground crew took over, Wing Commander Beaufort jumped out of the cockpit and strode towards the buildings. He paused when he saw the girls. 'Miss Chase. I thought we might have seen the last of you.'

'Good afternoon, sir,' Evie said. 'No, you won't get rid of me that easily. I wanted to thank you for passing me.'

'Why? You completed the test successfully, that's all there is to it. As long as you fly straight and keep your wings level you'll be fine.' He eyed the loaded-down car as Megan and Stella clambered out. 'Been shopping, girls?'

'No, just liberated a few things from my father's place in town. Make do and mend,' Evie said breezily. 'You should see the place we're billeted ...'

'It's not that bad.' Megan smiled apologetically at Beau.

Evie laughed. 'Well it's not what I'm used to.'

When she turned to Beau, he was studying her closely. 'You remind me of someone.'

'Really? People do say I'm the spitting image of Vivien Leigh.'

'Indeed, Miss Chase?' He tapped a cigarette on his battered silver case and lit it. 'Do you see yourself as the Scarlett O'Hara of Maidenhead?'

'This is the part where you say you don't give a damn.'

Beau smiled, plucked a strand of tobacco from his lip. 'That would be a little predictable. I was talking about my ex-fiancée.'

'Is that a compliment, sir?'

'No. Clearly you've never met Olivia.' He swung his parachute onto his shoulder and walked on.

'Ex?' Evie said curiously as Stella joined her.

'Be careful,' she said as they walked towards the offices. 'You don't want to be too familiar. These RAF chaps can be a bit prickly with civilian pilots – I should know, I was married to one. Show him some respect.'

'Nonsense. What does he want me to do? Curtsey every time he comes onto the airfield?' Evie pulled off her gloves as they went in. Instantly they noticed the atmosphere in the place. They joined the silent group of pilots in the mess, and watched as Miss Gold pinned a notice on the board.

'What's going on, Margie?' Stella whispered to the woman next to her.

'There's a bit of a flap. An aircraft's gone down,' she replied. 'Amy is missing.'

Squires Gate, 11.47 a.m.

There are things I miss of course. I would love to hold, and be held, smell the tomatoes in the greenhouse at home, taste a glass of cold champagne, feel the rain on my face. But I remember these things with dazzling clarity, and we are everywhere, that's what you realise as you take your last breath. Time is meaningless here. I can go back whenever I want, to my childhood, to the desert, to the arms of the men I have loved. All I have to do is think of my last days, and I am there again.

'The weather's closing in, Amy,' Pauline said to me on the telephone when she called me at Prestwick the day before I died. 'Come back by train.' The clipped head-girl tone got my dander up.

'No, I can do it. I shall stop at Squires Gate tonight on the way down. It will be a better day tomorrow.'

'Very well, but send Jennie on the train now. I have a Priority 1 and need her back sharpish.' Lucky for Jennie as it turned out. She was going to catch a lift south with me.

'What are you dicing with, Johnnie?' she asked as we left the Ops Room.

'Not much.' I shrugged on my flying jacket. I wish they had let me keep my astrakhan coat, but I was in uniform just like every other girl. It gets so cold when you're in the air. 'Ferry an Oxford to Kidlington, short stop in Blackpool. I'm seeing my sister Molly.'

It's Molly's belated Christmas present that they fished out of the drink after I went down. I had to laugh when the sailors on the Berkeley solemnly hung my new monogrammed silk knickers out to dry in the boiler room after my demise.

'I'll be glad to get going.' Jennie shivered.

'Me too. I was stuck up here over Christmas,' I said as she waved me off.

Each time I return to my last day, I kick myself now of course, what an unforgivable fool I feel. It is madness to fly this morning – the whole country is blanketed in freezing fog, but I shall 'press on regardless', as they say in the RAF. We pilots are all the same – we know every time we take off that this could be our last trip. Every flight is a gamble. If we don't smash into a cloud-bound hillside, we might be picked off like a defenceless lamb by a lone-wolf Messerschmitt with a gaping maw painted on its fuselage. But, after a while, when you have had a few scrapes and have seen friends not make it back, death loses its fear, its mystique. It becomes part of life.

'The plane's ready,' the rigger says, standing to attention, 'but the Duty Pilot says not to leave.' I check my watch. 11.47 a.m. I jump out, and hand him my lunch in a brown paper bag.

'I shan't be needing this where I'm going.' If I'm getting out of here today, against orders I shall be going over the top. My gut instinct is I can make it. Planes are needed urgently at the fighter stations. We have the right to say no, but in truth we fly all craft, anywhere. Ours is one of the most dangerous jobs in the war, yet few people know we exist.

He looks up at the impenetrable sky. 'Are you really sure, Miss? It's ten-tenths.'

'I know the cloud's on the deck, but I shall smell my way there.' I load my pigskin bag into the back, and look up as a dark car parks beside the runway. The passenger door opens and a man in a black fedora steps out. That is one of the theories, you see, that I was flying a top-secret mission. The missing hours. Apparently I was ferrying a spy into Europe, or helping a lover

escape. Was I? It was expressly forbidden for us to fly to the Continent but we bent rules, steadily broke new ground all the time.

Others think I was shot down by friend or foe, maybe even faked my own death. Perhaps I am still holed up in South America somewhere, laughing into my dotage. Or perhaps it was an elaborate suicide – after my disappearance someone came forward and said I had always predicted I would end up in the drink. They conjured the same stories about Amelia when she went down. Funny, isn't it, the truths and lies people weave around your life once you are not there to contradict them.

As I settle into the cockpit for the last time, I am in my element – senses heightened, adrenalin pumping through my veins. At last the door slams closed, the Oxford's propellers are swung and the twin engines sputter into life. I bump over the rough grass, everything rattling and creaking. Once I ease back, the wheels leave the earth for the last time, and I glide over the hedge. Soon I am in the air. Rising through the cloud is as unnerving as ever but then I break through and I am speeding over a dazzling white sea in glorious sunshine. This is more like it. Here you lose all sense of speed and time, of yourself even. Below the world is at war, but here I have a taste of the eternal as I tool along. It's bliss to be alone, the shadow of the plane skimming along the clouds, a luminous halo refracted around it. This is why we fly. This is the pilot's private ecstasy.

Up here, I am still 'Amy, wonderful Amy', who has soared over shark-infested waters, and flown eleven thousand miles in little more than a wooden crate with wings. I earned my money, but they had the cheek to call me the 'gimme gimme girl' for a while. Still, if you ride the bucking peaks and troughs of celebrity long enough you become a national treasure. If you have the sense to die in mysterious circumstances you become a legend.

After soaring beyond the clouds for a couple of hours, I realise I must have passed Kidlington. Still no break in the cloud. Now *my heaven has begun to feel like a prison. I don't panic immediately. There was enough fuel to fly for four and a half hours in all. There is still time. A strange calm settles as the minutes tick away. I check my fuel for the last time, and realise I must risk going down. I hold my breath as I descend slowly through the cloud. My ruddy cockpit ices up. Now I really can't see a thing. I have to go back, and as I ease the nose of the plane up, panic clutches at my stomach. I am trapped between heaven and earth. This is the first time I have ever really been afraid flying. But wait, what's that? Ahead I see a barrage balloon. Land! By this hour I calculate I am near the Kent coast. There's fuel left for another quarter of an hour. If I trim the plane to fly straight on out to sea, there will be no casualties and I can bail out safely.*

Now, as I descend silently through the sea of clouds towards eternity, I am nearly out of gas and completely out of luck. I know this is it. The descent lasts a lifetime, and my heart tightens on itself as I wait. I would rather die than be burnt or disfigured, so would most of the girls – our greatest fear is hitting the deck in a flamer. I am frozen on the stick, cold sweat trickling down my spine. That my life has come down to this – luck – is galling, when I have always directed my own fate. Land or water? Heads or tails? Life or death? We'll see.

7

The ferry pool at White Waltham was subdued. The pilots carried on their urgent work regardless, but the girls thought constantly of Amy.

'Is there still no news?' Megan rubbed her freezing hands together as she waited for the ground-school class to begin. 'We all know how dangerous this is, but I never thought ... of all of us, for Amy to go.'

Evie paled. 'I'm all for a bit of an adventure, but if a world-class pilot like Johnnie loses her life doing this ferrying lark, well, I'm not sure it's for me.' She frowned as Beau strode past. 'And it's not as if the natives are friendly either.'

'Morning, girls, come on in. We're waiting for you.' CFI MacMillan beckoned them into the training room.

'Come on.' Megan took Evie's arm. 'There's no way you're backing out now.' Reluctantly, Evie followed the other girls into class. As they took seats at the desks, the male pilots watched them with interest.

'What else are you going to do? Go home to your stepmother?' Stella whispered. She glanced over at a dark-haired pilot who was eyeing Evie up. 'Taken in the right spirit this will be fun. It's just like being back at school,' Stella said drily as Pauline strode in.

'Though there's less chance of being bumped off at school,' Evie whispered.

'Please sit down,' Pauline said briskly. 'I just wanted to welcome you all to White Waltham and congratulate you on joining the ATA.' She looked at each pilot in turn, making eye contact. 'The work you do here is vital to the war effort. As you may have heard, we have sadly lost First Officer Johnson.' She looked down at her hands. 'It is a sad day for the ATA, and for aviation. There will be a memorial service at St Martin in the Fields on the 14th, and I would encourage those of you not flying that day to attend.'

Pauline looked at the girls. 'I have always maintained that flying is the best career a woman can have, but let this be a reminder to you. ATA work is thrilling, but dangerous. You will fly unarmed and without instruments. We never, ever encourage our pilots to go "over the top" in bad weather, as Amy did. We would rather our pilots waited for it to clear up, however long that takes. The planes are needed urgently by our fighting squadrons – but it will always be your choice whether or not to fly.' She leant on the desk in front of her. 'Frankly, I would rather my pilots returned home safely. We can always replace a plane, but we can't replace you.' She looked directly at Evie. 'Now, I'll leave you in the capable hands of MacMillan's team. Good luck and welcome on board.'

'Crikey,' Megan whispered, 'if Amy crashed because she went over the top, what hope have we got?'

'She didn't crash.' One of the male pilots leant over. 'She ran out of fuel, pitched up in the drink a hundred miles off course.'

'Have they ... have they found her body?' Stella asked.

'No.' He shook his head. 'You should hear some of the stories going round the mess. People are saying she was ferrying a spy, or helping a German escape. Maybe she was shot down by a Messerschmitt—'

'Or friendly fire!' the man at his side chipped in.

'All of which is hearsay and tittle-tattle,' MacMillan said firmly. 'Right, welcome to the ATA. While you are with us, you will be flying with some of the finest pilots in this country, and indeed the world.' He paced in front of the blackboard. 'We have men and women joining us from all corners of the globe. We are a civilian outfit, but we count many RAF veterans among our number, men like Stewart Keith-Jopp. He may be over fifty and have only one eye and one arm, but he is one of the most capable and brave aviators I have ever had the fortune to serve with. You will come to learn that disability is no handicap to flying complex machines. Neither is sex an impediment.'

'Jolly good,' Evie whispered drolly.

'Now.' He pulled down a roller map of the country over the blackboard and picked up a long wooden pointer. 'There are at this time 800 airfields in the United Kingdom. We have ferry pools all over the country. Those of you based in White Waltham will be clearing planes from the Brooklands, Langley and Woodley factories mainly, so you will get a lot of Vickers, Hawkers and Magisters.'

What about Spitfires? Evie thought as she tapped her pencil on the desk impatiently.

'Each day you will report to your base and you will be issued with your chits. Most often you will be taxied to your first pick-up by the Anson. At the end of your day you will be collected and brought back to base if possible. If not you will take a night-train home.' Several pilots groaned. 'I know, not much fun at the best of times, but we need you back at base and operational as soon as possible. We have more work than we can handle at the moment. There won't be much rest. In any one day you may fly three, four, five different types of plane.'

'How much time off do we get sir?' one of the men asked.

'Time off?' MacMillan turned to him. 'You haven't even started yet. You'll have two days off each fortnight if you're lucky.' He tossed a small blue book onto each desk. 'Let's get on with work now shall we? Does anyone know what these are?'

'Ferry Pilot Notes, sir?' Stella read the yellow lettering on the cover.

'Well done. This is your personal ATA manual. Guard it with your life because it might just save yours. In these few pages are all the instructions you will need to fly any one of the aircraft the ATA ferries, from a Moth to a Lancaster.'

Evie flipped through the ring-bound 4 x 6 cards, each page crammed with small script describing the correct settings, speeds and configurations for countless types of aircraft. *They weren't joking when they said we'd be flying anything anywhere*, she thought.

'Many of your flights will be clearing new planes from factories to safer MUs—'

'MUs?' Stella asked.

'Maintenance units,' he said. 'There they will be fitted with finer elements.'

'Such as?'

'Armaments, radios ...'

'So it's true?' Stella slowly put her pen on the table. 'We fly alone?'

'Yes, Mrs Grainger.' He held her gaze. 'Will there be a problem with that?'

'No, sir.'

'You'll fly at under 2000 feet at all times. Let Miss Johnson's tragic accident be a reminder of the perils of going over the top.' He cleared his throat. 'Now, we all know pilots are allergic to the written word, so we've made these manuals as simple as possible. All we need is for you to get from A to B safely – straight and level, no aerobatics, no instrument flying.'

'But what if we get caught in cloud, sir?' Evie asked. 'Some of us have instrument training.'

'Do you have your rating?'

'No, sir.'

'I wouldn't rely on it then. You have so much to learn so we are not going to teach you one unnecessary fact. These,' he picked up a heavy white book, 'are the Handling Notes. There's one for each type of plane you will be expected to fly, and you should read them before you fly a new type.'

'Where are they kept, sir?' Megan looked up from the copious notes she was taking.

'In the engineering library. Each pool has one. The blue notes you keep with you at all times.' He tapped the cover of the little book. 'I repeat, at all times. Everything you need is here.'

'It seems awfully small,' Evie said doubtfully.

'Size isn't everything,' a pilot in the back row chuckled, setting off half the class.

'Settle down.' MacMillan tried not to smile. 'You'll see, Miss Chase. Pretty soon you'll be able to climb into any cockpit, check the engine and go.' He rolled up the map and took a piece of chalk from the ledge. 'As you know by now, you'll start on Class 1 light types, but eventually some of you will progress through up to Class 5 four-engine planes and Class 6 flying boats.' With a flourish he wrote 'Engines and Technical Aeronautics' on the board. 'For now, let's start with the basics. Your three-week ground school will cover meteorology, maps, tech, engines and navigation. I'm going to leave you in the capable hands of Captain Gribble to get on with your tech classes today.'

Evie rolled her eyes. When were they going to let them in the air?

'How on earth are we going to learn all this in a few weeks?' Evie said as the girls strolled into the mess after class. Her head was reeling with facts and figures. 'I've been Gribbleised.'

'Evie? Is that you?' An elegant girl in a Sidcot flying suit called from across the room.

'Joy?' They laughed and embraced. 'Why, I haven't seen you since the Magyar pilots' picnic!'

'It's been too, too long, darling.'

'Are you still dancing? Joy is the most marvellous ballet dancer,' she said to Stella and Megan.

'Gosh no, gave that up ages ago. What about you? Are you still seeing Clive?'

'That rat? No,' Evie tossed her hair. 'Didn't you hear? He's engaged to some dreadful horse-faced aristo from Northumbria.'

Trying to buy himself a title. The only good thing he did for me was encourage me to fly.'

'I never thought he was capable of keeping up with you.' She slipped her arm through Evie's. 'What about Peter? Is he still mooning over you?'

Evie shrugged. 'I wish he'd find someone. He still has this silly idea that we'll get engaged. I just don't think of him like that, but I can't bear to hurt his feelings, especially not at the moment.'

'I'm sure we can find someone to distract him,' Joy said. 'It seems like a different lifetime doesn't it? Debs' delights, skiing ...' Her face fell for a moment. 'But oh, this is such fun to have you here! You'll know several of the girls already,' she said, and glanced at Stella and Megan. 'I'm so sorry, we're old friends. I'm Joy Preston, and this is Honor, Margaret and Joan,' she added, as several of the women drinking orangeade and cups of tea smiled in welcome. Megan gazed longingly at the corner where Lettice Curtis was playing backgammon with Frankie, hoping for an introduction.

Joy picked up her cup of tea. 'Where are you staying?'

'A ghastly little cottage over at Cox Green,' Evie said.

'Well, listen, a few of us are going out tonight to the Riviera, why don't you all come along, meet the gang?' She glanced over Megan's shoulder. 'You'll come for a drink won't you, Beau?'

'I might drop in later,' he said.

'Do you know him?' Evie scowled as her gaze followed his retreating figure.

'Beau? Yes, I've known him for yonks,' Joy said. 'He was, or is, engaged to Olivia Shuster, have you met her? I can't keep up with them – the engagement's on, then it's off ...' Joy sipped her tea. 'Beau introduced her to me when we were skiing in Lech just before the war.'

'What's she like?'

'Very pretty girl, bit spoilt.' Joy said. 'I believe they're related on his father's side somehow, second cousins or something.' She leant in to Evie and whispered, 'Not many people round here know, but he's a count.'

'Really?' Evie watched him as he walked across the airfield towards a Hurricane. She frowned as she thought of how he had compared her to Olivia.

'Count Alexander Beaufort von Loewe,' Joy said. 'If you ask me, I think she wants to marry him for the title.'

'Well it certainly wouldn't be for his personality. I think he's the rudest man I've ever met.' Evie folded her arms. 'What happened with them?'

'I don't know, but I heard she's keen to win him back.'

'I can't imagine why. I'm not sure I do want to go dancing tonight if he'll be there.'

'Don't be a spoilsport, darling.' Joy dug her in the ribs. 'If our Wing Commander's not your cup of tea there are plenty of other lovely chaps around, and you have to make the most of it while you're training. Once you're ferrying you won't have time for parties, I promise you.'

8

As the girls spilled into the Riviera, laughing and talking, a young horn player rose to his feet, swinging out a Count Basie tune. The dance floor was jumping to the rhythm of the drums as Evie slipped off her velvet cape and handed it to the cloakroom attendant.

'I'll be there in a moment, I'm just going to powder my nose,' she said to the girls. She weaved through the crowd. *There are more men in uniform than dinner suits these days*, she thought, as a tall, auburn-haired RAF officer stepped aside to let her pass. He raised his eyebrows hopefully, met her gaze, but she simply said 'Thank you,' and walked on.

It was quieter in the ladies' cloakroom, the dance music muffled as the heavy mahogany door swung closed. Only one of the cubicles was busy Evie noticed as she padded across the soft, scarlet carpet. She could hear stifled sobs, and she paused, wondering whether she should say anything. *No*, she decided, *I always hate people to see me in a state.*

She slipped onto the plush stool in front of the low lights of the dressing table and clicked open her evening bag, tipping the contents onto the glass table top. Evie considered her reflection, and pulled a face. She sighed and rubbed at the dark circles beneath her eyes as she heard the bolt slide open on the cubicle. 'Eugh, I look ghastly,' she said as she picked up her lipstick.

'You don't. You look s-simply lovely.' A pale, platinum-blonde girl with red-rimmed eyes was looking at her.

'Oh, hello. I hope I didn't disturb you?'

'No, I'm fine,' she said unconvincingly.

'Can I help?'

'No.' The girl shook her head as she sat down next to Evie. 'But thank you.'

She was like a spirit, Evie thought – there was something ethereal about her. The bugle beads of her white dress shimmered against her luminous pale skin, her collarbones jutting as she inhaled deeply. A large opal gleamed on her ring finger as she dabbed at her eyes.

'I don't know what's got in to me,' the girl said as she tugged the diamond clip from her bob and clipped back the loose strands of her hair. 'Men do hate it when you make a scene. He's just s-so impossible.' She glanced at Evie's make-up. 'Actually, could I borrow a dab of powder?' Evie handed her the heavy gold compact. 'Thank you.' The girl skilfully covered the worst of her red nose. 'I left my bag at the bar when I stormed off.'

'Man trouble?' Evie said sympathetically.

'Just a silly argument with my fiancé.' As she stared at herself in the mirror, the girl's pupils dilated to deep pools of darkness. When she turned to Evie her eyes were unnervingly black against her pale skin, rimmed with a thin halo of ice blue. 'You know how it is.'

'I'm sure you'll make up,' Evie said as she dabbed perfume onto her wrists, behind her ears, the warm scent of leather, spice, jasmine and amber filling her senses.

'I don't know. I think I might have blown it this time. He's so difficult at the moment.' She shook her head as if she were trying to dispel her doubt. 'But he'll forgive me.' She pursed her lips into a tight, determined smile. 'He always does.' She turned to Evie. 'Is that Chanel?'

Evie held out her wrist. 'Cuir de Russie.'

The girl stood and smoothed her gown over her narrow hips. 'You are brave. I always go for something lighter and more feminine myself.'

Feminine? Evie thought indignantly. 'Well, good luck.' She caught the cool, calculating look in the girl's eyes as she appraised her reflection in the mirror.

The girl raised her hand, folded her long, bony fingers into her palm in a slow wave goodbye. 'Perhaps I'll see you later?'

Megan's eyes opened wide. The light from the mirror ball spinning above the dancers shifted over her. She watched the women in elegant evening dresses being swept around the shadows of the dance floor by men in uniform, and began to move in time to the big band tune. 'This place is amazing!'

A young soldier turned as she spoke. 'Would you care to dance?'

'Oh, I'd love to!' She took his arm.

Stella nudged Evie as she joined her. 'You look better.'

'Thanks.' The strap of Evie's evening shoe was already digging into her ankle and she was beginning to regret wearing such high heels. They watched the soldier swing Megan into the air, and the shifting light caught her face, her delighted smile. Evie felt time stand still for a moment. Stella laughed indulgently and said something to her. The moment passed, and the dance went on. 'Hmm?' Evie said, distracted.

'I said, we shall have to keep an eye on our little friend.' As Joy waved from the bar, Stella raised her hand in greeting. 'There they are.' The girls cut through the crowd.

'Hello, darling.' Joy kissed Evie. 'Your dress is divine!'

'Do you like it?' She smoothed the emerald satin gown at her collarbone just as Beau turned to hand a Martini to Joy. His eyes travelled from Evie's ankles up to her defiant expression. 'Good evening, sir.' She saluted.

'You're a civilian, Miss Chase, and I'm off duty,' he said. 'Can I get you girls a drink?'

'A Martini would be delightful.' Evie sat on a stool at the bar and pulled out her cigarette case from her bag. She offered him a Player's.

'Thank you.' He flicked open a book of matches on the bar, lighting the cigarettes.

'Evie and I are old pals, Beau,' Joy said. 'The last time I saw her, she had a darling little iguana draped over the shoulder of her evening gown.'

'Poor thing, he went everywhere with me for a while,' Evie said.

'It was terribly chic, darling! Whatever happened to him?'

'I broke down one night on the way back from a party and he fell into the engine bay.'

'No! How ghastly.'

Beau swirled the ice in his scotch. 'I've seen how you drive, Miss Chase. Perhaps the poor chap was taking the quick way out.'

'There you are, Alex darling.' The pale girl from the cloakroom reached across Beau and picked up a silver beaded purse from the bar. As her hand rested on his arm, he flinched.

'Olivia!' Joy said a little too brightly. 'What a lovely surprise.' The girls air-kissed.

'Are you still here?' Beau turned away from her, tapping his cigarette in the heavy crystal ashtray.

'Don't be like that, darling.' Olivia's eyes welled with tears again. 'I thought you might—'

'No, you didn't think, did you, Olivia?' he snapped. 'That's the problem. You just turn up out of the blue expecting everything to be back to normal. When frankly—'

'Now, now, children,' Joy interrupted. 'Let's not make a scene.'

Beau caught himself, glanced at her. 'Of course. Please excuse me.'

'I think it's best if I go.' Olivia's pale blue eyes grew calm as Beau handed Evie her cocktail. 'Will you walk me out, Alex?'

'Why?' His face was expressionless, but the tension showed in the flex of his jaw. 'You had no difficulty leaving before.'

Olivia turned her gaze from Beau to Evie. 'We haven't been introduced.' She offered her a dry, limp hand. 'Olivia Shuster. Alexander's fiancée.'

'Evie Chase,' she said. *Poor girl*, she thought as she shook her hand. *He really is being hateful to her.*

'Chase ...' Olivia tried to place her in this little group. 'Iron? Or is it steel?' She waved her hand dismissively. 'Horses? Something to do with racing?'

Evie returned her stare. 'I'm a pilot.'

Olivia raised her chin, stared down at her. 'Oh,' she said slowly, as if that explained a lot. 'Alex – Mummy and Daddy are expecting us for lunch next weekend,' she said to Beau without looking at him.

'I'm working.'

'Such a bore.' She pouted. 'You're always working these days.'

'There is a war on.'

Olivia glanced over her shoulder at him, the long beads of her dress swinging as she turned. 'Call me.'

What was all that about? Evie wondered, but before she had a chance to quiz Joy, the horn player blew a reveille, and as the band began to play 'Boogie Woogie Bugle Boy' Joy and Stella were pulled onto the dance floor by a couple of the RAF pilots.

'You're not dancing, Miss Chase?' Beau said finally.

'Maybe later.' She watched him curiously.

'I apologise for that little scene.' He shook his head and exhaled a plume of smoke. 'Olivia can be difficult.'

'I imagine you give as good as you get.' Evie stared at him until he met her gaze. 'I have a feeling we got off on rather a bad foot.'

'Do you think so?'

'You seem to be under the impression I'm a silly little girl.'

'You mean you're not?' He turned to her.

'Are you always this charming?'

'According to Olivia I have all the charm of a sabre-tooth tiger in need of root-canal work.'

Evie sipped her drink. 'From the little I've seen you'd give that tiger a run for its money.'

He pushed his empty glass away, trying not to smile. 'Why don't you go play with the boys, Miss Chase? I'm not in the mood to toy with "little girls" as you say.'

She slipped off her stool and stubbed out her cigarette. 'For a moment I thought you were going to tell me to go home and count my diamonds again.'

He gazed down at her. 'If I'm going to have to repeat everything twice, you'll never get through your training.'

Evie stalked away, fuming, to the dance floor, and tapped a tall, good-looking young pilot on the shoulder. He was only too delighted to dance with her, and she hoped Beau was watching as the officer swung her skilfully around in his arms. But when she spun around, she saw Beau had turned away, and was drinking alone at the bar.

'Are you having fun, darling?' Joy asked as she sat at their table when the song finished.

'Yes, it's marvellous to have a night out.' Evie tossed her bag onto the chair beside her. As she recovered her breath, her gaze travelled to where Beau stood alone at the bar. 'What's the story with our Wing Commander, or Count, or whatever he is? He's the most unfriendly man I've ever met.'

Joy laughed. 'Do you think so? You mustn't mind Beau. He used to be great fun, and I'm sure he will be again. He's had rather a tough time of it lately.'

'You mean the crash?'

'Well, I meant more all this business with Olivia.' Joy leant forwards. 'He wasn't expecting to see her tonight, you know, she just turned up. It's the first time he's seen her since he got out of hospital and I think it was rather a shock.'

'You mean she hadn't been to see him at all?'

Joy shook her head. 'She took the crash very badly. Walked out on him, called the wedding off.'

'Did she?' Evie said thoughtfully. 'That explains a lot.'

'From tonight's little drama it's obvious she's desperate for a second chance now, but he's saying it's over.' She sipped her cocktail. 'Then again, I've seen girls like Olivia manage to hang onto their man through sheer damn persistence. Once they get their hooks into a chap ...' Joy pulled a face like a wildcat, bunched her fingers up like paws. 'If Beau's having second thoughts I can't say I blame him.'

9

Bright winter sun filtered through the newly cleaned windows of the cottage as the girls slipped on their coats for church.

'I can't believe how nice this place is now.' Evie looked around the living room proudly. Every surface gleamed, and bright red gingham curtains cheered up the room, picking up the colours of the cushions liberated from Leo's flat. 'It's really rather satisfying, housework, isn't it?'

'You'll be offering the peasants cake next,' Stella said drily.

Evie threw a cushion at her. 'Do I sound that spoilt?'

'No, darling. But you do make me laugh. I can assure you the novelty of housework soon wears off. A lot of the girls were saying they just do the bits that show these days. They're too busy for anything else.' Stella straightened the cushion, patted it back into shape. 'This hovel jolly well should look nice the amount of time we spent cleaning at the weekend.' She checked her hair in the little shell-framed mirror they had picked up at a junk store in town. 'Where's Megan?'

'I don't know, she went out early. Heaven knows where she gets her energy from.'

'That's being a teenager, my dear.' Just as Stella slicked on some red lipstick, the front door flew open.

Megan burst into the room with a chicken under each arm.

'Look what I've found!'

'Where did you get them?' Evie screwed up her nose as the white hen struggled to break free, sending a cloud of dust motes into the air.

'I traded them with the farmer,' Megan said, laughing. 'When we were tidying up yesterday I noticed the old coop out at the back. You know what this means?'

'Fresh eggs!' Stella said.

'He says they're good layers.'

Evie glanced at her watch. 'Come on, we'd better get a move on. The service is in a couple of hours.'

As Evie started the car, Megan ran around to the back garden and put the chickens in the coop. 'What exactly did you trade with the farmer?' Evie asked as she jumped into the back seat.

'Not that!' She blushed. 'I said I'd give them a hand with the animals once in a while, that's all. They're short-handed with the men away, and apparently their land girl is not much cop. Spends her whole time mooning around in bed.' She leant forward conspiratorially. 'The farmer's wife reckons she's pregnant!' she whispered.

Evie sighed. 'Honestly. There's no excuse for getting yourself in the club these days. It's ridiculous. People are getting bumped off or knocked up right, left and centre.'

It was standing room only in St Martin in the Fields by the time the girls arrived. In the front pew a distinguished man in ATA uniform sat next to Pauline Gower, Badger and the other commanders. He was chatting over his shoulder with Beau, and Evie recognised his face from the papers. 'That's Pop d'Erlanger isn't it?' she whispered to Stella as the organ burst into life, wheezing out the opening bars of 'All Things Bright and Beautiful'.

'Commodore d'Erlanger to you,' Stella said.

'Look, there are the girls.' Evie pointed. 'Lois, Mona. I can't see Teddy anywhere.'

'He said to me yesterday that he believes in only "King and Country",' Megan whispered. 'And someone has to hold the fort.'

'Everyone else has turned out though,' Stella agreed, watching the vicar of White Waltham as he appeared from the vestry. At his side a young curate with dark wavy hair shepherded the choir boys to their stall. He reminded her of Gregory Peck. She pictured him more in a sharp double-breasted suit than vestments. As they sang the first hymn she found her eyes drawn again and again to the curate. There was something familiar about him.

'Lovely service,' Evie said to the vicar as they shook hands on the way out of the church. Stella was just behind her, and as she raised a white gloved hand to shake hands with the curate she found her heart was racing.

'I hope we'll see you again in White Waltham,' he said, and for a moment his clear, dark eyes met Stella's, before she was swept along as the congregation flooded out onto the church steps.

'Miss Chase?' Badger shook Evie's hand. 'So glad to see you decided to join us.'

'Thank you, sir.'

'Damn shame about Johnnie. A fine woman, and a fine pilot.' He pulled on his leather gloves.

'Is there any news about what happened?'

Badger shook his head. 'They haven't found her yet. Perhaps they never will.' He paused. 'There are all sorts of stories going round, but no one knows. Let it be a lesson to you, girls. Keep your wits about you.'

Thames Estuary, 3.37 p.m.

I was so close. I gambled and I lost. How was I to know boats transporting barrage balloons inland had been set adrift at sea after one of the craft went down? Ironically the boat was called the Carry On. *Balloons on the coast should have meant I could bail out there over land, while the plane carried on out to sea. Instead they drew me too far. I carried on too far.*

It's too late. Now I am down, flying low over the water, the engine revving, cutting, wings slipping, sliding towards a convoy of boats, and I am counting, one, two, three, the choppy grey Thames estuary below me. 'Don't let it hit a boat, please don't let it hit a boat,' I whisper, bracing myself for the moment to bail out, the nauseous sour taste of fear in my mouth. Then I am wrenching off the door. The plane flies on without me, and I fling myself out.

Oh God, the cold air. It takes my breath away. Some eyewitnesses say my parachute unfurls above me, the whoosh of the air dragging me up and up. For a moment I hang weightless in the air, snow falling around me, and think, This is how the birds feel. *England lies before me, dark and smoking, the Kentish countryside dotted with silver-grey balloons like a macabre celebration. Then I am falling, drifting down, anticipating the dark water. The plane, these eyewitnesses say, appeared to be under control as it came down,* making slow circles before hitting the water. Was there someone else in there? Perhaps that someone told me to save myself, that he would bring it down, take his chances. Others say I landed it myself, smacking the plane onto the water 'like a pancake', right between the Haslemere and a destroyer. I have heard the stories so often, sometimes I wonder myself.

Later, the captain of the destroyer is handed all they manage to rescue from the sea. He opens my bag. The contents are entirely dry – lipstick, keys, a wallet. He gasps. 'My God. It was Amy Johnson.'

There will be a telegraph to the house in Bridlington: 'Missing, believed killed'. There will be prayers in the Methodist chapel. In a week's time Ciss and Will make a toast to their lost daughter in the restaurant at Skindles, still hoping in their hearts that I will walk through the door at any moment. Father takes the five glasses, smashes them so that no one will drink from them again, and keeps the fragments of glass at our friends the Hofers for me.

That is all you have at the end of your life, fragments. Of all the seconds of your existence, how many do you have time to recall? A fraction.

I hear the great explosion of water, feel the turbulence as the plane goes down. But oh, the sea – the cold is pure pain now. I strike out, using my flight bag as a float.

'Help!' I gasp, the air catching in my throat. Then something rises up in me, I fight through the shock. 'Help!' Someone has heard me. Lights from a boat.

'Hold on, sir! We'll throw down some ropes.'

The wash slaps over me, freezing dark water. My teeth are chattering so hard I can barely cry out. 'Hurry, please hurry ...' The boat's name is HMS Haslemere, I focus on the letters, on the lights, but I cannot reach the ropes they throw to me. It is cold So cold, the darkness closing in. I blink, once, twice. A man dives from the deck, a rope around his waist, and he strikes out heroically towards me. He holds me in his arms for a moment. The last human touch I shall ever feel. But I am drifting away. They pull him back in, his body limp.

If Lieutenant Commander Fletcher had not died two days later without regaining consciousness, perhaps he could have told you whether there was another person in the sea with me that day, or even two. Some think it was the door, or my bag, that the sailors mistook for the torsos of men. People make mistakes. A gunner down the coast will claim to his dying day his regret at shooting down an unmarked plane – he believes it was me.

But I don't think I shall share my secrets. Mystery, conspiracy, keeps my name alive and I'm not ready for someone to put a full stop at the end of my story.

I was an ordinary woman who did extraordinary things. The first to qualify as a ground engineer. The first to fly to Australia single-handed. A million people lined the streets of London when I came home. I waved to them from an open-topped car like the Queen, the Queen of the Air. I was an International Adventurer. I was a woman. I was a pilot, no more, no less than the ATA girls whose names you have forgotten. Their joys, their loves, their losses, the dangers they faced were mine.

I will not leave these girls. I shall be their guardian angel, flying beside their Spitfires' wings. When they are looking for a break in the clouds, I shall be the wind that parts a safe course home. Shackleton talked of his fourth man. TS Eliot wrote of the other who walks beside you. We who have gone before are with you when you need us most. We are there holding our dying sons on the battlefields and beaches as they drown in their own blood. These women are my daughters, my sisters, and I shall be 'the other' flying with them, until this is over and we have won our peace.

I thought I was invincible, but it's funny how life plays tricks on you. Father ran a fish-processing factory in Hull; I spent my life fighting to stay in the air, and ended up in the drink just like the glass-eyed mackerel they used to chop up and can.

HMS Haslemere has come aground now. Dread cold seizes my limbs, stops the breath in my lungs. My suit is as heavy as armour, dragging me down, down, down. I hear the engines thrust, reverse, my eyes wide with shock as the stern rises above me, a dark cliff against the frozen, leaden sky. The cold, cold water swells, my body lifts, arms flung helplessly behind me like a rag doll. The boat surges. Propellers spinning, dragging me in to the darkness like Jonah to the whale. The lift, the wake, the chop, chop, chop of the blades. I cannot move, I cannot cry out, I am numb.

Then, suddenly, I am gone.

10

Stella stood patiently in the queue at White Waltham post office, holding the parcel for David. In front of her were two old ladies dressed in the Victorian fashion with long black skirts and high-necked white blouses.

'Morning, Miss Lee, Miss Ferguson. What can I do for you today?' the postmaster said.

'Good morning, Mr Hall,' the elder said. 'Two stamps please.'

Stella's mind drifted as she gazed down at the package. *Master David Grainger*, she thought. As she smoothed his name with her fingertip, the brown paper crinkling, snapshots of her baby came to her, stolen moments of happiness. She blinked quickly.

'Next,' the postmaster called. 'Next!'

Stella looked up finally. 'I'm sorry.'

'Cheer up, love.'

Her mother's voice came to her: *Pull yourself together, girl! Have a drink! For God's sake cheer up.* Cheer up? If anyone else told her to cheer up she would scream. But then, she was afraid if she began she would never be able to stop. She handed over the parcel. 'Do you sell air mail paper by any chance?'

'Sorry, Miss.' He shuffled a stack of letters. Stella's icy stare made him uncomfortable. 'You could try Mr Frisby in the newsagents.'

Stella walked through the village and found herself outside St Mary's Church. As much as she was enjoying living with the girls, she was glad to be alone with her thoughts for a while. In Singapore she had always had so much time to herself. Too much time perhaps. When Richard was away, she had loved the lazy shape of the days during her pregnancy. She remembered running her hand over the piles of neatly folded white vests and muslins in the linen press, feeling her child stirring at the touch of her hand on her stomach. She had felt full of anticipation, certain of the happy future that lay ahead for her family.

It was as if she was a different woman entirely then. The birth itself was a hazy memory. Disjointed fragments came back to her as she walked into the churchyard – the astonishing pain, the trauma her body suffered as they tried to save the baby. She glanced at a weathered gravestone near the path. Sometimes she wondered how close they had both come to death. Afterwards, once all the well-wishers had been and Richard had returned to his base, she had found herself alone with a small child, and she hadn't known what to do. When she looked at David, asleep in his cradle, she had wanted desperately to feel the love she knew she should feel in her heart, but instead she'd felt nothing.

She remembered hearing the sound of David's contented gurgling as the maid played with him while she painted or sewed on the shady veranda, her hands always trembling. Perhaps because her mother talked constantly, Stella loved the peace and silence of her home, the simple white walls and cool terracotta floors, the lush green garden. In the long, quiet hours, she had managed to convince herself she could cope. If she managed to keep the house tidy, and the baby fed then no one would notice what was wrong with her. *What kind of monster am I?* she remembered thinking. *What kind of mother doesn't love her child?* She waited day after agonising day for her spirits to lift, for love to fill her heart, but it never did. When her brother was killed in action, it was as if the earth fell away beneath her feet, and she plunged deeper into the darkness. *And then*, she thought, *I lost Richard*. That was how she liked to think of it. She lost him.

Without him, the silence that she had loved weighed heavily on her, like a palpable rock crushing her. Sometimes, she felt she could hardly breathe for the weight she carried with her. Just the memory of that time made her tense up, even now. Stella steadied herself as the blood sang in her ears, placed the palm of her hand against the rough bark of a tree in the churchyard. She would give anything, anything, to turn back time and be with Richard and their child as they had been in the first few moments together. She remembered the pride on her husband's face, the tender way he had stooped and kissed her forehead. *If only I could go back, I could make it right*, she thought. *If only* ... Stella was sure she would never know happiness again, that perhaps everyone is only allowed to know such joy once in a lifetime. And her moment had come and gone before she knew it. She had missed it. Her brief happiness had flown by unremarked.

Stella was carrying a sketchpad under one arm, and she settled down on a bench to draw the church. Whenever she had things on her mind she found sketching helped. As the lines and shading took shape, she relaxed, lost sense of time. When raindrops began to fall, it took her a moment to come round, to see the water seeping into the textured paper, blurring the pencil lines. Quickly she scooped up her things and ran to the steeply pitched church porch to wait out the shower. As she stood, shivering, listening to the rain on the tiles, she heard a voice echoing through the church. She turned to the door. It creaked slowly open at her touch and she crept in.

'And when we are surrounded by loss, we must remember to cherish that which we still have,' the voice intoned. 'The daily pleasures of friendship, community, the comfort of strangers.' Stella stepped softly through the church, her heels clicking on the tiles. The cool interior embraced her, the smell of beeswax and cut flowers, the rain drumming on the roof. 'We must treasure each day, and celebrate all He has given us—' The voice broke off as Stella appeared from the side aisle. Near the altar, an old lady in a paisley housecoat and a turban was dusting the choir stalls, and she looked up and smiled.

'Oh, hello,' the curate said.

'I'm sorry,' Stella said. 'Please don't let me disturb you. I was just sheltering from the rain.'

He jumped down from the pulpit and strode towards her. 'It's nice to see you again. You were at the memorial weren't you?'

'Yes, I was. It was a beautiful service.'

'Such a tragic loss.' He shook his head. 'Are you with the ATA too?'

'Yes, I'm a pilot.'

'You don't look like a pilot.' He tilted his head, smiled at her.

'I'm in disguise.'

'I thought you might be an artist.' He indicated the sketchbook. 'May I?'

Stella blushed, clutched the book to her chest. 'I'm not very good.'

'That's alright, neither am I.' When he came closer, she saw the amber flecks in his eyes. He took the book from her, and rested it on the pew edge. 'This is lovely.' He studied the sketch of the church. 'You have a very good eye.'

'Do you think so?' Stella felt the heat rising in her cheeks as she stood beside him. She traced the smooth polished wood of the pew with her fingertips. 'You can have it.'

He raised his gaze to hers. 'I couldn't possibly.'

'No, really.' She ripped the page from the sketchbook and handed it to him.

'Thank you, I don't know what to say.' He looked down at the book. A beautiful study of a sleeping baby was on the next page. 'Who's this?'

Stella touched the baby's cheek in the drawing. 'David, my son.'

'How old is he?'

'He was six months when I drew that. It was the last night I spent with him.'

'Oh dear, is he …?'

'No.' Stella cleared her throat uncomfortably. 'No, he's fine. He's with my husband's parents in Ireland.' She added. 'He … We were in Singapore, until Richard, my husband—'

'Your husband was killed?'

'I lost him.' Stella's gaze fell to the book, and she flicked quickly on through the pages. Luminous watercolours of tropical gardens, bright bougainvillea, sang in the half light of the church.

'These really are wonderful,' the curate said. 'You must miss all this.'

'Yes, yes I do.'

'I can hardly remember it.'

Stella glanced at him. 'You lived in Singapore?'

'Only for a few years when I was younger.'

'Where did you live?'

'Father had one of the old black and whites in Mount Pleasant—'

'Mount Pleasant?' she interrupted. 'That's where my parents live. Well, my mother and stepfather. My father died in India when I was six. We moved to Singapore when Mummy remarried.'

'What a small world! My name's Michael – Michael Forsyth.'

'Stella Grainger.' She shook his hand. 'When I saw you – the other day at the service for Amy – I had the strangest feeling I knew you.'

'Well, Stella Grainger, who knows?' His eyes creased with an easy smile. 'Just think, perhaps we went to the same birthday parties!' He glanced at the cleaning lady and whispered, 'I may even have seen you in your bathing costume.'

Stella laughed with surprise. 'If you did I was probably seven or eight years old.' She looked at the stained-glass window above them as bright winter sun shed multicoloured light across them like a cloak. 'The rain's stopped. I mustn't keep you from your sermon.'

'Oh, that old thing? I was sending myself to sleep.' Michael smiled mischievously. 'You must let me make you a coffee to say thank you for this beautiful drawing. I'm a bit of an artist myself. Perhaps you'd like to—'

'I thought for a moment you were going to ask me to come up and see your etchings!'

'Actually they're paintings, not etchings.' He took her elbow, guided her towards the church door. 'But you'll be perfectly safe. Mrs Biggs my housekeeper is at home.'

Stella checked her watch. 'I'm so sorry, I have to get back to the pool for a class. Perhaps another time?' She folded the sketchbook beneath her arm.

'I'd like that,' Michael said, and waved from the door as Stella walked away, sunlight glinting on the wet path beneath her feet.

11

'Morning, Daddy, off to work?' Evie breezed through the breakfast room, pinching a piece of bacon from his plate on the way past. She had learnt long ago that the best way to deal with her father when he was angry with her was to pretend nothing had happened.

'Evie? Where did you come from?' Leo looked up from the morning paper. He sat alone at the head of the vast polished mahogany dining table, dressed in his RAF uniform.

'It's a beautiful morning, I walked over from the cottage.' Evie was wearing jodhpurs, a crisp white shirt and long black riding boots. 'I've come to get Montgomery.'

'What do you mean get him?'

'There's a darling little stable at the cottage, and a paddock. Now the weather's getting better I'd like to ride him out each day. He's getting very bored over here with your geriatric racehorses.'

'Who are you calling geriatric?'

'Daddy, I think it's lovely that you've kept all your old champions but, be honest, they're practically toothless now. Monty needs a bit of fun.' *So do I*, she thought.

'Evie, I'm not happy about this.' His brow furrowed. 'I'm not happy at all—' Leo was interrupted by Virginia's arrival. She swept into the room wearing a lilac chiffon negligee and dressing gown, the marabou feathers around her collar picking up the deep purple and blue shadows under her eyes. She kissed the top of Leo's head, and poured herself a cup of coffee.

'Late night, Virginia?' Evie smiled tightly.

Her stepmother seemed on the point of saying something, but just waved her away, and sat gingerly at Leo's side, fingers pressed to her temple.

'You could be more polite to your stepmother.' Leo slowly put his cutlery down as Evie reached for a piece of toast.

'Why should I? She doesn't care about me, she never has.'

'That's not true.' Leo reached for his wife's hand.

'Thank you, darling,' Virginia said, adopting an expression of sweet resignation. 'I've done my best. I never wanted children ...'

'No, you never wanted me,' Evie said firmly, and strode out through the kitchen door.

'That girl.' Leo clenched his fist. 'I'm sorry, Virginia.'

'No, don't.' She kissed her fingertips, placed them on his lips. 'It's Evie who should apologise, not you. I hate to see you upset.'

'I can't believe she's going ahead with this ferrying lark. It's no job for a woman. Far too dangerous. She gets an idea in her head and there's no talking her out of it, she's just like ...' His voice trailed off.

'Just like Ingrid? That's what you were going to say, wasn't it?' Virginia smiled sweetly at him. 'Don't you worry.' Her voice took on a wheedling, little girl lilt as she stood and wrapped her arms around his neck. 'You're so busy at the Ministry, Daddy,' she kissed his cheek and he patted her hand. 'Baby will sort this out for you.'

'Evie won't listen.'

'I can be vewy, vewy persuasive,' Virginia whispered in his ear, before sashaying down the kitchen corridor.

She found Evie in the boot room, sorting through the coats. 'It won't last, you know,' Virginia said as she leant against the doorframe. She slid a gold case from her dressing-gown pocket and lit a cigarette. Evie ignored her. 'I said, it won't last, this ATA job.'

'You can't spoil this for me, Virginia,' Evie said as she pulled her heavy winter riding coat from the rack and slipped it on. 'Whether Daddy likes it or not, I'm an excellent pilot. Born to fly.'

'Born to fly?' Virginia tossed her head back as she laughed. 'Born with a silver spoon in your mouth more like. You'll get bored of roughing it eventually.'

Good grief, Evie thought, *not her as well. Is this really what people think of me? How can they assume just because I—*

'And another thing. You can forget about having your allowance restored. You may think just because you've always been able to wrap Leo around your little finger—'

Evie stepped closer to her. 'At least I'm earning my money, which is more than you've ever done.' She picked a crop from the stand by the door and flicked it against her leg impatiently. 'Bar the odd shilling on the nightstand of course ...'

Virginia's eyes widened in fury and she raised her hand.

'Go on!' Evie challenged, raising her chin. 'I know you,' she said quietly. 'I'm too old to be scared by you now.'

Virginia thrust her hand into the pocket of her dressing gown. 'Then you're old enough to stand on your own two feet.' She glanced at Evie as she turned away. 'You were never good for much, so if you can earn a few pennies flying ...'

Evie's heart twisted in her chest, an old familiar pain, but she pulled up the collar of her riding coat and smiled confidently. 'It's you who's no good for anything, Virginia. What do you do exactly? I don't think Daddy even sleeps with you any more does he?' Evie sensed she had hit home as Virginia's face twitched. She flung open the back door and a cold wind blew through the house as she turned to her stepmother. 'I feel sorry for you. You must be very unhappy to have made my life such a misery all these years.' She looked out across the frosty lawns to the stables, winter sun glistening on the pale, bare branches of the trees. In the distance she could see rain clouds. 'It doesn't matter any more. I have a job, and a life. I'm not coming back.'

'What about your father?'

'Daddy?' Evie turned to her. 'I shall always be there for him. But this,' she waved her hand, 'the house, the money, your lonely little gilded cage? You're welcome to it, Virginia. I hope it brings you everything you deserve.'

The crisp mid-February morning carried a hint of spring in the air. Evie strode across the kitchen gardens to the stables with a lightness in her step, her coat billowing around her. *Finally*, she thought. *After all this time I had the last word with Virginia!* Evie had always loved the stables – the warmth, the reassuring solidity of the horses. Montgomery had been her eighteenth birthday present from her father; a 17 hands stallion. Now as she strolled into the yard, he saw her and whinnied in greeting, tossing his head.

'Hello, old boy.' She held out a piece of carrot to him, and as his firm velvet lips nuzzled her palm she kissed his bowed head. She tugged his forelock. 'You're moving house today. Won't be quite as ritzy as this place, but we're all slumming it these days.' The groom led him out to the yard and saddled him up, giving Evie a boost up. Montgomery danced, shoes clattering on the cobbles. 'So you'll bring over some feed and hay in the trailer later to get us started?' she asked the groom.

'Yes, Miss Evelyn.' He checked the girth. 'I think Monty's been missing you. Been right off his food.'

She stroked the horse's powerful arched neck, the muscles smooth and firm beneath his gleaming chestnut hide. 'Don't know about you, but I'm in the mood to kick up my heels and be off,' she murmured in his ear.

'I'd watch him, Miss. He hasn't had a good gallop for a couple of days and you know how skittish he gets.'

'Right,' she said. Monty's ears pricked, his breath hung in a cloud as he exhaled quickly. As she dug her heels in, he flew out of the yard, and the sharp sound of metal on stone gave way to the steady drum of his hooves on crisp, frozen earth.

*

As Evie flew along the bridle paths to Cox Green, the wind whipped her hair and her coat fluttered behind her like a loose sail. She never wore a hat, in spite of her father's admonishments. On Montgomery, she felt free, like a bird – like she felt when she was flying. She whooped for joy, the cold air a pleasurable pain against her skin, in her lungs. She gave him his head, steam billowing from his nostrils. As he settled into a gallop up the final hill leading to the cottage, it felt as if they were one creature, his thundering hooves the echo of her beating heart. At the end of the bridleway, where two paths joined, Montgomery suddenly shied, reared up, legs flailing in the air.

'Good God!' someone yelled.

Evie cried out in surprise, used all her strength to stop herself from falling, but it was too late. She tumbled out of the saddle, landing flat on her back in the hedgerow. Montgomery wheeled, and thundered off across the open field, reins trailing and stirrups flapping wildly.

'Are you hurt?' a male voice asked.

Evie was winded. She lay still, checking herself for any pain. 'Only my pride,' she said and slowly raised her head to see Beau, doubled over, catching his breath. The air hung in a pale cloud around him. From his loose aertex shirt and plimsolls she guessed he had been running. 'You!' She squinted up at him, shielding her eyes from the sun. She noticed the dressing had gone from his cheek. All that was left was a fine scar beneath his cheekbone.

'I am sorry, Miss Chase, I didn't mean to startle you.' He offered her his hand, and pulled her up. She flinched. 'Is your wrist alright?' He checked it over, and for the first time she saw the injury to his arm clearly, the flash of burn fading against the smooth, muscular skin. She realised he was still holding her, and self-consciously they broke apart.

'That's perfectly alright.' She was panting still, her chest rising and falling. 'Monty didn't see you coming along the path. Perhaps we were both going too fast.'

Gently he pulled a stalk of grass from her hair. 'Why aren't you wearing a hat?'

'Don't you start too.' Evie brushed herself down.

Beau tracked Monty's path across the fields with his gaze. 'Stay here while I go and catch him.'

'Be careful – he doesn't like strangers.'

'Neither do I,' Beau called back to her as he jogged off across the field. He slowed as he reached the spot where the horse had stopped, beneath an old oak tree. She was amazed when she saw Monty allow him to take the reins and leap into the saddle. Beau trotted him around in a circle, before digging in his heels and galloping the horse across the field, clearing the hedge in an easy graceful leap. As he reined him in beside Evie, Monty tossed his head, nuzzled her hair.

'You bad boy,' she chided him.

'I said I was sorry.' A smile twitched on Beau's lips.

Evie's lips parted. 'Not you, him.'

'I see you didn't forsake horses for boys after all, Miss Chase.' He reached out his hand, stroked Monty's heaving flank, the hair dark with sweat.

'I told you, horses are far more reliable.' She rubbed her wrist; it was beginning to throb. 'That was very impressive.'

'I've been riding since I was a small boy. He's quite a horse for a girl. What is he, 17 hands?'

Evie nodded, biting her tongue at the 'for a girl' comment.

'Which way are you heading?' she asked.

'Back home.'

'Do you live near here?'

Beau pointed along the lane. 'I'm in a small cottage along that way. Ironically they gave me married quarters. I should have been by now ...' He looked down uncomfortably.

'How's tricks with Olivia? Have you patched everything up?'

Beau shook his head. 'She's insisting everything is back to normal. I don't think it ever can be.'

In the silence, all Evie could hear was Monty's heavy, rhythmic breath. She felt awkward suddenly. 'Listen, would you mind awfully riding him home for me? My wrist is rather painful.' Beau shifted back in the saddle and offered her his hand. 'Oh, I didn't mean ...'

'He's a big boy, I think he can handle both of us.' Beau's blue eyes sparkled. 'We can't have you walking home after a fall like that.' He slipped one foot out of the stirrups to allow her to spring up into the saddle in front of him.

'Well, this is cosy,' Evie said as she settled back in Beau's arms. They made their way slowly along the bridleway, sunlight dappling the catkin-laden trees above them as a song thrush called. They ducked their heads beneath a low branch. Evie reached up and brushed the soft flowers with her fingertips as they trembled in the breeze.

'It's funny isn't it?' she said. 'You get so caught up in this war, but the seasons just keep coming all the same.'

'I'll be glad when this winter is over. The cottage is bally freezing.'

'Ours too.' Evie felt the warmth of Beau's body against her back, and with his arms around her, she felt safe. It was as if the warmth were spreading through her, she felt the hair rising at the nape of her neck. The silence felt awkward again. As Evie searched for something to say, she hoped he couldn't see she was blushing. 'I've never seen anyone able to jump straight onto Monty,' she said finally. 'You must be very good with horses.'

'My family has a stud in France. I grew up around them. My mother says I could ride before I could walk.' Monty shied as a bird flew from the hedgerow, and Beau tightened the reins, steadying them. 'After the war I'm going to go home, take over the place.'

'You're French?' She turned her head towards him. 'Really? I wondered about your name. Beaufort von Loewe.'

'How did you …?'

'Joy told me, I hope you don't mind?'

'I'm half French. My father is German,' he said finally. 'That's why I use Beaufort. I've dropped the von Loewe. Most people seem to think I'm a spy.'

Evie turned her cheek to look at him, felt the bone and bristle of his jaw against her skin. 'And are you?' She felt him smile. 'How did you end up in England?'

'When my parents separated, my mother thought I was better off here.'

'I'm sorry.'

'Why? I was perfectly happy at boarding school. Then I went straight into the RAF.'

'Is your mother still alive?'

'Yes, she's in France. I worry about her, caught up in all of this,' he said.

Evie had seen the newsreels in the cinema a couple of nights earlier, the latest reports of the brutality and devastation on the Continent. The haunted faces stayed with her, kept her awake half the night.

'I haven't spoken to my father for years,' he said. 'He didn't have any time for me when I was younger, and now we're fighting on opposite sides. He's in the Luftwaffe. Not many men can say they were shot down by their father.'

'How do you know?'

Beau shifted in the saddle, guiding the horse on with his thighs as they crossed a frozen pool of water. Monty's shoes rang out, crunching through the ice. 'I don't know for certain, but I'm damn sure I recognised the paintwork on his plane. He's something of a hero among the Jerries, more hits than anyone. I've never seen so many crosses on a plane before.' She felt him tense as he talked.

'Surely he wouldn't have opened fire if he knew it was you?'

'Hans would shoot me down in a heartbeat. He's always hated me.'

'Hated you? Why?'

Beau fell silent. 'He adored my mother. Still does. I think he never wanted to share her with anyone, if that makes sense. Or, at least, not another man.' Beau frowned as he thought of his childhood, the dreaded sound of his father's boots on the nursery stairs when he had done something wrong; Hans' face contorted with sudden rage one moment, icy calm the next. His father's moods always changed like the flick of a switch.

'For years no one but me knew what he was really like,' he said quietly. 'He hid it very well. My mother had no idea.' He felt the sour taste of fear again as he remembered the swish of his father's heavy belt through the air, the still, tense moment before the searing pain. He took a deep breath, cold air filling his lungs. 'Ironically he's obsessed with the idea of the perfect family. He used to parade us around ...' He shook his head. 'That's why he was so pleased when Olivia and I became engaged.' Beau gently kicked Monty on. 'He still thinks it can be alright, that Françoise, my mother, will take him back.'

'Will she?'

'God, I hope not. Hans blames me for keeping them apart. He can't see it was him who destroyed the marriage.' Beau remembered the horror on his mother's face when she had walked into his bedroom unexpectedly one night. He remembered lifting his head from the floor, his eyes filled with tears of humiliation, the shadow of his father towering over him. And behind his father, Françoise's face, her screams. She had held him in her arms that night, bathed the lashes on his back, and rocked him to sleep.

'He sounds a bit bonkers if you don't mind me saying.'

Beau laughed quietly. 'You have no idea. That's why my mother kicked him out finally.'

'You're related to Olivia aren't you?'

'Distantly. On his side. That's the other thing – he's rather keen to keep the title and the Beaufort land in the family. His family.'

'But surely if your father's keen on her, that must rather put you off the whole thing?' Evie ducked as a low branch brushed over them. 'I know it would if I was in your boots. I can't bear being told what to do.'

'So I've noticed.' He smiled as Evie turned to him. 'It's not that. We practically grew up together. I spent a lot of my school holidays with her family.'

Evie had a sudden image of them, the blonde, athletic boy and the slender, fair girl. She pictured them by a lake, running through long grass, white butterflies rising into a clear sky.

'Maybe you're right. When I found out how delighted he was it did rather change things. And then I had my accident. Hans has a lot to answer for.'

'I can see how having a dogfight with your father might make things *difficult*,' she teased him.

Beau laughed. 'If it wasn't him, it was a damn fine pilot who got me.'

'This was during the Battle of Britain?' she said gently.

'Yes. Toughest day's flying I've ever had. I kept thinking the other chap had to run out of fuel soon, but he just kept on me .... I couldn't shake him off.'

'You managed to fly back to base?'

'Yes, I made it back to Debden, but my kite was on fire by the time I hit the deck. I owe my life to my ground crew.'

Evie glanced down at his arm. 'Does it hurt still?'

'This?' Beau flexed his hand. 'It's nothing.'

'Flesh wound?' Evie laughed. 'I wouldn't call what you've been through nothing.'

'I was damn lucky, compared to a lot of the chaps.'

'You look awfully well. I don't mean to be overly personal, sir.'

'That's perfectly alright.' He shifted slightly in the saddle. 'Thank you. It's a relief to be honest. I wasn't quite sure what would be under the bandages when they came off on Friday. The surgeons did a fine job with my face. Not quite ready for the Guinea Pig Club, am I? Once I'm fit again I'm hoping they'll let me back on active service. I've a few scores to settle.'

They rode in silence for a while. 'Have you lost a lot of friends?' she asked.

'More than I can bear to think about.'

Evie felt his head fall slightly. 'What's it like? Being in combat? The Russians let their girls fight. I wish they would let us.'

'No,' he said firmly. 'No you don't.' In the silence all Evie could hear was the sound of Monty's shoes on the hard earth. 'Have you ever seen a flock of swallows feeding on a cloud of insects?'

'Yes.'

'That's what a dogfight is like. Six, seven sorties a day, each a ghastly flurry, a feeding frenzy of wheeling birds. After a few weeks you are dead tired, too tired to get drunk and try to forget about it even.'

'But not too tired for romance? All the RAF chaps I've met ...'

'I can assure you that when you are on active duty, you can scarcely be bothered to look at a woman.'

'It must be glorious flying the Spitfires though.'

'They're wonderful.' He frowned. 'But there's nothing glorious about war. Sometimes I think with every kill, you lose a part of yourself. Every time some chap doesn't make it back ...' His voice trailed away. 'The best you can do is to get the job done, and try to stay sane.'

'Doesn't it help to talk about it? To get it out?'

'How?' Beau shook his head. 'This is part of me, part of all of us for the rest of our lives. It's changed everything. Sometimes I think we'll win our freedom, but we'll lose a part of our souls.'

Evie felt the tension in his body, sensed she should change the subject. 'So, do you speak German?'

'Fluently.'

'I'm surprised you're not a spy then,' she said lightly. 'Aryan good looks, fluent German, you'd be perfect.' She felt him relax.

'Are you teasing me again, Miss Chase?'

'Maybe.' She turned towards him, brushed a strand of hair from her face. 'You're quite different away from the base, you know.'

'Do you think so? Perhaps it's more the people than the base.'

'What do you mean?'

'Oh, nothing,' he said. 'Perhaps, as you say, horses are more reliable than people.'

'Well you're welcome to ride Monty whenever you want. I'll be keeping him in the stable here from now on.'

'Thank you,' he said. 'I'll take you up on that. It feels good to be back in the saddle.' He pointed down the lane. 'Is this it?'

'Yes. Why don't you come and have a spot of lunch with us? I've been practising my cooking and I'm dying for a new victim.'

Beau thought of the lonely tin of soup waiting for him in the larder at home. 'How can I resist?'

'The look on your face!' Evie whispered as Stella held her wrist under the cold tap. The kitchen was cosy after the ride, full of the rich scent of the steak and kidney pudding cooking in the range.

'Well I certainly didn't expect to see the two of you suddenly appear on horseback,' she murmured as Beau and Megan walked in the garden. 'Since when were you such good friends?'

'We're not. We just ran into one another. Literally.' Evie flinched as Stella pressed her thumb against her wrist, testing the bones. 'Where did you get to this morning?'

'Oh, nowhere. I wanted to catch the early post and just felt like a bit of a walk first thing.' Stella turned off the tap. 'I didn't sleep terribly well. A silly nightmare,' she said dismissively.

'I thought the kitchen looked clean when I came down this morning. Do you always do housework at midnight?'

Stella pulled a face. 'Very funny. I wanted to get ahead on the chores so I had time to sketch the church, actually. I bumped into Michael, the curate.'

'The curate?' Evie giggled. 'What, that dishy chap from the memorial you were making eyes at?'

'Yes, the curate,' Stella turned her wrist over sharply.

'Ow!' Evie cried out.

'Sorry. There, how does that feel?'

'Better.' Evie's wrist was numb with cold.

'I think it's just a sprain.'

'I'd be happy to take you into town if you'd like to see a doctor,' Beau said as he leant in the doorway. 'I do feel responsible for hurting you.'

'You, and every other man.' Evie tossed her hair.

'Cute.' Beau held her gaze. 'I mean it. I should have seen you coming.'

'Nonsense.' Evie flinched as Stella wrapped a bandage tightly around her wrist. 'We were both going too fast.'

'Shall we have some lunch?' Megan asked. 'Evie, have you seen? Someone's sent you a Valentine's card! I got two,' she said proudly.

Beau caught Evie's eye. 'If I'd have known, I would have brought you girls some flowers.'

'Have a seat, sir.' Evie offered Beau a chair. Her hand lingered for a moment by his shoulder. 'Would you mind getting the pie out for me, Meggie?'

Megan took a chequered cloth from the hook by the range and opened the door. 'Ooh, it smells good!' she said as she lifted the golden pie onto the table. 'I've been sorting the bean seeds for planting this morning, and my mouth's been watering like nobody's business thinking about lunch.'

'You girls are eating well. Thank you,' he said as Evie put a thick wedge of pie on his plate.

'Megan's our little star, aren't you?' Stella said. 'Eggs from the chickens, bartering cheese with the farmer. I don't know what she's doing for him on that farm but it's obviously working a treat.'

'Stop it!' Megan blushed. 'It's nothing like that. He's just glad of some help over there. I won't be able to do so much once we're ferrying, but he's been smashing. We're all set to plant turnips, carrots, all sorts.'

'Megan's digging for victory,' Evie said to Beau. 'Would you like a glass of Guinness, sir?' She pulled a bottle from the shelf and flipped off the top, wincing slightly.

'Here, let me,' Stella said and poured them each a small glass with a frothy head.

'Thanks.' He took a sip, and wiped his lip. 'How are you all enjoying your ground training?'

'Can't wait to get going, frankly,' Evie said.

'Having seen the speed at which you ride, Miss Chase, I'm not surprised.' He took a forkful of pie. 'That's why I shall be putting you through your paces in the trainer on Monday. I was going to pass you on to Nora but frankly I wouldn't inflict you on anyone else.'

Evie held his gaze as she cupped her chin on her hand. 'How's your pie? Sir.'

He smiled slowly. 'Delicious.'

'Is it true,' Stella interrupted, 'that the Luftwaffe is targeting the ATA?'

'Where did you hear that?' he said cautiously.

'Teddy and some of the boys were talking in the mess the other day,' Megan piped up.

'I wouldn't believe everything Parker says.'

Evie put her fork down. 'We're sitting ducks.'

'It's almost like they know when we're going up though. You don't think there's a spy at the base?' Stella asked

'I doubt it,' Beau said. 'It's too small. Everyone knows everyone.'

'But I heard there are spies everywhere,' Megan said excitedly. 'They're parachuting in disguised as vicars and nuns with their guns hidden under their vestments.'

'Don't be daft,' Evie said as she laughed.

'It's true! One was staying in a vicarage near here, and do you know how they caught him?' She leant into the table, lowered her voice. 'The vicar's daughter heard him going to the bathroom at night and he didn't pull the chain after … you know. He was signalling with mirrors from the upstairs window.'

'There are no spies in the ATA,' Beau said firmly. 'All I will say to you is to keep your eyes open when you are ferrying planes on the east coast. The Luftwaffe know the ATA are vulnerable, and if they get lucky and can pick one of you off, they will.'

'Well, it's ridiculous they won't let us have guns then,' Evie said. 'The women fighting for the Jerries even have a suicide squad planned. Not that I fancy that much.' She paused and looked at Beau.

'I think you are quite dangerous enough without weapons, Miss Chase,' he said. 'Let's get you safely in the air shall we before you start shooting everyone down?'

12

'This will do, Cullen.' Leo tapped on the glass. His driver pulled the Rolls to the side of Kingsway and parked outside the Air Ministry.

'Will you be needing the car tonight, sir?' Cullen asked as he opened the door and handed Leo his briefcase.

'No, I shall be staying in town tonight,' he said as he stepped out onto the crowded pavement. He pulled on a pair of supple tan leather gloves and held his hand out to help Evie from the car. 'What about you, darling? Can I get Cullen to drive you back to the airfield?'

'No thank you, Daddy.' She buttoned the collar of her black wool coat, and stared up at Adastral House. 'I have a few chores to do, and after I've picked up our uniforms I can just hop on the train.'

Cullen nodded in farewell and the car pulled out sedately into the traffic. 'Who'd have thought it, my little girl in uniform.' Leo frowned as he planted a kiss on her forehead. 'I'm sure you'll turn a few heads once you're all kitted out.'

'You look jolly smart yourself, Daddy.' Evie smoothed his lapel and patted the medals pinned to his jacket. 'Do you wish you were flying too?'

'Me? No, it's a young man's game. I'm quite happy with all the other stuffed shirts in the Ministry.'

'Or a young woman's game,' she corrected him. 'Are we alright now Daddy? You're not still mad at me?'

Leo's tough facade evaporated and his eyes filled with love as he gazed at her. 'I could never stay mad with you for long. I'm just worried about you, darling. I am glad you suggested driving up to town together today. I feel like I haven't seen you much lately.' He flicked the end of her nose gently with his index finger.

'Yes, well, I have no intention of coming home while Virginia is there.'

'I do wish you'd be kinder to your stepmother.'

Evie bit her tongue – she knew from experience it was hopeless trying to talk to her father about this. 'I had a feeling she would have been talking nonsense about me. You know I don't give a damn about all the loot, whatever Virginia says. All I care about is if you're in a blue funk with me.'

'You should care, Evie,' he said sternly. 'The only people who say they don't care about money are those who have never had to worry about paying the bills. You've never had to make your own way in the world.'

'Neither have you!'

Leo's brow furrowed. 'Lucky by name, lucky by nature. But my father never let me forget where we came from. I worry I've been too easy on you.'

'I do miss Grampy.'

'So do I, my dear, every single day.' Leo cleared his throat. 'Now, run along. You don't want to be late for your class this afternoon.' Evie kissed his smooth, cologne-scented cheek.

'See you soon, Daddy.'

Leo watched her disappear into the crowd heading towards Aldwych. Instead of going through the door to the Ministry, he stepped out into the road and hailed a cab. As they set off across town he settled back in his seat, his face set grimly.

A couple of hours later, Evie hobbled up Regent Street towards Austin Reed, her arms full of parcels. *Almost there*, she thought. As she leant against a red telephone box, she winced.

'Damn new shoes,' she muttered. The stiff patent leather had rubbed a blister on her heel.

'I say, Evie isn't it?' someone called. Evie turned to find Olivia walking towards her. She was immaculately dressed in a powder blue tailored coat and a hat with an elegant white feather that trembled against her cheek as she spoke.

Evie caught her breath and brushed aside a strand of hair that had stuck to her face. 'Olivia? How lovely to see you again.'

'Shopping?'

'I was just about to collect our uniforms,' she said proudly.

'Yes, I was hoping I might bump into you. When I spoke to Joy this morning she mentioned you were coming up to the tailors.' Olivia rummaged in her bag and pulled out a lace handkerchief. 'I couldn't bear to be in uniform myself, so ...' She waved her hand vaguely. 'Masculine.'

What's this about? Evie thought. *Why has she been talking to Joy about me?* She had the uneasy feeling Olivia had been hanging around Austin Reed all morning waiting for her to turn up. 'What are you doing for the war effort Olivia?'

'Oh, gosh, lots. Listen, I was just about to take some tea. Would you care to join me?'

Evie glanced at her watch. 'I only have ...'

Olivia tutted, and took her arm. 'There's plenty of time for you to pick up your uniforms and get back to Maidenhead. I have to pop into Liberty for a few things, why don't we have a cup of tea there?' She steered Evie towards the store. For someone who seemed so languid and ethereal Olivia had surprising strength.

The girls settled at a window seat and a waitress in a starched white apron came to take their order.

'Darjeeling please,' Evie said as she slipped off her heavy coat. Her blouse was sticking uncomfortably to her. She settled back on the plush chair and smiled, waiting for Olivia to come out with whatever was so important. Only her ramrod straight back gave away how on edge she felt. Whenever she was under pressure her old headmistress's words came back to her: *'Deportment, girls. A nice straight, confident back can fool the world and hide a multitude of sins.*' Evie waited. 'Gosh I feel like I've walked half of London this morning. I get up to town so rarely these days, we're very busy—'

'Mmm,' Olivia interrupted. She scanned the menu. 'Let's order some of those delicious little cakes they have here. My treat.'

'And tea, madam?' The waitress stood with her pencil poised. Olivia glared at her. 'Lemon and warm water for me. Not hot, warm,' she said emphatically. She gazed after the girl as she retreated. 'I don't know where they get these girls. I've been coming here with Mummy for yonks, but it's like the whole country is going to pot at the moment.'

Evie watched her warily. 'Well, this is nice. I haven't had a chance to stop all morning.'

'Do they work you hard, the ATA?' Olivia asked suddenly.

'Yes, it's non-stop. Once we're trained up we'll be lucky to get a day off each fortnight from what I've been told.'

'That's interesting.' Olivia pursed her lips as the waitress placed a cup of steaming water in front of her, the spoon rattling in the saucer. 'Be careful!' she said tetchily.

'Sorry, madam.' The girl cautiously set a bowl of lemon slices beside the cup.

'Thank you,' Evie said as she took the pot of tea. A tier of elaborate little cream cakes was placed between them. 'These do look good,' she said as she helped herself to a tiny scone. 'What a treat.' As she took a bite, she noticed Olivia was toying with her cake, breaking it into tiny pieces with her fork without eating a single morsel. 'Do you live in town?'

'Yes, I have a pied-à-terre near here.' Evie noticed that when Olivia spoke, her eyes rolled upwards occasionally. 'Mummy and Daddy have a small estate in Norfolk.'

'Lucky you. What a beautiful place to grow up.' Evie adjusted her vision of Olivia and Beau as children, imagined them boating on the Broads, or racing across the wide flat sands at Holkham. 'Your fiancé, Beau,' she said awkwardly, 'he mentioned that he spent his holidays with your family.'

'Did he?' Olivia's eyes locked onto hers and she stopped

fiddling with her cake. 'Dear Alex.' She laughed, a tinkling coquettish sound. She glanced at the table next to them, where two soldiers sat talking quietly. One of the men looked over and smiled. Olivia stabbed at her cream cake, showering choux pastry as she leant towards Evie. 'I do wish they would stop gawping at us, don't you? It's so tiresome.'

Evie looked at them. 'They're harmless enough.' She tried to guess Olivia's age – eighteen, perhaps nineteen? Something about this impromptu tea party reminded Evie of the family dinners where she ended up sitting at the children's table entertaining her little cousins. 'Why did you say it was interesting we work so hard?'

'Hm?' Olivia waved the steam from her cup as she sipped elegantly at her water. Her eyes flickered. 'It's Alex ... or Beau as you all call him.'

'Actually I call him sir.'

'Do you? How amusing.' When she laughed, Evie thought of the peal of tiny bells. 'He's been saying he can't possibly come and see me, he's working round the clock. I thought he was giving me the brush off.' She paused. 'Or that he was seeing someone else.'

So that's what this is about, Evie thought. 'I hardly know him ...' she said, and set down her cup of tea.

'Oh! No!' Olivia laughed, her tinkling little laugh grating on Evie's nerves now. 'You? Not you, my dear. You're not his type at all.'

'Meaning?'

'Please don't be offended.' Olivia patted her hand chummily. 'I just meant Alex prefers—'

'Someone like you?'

Two bright spots of colour rose in Olivia's cheeks. 'We grew up together, Alex and I. Of course he's a lot older than me. He was more like an elder brother at first.' Her eyes flickered. 'I've been such a fool. His parents adore me.' She tossed her hair. 'I just can't bear the thought of losing him. We are meant to be together. I will be the Countess von Loewe. It's my destiny. Alex will come back to me.'

114

'Really?' Evie extricated her hand. 'I heard you ran out on him.'

Olivia glared at her. 'Did Alex say that? That's nonsense. I was scared, that was all. I didn't think I could cope.' She brushed the petals of the flowers on the table. 'Even if he wasn't himself – I mean physically – any more, our children would still be beautiful and pure. Oh we've talked and talked about the gorgeous babies we'll have together.'

Pure? Evie thought. With a dawning horror she realised what Olivia was talking about. She thought of the German propaganda films she had seen, of flaxen Aryan youths striding wholesomely through the countryside.

'That's what you meant, isn't it?' She gathered up her parcels. 'You said I'm not Beau's type. What you meant was I'm ... too dark!'

'Hush!' Olivia glanced nervously around. 'I just meant that our families want the blood line of our children to be unblemished. Uncle Hans says—'

'But he's a Nazi.' Evie's eyes widened in horror. 'You're a sympathiser aren't you?' she said.

Olivia folded her hands in her lap. 'My father and Uncle Hans are very close. They ... we, share certain ideologies.'

'We? You mean you and Beau?' Evie's heart was racing. 'I'll have you know my mother is Danish, and my father's family is Jewish. I may not be "pure" like you, but I'm damn proud of my family and who I am.'

'Oh dear, I've upset you,' Olivia said limply. 'All I wanted was to be your friend. You seemed so kind the other night, and I thought ...' She hesitated. 'I thought you might be able to tell me what Beau gets up to.'

'You want me to spy on your fiancé?' Evie said incredulously. She pulled on her coat. 'Ridiculous! Why don't you grow up and ask him yourself what's going on Olivia?'

'Yes, yes ... I'm quite sure you're right.'

'As for your precious Beau, or Alex, or whatever you call him, he may be making love to half the women at White Waltham as far as I know, but I wouldn't touch him if he was the last man on earth.' Evie tossed a few coins onto the table with a flourish. 'Good day.'

As she watched Evie leave, a satisfied smile crept over Olivia's lips.

13

The girls marched through the offices side by side. In their new uniforms they felt ten feet tall. One of the men couldn't help wolf whistling as they walked past, and every head turned.

'Aye, aye – here comes the beauty chorus,' he said to Doyle as they stepped aside to let the girls pass.

'Oh God, I love our uniforms!' Megan whispered as they signed the students' attendance book. 'I'm going to wear mine even on my day off!'

'Good morning, everyone,' Badger said as the class settled down, chairs scraping on the lino floor. Someone sneezed. 'I'd take a whisky and aspirin for that, laddie. We don't want you falling sick on us now.'

'Yes, sir,' the man said.

'Right, chaps,' he said, and paused, looking directly at Evie, 'and girls. We've reached the point you have all been waiting for. Congratulations on passing your ground-school tests. Captain Gribble has signed you off, and it is now time for your cross-country training. You will all be flying dual then solo in the Magister. As cadets we expect you to complete thirty cross-country flights solo before we admit you to the ferry pool. You will also fly dual then solo in the Miles Master, before progressing to the Harvard—'

'Is that the one that sounds like an angry bee?' Megan whispered to Evie.

'Now,' Badger continued, 'you have each been assigned an instructor. Because we urgently need fresh blood, as it were, Nora will be working with several other pilots to train you.' Through the sea of heads, Evie caught Beau's eye.

Nora stood, and shuffled through her papers. 'Thank you, sir. Let's get cracking. Will those pilots flying this morning please change and meet their instructors on the field.'

Evie's stomach tensed with excitement. 'That's us then, girls,' she said, as the meeting broke up and the pilots filed out of the room.

They changed quickly in the cloakroom. As Evie touched up her lipstick in the mirror, Megan slipped out of her pleated skirt. 'This lovely uniform,' she said as she carefully folded her skirt in the locker, 'all this and £26 a year, I feel like I'm dreaming.'

Evie shrugged on her heavy black leather sheepskin jacket over her Sidcot suit. 'I wish this was blue,' she said as she turned in front of the mirror. 'Do you think ...?'

Stella laughed as she fastened her high boots. 'It's RAF regulation, Evie, not a fashion statement.'

'I know, darling, but black and navy.'

'Your shirts are wizzo,' Megan said, touching the soft fabric of Evie's spare shirt in the locker. Evie had turned the tiny space into a miniature version of her dressing table. A beaded evening dress glittered in the shadows at the back, and beside her ferry notes were scattered a gold lipstick and a bottle of Chanel Cuir de Russie.

'Well, it's such a relief that we could at least choose our own shirts and ties,' she said. 'But I didn't go quite as far as Wendy.'

'Who?' Megan said as she wriggled into her flight suit.

'Audrey Sale-Barker,' Evie said. 'She had her uniform made up in Savile Row. Haven't you seen it? It has a scarlet lining.' She brushed down her jacket before hanging it up, imagining the day when there would be gold wings in the empty space.

'Right,' Stella said. 'Everything tiggerty-boo?'

The girls linked arms. 'Let's go and show them what we're made of,' Evie said.

A haze of tobacco smoke hung like a cloud across the mess ceiling as Evie pushed her way through the crowd after her flight. Several of the pilots were clustered around the stoves for warmth. A paper dart shot across the room as she walked past, and she saw Miss Gold the secretary pinning a lost property notice on the board. Evie was freezing, and dying for a cup of tea. She couldn't see Stella or Megan, so she joined the queue and waited patiently, rubbing her arms to warm up.

'Don't give me your "Hi babe" look, Arthur Smith,' Jean said from behind the counter.

'Come on, Jeanie, you know you want to go out dancing with me Friday. We could have a couple of pints at the Beehive first…'

Evie peered around the side of the queue and saw one of the engineers leaning against the counter, his hat at a jaunty angle. He picked up a cake, but Jean smacked his hand.

'Taking liberties like that. Get your filthy oily hands off my scones,' she said.

Evie suppressed a laugh.

'There you are!' Stella joined her in the queue. 'How did you get on?'

'Fine,' Evie said. 'Old misery guts didn't say much, but at least I didn't get told off this time.' She didn't like to admit how much she had enjoyed flying with Beau again, the sensation that he was right behind her. She had to force herself to concentrate on his instructions because all she could think about was the ride home on Monty. She had thought after lunch the other day he might have been more friendly, but he had closed off again. 'I mentioned I bumped into his fiancée the other day in town, but he just cut me dead.' Evie flushed angrily at the thought of her confrontation with Olivia. As Beau debriefed her after the flight, she had looked at him and wondered if he really did have the same twisted views as Olivia. She couldn't make sense of it at all. 'How did you get on?'

'Nora is a marvellous instructor,' Stella said. 'She just gives you so much confidence.'

Lucky you, Evie thought.

'To be honest it was the first time I've really enjoyed myself flying. I was always so nervous with Richard, worried that I had to impress him.' She hesitated. 'Nora said she couldn't believe I only had 250 hours.'

'Good for you.'

'What's going on?' Stella craned her head above the queue. 'Is there a hold-up?'

'Just a drink then? I'll pick you up at eight.' Arthur tried again.

'Here's your char.' Jean thumped a mug of tea in front of him. 'Now move along and behave yourself.'

'Give us a kiss!'

'Arthur!' Jean blushed as several of the pilots whistled. 'Behave yourself.'

'That's not what you said on Saturday at the Jolly Farmer.'

As Evie reached the counter she saw a small posy of violets on the counter, tied with a purple velvet ribbon. 'Looks like spring has sprung,' she whispered to Stella.

'Romance in the ATA?' She giggled. 'It's all getting a bit fruity.'

'What's that you say?' Jean looked at her.

Stella stopped laughing. 'Sorry, Jean, we were just talking about fruit—'

'Oranges,' Evie said quickly. 'We were just discussing the best way to preserve them. Thick- or thin-shred marmalade?'

'My ma swears by thick,' Jean said as she poured their tea.

'Thick it is then.' Stella bit her lip. 'Thank you, Jean.'

The girls managed to hold in their laughter until they were at their table.

'Oh,' Evie gasped. 'It's not fair. Even Jean is being romanced. Look at us, in the prime of our life, sitting at home night after night reading our tech manuals.'

'We haven't got the time for romance, darling. There are planes to fly.' Stella sipped her tea. 'Did you hear? One of our Ansons rammed a Heinkel. Smashed the thing to pieces.'

'Really? Who was the pilot?'

'I don't know, but Jerry had better watch out. We may be unarmed but we're still dangerous.'

14

The days passed quickly as the girls immersed themselves in training. They flew until dusk, and often Evie and Beau returned to base just as everything was closing up, weary figures in silhouette streaming from the offices and huts to the coaches for their journey home. Evie found she looked forward to flying with Beau more and more. She soloed after ten hours' instruction with him, but when she flew alone on her cross-country trips it was Beau's voice she heard talking her calmly through the procedures. In spite of herself, she found she missed him as she performed endless circuits and bumps, and soared high above the mosaic of fields below. Yet when she thought of him, and Olivia, doubts nagged at her. She wanted to ask him why Olivia had been so cruel, but every time she imagined having it out with him, she faltered. Evie was ashamed at how much Olivia's words had stung.

'He's an enigma,' she said to Megan as she unpacked the groceries from the market. 'I've never met anyone quite like him. He's arrogant, moody ...'

'Sounds like you've met your match,' Megan laughed as Evie passed her the last of the packets from her basket.

'Oh, nonsense. I can hold my own with our Wing Commander.' Evie hung her coat on the pegs by the back door.

'How are you getting on?'

'Not too bad,' Megan said. 'I think I'll get my wings—'

Evie glanced at her. 'Is everything OK?'

'Oh, it's nothing really. Just some of the men teasing me.' The colour rose in her cheeks. 'One of them called me Pilot Officer Prune the other day when I messed something up, and now wherever I go it's "Hello Pruney". I'm not that bad. I don't get everything wrong. It's just taken me a while to get to grips with the technical bits.'

'You passed your exams.'

'Just. I wouldn't have if you hadn't helped me understand everything. Everything comes easily to you, you're so lucky.' Her eyes fell. 'I wish I was more like you. You came top of the class.'

'Well, I'm a girly swot aren't I?' Evie nudged her. 'You'll be fine with whatever else they throw at us,' she said kindly.

'Yes, yes I will,' Megan said.

Evie pulled a face. 'Gosh, I'm dead beat. I tell you something, I am sick to death of food queues and shopping bags.' She kicked off her shoes. 'When I popped into Fortnum & Mason's last leave day, their displays were dazzling, but it was all condiments. I want a good roast chicken.' She licked her lips as she imagined a crispy golden bird fresh from the oven.

'Hands off my hens!' Megan laughed. 'How about eggs instead? I see you managed to get a bit of extra butter.'

Evie perched on one of the wobbly old kitchen stools. 'It's all about buying by personality, darling,' she said as she lit a cigarette, resting her head against the wall. She tapped her lighter on the red Formica table. 'I've always made sure to be charming to shop people. Imagine how tedious their work is, and how ghastly most people are to them.'

'Do you miss being able to buy nice things? I mean, you're so—'

'Rich?' Evie exhaled a plume of smoke. 'No, I don't. Anyway I'm not rich. Daddy has always been incredibly strict about cash. If I wanted something nice I had to save up for it. I won't get a bean of my own money until I'm twenty-one.'

'I just assumed ...'

'Yes, well, it seems a lot of people have made the wrong assumptions about me.' She flicked her cigarette. 'Now Virginia has arranged for my allowance to be cut off, I'm bumping along on my salary just like everyone else. We all have to do what we can.'

'Hello, darling, how did you get on? Shall I fix us some lunch?' Stella swung through the kitchen laden down with card and paper.

'No, don't worry, I'll rustle something up in a minute.'

'Are you done with that copy of *Tatler*? I'm just sorting out the salvage.'

'Yes thanks.' Evie stubbed out her cigarette and padded over to the pantry. 'How about an omelette?' she called.

'Sounds good. I'll just go and finish up the laundry,' Stella said.

'Thank goodness she's cheered up,' Megan whispered.

'What do you mean?'

'Ooh, she really snapped at me this morning.'

'I'm sure she didn't mean it. Everyone is tired and on edge at the moment.'

Megan frowned. 'No, she was really horrible. "What have you got to be so bloody cheerful about?" That's what she said. As if it's a crime to be happy.'

Evie could see Stella moving around in the lean-to, her shadow just visible through the opaque glass in the door as she lowered laundry into the tub. 'I wouldn't let it bother you, darling. Stella's only really content when she's doing something, it seems to me. When she's mooching around, well, perhaps her thoughts get too much for her. Imagine what it's like to lose your husband, and then to have to send your baby away.'

As Megan laid the table, Evie whisked eggs and set about cooking lunch. The girls looked up as someone knocked on the front door.

'I'll go. Are you expecting anyone?' Megan asked as she hurried to answer it.

'No.' Evie wiped her hands on her apron.

Megan's voice drifted through to the kitchen. 'Hello, can I help you?' she said. 'Yes, do come in.' As she pushed open the door, sunlight spread across the floor of the living room. A dark figure stepped in and removed his hat.

'Hello,' Michael said. 'I do hope I'm not disturbing you.' As he unwound his scarf and Evie saw his dog collar she put two and two together.

'Not at all. You must be Michael? Stella's just in the dhobi room if you want to go through.' She indicated the back of the cottage with a toss of her head as she cooked.

Once Michael was safely out of the way, Megan scampered over. 'Blimey, he's a bit of a dreamboat for a vicar.'

'I know!' Evie flipped the omelette onto a plate and cut it in two. 'Still, from what Stella said to me the other day, they're just friends.'

'It's a shame. It would be nice to see her cheer up a bit.'

'I'm sure she knows what she's doing. It's probably too soon after Richard for her to be out romancing, even with a vicar. Shall we start? I have a feeling we won't be seeing Stella for a while.'

'East of the sun ...' Stella sang under her breath as she scrubbed the sheets on the board. She stopped to wipe a strand of hair from her face. At her side the woollens were soaking in Lux, the fresh scent of soap powder filling the air. She sensed someone watching, and swivelled around quickly.

'Hello,' Michael said.

'Michael! What a lovely surprise. I'm sorry, I must look a frightful mess.'

'No, not at all.' He smiled as he stepped closer to her. The light danced over them, filtered softly through the opaque roof of the laundry room. 'You have a little ...' He hesitated, reached up, almost touched her face.

Stella brushed the fine bubbles away. 'Thank you.'

'I hope you don't mind me dropping in unannounced, but you don't have a telephone, and I was visiting one of the land girls at the farm.'

'No, no, not at all.' Stella tidied away a packet of Vim and a cleaning cloth by the old sink.

'I brought you that book about Stanley Spencer I mentioned.' Michael slipped a slim volume from his coat pocket.

'Thank you,' she said again, awkwardly wiping her raw, red hands on a cloth and taking it from him. She flicked through the images. 'These are beautiful.'

'I thought, perhaps ... If you haven't seen his work at Cookham. Would you like to ...'

'Oh, yes, very much,' she met his gaze.

'One day when the weather clears up.'

'Perhaps we could cycle up there?'

'That would be marvellous.'

She tucked the book into the pocket of her apron. 'Would you like to stay for some lunch?'

'I'd love to, but I have to get back to White Waltham. Parish meeting.'

She tried to hide her disappointment. 'Another time.'

'How are you?' he asked as she led him around the outside of the house. The birds were singing in the crisp air, the first leaves emerging from the bare trees, shimmering in the sunlight.

'Busy,' she said. 'Flying every day now, and the final test is coming up.'

Stella paused by the gate.

'Well, do call in and see me again soon.' Michael's smile creased his eyes as he gazed down at her. 'I mean it, anytime you're passing. It's so nice to find a kindred spirit here. There aren't many people I can talk to about art, and Singapore.'

'Yes, I'm so glad we're friends.'

Michael hesitated. 'Yes. Yes, absolutely.' He put his hat on as he stepped out into the lane and turned to her, smiled shyly. 'If you can persuade your friends to come along to St Mary's on a Sunday, the vicar would be delighted to see you. So would I.'

Stella leant against the gatepost, watching as Michael walked up the lane, head bent against the chill breeze. Stalin chirruped a greeting and wound himself around her ankles. 'Where have you been?' she asked. She knew better than to try and pick him up – the girls all had the scars to prove he wasn't mellowing with domesticity. As he reached the road, Michael turned and looked back, raised his hand. 'See you soon,' Stella called as she waved, the wind catching her words.

15

On the day of her final test, Evie paced nervously outside the offices at White Waltham, smoking a cigarette while she waited for her instructor. From inside, the sound of raised voices drifted out to her.

'I don't ruddy care what the rumours are ...' she heard as the door opened. She moved closer to hear what was going on.

'Gentlemen!' She heard Pauline Gower's voice. 'Would you mind keeping it down? Some of us have a war of our own to deal with.'

'I'm sorry, Commander.'

With a start, Evie realised it was Beau.

'What's this all about?' Pauline said.

'This ... this buffoon, Parker, has been implying I'm some kind of spy!' he exploded.

'I can assure you I haven't,' Teddy said. Evie could picture the expression on his face as he spoke. Smooth, blank eyed like a pike.

'I do hope not,' Pauline said firmly.

'I merely mentioned it was interesting that Wing Commander Beaufort's father was in the Luftwaffe, and increasingly Jerry seems to know our movements. These Germans are clever chaps—'

'Why you...!' Beau shouted.

'Beaufort!' Pauline barked.

'How did you find that out anyway? I haven't told a soul.'

Evie's stomach lurched because she knew what was coming next.

'I had a most interesting conversation with Miss Chase this morning over coffee.'

'Did you indeed?'

Evie could hear from his voice how furious Beau was. She felt nauseous, her blood ran cold. *Idiot*, she said to herself, *you ruddy idiot.*

She had been sitting with Megan in the mess, helping her run over her notes before the test when Teddy sauntered over.

'Mind if I join you Miss Chase?'

'Not at all,' she said reluctantly.

Teddy patted his pocket. 'Damn, I've left my cigarettes in the office. Do you mind?' Before Evie could answer he reached across and took a Player's from her case. 'Final tests today, girls?'

'Yes,' she said, barely looking up from the books.

'I wouldn't worry. All the chaps are the same, and very soon they are flying anything from a Moth to a Lanc in a day.'

Evie glanced up. 'Why can't women fly operational aircraft? It's not fair.'

'Miss Chase, you can pout and stamp your pretty little heels as much as you want, but flying fighter planes is beyond a woman's physical and mental capabilities.'

Evie dug her nails into the palm of her hand. Calmly she raised an eyebrow as she looked at him. 'Oh really, Teddy? We'll see.' She gathered her books. 'Come on, Megan, let's get ready.'

Teddy stretched out, took a drag of his cigarette. 'How are you getting on with old Beau?'

'Fine.' Evie hitched her jacket over her shoulder. She knew Teddy was digging for something and she wasn't about to land Beau in trouble.

'I never know what to make of the chap.' Teddy inspected his nails. 'I heard him talking German with some of the foreign pilots the other day.'

'Well, what's funny about that?' Megan interrupted. 'He's German.' Evie scowled at her, willing her to stop talking.

'Is he?' Teddy said smoothly. 'Well, that explains a few things. Surprised he's flying on our side.'

Megan tried to make amends. 'His father is flying with the Luftwaffe, but his mother is French.' She nodded, full of authority.

Now, Evie cringed as she heard the anger in Beau's voice. 'Parker – you and Miss Chase would do well to learn one shouldn't listen to gossip. Careless talk costs lives.'

'Don't throw propaganda at me!' Teddy yelled as the door swung open. Evie ducked back against the wall. 'I've got my eye on you, Beaufort, always knew there was something off about you.'

'That's enough,' Pauline said, calm but firm. 'May I remind you of the ATA ethos, gentlemen?'

'But—' Teddy interrupted.

'There is no room for personal grudges or tittle-tattle here,' she said. 'We are all far too busy. We work as a team.'

'Thank you, Commander,' Beau said. He turned to Teddy. 'I may be half German, Parker, but don't doubt for a moment that I'm batting for the British in this war.'

Beau strode out onto the airfield. His head snapped around. 'Are you coming?'

'Where?' Evie looked uncertain.

'Your test, Miss Chase. Unless of course you think I'm about to kidnap you and whisk you away to Berlin.'

'I thought Nora was doing my test. Are you …?'

'Nora is off sick. I shall be deciding whether or not you get your wings.' He zipped up his flying jacket. 'Of course if you're genuinely worried I'm a spy, you can ask for someone else.'

'No, don't be silly.'

'It is you, Miss Chase, who are silly.' He walked closer to her. 'A silly girl gossiping about things she knows nothing about.'

'Now just a minute! It wasn't my—'

'Are you saying Teddy was lying?'

'No.' She thought quickly. She couldn't tell Beau it was Megan who had blabbed. She could handle his bad temper but the thought of him bawling Megan out was unbearable. Her confidence was shaky enough already.

'Forget it.' He frowned as Teddy appeared at the door to the offices. 'Come on, before I change my mind and fail you automatically.' Beau marched off towards the waiting aircraft. Just at that moment a Bentley roared to a standstill outside the offices.

'Oh no,' Evie said, 'just what I need.'

Leo stepped out of the driving seat. 'Hello, darling.' He kissed her. 'Are we early?'

'Early?'

'I bumped into Badger in Maidenhead and he said you had your test today. We thought we'd surprise you.'

'We?' Evie looked up as Virginia appeared on the other side of the car.

'Mr Chase?' Teddy sauntered over and shook his hand. 'Delighted to meet you. I'm Parker. Perhaps you'd like to come and watch Evie's test flight from the Ops Room? I have some spare binoculars.'

Evie wanted to curl up in a ball. She could see Beau waiting impatiently by the aircraft. 'I have to go,' she said, backing away.

'Good luck, darling!' Leo called after her as she broke into a run.

'Quite ready are you?' Beau folded his arms. 'Of course if you're too busy socialising ...'

'Sorry,' Evie said, catching her breath as she jumped into the cockpit of the trainer. 'Why we have to do this when I've completed thirty cross-country trips by myself ...'

'Procedure, Miss Chase. Procedure.' Beau climbed in behind her. 'Visibility?'

Evie checked the spire of Shottesbrooke Church. 'Clear for two miles,' she said. She glanced over at the curved window of the Ops Room. There she saw Leo and Teddy with binoculars and the flash of Virginia's scarlet dress in the background. 'I'm ready if you are, sir.' It was a relief when the propeller turned and the engine burst into life. She wanted to be free, soaring above the earth. More than anything she didn't want Beau to be angry with her.

The test passed in a haze. As Beau called instructions to her down the speaker tube, she put the aircraft through its paces as if she were a machine. Beau tested her skills to the limit, made her recover from terrifying mid-air stalls, perform forced landings until she got it absolutely right. Always, nearby, was his voice – calm, intimate, reassuring, so different from the man she knew on the ground. It was almost a surprise to find herself safely back at White Waltham, the plane bumping across the grass, slowing gradually from 40 mph until it came to a standstill near the hangar.

As the ground crew slipped the chocks under the wheels, she lifted herself awkwardly from the cockpit. Beau was already on the ground, finishing his notes.

'So?' Evie could hardly look at him.

'Frankly, Miss Chase, you have a certain amount of ability, an overdose of self-confidence, a lack of experience and a dislike of taking orders. In short, you're a menace.'

'Charm will get you everywhere, Wing Commander. Do I pass?'

'They've let a narcoleptic in so no doubt they'll take you.'

Evie smiled, but Beau wasn't laughing. 'I am sorry, sir,' she said. 'I—'

He held up his hand. 'Save the platitudes, Miss Chase. There's nothing I dislike more than gossip. I had begun to think you were different, but clearly you're not.' He strode away towards the offices.

Evie leant back against the aircraft and hung her head. Far from feeling elated, she felt as if she was about to burst into tears. She stood there for a few minutes, gathering the strength to face Virginia.

As Evie strode through the corridor several of the pilots clapped her on the back. 'Well done, darling!' Joy said as she hurried past on the way to a waiting Anson.

'How do you know?' Evie frowned.

'Beau told Chief Ops Officer Wood, he told Teddy—'

'Teddy told Daddy—'

'And now Virginia is handing out the most delicious cake in the mess.'

'She's what?' Evie said furiously. She pushed through the crowd to see Virginia flirting outrageously with the male pilots as she handed out slices from a large iced sponge cake. Evie marched over to her. 'What do you think you're doing?'

'Evie!' Virginia simpered. 'Congratulations, darling.' She offered her a paper napkin with a piece of cake.

Evie stared at it incredulously. 'What is this Virginia? Let them eat cake?' The crowd fell silent around them. 'This has nothing to do with you ...' Evie was so angry she could hardly force the words out. 'And here you are basking in all the glory.'

Virginia leant towards her, the smile never leaving her scarlet lips as she hissed, 'Glory? What glory? Don't show yourself up. You've passed some silly little test. I did it to make Leo happy, if you must know. You know how upset he was that you took this job. He wants to make peace.' As Virginia leant back she spotted the diamond earrings Evie was wearing. 'Help yourself, boys!' She waved her hand at the cake. As the conversations resumed, she took Evie's arm and pulled her aside. 'I've been looking for those.'

Evie touched her ear. 'These earrings were my mother's.'

'Your father bought them, therefore they are mine.'

'I won't forget this.' Evie hurled the cake to the floor, and pulled off the earrings.

'Whoops-a-daisy,' Virginia said brightly, pocketing the earrings as Leo and Beau walked over.

'Well done, darling!' Leo spread his arms wide and embraced her. His eyes fell to the cake on the floor. 'Oh dear ...'

'Evie had a little accident.' Virginia lowered her lashes.

Evie rounded on her. 'You lying—'

'Miss Chase!' Beau barked at her.

'But she—'

'I don't give a damn. You're a member of the ATA now. Your behaviour reflects on everyone, and you'll show your mother some respect.' Beau handed Evie a pair of gold wings. 'I wanted to give you these myself.'

Evie looked down at the wings gleaming in the palm of her hand. She needed some air. 'Thank you,' she said, unable to look at him. She turned to her father, eyes glistening, angry. 'Goodbye, Daddy,' she said.

He hugged her tightly. 'In spite of everything I said, I'm very proud of you, Evie.' She nodded, and walked away.

'I'm sorry, sir,' Beau said to Leo as he watched her push her way through the mess, head held high.

'Don't be silly, Alex. I'm sure it's nothing. Evie will calm down. She's always been like a bottle of champagne when she's angry – "pop" and it's all over.' He glanced uncertainly at Virginia as she flirted with a couple of the pilots. 'Well, it's good to see you again, old boy. You were with a very pretty blonde last time I saw you.'

'My fiancée.'

'Is she well?'

'As far as I know.'

'Oh, I'm sorry. I hadn't realised ...'

'It's all rather a mess. She walked out on me. Now she's changed her mind.'

'Woman's prerogative, old boy. They like to keep us guessing.' At the sound of her high, cascading laugh, Leo turned to his wife. 'Virginia, why don't you take the rest of the cake to the offices and see if any of those ground wallahs fancy a piece?' Reluctantly, she scooped up the plate and sashayed past Beau. When she had gone, Leo offered him a cigarette. 'How are you, Alex? Last time we had a proper chance to talk was in Gstaad, before this mess blew up. Damn shame about your accident. You haven't changed a bit, you know. I heard you were all smashed up but you're as annoyingly handsome as ever.'

Beau laughed drily. 'I was lucky. It looked worse than it was, and McIndoe's surgeons did a tremendous job.' He took a drag of his cigarette.

'So, will you marry now you've recovered?'

'Olivia wants to reconcile, but I don't know. If your fiancée isn't there when you need her most, it doesn't say much for your future together.'

'Oh dear,' Leo said. 'Don't let it make you bitter, Alex. A lot of these young girls can't cope with the realities of war. If I were you I'd give her another chance. Good women are hard to find.'

'The voice of experience?' Beau smiled as he exhaled. 'I'll be back on ops soon enough. That will take my mind off it.'

'Is that what you want? To fly in combat again?'

He shrugged. 'What else is there? I certainly don't want to stay around here any longer than I have to. These silly girls and their gossip.' He pointed at Teddy. 'See that buffoon over there? Your daughter informed him my father is flying with the Luftwaffe, and he took it upon himself to tell the whole bally pool I'm a spy.'

Leo couldn't help laughing. 'Alex, you know who – and what – you are. You're a grown man now, no longer in Hans' considerable shadow.' He looked at Beau. 'Are you sure it was Evie? If there's one thing I know about my daughter it's that you can trust her implicitly. She's straight as a die. Always has been.'

Beau looked unconvinced. 'Anyway, I'll be glad to get out of here and back to my squadron.'

'You know,' Leo said, 'there are plenty of other options for a pilot of your calibre.'

'Such as?'

'Not here.' Leo took him to one side. 'I was talking to an old friend at my Club in London the other night. I think Pickard may have something that would suit you down to the ground. Why don't you come around to the house for a drink one night? I have a few chaps I'd like you to meet.' Leo took a deep drag of his cigarette. 'So, how's my little girl doing?'

Beau smiled. 'Miss Chase takes after her father.'

'I hope not. I always thought she had more of her mother in her.'

'They don't look very alike.'

'Virginia isn't her mother. No.' Leo's eyes took on a sad look. 'Ingrid ...' He exhaled deeply. 'Well, she was a wonderful woman. Sensible too. She wouldn't put up with my playing around. Evie's like her.'

'She needs to learn to control herself.' Beau beckoned to Jean to come and clear up the cake from the floor.

'At least she had the balls to tell us to stick the money ...'

Beau glanced at him. 'Pardon?'

'I told her not to join up. As far as she knows, thanks to Virginia, she's cut off without a penny, no allowance, nothing. She has principles, my girl, just like her mother. I lost Ingrid but I won't lose Evie. Take care of her will you, Alex?'

'Yes, sir,' he said as they shook hands, and Leo went to join his wife.

'Peace offering.' Teddy slipped a slice of cake in front of Evie. She was sitting on the bonnet of her car, her arms folded around her knees.

'Eugh, take it away. I loathe icing and she knows it.'

'Did I get you in trouble?'

'Yes you did as a matter of fact.'

'Let me make it up to you.' He perched on the wheel arch. 'How about dinner tonight? We could celebrate your test.' He pointed at Evie's newly acquired wings on her jacket. 'Aren't you pleased?'

Evie groaned inwardly at the thought. Dinner with Teddy was the last thing she wanted. She began to make an excuse but just then Beau marched out onto the field. 'Of course I am, I'm delighted,' she said clearly so that Beau could hear. 'A celebratory dinner would be lovely, Teddy, thank you.' She kept her eyes on Beau all the time.

Teddy leant closer to her. 'Shall I pick you up at eight?'

'Why don't I meet you in town? Sunny's nightclub perhaps?'

'Independent, eh?' He ran his thumb across his moustache. 'I like that in a girl.' As he walked away, Beau followed him with his gaze.

'Aren't you going to congratulate me?' Evie asked Beau.

'On what, Miss Chase – your wings, or stepping out with a jackass?'

Coolly, she walked over. 'Both, perhaps.'

'I would have credited you with more taste. You could do better than a man like Parker.'

'Do you think so? How surprising.' She thought angrily of Olivia's hurtful comments. 'I think he's perfectly charming.'

Beau put his hands on his hips. 'Good luck.'

'What for?'

'If you're fool enough to step out with him, you'll need all the luck you can get.'

Evie turned away from him, glanced back over her shoulder. 'Why, Wing Commander, from the look on your face, anyone would think you cared.' She jumped into the Aston and roared off, certain this time that he was watching her, even before she looked in the rear-view mirror and saw him standing alone, looking after her as she drove away.

16

'Thanks, Jim.' Stella jumped down from the Anson, dragging her flight bag after her. The pilots who had been playing chess during the taxi flight were packing up their game in the back.

Jim Mollison climbed out of the cockpit. 'So, how was your first day?'

'Tiring.' Stella rubbed the back of her hand across her forehead.

'You'll get used to it.' White Waltham was closing up for the night, and they were the last aircraft in. Jim offered her a cigarette as they walked towards the offices.

Stella shook her head. 'No thanks. Any news about Amy?'

Jim paused, his lighter flaring in the half light. 'I don't think we'll ever really know what happened,' he said quietly. He held the door open for Stella as they walked in. 'It's funny. Sometimes I get the feeling she's still around.'

'You don't strike me as the superstitious type.'

'Most pilots are. Spend enough time in the air and your mind starts to play tricks on you.'

Stella laughed. 'You should talk to Evie. She's convinced she's got a guardian angel.'

'Lucky girl. Pilots have always believed in cockpit gremlins. Sometimes they fiddle around with your gauges, sometimes the good ones blow a hole in the cloud cover to get you safely home.'

'Stella!' Megan raced over to them. 'Did you hear? Evie got her wings,' she said as Jim walked away.

'Good for her.' Stella handed her signed chits in to the office.

'I'm that nervous. What if I don't get mine? I couldn't bear it if you and Evie are flying and I'm not. My test's in the morning, and I've got so much to learn tonight. Evie says she'll help me, mind, but she's going out with Teddy and she won't be back till late …'

Stella tuned out Megan's voice as they walked towards the mess. Every bone in her body ached. All she wanted now was a searingly hot bath, and sleep.

'Oh, I almost forgot.' Megan pulled an airmail letter from her pocket. 'This came for you this morning. It's from Singapore.'

Stella stared wordlessly at the envelope in her hand. She recognised her mother's handwriting.

'Aren't you going to open it?' Megan said. 'The stamps are lovely. Can I have them to send to my da? You know, he's got a lovely collection he has, stamps from all over the world.'

'How on earth would I know that?' Stella stuffed the envelope into the pocket of her Sidcot suit.

Megan bit her lip. 'Don't be like that, Stella, I only meant—'

'For God's sake will you stop going on at me? Chat, chat, chat,' Stella mimed, her fingers snapping like a jaw. 'Don't you ever stop talking?' She dumped her parachute by the door to the Ladies, and pushed her way in.

Alone in the cloakroom, Stella unzipped her flying jacket and let it fall to the floor. She ran a steaming basin of water, leaning against the edge. While it filled, she raised her head wearily, and wiped away the condensation on the mirror. Her skin was pale, and her eyes were sunken with dark rings beneath them. *I hardly recognise myself*, she thought.

She remembered lying on the cool lawn outside her parents' house the night she met Richard, gazing up at the endless velvet black tropical sky with him. Her hand was tanned against the white cotton sleeve of her dress as she pointed out the constellations. There were voices on the veranda, the sounds of a party in full swing. She knew her mother would be watching her like a hawk, but she didn't care. The handsome Squadron Leader had asked her to dance – her! – when there were so many pretty girls he could have chosen. They had danced all night. She had jasmine in her hair, and as they lay beside the pool, stars sparkled on the water, paper lanterns swayed gently in the breeze. He hadn't kissed her that night, though she had wanted him to.

She looked down at the rippling water, turned the tap off. Stella could hear people leaving for the night outside, the sounds of doors slamming, engines fading away across the airfield. In the silence, the tap dripped rhythmically, echoing around the empty cloakroom. Stella ran her fingers through her hair, and wondered what her mother would think of the short, platinum bob. *Mummy always loved my long hair*, she thought. *So did Richard.* As she looked at herself, she remembered the night she had taken the shears from her sewing table and hacked her hair off, her waist-length golden curls tumbling onto the white tiled floor. The buzz of the cicadas in the long grass beyond her bedroom window had seemed to intensify; her skin had been slick with sweat.

Stella's gaze fell to the floor. The muddy tiles beneath her boots made her anxious. She thought of her little house, how clean it had been when she left. How many sleepless nights had she spent polishing and tidying, patting cushions that did not need plumping into shape? She felt far from home, utterly alone. Stella fought to control herself, to suppress the anguish that tightened at her throat like a hand. She rolled up her sleeves, plunged her hands into the hot water and held them there. As the chill began to leave them, she raised her hands to her face, wiped her lips, tried to rub some colour into her cheeks.

What does Michael see when he looks at me? She thought. She wondered if she could trust him. Perhaps she could talk to him, confide in him. She tried to imagine telling him everything. How could she explain this bleak feeling to someone as happy-go-lucky as him? Sometimes she felt as if she were at the end of a dark tunnel, utterly alone, the emptiness pressing in on her. It took all her strength just to get up in the morning and face another day, not to give in to the crushing loneliness. *I don't want to spoil it. He's the first person who has made me feel normal in a long time.* As she thought of their conversations about painting, their jokes about their shared experiences of childhood, she smiled. They were like bright moments in the relentless, dark days. With him, she felt like her old self. Her friendship with Michael gave her hope.

Talking to him about Singapore helped her feel less homesick. As she scrubbed her hands, she thought of all she missed. She remembered the maid podding beans on the steps of the house, tossing empty shells to the earth, a gecko scuttling away. She longed for the searing colour of the place, for the bustle of Arab Street, where she had bought iridescent silks for their bedroom and muslin for nursery drapes. Her mouth was parched. What she wouldn't give for a gin and tonic – ice chinking, lemon, bubbles fizzing. She remembered her honeymoon night then, the chatter of the mynah birds in Raffles and the crunch of peanut shells underfoot in the hotel bar, how they had imagined Somerset Maugham holding court in the corner as she laughed and chatted with Richard. She remembered walking hand in hand with him through the shaded colonnades to their room, the cerise orchids of her bouquet vivid against the white silk of her dress.

Her hands were still cold, and her feet felt like ice. She sat on the bench and dried her fingers, rubbing them again and again until her skin was completely clean and bright pink. Stella closed her eyes, the towel falling to her lap. She tried to summon the energy to move, but she could have slept where she sat. She remembered how, when David's whooping cough had looked as if it was turning into pneumonia, and he had been rushed to the Mission Hospital, she had looked at the neat rows of beds with their clean white sheets and wished she could curl up beside him. She had wished that someone would take care of her too. She had wished that she could sleep.

'Sweet dreams, sunny Jim,' she had said as she kissed her sleeping baby one last time, breathing in the scent of him. That was what Richard said to him every night as they tucked him in. Sweet dreams, sunny Jim. She closed her eyes tight, fighting the tears, the longing to hold him to her. *He's better off without me*, she told herself. *He'll be safer there.*

Stella felt the envelope in her pocket crinkle as she shifted, resting her head against the wall. Reluctantly, she pulled it out, and slit it open with her thumbnail.

'Stella,' the letter began. *No 'Dear Stella', or 'Darling'*, she thought. 'We are very worried about you. Richard's parents sent a telegram to let us know that David is safe. What on earth do you think you are doing? Have you lost your senses? Richard says ...'

The cloakroom door opened, and Megan poked her head around. Stella stuffed the letter in her pocket.

'I'm going,' Megan said in a small voice. 'Bill Harben's giving me a lift.'

As she looked at the hurt expression in Megan's eyes, Stella felt like she had kicked a puppy. 'As long as he hasn't got that ruddy cheetah in the car, I'll come with you.' Stella forced herself to her feet, and put her arm around her friend. 'Sorry.'

'I didn't mean to—'

'Let's get home.' Stella picked up her leather jacket and slung it over her shoulder. 'Is Evie really going on a date with Teddy?'

'I know! She must be bonkers.'

Bonkers. Maybe I am, Stella thought. As they walked out across the airfield to Harben's car, her mother's words looped unnervingly around her mind. *Have you lost your senses?*

17

Evie paused at the top of the stairs, her fingertips resting on the brass banister as she gazed across the nightclub. Through the haze of smoke, she caught Teddy's eye. He was seated alone at a table for two near the dance floor, a pool of rosy light spilling from the red-shaded lamp beside him. As he stood and adjusted his bow tie, Evie walked down the plush red carpeted steps, a jazz melody and the scent of hot bodies, cheap perfume and stale cigarettes rising to meet her.

'Here we go,' she said under her breath. She had regretted taking Teddy up on his offer the moment she had cooled off on the drive home, but she was determined to go through with the date. The heels of her satin evening shoes tapped on the parquet as she walked towards him.

'Miss Chase.' Teddy took her arm as he pulled back the chair for her. His eyes were bright and hopeful. 'Evie.'

'Thank you, Teddy,' she said, perching on the edge of her seat, her back ramrod straight.

He settled comfortably on the chair opposite, crossed his leg towards her. Evie inched away. 'It's quite jolly tonight,' she said, gazing out across the shadowy figures on the dance floor.

'Rather more intimate than the Riviera.' Teddy clicked his

fingers towards the white-jacketed waiter. 'Of course, not what you're used to I imagine?'

Evie pursed her lips as he beckoned impatiently at the waiter. She wished people would stop making assumptions about her. It wasn't as if she spent every night at the 400. This was a rare night out these days, and she was determined to enjoy herself. She looked at Teddy, and tried to ignore the overbearing way he was talking to the waiter. *Maybe he's nervous*, she thought. Leo had always told her you can find something good in anyone you meet. She decided to give Teddy a chance. He'd certainly made an effort – his evening shirt was immaculate, and it looked as if he'd had a haircut. *In this light, he's almost handsome.* She thought about the conversation with Stella she'd had that evening.

'Teddy? Good looking? If you like that kind of thing,' Stella had said to her as she was getting ready. 'Not my cup of tea.'

'Mine neither, really.' Evie frowned as she checked her reflection in the mirror.

Stella glanced up from the magazine she was flicking through on Evie's bed. 'So why on earth are you going out with him?'

'Looks aren't everything. Anyway, it's complicated.' Evie rifled through her jewellery box. 'It might be fun. Teddy's perfectly charming, and I haven't been out dancing for ages.' She clipped a diamanté cuff around the long black velvet sleeve of her dress. 'There. What do you think?'

'It's a bit …' Stella hesitated. 'Well, you're very welcome to borrow the frock, but it's rather funereal for you.'

'Don't want to give Teddy too much encouragement, do I?' Evie winked at her as she walked to the door.

'I doubt he'll need any,' Stella murmured as she returned to her magazine.

'Finally!' Teddy barked. 'It would be quicker if I fetched the menus myself.'

Evie was jolted back to the moment.

'Will you be dining with us tonight, sir?' The waiter offered Evie a menu.

'I'm really not very—' she began.

'Yes.' Teddy waved the menus away. 'The lamb is excellent,' he said to Evie. 'We'll have the lamb. Make sure it's well done.'

Evie bit her lip and reached for her cigarettes. *Not a good start*, she thought.

'A bottle of champagne perhaps?' the waiter ventured. His eyes were stony as he smiled at Teddy.

'Champagne? On a first date?' He laughed a little too hard. 'I don't think so. Bally rip-off, I've seen your prices. And it's an early start in the morning.' Teddy glanced at Evie. 'Unless …'

Evie noticed his hand had unconsciously slipped to his wallet. 'I'd love a glass actually.'

'Would you like to see the list, sir? Just to check the—'

'No, that's perfectly alright.' Evie smiled at the waiter. 'The house champagne will be fine.'

'And I'd like another beer.' Teddy glared after him as he walked away. 'Don't know where they get these chaps. Still, don't suppose they can find the staff with all the decent men away fighting,' he said loudly.

Evie glanced at the empty pint glass on the table. She wondered how many beers he had already had before she arrived. 'So, Teddy,' she said. 'Tell me about yourself.'

He leant towards her. 'What would you like to know?'

'Well, what do you like to do when you're not working?' Evie turned away, pretending to look at the dancing couples. She was finding the conversation hard work. 'I love to dance, do you?'

'I would ask you,' he said, 'but I'm not much cop with this old thing.' He tapped his leg.

'How did your accident happen? Were you in combat?'

Teddy fiddled with his cutlery. 'Don't really like to discuss it, if you don't mind.'

'Of course.' Evie thought of her conversation with Beau about the stress pilots endured in dogfights. 'I quite understand. It was insensitive of me.' She patted Teddy's hand, pulling hers away just as he reached for her. 'Oh good, our drinks,' she said brightly as the waiter placed a flute of champagne beside her. 'Thank you.' She raised her glass to Teddy. 'Cheers.'

'Bottoms up.' He drank quickly, and the glass was half empty by the time he put it down. 'Congratulations—' He broke off to belch, covering his mouth with the back of his hand. 'Excuse me. Better out than in, as Mother says.'

'Do your parents live near here?' Evie peeked surreptitiously at her watch.

'Just up the road. My father died during the Great War, so it's just me and Mother.'

'That's very good of you, looking after her like that.' Evie leant back as the waitress slid a plate of greasy lamb and grey potatoes in front of her. It was the last thing she felt like eating.

'Mother enjoys spoiling me, but we take care of each other really,' Teddy said, smacking his lips as he looked at the plate. 'Thank you, Alice,' he said to the waitress. 'Do you have any brown sauce?'

'Anything for you, Teddy.'

His head craned around to follow her as she walked away.

When it wasn't offered, Evie helped herself to mint sauce. 'You've never married?'

'Why would I marry while I've got Mother at home to do my washing and meals?' He laughed awkwardly as he took a big forkful of lamb, gravy soaking his moustache. 'No, I'm not short of company, if you know what I mean. Maybe once she goes I'll choose some lucky lady.' He dabbed at his mouth with his napkin, gazing up at the waitress as she placed a bottle of sauce on the table. 'Thank you.' He patted her on the backside.

As the waitress sauntered away swinging her hips, Evie's eyes opened in disbelief. She tried to laugh it off. 'It sounds like you have it all worked out, Teddy. But, what about love?'

'Love?' He laughed. 'The moon in June, and hearts and flowers?' He shook his head. 'Women's stuff.'

Evie washed down a mouthful of the lamb with a sip of warm champagne. 'Do you think so?'

'There was one girl.' He paused, cutlery in mid-air. 'I did think for a time she might be the one ...' As Teddy talked on about his ex-girlfriend, he ate steadily and soon cleared his plate. Evie's eyes had glazed over, and when he finally let his knife and fork fall onto his plate with a clatter, she jumped. 'But Mother didn't take to her, so that was that.' Teddy took a swig of his beer. 'Excellent grub,' he said. 'Are you not hungry?' He eyed Evie's half-eaten meal.

'Not terribly.'

'I know what you girls are like, always watching your figure. Don't want to run to fat, do you, sitting around in the cockpit all day.' He licked his lips. 'Would you mind if I ...?'

It took Evie a moment to realise what he was angling for. 'Oh! The lamb? Gosh, you do have a healthy appetite. Um, yes, help yourself.' They swapped plates. 'It's quite exhausting, actually, flying all day.'

Teddy shook his head, swallowing a large mouthful. 'It's no job for a woman.'

Evie blinked. 'I beg your pardon?'

'Don't get me wrong.' He held up his hands. 'Lord knows our fighting squadrons need all the help they can get, and the ATA has got to take any pilot capable of shifting the aircraft. It just does the chaps' morale no good having girls around the place.'

'What do you mean?' Evie sat back and folded her arms.

'Well, imagine how it feels to a man to see a chit of a girl delivering their aircraft.' Teddy drained his glass. 'It's not right. The natural order of things is for women to support their men.'

'Rather than working side by side you mean?' Evie was determined not to lose her temper.

'The trainers are one thing, but they'll never allow girls to fly the fighters, let alone the big four-engined Lancs, whatever people like Pauline think.'

Evie drummed her fingers on the table. 'Do you want to bet?'

'Gambling girl, eh?' Teddy said.

'I bet you ten shillings the girls will be flying operational aircraft by the summer.' She held out her hand to him.

'Ten bob? A bit steep ... but it will never happen.' They shook on it. 'Suppose it runs in the blood.'

'Sorry?'

'Gambling. Your father, he was a jockey wasn't he?'

'Yes, he was,' she said coolly.

'That's what I call a job, gallivanting round the racetrack. Don't suppose he ever had to do a proper day's work in his life.'

'Talking of work, I really must get home.' Evie faked a yawn. 'Early start, as you said.'

'No pudding?' Teddy looked put out, but he signalled to the waiter for the bill.

'Anyway, Daddy was very successful in his own right.'

'It must be nice, though, having all that behind you. I can't imagine you're doing this ferrying lark for the money.' It took him a couple of attempts to get his hand into his jacket pocket. 'I must admit, I was surprised you agreed to come out for dinner with me tonight.'

'Why?'

'Well, a girl like you—' He stopped as the waiter appeared at their table.

'Sir.' The waiter slipped the billfold onto Teddy's side plate.

Teddy flipped open the leather case. 'Good grief,' he said. 'Tap water next time, Evie.' He laughed at his own joke as he opened his wallet.

'Let's go Dutch, shall we, Teddy?' Evie said.

'Really?' He swayed slightly as he looked at her. 'I know some of you girls are frightful bluestockings, but this is one modern innovation I approve of.' He tossed a note on top of the bill, and Evie slipped another in.

'Keep the change,' she said as she handed it to the waiter.

It was dark on the street, only a faint silvery light from the crescent moon shining down.

'Thank you, Teddy,' Evie said as she pulled her gloves on. 'This was ... Well, it was lovely to have a night out.'

'There's a new picture on at the cinema this weekend if you

fancy it?' Teddy said. He slipped his arm around her as they walked along the pavement.

'Thank you.' Evie moved aside. 'But I'm going to be awfully busy now I'm flying.'

'Come on,' he cajoled. 'You're never too busy to have a little fun.' He stepped in front of her, pinned her against the wall with his arm. 'Besides, I can make your life a lot easier, if you know what I mean. I can make sure you get all the best jobs, see you have plenty of time to enjoy yourself ...'

Evie recoiled, shrank against the cold, wet bricks. 'I must be getting back. The girls are waiting up for me.'

'Evie,' he murmured, brushing her neck with his lips. His breath was hot, heavy with the smell of beer. His hand fumbled at her coat as he pushed himself against her. 'You're so pretty.'

She turned her face as he tried to force his mouth on hers, grazing her lip with his teeth. 'Teddy,' she said firmly, pushing him away. 'I want to go now.'

'Just a bit of a kiss and a cuddle,' he whispered, his lips close to her ear. 'I'm randy as hell, can't you feel ...'

'I said no.' She gave him a shove, and Teddy staggered back onto the pavement. Evie's heart thumped in her chest, and she looked frantically around the deserted street.

Teddy followed her gaze, and a sly smile crept over his lips. 'I know your sort,' he said as he stepped towards her. 'Say one thing, and mean another. It's alright, you don't have to play hard to get with me.'

'I can assure you I'm not playing games.' Evie fumbled in her bag for her keys. At least if he made another lunge for her, she'd be prepared.

'Let me walk you back to your car.' He grabbed at her arm, held her tightly by her wrist.

'Teddy, you're hurting me,' she said.

'Hey, Evie?' A man called from the doorway of the nightclub. 'Is that you?'

A small crowd spilled out onto the pavement.

Evie recognised him as one of the engineers from the airfield.

'Hello, Reg,' she said.

'Everything alright?' he asked as he walked over to them. He eyed Teddy cautiously.

'Clear off, Reg,' Teddy said. 'This is none of your business.'

'Actually, I'm having a bit of car trouble,' Evie interrupted. 'Would you mind taking a look at it for me?'

'Sure.' He took Evie's arm from Teddy. 'Night, sir.'

'Goodnight, Teddy,' she called as they walked towards her car.

'I'd watch yourself with him, Evie,' Reg said once they were out of earshot.

'Teddy?' Her hand shook as she opened the door of the Aston Martin. It started first time. 'He's a buffoon. It was good you came along when you did, but I could have handled him.'

'I don't know, Miss. I've heard things,' he said as he leant down on the roof to talk to her. In the distance they saw Teddy walking alone along the middle of the road into town. 'Apparently he can be a nasty piece of work if he's crossed.'

'Thanks for the warning, but I can take care of myself,' Evie said, and she waved as she drove off into the night.

SPRING

18

'A little bird told me you went out with Teddy last week,' Joan said as she waited with Evie for the chits to be put out in the Ops Corridor.

'Does everyone know everything around here?' Evie groaned. 'Oh Lord, he's coming over.' She pretended to check through the rail vouchers and float money she had just been issued with.

'Morning, ladies.' Teddy leant against the polished wood counter, pinning Evie in with his arm. 'Super time the other night. Perhaps you'd like to—'

'I'm sorry, I'm going to be frightfully busy now I'm ferrying.'

'I haven't suggested a day yet. We do let you have some leave.'

'I know.' Evie forced a tight smile. 'I promised Daddy I'd help my stepmother out at home when I'm not flying. For the foreseeable future. She's poorly … in bed.'

'What a shame,' Teddy said, releasing her from the counter. 'Well, you know where I am if you change your mind.'

'What was that all about?' Joan whispered.

'Oh God, it was ghastly. He made a lunge for me after dinner.'

'Teddy? Well, you wouldn't be the first by all accounts.' Joan looked at Evie. 'Are you OK? He didn't …?'

'I'm fine,' Evie folded her arms.

'Don't take it to heart. What is it they say – you have to kiss a lot of frogs.'

Evie grimaced. 'I didn't kiss him, though he gave it his best shot.' She looked sad for a moment. 'I'm done with frogs. It would just be so nice to have someone special.'

'I'm quite sure there's a lovely chap just waiting to sweep you off your feet,' Joan said kindly. 'I can just picture you with a brood of children.'

Evie laughed at the thought. 'I used to believe in all that you know – love at first sight, living happily ever after. I'm not so sure any more.'

'Well, soon you'll be so tired from flying you won't have a chance to think about romance.'

'What about you? Do you think you'll settle down after all this?'

'Marriage?' Joan shook her head. 'Flying comes first, and it always will.' She looked down at the empty shelf. 'They're late with the chitties this morning. Shall we get a cup of tea?'

The mess was quiet; exhausted pilots sat in silence as Jean stacked the cups and saucers ready for the day, the tea urn glugging, hissing steam behind the counter.

'Is this your first?' Joan asked as they settled down near the window.

'Yes, I'm nervous as hell.' Evie scanned her notes.

'You'll be fine. You're an excellent pilot from what I've seen.'

The Ops Room hatch slid open. 'Chits are out,' one of the pilots called, and everyone trooped through to the corridor.

'Typical, just as we get our tea,' Evie said, scrambling to her feet. On the long, polished shelf the day's ferrying instructions were laid out. She spotted her name on a chit and picked it up.

'Wellington from Brooklands,' one of the Polish pilots said. 'Again. What have you got?' he asked his friend.

'Beaufort to Chobham.'

'So, what are you dicing with?' Joan asked Evie.

'A Puss Moth down to No. 2, Whitchurch, and a Magister

back here. I'm glad it's a simple day with only two flights. I heard from some of the girls you might get four, five flights a day eventually, all with different aircraft.'

'Oh you don't need to worry about that. With single-engined types all you really need to know is the take-off speed, and the landing and stalling speeds. You'll get used to it.' Joan checked her chit over. 'You'll have fun down at Whitchurch. Super crowd of boys in Bristol. Just remember mess etiquette when you're away from home.'

'Sorry?' Evie looked at her quizzically.

'Smoking only at tea, don't monopolise the radio or papers, don't shoot a line because the RAF chaps always have better stories, and if a Wing Commander comes in, stand up and call him sir.'

Evie thought awkwardly of the day she had addressed Beau by his nickname. 'Where are you off to?' she asked.

'Anson to Debden is my first, then you don't want to know. I'll be lucky if I make it back home tonight. Still, at least if I end up at one of the American bases the food is good and I can stock up on lipstick and stockings.'

'Really? Thanks for the tip.' Evie made a mental note.

'To be honest it's quite fun if you get stuck out in the right place, and they do give you a pound for your expenses. It's those ghastly night trains you need to avoid.' Joan fastened her flying jacket. 'Hope it all goes well. Make sure you watch the weather today.'

Evie looked through the hatch and across to the high curved windows of the Ops Room. She knew they were only supposed to fly if there was 1000 yards visibility, and she gazed out across the airfield and up at the clouds with suspicion. On a blackboard covering one wall of the Ops Room, people were chalking up the day's flights beside each pilot's name. She caught Teddy's eye accidentally and looked away. 'The sky looks clear enough at the moment. What's the forecast?'

'Perfectly good – which should always make you suspicious.' Joan winked. 'Be careful, we don't want you to get caught out on your first run. Good luck!' she called over her shoulder.

One of the pilots pushed past Evie to the window. 'Come on, Teddy, I've had five Hurricanes this week. Why not a Mustang?'

'Sorry, Doyle.' Teddy marched over. 'I had to give it to someone, old boy.' With that he slid the window closed.

Evie went to her locker for fresh maps and a splash of perfume. As she touched up her lipstick, she glanced proudly at her gold wings. *This is it*, she thought, *Third Officer Chase. Let's show these boys what we can do.* She checked in at the Meteorological Office just to be certain, but the forecast was fine for the morning, clouding up later. The air was brisk and clear, a light breeze lifting her hair as she walked to her plane. In the cockpit she settled in, pulled up the collar of her flying jacket. By now she knew just how cold she would be by the end of the flight. The engine started first time, and she gave the ground crew the thumbs up. As she turned the Puss Moth down the runway, Evie ran through her checks as easily as she had recited the ABC as a child.

'Right, full throttle for take-off, and ...' The aircraft lifted, and her heart soared with it as she skimmed above the tree-lined lane on the west boundary of the airfield. As the ground fell away beneath her, the trees and houses growing smaller, she whooped for joy. This was what all the girls talked about, the secret joy that made all the risks they took worthwhile.

Nothing seemed to matter once she was in the air. Her argument with Beau, her dreadful date with Teddy, everything just evaporated as she settled in to the flight. She checked the map and set a clear course for Bristol. 'Oh, she flies through the air with the greatest of ease ...' she sang at the top of her voice. She was so engrossed in her own world that she didn't notice the large bank of cloud ahead. Before she knew what was happening, silver wisps flitted past, and soon the plane was engulfed. *Damn, where did that come from?* she thought. Quickly she ran through her options. She bit her lip as she checked her map. Where was she exactly? If she went down, there was always the chance there might be a steep hill or a barrage balloon just below her. It was too dangerous. The only option was to go up, and hope there was a break in the cloud where she could come down and find the nearest airfield. She eased back on the joystick and the nose of the plane lifted. It seemed like a lifetime until she broke through the thick cloud and bright sunlight flooded the cockpit.

Once she was above the clouds, she breathed easily again, though her heart was still racing. *Right, Evie*, she told herself, *calm down*. Beau's voice came to her: *Don't panic. Think.* She checked her compass and map. If she continued west, she would make Bristol in about thirty minutes, she calculated. Even if there was no break in the cloud, she could come down just after that and swing back east over the water and navigate from the coast. The shadow of the plane flitted along the cloud bank beneath her. *It's beautiful*, she thought, and wondered if this was how Amy had felt as she tried to find a way through to safety.

After half an hour, there was still no break in the cloud. The minutes ticked away relentlessly. She knew if she flew on much longer she wouldn't have enough fuel to make it back to the airfield. *Please God, don't let me cock up on my first flight*, she prayed silently, and as she did her panic gave way to a feeling of calm. She knew she was flying alone, but she had the strangest sense someone was with her. Her heart pounding, she banked the plane into a 180 degree turn, and began to descend. Cloud engulfed her, and again she was flying blind. Down, down, the cloud seemed to last forever, but still she was calm. She had a very real feeling that she would get through this. The cloud broke and she found herself skimming above the sea in the driving rain. She screwed up her eyes, tried to make out the coast. She could see land up ahead, but had no idea how far off course she had drifted.

If I'm too far south, she thought. *I should see the estuary up ahead. Please let me see the estuary up ahead.* Beneath her, the Bristol Channel was choppy and grey. There was no way she wanted to ditch in that if she could avoid it.

At last she saw the mouth of the River Severn beneath her, and she banked the plane around.

'Yes!' she said under her breath, and followed it in. 'Thank you, thank you, thank you,' she whispered as she made out the factory at Filton and the Whitchurch airfield ahead of her. It was chock-a-block with aircraft, and as she was flying without a radio she did a couple of circuits to make sure there were no other pilots waiting to land. As she straightened up for the final approach, she was shaking with adrenalin. *Right, flaps down*, she thought. *Ease the old girl down to 65 mph*. The runway was slick with rain as she landed, and water sprayed from beneath the wheels. She taxied over to a spot some way from the hangars, and as she turned the engine off all she could hear was the rush of blood in her veins, the thud of her heart and the drumming rain on the wings. 'Thank you,' she said quietly.

From the offices, a figure emerged, sheltering under a mac as he sprinted across the runway towards her. Determined not to show how shaken up she was, Evie quickly powdered her nose with a trembling hand. As she climbed out of her seat to greet him, her knees buckled.

'Are you OK, Miss?' he called out.

'Fine,' she said breezily, pretending to check the wing. 'Thought I saw something on the approach.'

'Well it must have been your guardian angel.' The pilot smiled up at her and cocked his cap back at an angle. 'Boy, they said a pretty girl was going to be delivering a plane, and they were right.' He took her flight bag and offered her his hand. Evie jumped down from the cockpit into his arms. 'Here.' He draped the mac over her head.

'Thank you. Are you American?'

'Yes, ma'am!' He saluted. The rain ran over his tanned face, slicking his wild dark hair to his head. 'Pilot Officer Jack Whitman, US Eagle Squadron No. 71, based in Kirton. I'm fighting with your boys, convoy work mostly,' he explained as they ran for shelter. 'There are only a few of us Yanks over here. My grandfather was British so I thought I'd do my bit for you guys.'

'A pioneer?' she said. 'I thought for a moment I had overshot the mark and ended up in New York.'

'No, ma'am, welcome to Bristol.'

As they paused in the porch to catch their breath, Evie laughed. 'Do stop calling me ma'am, you make me feel like an old woman!'

A gust of wind blew a puddle of water off the porch roof, and he pulled her close to him to avoid it. 'You sure don't feel like an old woman to me.'

'Right now I feel lucky to be alive,' she murmured as the rain fell around them. The blood rushed in her veins, and a warm wave of desire pulsed through her.

'Why don't we get you out of your wet things?'

Evie hesitated, smiled. 'I'd like that.'

In the offices the Duty Pilot signed Evie's chit for the plane. As Jack pushed the door open, music and voices drifted out from the mess.

'I'm flying Hurricanes. What are you on?' he said.

'Single-engine trainers at the moment. I've just got my wings.' Evie ran her hand through her wet hair. 'In fact this is my first flight.'

'Well you picked a hell of a day for it.' He guided her through the crowd. 'Where are you based?'

'White Waltham.'

'Do you know Stewart Updike? You should look him up. He's a good guy. Well he's a Yank so he would be.' Jack grinned down at her, his teeth white and even. 'If all the girls at your pool are as pretty as you maybe I'll drop in there and see Stewart next time I have some leave.'

'That would be fun,' Evie said lightly. 'Are you on leave at the moment?'

'No, I was out on cross-country manoeuvres, trying out a Spit. We're going to be switching to them soon. Man, they're great to fly – no bad habits at all, though I had a bit of a prang. When the weather closed in I thought I'd head here because I know a few of the guys and Taff's one of the best engineers around. He's fixing my kite at the moment.'

'How did you end up in England?'

'Well, my dad got in with Charles Sweeny's lot – he brought us over here.'

'Have you always flown?'

'Well, ma'am ... Evie.' He smiled. 'I'm 20/20 and could give them 300 hours crop-dusting time and they seemed pleased enough.'

'Do you like the Spits? I do hope they'll let us fly them soon.'

'Why, they're a great plane – a little lively. I'm more used to the Hurricanes to be honest with you.' Jack scanned the mess. 'Did you know we've got some of your ATA fellows here already?' he said.

'You have?'

'Yeah, the whole country's shut down. Something to do with a sudden high dew point. They'll be glad to see you.'

'Or maybe not,' Evie murmured as she recognised Beau at the counter, still in his flying jacket and Sidcot suit. 'Hello, sir,' she said clearly as she slipped onto the stool beside him.

'Evie,' he said. 'Thank God.'

Evie? She thought. 'I made it, but only just.' She smiled bravely.

'Cut the flannel. Now's not the time to shoot a line,' he said. 'Haven't you heard? The whole country's down. We've lost a lot of pilots. When I saw you were heading down here, and it was your first flight ...'

Evie was aware that Jack was listening to every word and she didn't like the way Beau had cut her down again. 'I didn't know you cared, Beau,' she smiled flirtatiously, flashing her eyes at Jack.

Beau put his coffee cup down. 'As your instructor I feel responsible. As you would for a child.' He frowned. 'And I've told you before, don't call me Beau.'

'Sorry. Well, don't call me Evie. It's Third Officer Chase to you, sir,' she called after him as he strode out of the mess.

'Friendly guy, huh?' Jack leant back against the counter and offered her a cigarette.

'Thank you,' Evie cupped his hand as he gave her a light and raised her eyes to his.

'So what's the deal?' he asked quietly. 'Are you and he ...?'

'Us?' Evie laughed incredulously. 'You must be joking. No, I'm footloose and fancy free.' She crossed her leg towards Jack, wishing she was wearing her uniform rather than her flying suit and boots.

'Now that,' Jack leant towards her, 'is the best news I've heard all day.'

In the cloakroom, Evie slipped out of her wet flying suit, and pulled her uniform out of the bag. She hung it near the steaming basin of water to try to get the creases out, and brushed her hair. In the mirror she checked her reflection, powdered her nose and applied a flash of dark kohl over each eyelid. Her lipstick was still fine, so she just smudged her lips together, running her tongue over her teeth. She thought of Jack's dazzling smile, and desire rushed through her again.

Evie took a step back, turned this way and that in front of the mirror, straightening the straps of her camisole. *An American,* she thought, remembering how it felt when he had pulled her to him in the porch. Jack seemed so vital, full of life and energy. *Not like old Beau,* she thought, and poked out her tongue. She pulled a precious pair of black silk stockings from the bag and slipped one on, fastening the top at her garter belt. Just as she put the other one on, and raised her leg to the basin to smooth the stocking over her thigh, the door flew open.

'Man, it's like a Turkish steam bath in here!' Jack froze as he saw her, and blew a long, slow whistle.

'I'm sorry, I thought I locked the door,' Evie said coolly, putting her hands on her hips.

'You did, probably.' Jack's gaze held hers. 'It doesn't work. Ever since they've been sending beautiful half-naked pilots down here, some jerk decided it would be fun to break the lock. I don't know why.'

'I see.'

'Oh no! It wasn't me,' he protested. 'I didn't know you were in here. I just really need to ... Do you mind?' He pointed at the cubicle.

'Be my guest.' Evie hoped she looked calmer than she felt. Once he had locked the loo door, she raced to get her uniform on.

'Nothing's moving tonight,' he called out to her. 'A few of the guys are going to the pub up the road for dinner, do you want to come along?'

'I'd love to,' she said. 'I'm ravenous.'

Just as she settled her cap on her head, the door opened again and Beau stepped in. When he opened his mouth to speak, the loo flushed and he looked over at the cubicle. Jack emerged, a little startled when he saw the other man.

Beau frowned. 'Miss Chase, it's clearing up enough out there for me to make it back. I'm going to White Waltham tonight. If you want to come back with me, I can give you a lift and one of the other pilots can bring your aircraft in the morning. It's been a hell of a day.'

Evie looked at Jack. He was gazing at her, eyes full of barely concealed desire. 'No, thank you, Wing Commander. I wouldn't dream of failing to complete my first mission. I'll fly back in the morning.'

Beau folded his arms. 'Will you indeed?'

'Yes, sir. You can count on me.'

'Fine. Give the pool a ring – Littlewick Green 258. Tell them you'll be back tomorrow.' He glared at Jack and strode out of the cloakroom.

As the door banged shut behind him, Jack offered her his arm. 'Shall we?'

19

'Oh, that was good.' Evie sighed as she settled back in her chair beside the fire. 'How lucky having this place on the doorstep. The food is marvellous.' The old beamed pub was busy, humming with voices. The pilots they had come with were busy playing billiards in the back room, and they were alone now. The fire gleamed on the polished brass pots that hung from the rafters, and an old Labrador snored contentedly beside the bar.

'I'm glad you like it,' Jack said. His finger traced the side of her hand, and as she looked at him the firelight flickered in his eyes.

'You must think I'm a greedy pig,' Evie smiled. She hadn't laughed so much in a long time. There was something easy about Jack's company. She sipped her glass of beer as the landlord rang the bell for last orders. 'Oh dear,' she said. 'Is it closing time already?' The evening had flown by.

'That's OK,' Jack took her hand. 'George is pretty relaxed with his residents.'

'You're staying here?' At his touch, Evie felt the hair rise at the nape of her neck.

'Best billet in town. I booked in the minute I knew I'd be stuck here for the night.'

'Do you think he has a spare room? I need somewhere to stay.'

'Nope, but you're welcome to share mine,' Jack said.

'Do you Yanks think English girls are that easy?'

He leant towards her. 'Easy? No. But I think you're the most dazzling girl I've seen in my life.'

Evie's breath was light and fast. 'Flattery won't make me sleep with you.'

'Who said anything about sleeping?' He traced her jaw with his fingertip. 'Stay with me,' he said.

Evie felt the blood pulse in her veins, warmed by the fire, the closeness of him. 'Stay,' he said again. 'I won't do anything you don't want me to.'

Jack led her up the creaking wooden staircase to the attic rooms. Gradually the noise of the pub diminished beneath them. He held her hand tight, fingers interlocked, his thumb impatiently caressing hers. As they reached his door, he took her in his arms. His kiss took her breath away, the hunger and desire. They stumbled against the wall.

'Jack … I can't.' Evie's head swam as he pressed his lips to hers, his hand at the nape of her neck.

'Why? Evie, baby … Is this your first time? Is that it?'

'Yes, I've never …'

He looked deep into her eyes. 'Me too,' he said.

She threw back her head, her neck arching up to his lips. 'I don't believe you for a moment,' she said, laughing softly.

'Well, maybe not the first. But it's the first time it feels like this.'

'You shoot a good line, Jack Whitman.' She cupped his cheek in her hand.

Jack placed his hand flat against the wall, rested his head on hers as he caught his breath. 'Damn, you're beautiful. Will you marry me?'

'Are you mad?' Evie's eyes flew open. 'We only met a few hours ago.'

'Madly in love with you,' he murmured, kissing the arch of her brow, her eyelids, her mouth. 'Marry me,' he insisted. He took her face in his hands. 'I'm serious. I fell for you the moment

I saw you step out of that Puss Moth.' He pulled her closer to him. 'Then when I saw you in your underwear ...'

She raised an eyebrow. 'You thought I'd fall into bed with you?'

'Hell no.' He grinned. 'But I thought it was worth a shot.' He kissed her quickly, and unlocked the door. 'Stay here a minute.' He disappeared into the room, and Evie could hear him tidying up. Jack reappeared and waved an old blue toothbrush before he slipped it into his pocket. 'All yours.'

'Where will you sleep?'

'I'll bunk down with one of the guys. Don't worry about me.' He pressed her fingers to his lips, backed away, holding her hand for as long as he could. 'Marry me.' He said it like a dare.

'Good night, Jack.'

'Marry me!'

'Ask me in the morning.' She shook her head, smiling, as he whooped with laughter and ran downstairs. Evie closed the bedroom door behind her, and leant against it, listening to the beat of her heart.

*

'Hey, Evie!' Jack ran over as she walked out of the airfield offices. 'Where did you get to? I was going to treat you to breakfast this morning.'

'I wanted to see if the Magister was ready.'

'So you would have just run out without saying goodbye?' He looked crestfallen.

Evie glanced around. No one was looking. 'Of course I would have said goodbye.' She kissed him softly on the cheek, their lips drifting close to one another for a moment.

'Did you sleep well?'

'Thank you. It was kind of you to let me have your room. I paid George on the way out.'

'You didn't need to do that.'

'It was the least I could do after making you sleep with your friend.'

'I didn't. Red snored all night, and I couldn't sleep anyway for thinking of you.' The office door banged open, and Evie stepped away.

'Do you really have to go?' Jack asked her as he followed her across the airfield.

'Yes. I'd love to stay, but this old girl was supposed to be back at White Waltham yesterday.'

'Will I see you again?' He gave her a hand up into the cockpit.

'You can count on it.' Evie pulled on her leather flying helmet and waved goodbye as Jack stepped back. She felt light, giddy with happiness. Her body ached and hummed with life. *Concentrate, Evie*, she thought, and waved again as he turned to look at her. She flooded the carburettor. *OK, ignition switches on ...*

Nothing happened, just a dull clud, clud, clud. *That's odd*, she thought, and tried to start the engine again.

'Everything OK, baby?' Jack strolled over, one hand in his pocket.

'I don't understand.' Evie's brow furrowed. 'I know it needs repairs but they wouldn't send me out to ferry a plane that won't start, surely?'

'Why don't you jump out and we'll get one of the guys to take a look.' Jack whistled, waved his arm towards the hangar, where a group of engineers were brewing a pot of tea. 'Hey, Taff, would you take a look at Miss Chase's plane?'

Evie stood beside the Magister, listening as the engineer tried again to turn the engine over. It caught, thud, thud, clump. He shook his head.

'Sorry, Miss, looks like you're stuck here.'

'What do you think it is, Taff?' Jack leant against the hangar.

'Don't know, sir, but we'll have a shufti,' he said with his head in the engine. 'The old girl must like it here.'

'Well, do your best. If you have any luck, give the pub a call, Taff – Miss Chase has a room there.' He glanced at Evie. 'It's my day off today. I don't have to be back at Kirton just yet.' He guided her towards the offices. 'How about I show you round the place?'

'I'd like that,' she said. 'But what about the—'

'I'll ask the Duty Pilot to put a call in to White Waltham Ops Room, tell them you're tied up down here.'

Evie could tell from the Duty Pilot's reaction on the phone that Teddy was annoyed but she didn't care.

'Listen, Parker,' he said, calmly chewing the stalk of his pipe. 'Our chaps are doing their best ...'

Jack was standing just behind her. It felt as if the air between them was charged. Evie was sure the Duty Pilot had to notice something, but he just carried on talking to Teddy.

Jack leant forward, his eyes on the other man. 'Let's get out of here,' he whispered to her, his lips brushing her ear. Casually she clasped her hands behind her back. The Duty Pilot slammed the phone down.

'Right, they're not happy, but I've explained the engineers are on the job.'

'Thank you, sir.'

He puffed on his pipe, looked from Evie to Jack. 'Where are you staying, Miss Chase, if I need to get hold of you?'

'She's staying at the pub, sir,' Jack cut in. 'I gave her my room and bunked down with the guys.'

'Very chivalrous of you, Whitman,' he said drily. 'Well I can see you're in good hands.' He waved them away.

'Taff's lent me his bike,' Jack said as they walked across the car park. 'I can pick you up around the corner if you don't want everyone gossiping?' He zipped up his flying jacket. Evie walked on, flashing him a quick smile over her shoulder.

It was a beautiful morning. The world seemed newly minted, and as she strolled down the lane Evie whistled a tune. At the roar of a motorbike, she turned and stuck out her thumb.

Jack pulled up beside her. 'Morning, Miss. Can I give you a ride?'

'I don't know. My father always told me not to go with strangers.'

He pulled her to him. 'I'm not a stranger so your father can rest easy. I'm your fiancé.'

'Since when?' she said, laughing.

'Since we fell madly in love.'

'I told you to ask me again in the morning.' She pressed her palm flat against his chest, the firm leather of his jacket warm against her skin.

'I'm asking,' he said.

'Maybe.'

Jack revved the engine. 'Maybe? Jeez, woman, what have I got to do to convince you?'

'It's crazy, I hardly know you.'

'What's that got to do with anything? I knew you were the one for me the moment I saw you.' He hunkered down, eye to eye with her. 'Marry me.'

Evie jumped on the bike behind him. 'I said, maybe.' As she wrapped her arms around him, she tickled him.

'Hey! Stop it,' Jack was soon helpless with laughter.

Evie caught her breath, and grinned. 'Come on. Let's have some fun.'

They rode for miles through the countryside, and as Evie clung to Jack, the wind whipping her face, she thought she hadn't felt so alive for months. At midday, Jack waited in the pub downstairs as Evie tidied up. She dressed quickly and joined him in the empty bar. He was on the telephone.

'No luck, Taff?' he said. 'OK, well we've done the scenic route so now I'm going to take Miss Chase out for the grand tour in town. Speak to you later.'

He hung up and took her hand. 'Sorry, they're still working on the Magister. Looks like you'll be stuck with me for a while.'

'What a shame.' She pulled a face.

'Are you hungry?'

'Famished.'

He offered her his arm. 'George doesn't do lunches so we'll go into town.'

The motorbike sped along the clear roads into Clifton, past the elegant rows of stucco-fronted houses and out to the edge of the gorge. Jack parked up near a pub with a breathtaking view of the suspension bridge.

'This is beautiful.' Evie shielded her eyes from the sun. Jack noticed several men turn admiringly in her direction, and he put his arm around her, proud and protective.

'Let's find a quiet table,' he said. 'It's not safe to leave you out here while I get the drinks.'

They chose a spot far from the other diners. The light inside the pub was dim, and the good food made Evie drowsy. She would have liked to curl up on the old velvet sofa and sleep in his arms. They talked for hours, filling in all the spaces and questions – families, first loves, heartbreaks and dreams.

'When I go back to America, I'm going to run the ranch,' he said.

'You're a cowboy?' Evie laughed. 'I'm in love with a real American cowboy.'

Jack raised an eyebrow, leant closer to her. 'In love?'

'I didn't mean …' Evie blushed.

'You said it! You love me!' Jack smiled broadly as he took her hand.

'It just slipped out.'

'It's too late, you've done it now.' He kissed her softly. 'Well, it's just as well because I'm sure in love with you.'

'Are all cowboys as mad as you?'

'Yep, most of them. It's all that sun on our heads out riding all day.' He pulled a crazy face. 'We raise cattle in Montana – it's the most beautiful place on earth, you'll love it.' As Evie listened, he talked to her of vast green plains, of family land that stretched as far as the eye could see. 'It's not like you're cut off either. With the airstrip and planes, we can fly in and out whenever we want. We can go to New York, Chicago …'

Visions of cities Evie had only heard about and seen on newsreels danced in her imagination. It was exhilarating to think of the future when recently so much of her life had been caught up in the moment. It felt daring.

'Shall we take a walk?' Jack said.

'Yes, let's.' Evie raised her head from his shoulder. 'I'll fall asleep if we stay here.'

'I'm sorry.' His face fell. 'I'm boring you, yacking away.'

'No!' She laughed. 'I'm just tired for some reason.'

'Didn't get much sleep, huh?'

She nudged him playfully. 'I can sleep when I get home.'

Hand in hand they strolled out onto the street, browsing the windows of the old shops. Jack paused outside an antiques store, looked at the tray of diamond rings in the window. Evie caught their reflection in the old, dimpled glass, Jack's handsome face close to hers as he studied the rings. She felt as if she were in a dream – how could happiness arrive so suddenly, so unexpectedly?

'That's beautiful.' He pointed at a large sapphire.

'They're all lovely,' Evie said.

'Pick one.' He slipped his arm around her.

'Jack. It's all too fast ...'

'The world won't wait for us, Evie. You have to take every chance of happiness you get these days.' Jack's eyes were uncertain, full of pain as he turned to her. 'I've seen too many good guys killed before they have a chance to—'

'Don't.' She placed her fingertips on his lips. 'We have a whole lifetime ahead of us. There's no hurry. We can get to know one another better.'

Jack shook his head. 'I know you. I know what I feel in here.' He balled her hand in his fist and placed it against his heart. 'I've waited my whole life for you.' He kissed her then. 'I love you, Evelyn Maud.'

'Don't remind me of my ghastly middle name!' she said, giggling.

'It's beautiful! Everything about you is beautiful, Evelyn Maud.' Jack doubled over laughing as Evie poked him in the ribs. 'I bet you by the time you go home you'll have agreed to marry me, and when you do I want a ring to put on your finger so every other guy knows we're together.' He pulled her, laughing, into the store.

A grey-haired woman in a heather tweed suit rose stiffly from the stool behind the counter.

'Good afternoon,' Jack said as he tucked his cap under his arm. He put his arm around Evie, and she looked up at him. 'May we look at the rings you have in the window?'

The woman smiled. It made her feel young again to see a couple so obviously in love. She unlocked the display and put the black velvet tray of rings on the counter. 'What price were you looking for, sir?'

'Doesn't matter,' he said, gazing at Evie. 'Nothing is too good for my girl.'

That night as they danced in the bar to a Frank Sinatra record, Jack had the sapphire ring in a leather box in his pocket. They knew time was running out for them. If Taff couldn't get the plane working in the morning, White Waltham would be sure to send an Anson to pick Evie up and get her back to base.

'Let's go to bed,' he murmured. When she looked at him, her eyes were heavy lidded, sated, tired. They leant against one another as they walked upstairs. Jack threw open the windows to a star-filled sky, Sinatra drifting up from the bar below. Evie wrapped her arms around him, leant her head against his back.

'I don't want this night to end,' she said.

He turned to her. 'This is just the beginning.' Jack kissed her, his lips, his tongue urgent, his hands in her hair. 'Stay with me.'

'Jack, I can't ...'

He caught his breath. 'Please, baby. Can't you tell how much I love you?'

'Jack, it's not that.' She stroked his face. 'I just always imagined my first time would be perfect. I always promised myself I'd wait until I was married.'

Jack sighed. 'I respect that.' He held her tightly, buried his face in her hair. 'Let me stay though. I won't try anything on. Just let me sleep on the sofa here. Who knows when I'll be able to get over to see you again, and I can't stand the thought of another night alone knowing you're so close.'

Evie glanced up at him. 'Promise?'

He kissed her. 'Promise.'

They talked through the night, Evie curled up in the soft, creaking old bed, and Jack nearby on the sofa. They shared their hopes and dreams, everything they longed to see and do when the war was over.

'I can't wait for you to meet my folks. They'll love you,' he said sleepily. 'Mom always wanted a daughter, and none of my brothers have married yet.'

Evie propped her head on her hand. 'How many do you have again?'

'Three. I'm the youngest.'

'It's funny, isn't it? We'll both be twenty-one this year.'

'I'm still older than you.'

'Just.'

Jack reached out to her, their fingertips touched. 'I'm going to build us a house, Evie. There's a patch of land I've had my eye on my whole life. I'm going to give you and our kids—'

'Steady on!' Evie smiled. 'We're not even married yet.'

'I want girls just as cute as you.'

'Cute? You really don't know me well yet. They'll be monstrous little tomboys if they're anything like me.'

'We'll be so happy, Evie. It's going to be the best adventure of our lives. After this damn war is over, we're going to travel, see the world together.' He yawned, let her hand fall. 'All I want is to take you home.' As Jack's words washed over her in the darkness, she must have fallen asleep, because when she woke at dawn, he was lying on his side breathing peacefully.

Evie propped herself up on her arm, watching him sleep. She tried to imagine waking up next to him every morning for the rest of her life, and smiled. Images of a white clapboard house came to her mind. She pictured herself sitting beside Jack on a swing seat on the porch, watching a troop of children running wild and free across green fields, running home. Evie thought of Jack's parents, his warm, gentle mother, how his eyes filled with love when he spoke of her. It was everything she had ever wanted – a family, a home of her own.

Jack's eyes flickered gently beneath their lids as he slept. Evie didn't want to miss a moment, she didn't want the dawn to come. She wished they could stay together like this forever.

'No,' he murmured in his sleep. His face contorted, fists clenched. 'Hell,' he thrashed out.

'Hey,' she said softly. She slipped out of bed and padded over. She touched his face. 'Jack, wake up. It's only a dream. Jack …'

His eyes blinked open sleepily, but he was breathing hard. As he came round, he turned to her. 'Hi, beautiful.' He brushed her cheek with his fingertips. 'I'm sorry, did I wake you?'

'No, I was awake. You were dreaming,' she murmured sleepily, as she curled up on the floor beside him, laid her head against his chest.

'I was flying,' he said, his voice low and broken. 'Damn Jerries all over the place.' He stroked her hair.

'It was only a dream.'

Jack straightened her cap for her, his eyes dancing as he saluted. He offered her his arm, and they walked in companionable silence to the base.

'No luck with this one, Jack,' Taff called out to them. Tools lay scattered around the fuselage of the Magister. 'Your Spit is all ready to go though.'

'Thanks, Taff,' Jack said. He turned to Evie. 'Thing is with a Hurricane you know where you are, its strength is all inside. With my little Spitty, her skin's all part of the strength. I thought it might have to go back to Vickers but I trust Taff.' Jack looked around. The base was quiet, only ground crew milling about. 'Why don't you get yourself a coffee while I get changed?'

She waited in the mess, watching an endless stream of aircraft taking off and landing. Jack reappeared in his flight suit with two other men and a pretty brunette WAAF. 'Guys, this is Evie

Chase, my girl,' he said proudly. 'Listen, we've got to go up and do some manoeuvres. Have you ever been in a Spitfire?'

'A Spitfire?' Evie's eyes widened. 'No, but I'd love to ...' She thought for a moment. 'But how? They're single-seaters and I can't fly one myself yet.'

'Come on.' Jack took her hand. 'I'm going to slip you in my pocket.' He led her to the hangar where the blue-nosed Spitfire was waiting for him, and checked the coast was clear. Jack clambered into the cockpit and beckoned for her to join him.

Evie ran her hand across the sensuous curve of the wing. 'You're mad! I'm not flying in this with you.' She glanced over to see the young WAAF squeezing into the plane next door with Jack's friend. The cockpit was tight, barely shoulder width. 'Is it safe?'

'Sure. You're only little, and I've seen guys do this before.'

Evie shook her head. 'No, you're officially bonkers. I'm going to sit this one out, chaps.'

Jack signalled to Taff. 'Miss Chase doesn't fancy taking her chances with me this morning. Would you mind giving her a ride up to the bridge? I'm planning a little fly past for her.' Evie looked at him curiously as he fastened his helmet. 'Listen, I'm going to make you a little bet. If this is the best damn Spitfire flying you've ever seen, you are going to say yes to me. Deal?'

Evie heard the power surge through the plane. It made the hairs stand up on the back of her neck. As Jack began to move forward, she yelled, 'Deal!'

It was a gin-clear day, blue skies stretching out to sea. The three men put the planes through their paces, skimming above the water. They turned, headed along the estuary. Taff pulled up in a pub car park overlooking the river, and Evie clambered off the motorbike.

'Oh ... I know what he's going to do,' Taff said, watching the aircraft swoop low over the water.

'What?' Evie looked at the Severn Railway Bridge just ahead. 'No! He wouldn't!'

'I heard so many pilots have done this there's a policeman

172

permanently stationed in the beer garden up here taking down numbers,' Taff shouted above the noise of their engines. 'Let's hope for their sakes he's not on duty so early.'

Evie's eyes widened as the planes got closer to the bridge. 'They'll never make it!'

'Well, they say there's thirty feet less clearance at high tide,' Taff teased her. 'Do you reckon they'll get lucky?'

The three Spitfires came abreast, and Jack looked from left to right as each pilot gave the thumbs up. They descended low over the water.

'They're crazy!' Evie shouted, breathless with fear and excitement. The planes sped closer, each pilot choosing his span.

From his cockpit Jack peered down at the riverside, checking Evie was there. 'I'm crazy for you, Evie,' he yelled. He didn't care that she couldn't possibly hear him. 'Marry me!'

'Surely they're not going to!' she exclaimed to Taff as they dropped even lower.

Jack levelled his wings as the piers of the bridge drew closer. 'Marry me!'

'No!' she said under her breath. 'They'll never make it, Taff.'

Jack let out a whoop of pure joy, and the Spitfires skimmed under the bridge at 300 mph, wingtips almost touching the spans as the incredulous faces of passengers on the London train looked down from the bridge above.

When they landed, Evie and Taff were waiting for them. Jack's friend checked there were no senior officers around, and his girl jumped out onto the runway.

'That was incredible!' She laughed, loosening her hair. 'You should have come!' she said to Evie. 'You don't know what you missed.'

Jack's plane taxied over and he leapt out. 'Well? What do you think?'

'Yes,' Evie said.

'Yes?'

She wrapped her arms around him, kissed him full on the lips. 'I'm saying yes.'

Jack's face creased into a delighted smile, and he pulled the ring box from his pocket. He went down on one knee, and offered the sapphire to her. As she smiled and he slipped the ring onto her finger, a cheer went up in the hangar.

Taff walked over, wiping his hands on an oily rag. 'Congratulations,' he said. 'Well, Miss, looks like you're all set for takeoff. Just as well, your pool's been on the line.'

'Really?' She couldn't hide her disappointment.

'Hey,' Jack kissed her forehead. 'A few weeks, that's all. I'm going to be up at White Waltham every chance I get from now on.'

20

Stella stretched out on the threadbare Persian rug, the coal fire warming her toes. A Chopin nocturne played softly on the gramophone as the wind rattled the sash windows, and the spring rain fell outside.

'Here we are,' Michael said as he carried over a stack of books. He sat beside her on the floor and flicked through the pages. 'This is what I was talking about. Look how Turner builds the washes and glazes.' He placed a reproduction of a luminous watercolour in front of Stella.

'It's beautiful,' she said as she swirled her paintbrush in the jam jar of water at her side. Paints and sketchbooks lay scattered around them. 'I don't think I'll ever really master it.'

'Of course you will.' He turned to her, smiling.

Stella reached for her watercolour block, stroked the soft brush across the paper, soaking it with water. She chose a finer brush, circled the tip in a rosy block of pigment. 'I'm so glad I bumped into you this afternoon. I was at a bit of a loose end.'

'Where were you going?' Michael watched as she began to build up the colours of a sunset in transparent layers. 'You were soaked to the skin.'

'I just felt like walking.' Stella hesitated, her brush poised over the paper. 'Don't you ever feel like that?'

'All the time.' He looked up at her. 'Sometimes I get so fed up, stuck here listening to parishioners' problems—'

Stella blinked, looked away. 'It must be awfully tiresome.' She was glad she hadn't bothered him with how she had been feeling.

'Not really.' Michael laid his arm back against the old leather Chesterfield sofa, traced the smooth indentation of a button with his finger. 'I enjoy helping people. I just wish I could do more. I'm thinking of signing up.'

'No.' She turned quickly to him. 'You can't …' Stella bit her lip.

'I wouldn't fight, of course,' he said. 'You know how I feel about that. But as a chaplain, perhaps I could really do some good.'

Stella hated the thought of him anywhere near the front line. 'I think you're being a great help to people right where you are. So many families have been torn apart by this damn war.'

'Have you heard from yours?'

'Sorry?'

'Your parents – I wondered if you had heard from them?'

Stella shook her head. 'Not for a while. I had a letter from Mother.'

'How did they take it, when you decided to join the ATA?'

She hesitated. 'I didn't tell them,' she said quietly as she swirled her brush in the water.

Michael's eyes widened. 'You didn't tell them?'

'No. After Richard …' She twisted the gold band on her ring finger. 'I booked a passage for me and David, and just left.'

'They must have been worried sick.' Michael saw her hand was shaking and took it gently in his. 'Stella, what happened?'

She blinked, looked towards the fire. 'Do you know what Mother said, in her letter? "Have you lost your senses?" Sometimes, I think … maybe I have.' She tried to laugh it off, but Michael's face was full of concern as she turned to him.

'It will get easier,' he said. 'I've seen so many young women who have lost their husbands. Grief can take months, years to work its course. It's perfectly normal to feel very blue, very angry.'

'Angry?' Stella thought for a moment. 'I haven't felt angry, not at all. I don't feel …' She struggled to put into words the relentless darkness she carried with her. 'I can't imagine feeling normal ever again.'

'You will,' he said kindly. 'You'll start again.'

'Who would even look at me? I'm such a frightful mess, and I've a young baby.'

Michael glanced down at his hand, holding hers. 'You are—' He was interrupted by a knock on the door. 'Come in.'

'Brought your tea, Mr Forsyth,' the housekeeper said as she bustled in. She laid a tray on the coffee table, the cups clattering. Her mouth twisted as she looked at Stella. 'There's no cake, I'm afraid, but I put an extra bag in the pot as you have company.'

'Thank you, Mrs Biggs.'

'Would you like me to tidy up in here now, sir, or would I be disturbing you?'

Stella sensed the woman's disapproval, and she stood, smoothing down her skirt. She turned away from her, pretended to scan the books on the shelves.

'No, that's perfectly alright,' Michael said. 'If you've done the other rooms you can finish for today. I left your money under the tea caddy.'

'Thank you, Mr Forsyth.' She patted her hair, her gaze directed towards where Stella stood looking at a painting on the wall.

'No, thank *you*, Mrs Biggs,' he said pointedly. The housekeeper left, muttering under her breath. As the door closed, Michael laughed. 'You must excuse my housekeeper,' he said to Stella. 'She's remarkable. Sometimes she has entire conversations with herself. She's a good cleaner, but she'd take over my whole life if she had the chance.' He poured a cup of tea and carried it over to Stella. 'She doesn't like it when I have company.'

She took the cup from him. 'Thank you.' As he stood close to her, Stella caught the clean, citrus scent of eau de cologne. 'Do you entertain many young women then?' She turned to look at the painting again.

'Only beautiful pilots who need rescuing from rainstorms.'

The heat rose in her cheeks. 'This is lovely. Is it a Spencer?'

'Yes.'

'I recognise his work from the book you lent me.'

'Did you enjoy it?'

'Very much. I've been meaning to give it back to you at church.'

'You know you can drop in anytime, don't you?' Michael smiled as she turned to him. 'I'm always here if you would like to talk. It really does help.'

Stella hesitated. She wanted so desperately to tell him everything.

'That's what I'm here for,' he went on. 'That's my job.'

Sometimes I get so fed up, stuck here listening to parishioners' problems. Stella glanced at the window as she thought of his words. Bright sunlight broke through the slate grey clouds, sparkled on the fresh leaves shifting in the breeze. 'Of course it is, and you're very good at it. I feel so much better.'

'I didn't mean—'

'The rain has stopped,' she said. 'Thank you for the tea. I mustn't take up any more of your time.'

'Would you like to take that trip out to Cookham soon?' Michael said as she slipped on her shoes by the fireside.

Stella ran a hand through her damp hair. 'Yes, I'd like that.' She forced a bright smile. 'I'd like that very much.'

21

'Where the hell have you been?' Beau demanded as Evie walked into the Ops Corridor.

'I thought you'd be pleased to see me, sir.' Evie dumped her parachute on the floor. 'Better late than never, isn't that what we're always told?'

'It's a bad show on your first flight. That twerp Teddy's completely lost his wool over this one.'

Evie wasn't going to let Beau spoil her good mood. She had been buzzing with happiness the whole flight. 'But the Magister—'

'Are you telling me it takes two days for the engineers to fix a simple mechanical fault?'

'How do I know?'

'It's your job to know, Miss Chase.'

'Hello, Evie!' Megan stopped on her way past. 'Good to see you!'

At least someone thinks so, Evie thought. As Evie ran her hand through her hair, shaking it loose from her flying cap, Megan spotted the ring on her finger, and grabbed her hand.

'Evie! Are you …?'

'Shh. I'll tell you about it later.' Megan raced out to her aircraft, and Evie turned to Beau. 'Well, I'm sorry, sir. It won't happen again.'

'Make sure it doesn't.' He looked solemnly at her. 'I see congratulations are in order. At least that Yank has the decency to make an honest woman of you.'

'What do you mean by that?'

'You seem to get through men as quickly as you do aircraft. I would be careful, Miss Chase, you're getting something of a reputation.' He took her to one side as some pilots pushed past. 'You need to consider your position here. Gallivanting around the countryside is no way for a new officer to behave. You girls are under a spotlight. The slightest hint of a scandal and you will all get a bad name, do you understand?'

'Evie!' Stella called out from the queue by the counter in the mess. 'We thought you'd got lost.'

'Very funny.' Evie was still smarting from Beau's warning, but she was determined not to show it.

'Welcome back. We have missed you.' Stella gave her a hug. 'So, what have you been up to?' As Evie raised her left hand, the sapphire sparkling in the sunlight, Stella's mouth fell open in surprise. 'No!'

'Congratulations, Miss,' Jean said as the girls clustered around to look at Evie's ring.

'Thank you, Jean. These look good.' Evie chose a slice of fruit cake from the display.

'Well, when I saw how much everyone liked the cake your mother—'

Evie's face clouded. 'Stepmother.'

'I thought why not bake a few cakes at home and bring them in? Make a few coppers.'

Evie took a bite. 'Delicious.'

'Who is he?' Stella asked as they found a spare table. They flopped down in the armchairs and Evie told her the whole story. 'Oh it's so romantic,' she sighed. 'An American.' She rested her chin on her hands. 'What's he like?'

'Gorgeous,' Evie said thoughtfully. 'Handsome, funny, kind. He's rather mad and impulsive ...'

'So are you,' Stella said.

'Jack said we could be twins, we're so in tune with one another.' She took a sip of Stella's hot orangeade. 'How's it been here?'

'Busy.' Her face fell. 'They lost dozens of pilots the day you got caught in Bristol. I finally headed back here, and even then I had to do a steep bank to miss Shottesbrooke. Almost took half the church with me.'

'I had the strangest feeling when I was flying into Whitchurch,' Evie turned the cup in her hands. 'I know it's silly, but do you ever feel like you have someone flying with you, even when you're alone?'

'Not your guardian angel again?' she said. 'Poppycock. It's concentration and endurance gets you in.'

'I don't know,' Evie said. 'It's a funny old game.'

'Nothing funny about it,' Teddy interrupted. 'Glad you decided to join us, Miss Chase. Hear you're marrying some Yank, is that right?' He leant uncomfortably close to her. 'A British chap not good enough for you, eh?'

Instead of recoiling, Evie leant closer to him, whispered in his ear. 'I should have slapped you that night you made a pass at me, and if you don't back off I'll do it now and tell the whole base what a cad and a bounder you are.'

'I'd watch him, Evie, he's got it in for you,' Stella said as he stormed off.

'I can handle him.' Evie glanced up as a pilot walked into the mess. 'Hello, Stewart,' she called. 'I just met a friend of yours, Jack Whitman.'

'Jack? Hell, fancy that. How's he doing?'

'Rather well as it happens. We've just become engaged.'

'Congratulations, Evie.' He shook her hand.

'How are things with you?'

'I just had a lousy flight. It was a P40 Tomahawk I. Did you know they have a French throttle?'

Evie shook her head. 'Nope.'

'Neither did I till I read the notes. It's like easing off the gas in a car to speed up. Listen, I've got to run, but let's have a drink to celebrate later.'

'A reverse throttle? Most unnatural.' Stella sipped her tea. 'I had a dicey one too. I had to deliver a Magister to a new MU. You know how they tie the trees back at the perimeter of these places when they're being built, then release the trees to hide the unit? The last time I flew over there the trees were tied back and the strip was nice and clear. This time I couldn't find the bally place. I had to do a short stop bang on the field, it was a close-run thing.'

'You're doing so well,' Evie said. 'You'll be a Second Officer before you know it.'

Stella blushed. 'Sometimes I feel that there's a peace in doing something worthwhile. I probably sound awfully silly.'

'No, I know what you mean,' Evie said. 'How are things at the house?'

'We have eggs! Megan's very excited. She spends hours out there talking to the hens. I think Meggie finds them better company than me.'

'Don't be daft,' Evie said. 'It is good to be home,' she sighed and closed her eyes, wondering when she would see Jack again.

22

The girls had slept late, exhausted after days spent ferrying planes all over the country, and several unlucky nights lurching home on the dreaded pitch-black night-trains. They had only a couple of days off, but for once their leave worked out with Jack's. His imminent arrival caused a buzz of excitement. It had been a beautiful day – soft rain in the early afternoon clearing to a golden sunset. Evie had spent the afternoon cooking and baking for Jack's arrival, the chickens clucking contentedly in the garden, Stalin dozing in a patch of sunlight on the kitchen windowsill. Now the house was filled with the delicious scent of boeuf bourguignon bubbling away in the range.

Evie had arranged that they would meet friends at the Riviera that night. Cocktail gowns lay scattered over every surface in Stella's bedroom, and the three outfits the girls had selected hung carefully by the full-length mirror.

Megan lay on her stomach on the bed, her chin cupped in her hand. 'Evie …'

'Mmm?' she replied distractedly. She was painting her nails scarlet, leaving the moons white.

'You and Jack, did you …' Megan blushed. 'Did you do "it"?'

Evie laughed. 'What do you mean "it"? Did we make love?'

'Did you, Evie?' Stella rolled on the bed next to Megan. 'Did he clutch you in his manly arms?' She hugged a pillow to her face, laughing.

'Oh shut up, you're just teasing me!' Megan's bottom lip stuck out.

'Sorry, darling.' She tossed the pillow at her.

'Stella's the old married woman,' Evie said. 'You should be asking her about this kind of thing, not me.'

'Hardly,' Stella said. 'I can barely remember what "it's" like.' Her eyes fell for a moment.

'So … what is it like?' Megan asked finally.

Evie glanced up from her nails. 'You mean you haven't either? What about this chap of yours at home?'

'Bill?' Megan shook her head. 'No, we've kissed, that's all.'

'Well, I always wanted the first time to be special. I'm glad we're waiting for our wedding night.' Evie's eyes twinkled mischievously. 'Listen to this though.' She unfolded a letter from her dressing-gown pocket. 'My darling girl—'

'Oh,' Megan sighed. 'I wish someone would call me their darling girl.'

'I'm back on ops, and missing the future Mrs Jack Whitman terribly.' Evie glanced up from the letter. '"Mrs Jack Whitman", I like that.' She skimmed through the letter. 'I'm all trussed up in my Mae West, ready to scramble, but I'd rather be in my birthday suit with you …'

Megan screamed with laughter, balling a handkerchief into her mouth. There was a sudden knock on the door.

'He's here!' Evie leapt up, fanning her nails. Her stomach tightened with excitement. She pulled her red silk kimono around her, ducked down to look in the dressing-table mirror. 'How do I look?'

'Beautiful.' Stella smiled. 'Well go on, don't keep the boy waiting!'

'Hello,' Jack called. 'Anyone home?'

Evie flung open the bedroom window, and looked down, the dark waves of her hair framing her face. Jack took his cap off, gazed up at her. In his hand there was a bouquet of white roses. 'There you are!' he said.

She flashed him a dazzling smile. 'Wait there.' She ran downstairs, and threw open the front door. Jack took her in his arms. 'Missed me?'

'You bet,' he murmured, as Evie kissed his tired eyes, the dark circles new to her.

Megan paused on the staircase. 'It's so romantic,' she sighed. They seemed an impossibly glamorous couple to her, Jack in his uniform, Evie in her beautiful scarlet gown with the roses in her hand.

'Come and meet the girls.' Evie hugged the flowers to her chest. 'Stella, Megan, this is my fiancé, Jack Whitman.'

'That sounds good.' He slipped his arm around her waist. 'It's a pleasure to meet you both. Evie's told me all about you.' Jack winked as Megan self-consciously touched the rags in her hair. 'If she'd told me how pretty you both are I would have brought some of the guys with me.'

Jack enjoyed the attention of the girls. He had been through a tough few days' combat and it was a relief to be in a peaceful cottage, his girl piling his plate high with stew, a cool glass of beer beside him. After dinner Stella and Megan retreated upstairs and Jack sat in his shirtsleeves by the stove listening to a Sinatra record he had bought especially for Evie. 'Tell you something, this war sure makes you appreciate the simple pleasures in life.' He held his hand out to her. 'I'll always think of you when I hear "East of the Sun",' he said as she slipped onto his lap. 'Now you can play it whenever you want.'

'They played it that night in the pub, do you remember?'

'It's our song.' He affectionately flicked the end of her nose with his finger. 'What's up with the cat?' Stalin glared at him from under the sofa.

'You're in his chair.'

'Yeah? Well, mister, you're going to have to get used to having another guy around the house.' Evie kissed the top of his head. He cupped her jaw, brought her lips to his. 'Baby, do we have to go out tonight? I have to go back to the base tomorrow.'

'I thought it would be fun for you to meet some of my friends. I've been boring them all senseless telling them how wonderful you are.'

'You have?' He grinned.

'Of course!' She stroked his thick, dark hair away from his forehead. 'You do look tired, darling. How's it been?'

'Busy,' he said.

'Have they moved you to Martlesham yet?'

'Early April they reckon.'

'You will be careful won't you?'

'Don't worry about me.' His eyes crinkled as he smiled. 'Listen, I've been thinking, I want to ask your dad for your hand in marriage.'

'Why?' she said coolly. 'It's not his to give.'

'Evie, I want to do this properly.' He stroked her cheek. 'You're an old-fashioned girl and I respect that.'

'You mean, about making love?' She blushed. 'I hope it's not too hard, waiting.'

Jack broke into a wide grin. 'Baby, you have no idea … But it will be worth it. As soon as I have the all clear from Mr Chase, we'll set a date.'

'Oh, fine,' she said reluctantly. 'But not tonight, please? There's so little time and I just want to enjoy being with you.'

'OK, I'll write him. Maybe we can hook up next time.' Jack settled back in the chair. 'I bumped into one of your guys at the 43 Club last night.'

'So that's why you look so tired!' She pulled a face and laughed. 'Who was it?'

'Jim Mollison. He's a fun guy, had us all in stitches. Man, he has some good stories.'

Evie nudged him in the ribs. 'What were you doing in Soho?' She knew the club's louche reputation. 'Six floors of celebrities, drugs, aristos and sex from what I've heard. I wouldn't have thought it was your kind of place.' As Jack stretched, she saw the flash of his bright green socks above his boots. She began to wonder whether there was another side to him.

Jack shrugged, hiding his guilt. 'We were just letting off some steam.' His head still throbbed from the all-night bender. 'It was kind of wild. We ended up in Mayfair with a bunch of guys from home. They water-bombed the hotel stairs with their shower curtain.'

'Sounds like quite a night. Any girls?'

Jack rubbed his nose and yawned. 'Nah, nobody to touch you.' He thought of the pretty blonde Polish WAAF he had left sleeping in her bedsit that morning. What was one night, after all?

'Come on, lovebirds.' Stella appeared in the doorway wearing a midnight blue satin gown.

'Boy, I have to be the luckiest guy alive going out on the town with you three girls.' Jack straightened his tie as Evie stood and smoothed the silver silk of her favourite Schiaparelli gown.

As the girls found a table at the Riviera, Jack went to the bar to fetch a bottle of champagne. While he was waiting to pay, Beau arrived.

'Hey, you're the guy who was in Bristol with Evie? Pilot Officer Jack Whitman, sir.' He held out his hand to Beau. 'I have to thank you for not taking her home with you that night.'

'Congratulations on your engagement,' he said.

Jack clapped him on the back. 'Won't you come and have a drink with us?' He nodded towards the table where the girls sat.

'I don't think—'

'I insist. If it wasn't for you we might not be together.'

Beau helped Jack carry five champagne glasses to the table. 'Good evening, girls,' he said.

'Wing Commander.' Evie gazed up at him. 'I haven't seen you for a while. Is Olivia not with you?' For a moment their eyes met. The champagne cork went off with a loud pop, and as everyone cheered, Evie looked away uncomfortably.

'I'd like to make a toast,' Jack said, 'to the most beautiful girl in the world. I'm the luckiest guy alive. To Evie!'

'To Evie,' they all said. As she looked up, she felt Beau watching her still.

'What's it like flying in combat, Jack?' Megan asked him.

'Well ...' He stretched back in his seat. 'Our squadron is flying Hurricanes, but the Spits are coming soon. We're all volunteers.'

'It's so brave of you,' Megan said. 'Fancy fighting in another country's war.'

'This is everyone's war,' Beau said steadily. He took a battered silver cigarette case from his breast pocket and offered it round.

'Thank you,' Evie said. As he lit her cigarette, their hands touched. She hoped Jack wasn't about to shoot a line, or worse that Beau would show him up.

'My feeling exactly, sir,' Jack said. 'I've been in since the early days with Shorty and Red and the guys. They've moved us around a bit, but once we're over at Martlesham I'm going to get me a couple of Jerries if it's the last thing I do.'

Evie knew from the expression on his face that Beau was thinking, *It may well be.*

'You must have seen some action?' Stella asked.

'Sure. Man, I came close the other day.' Jack tucked his hands behind his head. 'We were doing convoy work over the North Sea. We were jumped by two or three dozen Me109s while we were off the coast of France. I saw a Jerry cutting through the bombers. I got a couple of bursts in ...' Jack's voice drifted over Evie. Beau smoked quietly as the story unfolded. 'It felt like he was taking a piggyback.' He winked, and Megan giggled. 'Next time I'll get him.' Jack drained his glass. 'Those squareheads are wily. You've gotta stay in formation, look out for your buddies. The ones who go off alone are the ones who get in trouble. They're sitting ducks for Jerry.'

'We always fly alone.' Evie turned a book of matches over in her fingers. 'I can't wait to fly the Spits.'

'D'you reckon that will happen, baby? It's a hell of a plane for a—'

'For a woman?' Stella said frostily.

Jack held his hands up in defence. 'Hey, back me up on this, sir.'

Beau stubbed out his cigarette. 'Frankly, I would be delighted to have either Miss Chase or Mrs Grainger on my wing.'

Megan's face fell at his omission, and Jack noticed. 'Right, Meggie, how about I show you how we dance in America?' He took her hand and spun her towards the dance floor.

'I'm just going to powder my nose,' Stella said.

'Would you care to dance, Miss Chase?' Beau asked her. 'If I may?' he asked Jack.

'Sure, sir,' he called, before Evie had a chance to object.

The band was playing 'Stardust' as Beau led her to the floor, couples moving slowly to the music, lost in one another's arms, the mirror-ball lights swirling around them. Evie's heart was beating fast as Beau took her hand and slipped his arm around her waist. Through the thin satin of her gown she could feel the heat of his hand on the small of her back. She was surprised how well he danced, easily, with a natural strength and grace.

'I'm sorry about Jack,' she said. 'He does like to shoot a line. It was good of you not to show him up.'

'There are two types of fighter pilot, Miss Chase. You're either an ace, or a target.'

'And which is Jack?'

'He's young,' Beau said 'Perhaps he'll learn.'

'He's the same age as me.'

'You seem older.'

'Is that what you class as a compliment, sir?'

'It's as close as you'll get tonight.'

Evie smiled. 'You're hardly ancient yourself.'

'I'm twenty-nine, in case you're fishing.' He sighed. 'But when I see a wet-behind-the-ears stooge like your fiancé I feel twice that.'

'You don't seem terribly happy for me, Wing Commander,' she said finally, her head resting lightly against his cheek.

'Are you sure about that boy, Miss Chase?'

'Yes, yes I am,' she said defiantly.

He turned his head slightly to look at her, his dazzling blue eyes close to hers. 'Then I am happy for you.' As they danced on, he held her a little closer, the music and shimmering light moving around them, within them.

'Jack says we have to take every chance of happiness we can at the moment. Do you think he's right?'

'Happiness? In my experience it's ephemeral, Miss Chase.' His head turned, his lips close to her ear now. 'Often you don't appreciate you had a chance of it until it is too late.'

As Beau exhaled, Evie felt his warm breath against her temple. He smelt good to her – tobacco, leather, eau de cologne. She felt a rush of sensation, a warmth that made the hair at the nape of her neck rise, and her stomach melt away.

'It's never too late.'

'You seem to have a natural talent for happiness, which I lack.' He hesitated. 'I just hope you're not rushing into this.'

Evie laughed lightly. 'I know what I'm doing, sir.'

'Do you?' He turned his face to look at her. 'Lord knows I'm the last person to be giving advice on affairs of the heart, but sometimes you need to know when to rein yourself in.'

Evie met his gaze. His lips were close to hers. 'You're talking like I'm a wild horse that needs breaking, sir.'

The sparkling air swam between them. As the song ended and the couples began to leave the floor, they stood, caught in the moment.

Beau's hand fell away and he led her to the now empty table. Evie felt hot. She reached for her champagne, the cold bubbles dancing on her tongue.

Beau lit two cigarettes and passed one to her. 'You do need to consider your reputation, Miss Chase,' he said.

'What do you mean my "reputation"?' Her temper flared. 'You're not my father.'

'Thank God.' He blew a cloud of smoke into the air. 'It's simply not the same for men and women.' He leant towards her. 'Perhaps if you concentrated on being a good pilot instead of bedding pilots ...'

'I beg your pardon?' She glared at him.

'First Teddy, now this Yank. You've been in the ATA barely a couple of months. I had you down as more than—'

'How dare you!' She slammed her glass down on the table. 'I most certainly did not sleep with Teddy. Is that what he's been saying?'

'From what I've heard he's telling everyone you are a "tigress" in bed. Strangely believable …' Beau wiped up the champagne she had spilt with a linen napkin.

'Believe what you want, but he's lying.' She fought to control her anger. 'What do I need to do? Get old Doc Barbour to confirm my virginity? Wouldn't he just love that.' She leant towards Beau. 'Or perhaps once the great event has occurred I could ask Miss Gold to post a notice on the Lost Property board?' Evie held his gaze until Beau looked away.

'I'm sorry. Clearly I owe you an apology.' He pushed back his chair. 'Good evening, Miss Chase. My congratulations … and my apologies, again.' As Beau walked away, Jack and Megan came back to the table.

'Is he leaving already?' Jack held out Megan's chair for her. 'That's no fun.' He went after Beau.

'Hey, sir.' He tapped him on the shoulder. 'Help me out here. I can't dance with three women all night!'

'I wouldn't worry about that. There are always plenty of men sniffing around our ATA girls.' Beau handed his ticket to the coat-check girl. 'By the way, you should know that a certain Ops Officer, Edward Parker, is spreading rumours about your fiancée.' He looked over at Evie. 'If she was my girl, I'd punch his lights out.'

Jack's face hardened. 'Thanks for the tip.'

23

At dawn, Evie woke alone. She padded downstairs to wake Jack, but the sofa was empty. She stretched out her hand, felt the warm indentation in the cushions where he had lain. In the half light as she turned, she saw him, sitting in his vest and boxer shorts by the kitchen window, his face turned away from her. The dawn light flared around him. 'Jack?'

'Hey.' He turned and smiled at her. 'You're awake.'

'What time is it?'

'I've got to go, baby.'

'Already?'

He walked across the room, took her in his arms. As he kissed her, his skin was cool and fresh against hers; she tasted shaving soap on his lips. Jack sighed, enveloped her in his arms.

'You are a very hard girl to say goodbye to.' He kissed her forehead, and gathered up his clothes. As he buckled his trousers, Evie handed him his flight bag. After the weeks of anticipation, it had all gone so quickly. She couldn't believe he was leaving already. 'Why don't you get some more sleep?' he said.

'But I want to see you off.'

'No, it's fine. I want to remember you like this.' He slipped his hand around the curve of her waist. 'Damn, I'm going to miss you.' He broke away from her, pulled his boots on.

'When will I see you again?'

'Soon, I promise. Once I've written to your dad, we can set a date.' Jack buttoned up his shirt and shrugged on his jacket. 'The next time I see you, you're going to be walking down the aisle, Mrs Whitman.'

Evie followed him to the door. As it swung open a cold draught lifted the hem of her kimono, danced around her bare feet. Her eyes scanned his face urgently. She wanted to remember everything about these few snatched hours together. This handful of memories had to last the days and weeks until they were together again. 'I can't bear it.' She buried her head on his chest. 'It's too soon.'

'Hey, don't be blue.' He gently lifted her hand to his lips, kissed her engagement ring. 'The time will fly by. Just think of everything you have to plan – dresses, bridesmaids ...'

'Stella and Megan will be my flower girls. I thought I'd ask my godmother Mary to be my Matron of Honour.'

'Sounds swell.' Jack looked out at the sky. 'Red sky in morning, isn't that what you guys say?' He pulled on his cap. 'Go back to bed, baby, don't get cold.'

'I love you, Jack,' Evie called after him. He turned to her as he walked, and grinned as he flicked a salute.

As Jack waited in the mess at White Waltham for his ferry back to Kirton, an orderly marched in. 'Excuse me, Officer Parker ...'

'Yes? What is it?' Teddy snapped, not bothering to look up from his paper.

Once the orderly had gone, Jack strode over and stood in front of him. 'Excuse me sir, are you Edward Parker?'

'Yes. Do I know you?'

'May I have a word with you?'

Teddy flicked his paper with irritation. 'I'm extremely busy. What is it?'

'I'd like to have a word with you – outside.'

'Very well.' As Teddy followed Jack, he signalled to Doyle and Stent.

Around the side of the hangar, Jack turned on him. 'Do you know who I am?'

'No, I don't,' Teddy sneered. 'You Yanks all look and sound the same to me.'

Jack stepped up close. 'You know my fiancée, Evelyn, then.'

'Oh yes, Evie.' A slow, dangerous smile flickered on his face. 'I know her.' He glanced at Doyle. 'I know her very well.'

'You're a liar.' Jack landed a quick punch in the eye that caught Teddy off guard. He staggered back, tongued his cheek, tasted blood. Doyle and Stent leapt on Jack, pinned his arms back against the wall.

'Liar, am I?' Teddy drawled, his face close to Jack's as he struggled. He punched him hard in the stomach, and Jack's head fell forward as he gasped for breath. 'Let me tell you something. This is no place for women. They're all spoilt brats and trick flying whores. Women like your fiancée think they're better than the ordinary woman but she's nothing but a little prick tease just like the rest of them.'

Jack roared, struggled to get free but the men were too strong.

Teddy rolled his head, loosened up his shoulders. 'Why don't you fuck off back to America?' He punched Jack hard, a right hook that spun his head around to the side, a spray of blood and spittle arcing from his lips. As Doyle and Stent released him, Jack slid to the floor.

'What the hell is going on here?' Beau did a double take as he strode past to the Anson waiting on the runway.

'None of your business, Beaufort,' Teddy said, striding towards him. 'I'm going to get that Yank fired for attacking an officer if it's the last thing I do.'

'I wouldn't do that.' Beau blocked his path. 'If you want everyone to know you are a bully, a cad and a coward, go right ahead. I'd be delighted to let the entire pool know what a liar you are.' Teddy swore under his breath, and Beau marched over to Jack, helped him to his feet.

'Are you alright?'

'What a prick.' Jack's eye was closing already, and he smarted as he put his hand to his face. 'He got his goons to hold me down.'

'He's always been an arsehole.' Beau watched the three men disappear around the corner. 'I'm supposed to be dropping you in Kirton on my way up to Scotland. Are you sure you want to fly?'

'Yeah, I'll be fine.' His legs gave way as he started to walk. 'Man, you always forget how much it hurts getting punched.'

'Know what you mean.' Beau laughed. 'Not like the movies is it? You go down, you stay down.' He put his arm around Jack's waist and took his weight as they crossed the airfield. 'When's your next mission?'

'Tomorrow they reckon.'

'I'd get yourself checked out. You might have concussion.'

'Nah, I'll be fine. Just a bit of a shiner.' Jack paused by the Anson. 'Thank you for telling me about him. Jerks like that give the rest of us a bad name.' They shook hands. 'Listen, can you do me a favour?'

'Of course.'

'Would you keep an eye on Evie for me?'

'Funny, you're the second person to ask me to do that.' Beau gave Jack a hand up into the plane. 'Miss Chase is more than capable of looking after herself.'

'Can you just make sure she's OK, sir? I don't want him giving her any trouble because of this.'

'Don't worry,' Beau said, 'I'll take care of her.'

24

Evie sat on the back doorstep of the cottage in a pool of sunlight, plucking a pigeon to make a pie for supper. She was wearing a broad-brimmed felt fedora, and a thick argyle jumper over her silk nightgown against the crisp spring air. When she'd got up she had pulled on a pair of knitted socks up over her knees, and a pair of jodhpur boots, and she hadn't bothered to change.

'I take it you're not coming to church?' Stella said as she strolled into the kitchen. 'That's rather an eclectic look.'

Evie turned her head. 'Very funny. You look nice.'

'Thank you. Michael is coming to pick us up.' Stella smoothed her hair in the mirror.

'Is Megan going too? I thought she was Methodist.'

'She is. She normally goes to the chapel but I could do with some moral support.'

'Why's that?'

'Mike's housekeeper doesn't like me. Mrs Biggs keeps giving me the evil eye each Sunday. If looks could kill! She's a funny woman. Mike and I are friends – that's all. Still, let them gossip. I don't care.'

Evie's eyes twinkled. 'At least with a couple of you there it will look less suspicious.' When Stella ignored her teasing, Evie glanced up. She could see from the set of her face she was in one of her moods. 'Will you be home for lunch?'

'I don't know,' she said as she poked irritably at her hat. 'We might just go to the Barn for a bite afterwards.' Stella frowned as she looked at the pigeon. 'To be honest that doesn't look very appetising.'

Evie waved the bird in her direction. 'You don't get away with it that easily. It's pigeon pie for supper. Take it or leave it.' Evie turned back to the plucking. It was not a pleasant job and she winced slightly as she pulled clumps of feathers from the scrawny bird. The farmer had given it to Megan, and she was loathe to disappoint her by not cooking something with it.

'Eugh, hateful bird,' she said. She was upset about Jack's fight still, and worried about him. *Why on earth did he get into a fight?* she thought. The news had spread quickly through the pool – she'd heard Teddy was flaunting his black eye like a war wound. She threw the little bird down in frustration. She was looking forward to getting back to work tomorrow. Her day's leave without Jack had dragged, and she was missing him. She had helped Megan plant carrots and cauliflowers, and they fixed the wire on the chicken coop where the fox had tried to get in. It helped to stay busy, but she felt Jack's absence keenly. She leant against the doorframe and lit a cigarette. 'I think I'll go for a ride once you're in the oven,' she said to the pigeon.

There was a brisk knock at the front door, and Michael stepped in. 'Morning,' he said when he saw Stella. 'You do look smart. Are you all ready?'

Megan clattered downstairs. 'Hello, Michael, I thought I heard the pony and trap. What fun!' She raced outside.

Evie brushed the feathers from her lap. 'Are you joining us, Evie?' Michael asked doubtfully.

'Sorry … pigeon.' She gestured vaguely at the mangled little bird on the doorstep. 'I've never done this before.'

'Evie's not coming.' Stella took Michael's arm. 'She's a bit tired,' she winked at Evie. 'Jack, her fiancé, came to stay this weekend.'

'Came to stay?' Michael coloured. 'Oh, you mean they …?'

'No she does not mean that!' Evie put her hands on her hips indignantly. 'Why does everyone assume I'm some floozie?'

'Hold on.' Evie cursed as she pushed the bit into Monty's mouth. He tossed his head impatiently. 'I know, I want to get out of here too. Why do so many people make assumptions about me, Monty?' She tugged his forelock clear of the bridle, and kissed his nose. *I don't do that, do I?* she thought. *I take people as they are. I don't jump to conclusions.* Beau's words at the Riviera had stung her. She wished she didn't care so much about his good opinion. As she stroked the horse, her engagement ring shone in the midday sun. *It's nonsense,* she told herself. *I have to get myself back on form. All these bally idiots have knocked my confidence, that's all. I'll show them.* As she leapt into the saddle, Evie imagined herself walking down the aisle of All Saints on Leo's arm, saw Jack turn by the altar and smile at her. She pictured an elegant white dress, her grandmother's intricate lace veil. *I just want it to be simple, and beautiful,* she thought. *Orange blossom, old roses for my bouquet. Perhaps we could marry in the late afternoon, and the church could be filled with white candles.*

'Come on, Monty,' she said as she dug in her heels. 'Time to pay Daddy a visit.'

The moment Evie clattered into the stable yard at her father's house she spotted Leo and Virginia on the pool terrace having pre-lunch drinks with Mary. She kicked Monty on along the gravel path, cleared the box hedge and cantered across the lawn.

Leo clapped his hands as she reined in beside the steps. 'Splendid!' he said, laughing in delight as he walked down to her. 'Just in time for lunch.'

'Thank you but I'm not stopping, Daddy.'

'What *are* you wearing?' Virginia said, her upper lip curling in distaste.

Evie looked down at her moth-eaten jumper. She had simply

pulled a pair of jodhpurs on over her nightie and set off. She tipped the fedora back defiantly with her index finger, and ignored her.

Leo rummaged through his pockets and gave Monty a peppermint. 'It's good to see you, darling. How are you—'

'I'm fine,' Evie said. She wanted very much to give him a hug, but at that moment Virginia walked over and slipped a proprietorial arm through his. 'In fact I have some good news.'

'I told you she'd be in the club before long.' Virginia sighed.

'Actually I'm getting married.' Evie held up her hand to show them the ring.

'Married?' Leo looked stunned.

'You don't know him. Jack's going to write to you – he wants to do everything properly and ask your permission. He's an American.'

'Marvellous …' Virginia rolled her eyes.

'His name is Jack Whitman, and after the war we shall live in Montana together.'

'Do you love him?' Leo asked.

'Yes.'

'How will he support you?'

'His family own a ranch.' Evie had expected Leo to explode and had readied herself for a fight, but he seemed strangely subdued.

'I'm …' He hesitated. 'I'm just going to get you a glass of champagne. We should make a toast.'

'The simple life, eh?' Virginia inspected her glossy red nails once he had gone.

'You'll never see me again,' Evie said quietly to her. 'Are you happy now?'

'Delirious.' Virginia squinted as she looked up at Evie, and pulled a pair of sunglasses from her pocket. 'You know you'll never be happy with that kind of life.'

'What do you know?' She saw Leo was busy handing Mary a flute of champagne, so she leant closer to her stepmother. 'How does it feel to be you, Virginia?' she whispered. 'Have you ever felt really alive, and happy, and in love?'

'This isn't love, you foolish girl, it's infatuation, a whirlwind romance.'

Evie flinched. She was too close to the truth. 'Nonsense.'

'How long have you known this boy? Or is he a man?'

'A few weeks. Long enough—'

Virginia cut her off. 'This is so typical of you. You take all this for granted.' She waved her hand across the beautiful vista of the house and grounds. 'You're playing at roughing it with your little friends in that pathetic cottage, and now you're playing at romance.'

'I'm not playing,' Evie whispered. 'This is my life, and I choose how to live it.' She glanced up; Leo was coming over. 'I was born to "all this", at least I didn't claw my way up to it on my back.'

As Virginia opened her mouth to speak, Leo handed her a glass of champagne, and gave one to Evie. 'Congratulations, darling! I wish you every happiness.'

There was something new in Leo's eyes that unsettled Evie. She was unnerved by his calm reaction too. Evie drained her glass, and handed it back to him as Virginia stormed off towards the house without another word. 'Thank you, Daddy,' she said, and wheeled Monty around. 'Hello, Mary,' she called. 'I am sorry I can't stop.'

She raised her glass. 'Congratulations, darling.'

'Can I come and see you next week? I was rather hoping you'd be my Matron of Honour.'

Mary blew her a kiss. 'It would be my pleasure.'

25

Evie rode for hours, trying to shake off her bad mood. As she finally thundered across the country lanes towards home, her thoughts turned to Jack. She guessed he must have been defending her honour but she couldn't figure out how he knew about Teddy's lies because she had never told him, and the only person she had talked about it with was ... 'Beau,' she said aloud as she spotted his Triumph motorbike parked outside a pretty white cottage on the edge of the field. She wheeled Montgomery around and trotted over. At the gate she jumped down and tethered the horse.

It's so unlike him to gossip, why on earth would he have told Jack? Evie thought angrily as she pushed the gate open and strode along a brick path lined with yellow and purple crocuses. *He must have known he'd pick a fight with Teddy.* When no one answered her furious knocking she pushed open the door of the cottage. Wagner's *Tristan und Isolde* blasted full volume from the gramophone in the living room.

'Hello?' she called. *Well this is very Bayreuth isn't it?* She walked uncertainly through the house as the music swelled around her. Apart from a few books on the kitchen table and an empty whisky bottle on the draining board, the shabbily furnished house might have been uninhabited. It was immaculately clean but totally impersonal. Evie pursed her lips as she thought, *I like what he's done with the place.* 'Hello?' she tried again. The back door was open, so she strode outside, her temper rising. An overgrown pergola choked with brambles blocked her view but she could hear raised voices in the garden.

'I don't care. How many times—'

'Alex, darling—'

'Olivia, you weren't there when I needed you most. You don't want me, you never loved me—'

'But I do! Don't you see? Last night, when I thought I was going to die, everything became clear.'

Evie hesitated for a moment, began to back away towards the kitchen. Her boot knocked a rake standing by the back door, and it fell to the floor with a clatter.

'Who's there?' Beau yelled.

Damn, Evie thought, her heart beating fast. It was too late now. 'It's me, sir, Evie.' She took a deep breath and strode through the pergola with a confident smile. The moment she saw Beau, it faded.

'Sir?' She froze in her tracks. 'What's happened?'

He was slumped on a wooden bench in the garden, a half-empty bottle of whisky at his side. His eyes were red. When he turned to Evie, she saw the grief there. Olivia was on her knees at his side. Angrily, Beau snatched away his hand from hers and wiped at his cheeks with the heel of his palm.

Olivia glared at Evie, her pale eyes smudged with mascara. 'What's she doing here?'

'Hello again,' Evie said pleasantly. 'We're neighbours. I thought Wing Commander Beaufort was alone.'

'I bet you did. Do all your pupils make social visits, Alex?'

Evie ignored her and turned to Beau. 'Is there anything I can do?'

'Go away, Miss Chase. It's not a good time, as you can see.'

'Surely I can help?'

'Just go.'

Olivia got to her feet, glared at Evie. 'You heard him,' she said.

'I meant both of you. Go on, leave me alone,' he yelled.

Olivia turned to him, the colour rising in her cheeks. 'How dare you? How dare you t-talk to me like that?' she stammered, her eyes flickering wildly before she ran from the garden. A moment later, Evie heard the distant throb of a car engine roaring to life.

Beau slumped on the bench, his head in his hands. 'I wish everyone would just ruddy well leave me alone.'

Evie folded her arms. 'Isn't it rather tragic, drinking alone, sir?'

Blearily he looked up at her. 'Olivia doesn't drink. If you insist, there's another glass in the kitchen.'

When she returned, Beau poured her a large shot of whisky. 'Cheers,' he said. As he lit a cigarette, Evie stretched out on the grass at his feet, turned her face to the evening sun. In the silence, all she could hear was birdsong.

'It's such a bloody mess,' he said finally.

'What is?'

'Me. Olivia ...' He shook his head. 'You know, she was nearly killed last night.'

She looked remarkably well to me, Evie thought. 'What happened?'

'Her mother rang the airfield in hysterics this morning.' He took a hit of whisky. 'I'd been stuck out all night on one of those bloody trains, but Olivia was in the Café de Paris apparently. Probably with some boyfriend or other.'

'The bomb?' Evie had heard on the BBC Home Service that thirty-four people had been killed, including the bandleader Snake Hips Johnson.

'Ironic, isn't it? She's scared of everything. It was the only club she'd still go to because they said it was bombproof. The bastard got lucky, dropped a bomb straight down through the Rialto's roof.' He exhaled, the plume of smoke blue against the sky. 'Of course I went straight up to town. She was in hospital, not a scratch on her, luckily.'

'Poor thing. It must have been ghastly.'

'Now of course she's saying it's made her realise how much she loves me, how foolish she's been.'

Evie sipped her drink, the Scotch warming her throat. She swirled the glass. 'Will you marry her then?'

'I feel responsible for her. And the family ...'

'Responsibility isn't love,' Evie said quietly.

'Even when we were children, she needed me. I wanted to protect her.' Evie waited for him to go on. 'She left me, you know. She couldn't cope with how I looked after I was shot down.' Evie had never seen him like this. The guardedness stripped away. 'Just when I needed *her* for a change, she abandoned me.'

'That must have been hard.'

'I should have known better. I knew what she was like when I asked her to marry me.'

'Why did you then?'

'Because she was beautiful, and impulsive. Because she drove me mad.' He hesitated. 'But if she truly loved me, she would have stood by me, wouldn't she?'

Evie's heart filled with compassion. 'Yes, sir, she would.'

'She doesn't love me, not really. She loves the prestige, and the title, and all the rubbish I couldn't give a damn about.'

As he broke down, Evie instinctively clambered up onto the bench beside him, put her arms around him, held him close as he wept. *And the pure children*, she thought angrily, *don't forget about them.*

After a time, he caught his breath. 'Christ, I'm sorry. I don't know what's got into me. It really threw me that she could have been injured, or killed.'

'Never apologise, never explain.' Evie smiled. 'So what will you do?'

'I don't know. Break it off as cleanly as I can. She's not the girl I thought she was.' He shook his head. 'The stupid thing is, as soon as she heard I'd recovered, that I wasn't some kind of a monster under those bandages ...'

204

'Hardly.' Evie gently wiped away the tears from his cheek with her thumb.

'She's been trying to get me to take her back for months now. Maybe if I had, she'd have been here last night instead. Christ, she could have been killed.'

'Shh. You can't blame yourself.' She soothed him like a child, stroking his thick blonde hair. 'It's madness at the moment.' She sighed, gazed out across the fields. 'I can't make any sense of the world. There's as much chance of getting bumped off here as in town.' It grew darker, dusk falling as she held him. Gradually, she felt him relax, his breath slowing as he composed himself. 'All we can do is live for the day. God knows, each one could be our last,' Evie said. As she turned to him, his jaw brushed her cheek.

'Evie—' he said, his voice low.

'I must go,' she said. 'It's getting dark.' She stood quickly, started to walk away. 'I'm sorry. I hope you sort it all out.'

'Wait, let me walk you to the door.' He rose unsteadily.

'Why don't I take you to bed?' She walked back.

'That's the best offer I've had in a long time.'

'You're drunk, sir.' She hooked her arm around him and guided him indoors.

'Did you walk here?'

'No, I was out for a ride, and I saw your motorbike.'

Beau looked through the front door and saw Monty tethered to the front fence. 'You ride that horse too hard,' he said. 'He'll catch a chill.' Monty whinnied and tossed his head.

'I think he's agreeing with you.'

'Go on.' Beau clutched the banister. 'I'll be fine. Take care of him.'

'If you're sure?'

In the silence, the record looped around on the gramophone and the long-case clock on the landing ticked on. Beau's head rested against hers for a moment. 'Thank you, Miss Chase,' he said. As he turned to walk upstairs, he stumbled.

Evie sighed. 'Come on.' She tucked her arm around his waist and helped him to his room. He collapsed on the bed.

'I'm sorry,' he said.

'I told you, never apologise, never explain.'

He laughed softly. 'You do come out with the strangest things. I don't normally drink like this. It's just I haven't slept for forty-eight hours, then this ...'

Evie poured Beau a glass of water and pulled the blanket over him. 'Sleep well, sir.' She turned out the light.

'Thank you,' he said. 'Wait. You never told me why you're here.'

She paused at the door. 'It can wait.'

26

The days and weeks flew by as Evie and the girls worked flat out. Their paths rarely crossed now they were so busy, but Evie had made friends with some of the other pilots at the pool and was happy enough to spend her leave nights in town or at the Coach and Horses with the ATA crew. With the arrival of April, at last the weather began to improve, and as she flew she imagined the summer to come – lazy days in the sunshine with Jack, swimming in the Thames, boating. There had been a few letters, but she hadn't managed to see him since his last visit. Somehow their leave days never worked out. She missed him, but she threw herself into work. She was conscious that Stella had already done the conversion course for flying complex single-engine aircraft and she wanted to do the same. When the Spitfires came, Evie wanted to be ready.

First thing one morning, Jim Mollison flew Evie and several other pilots to Langley to clear some Hawker Harts. As they soared over White Waltham, the cherry orchards along the road were ablaze with blossom. Evie stepped up to the cockpit to keep Jim company.

'I met your fiancé a few weeks ago,' he said.

'Jack mentioned he had bumped into you.'

'Nice guy. We had quite a party.'

'Did you indeed?'

The Anson hit some turbulence, and Jim checked his instruments. 'This old girl almost didn't get going this morning. Reg and Sheila found a nest in the cowling of this one when they were running their checks.'

'Is it right you're being posted to another pool?'

'No, I've just got a bit of work to do for a few months. I'll be back though, I like it here.' Jim winked at her. 'How's that guardian angel of yours?'

'Busy,' Evie said, laughing. 'Very busy.'

Having made her first delivery to a fighter squadron in East Anglia, Evie took a break at the station's mess and spotted Joy over by the fireplace chatting to a couple of RAF pilots.

'Hello, darling!' Joy called. 'Glorious day, isn't it?'

'Makes you remember why we all fell for flying in the first place,' Evie said as she gulped down her scalding tea.

'Where are you off next?'

'Miles Master to Debden. I must dash.' She checked her watch. 'Perhaps I'll see you later?'

'Definitely. Last one home gets the Martinis.' Joy's face danced with amusement. 'Oh, by the way, I saw Olivia at a party a few nights ago. She was asking an awful lot of questions about you.'

Evie shifted her parachute onto her shoulder. 'Me?'

Joy laughed. 'Yes, darling. I'd watch my back if I were you. She's got it into her head that you and Beau are having some grand passion and you're the reason he won't take her back!'

'How ridiculous!' Evie said indignantly. 'I hope you told her I'm happily engaged to another man?'

'Well, that's never stopped some people.'

As Evie clambered into her plane she was seething. She recalled her last run-in with Olivia and thought how it must have looked. She decided to put the record straight the next time she saw her. *As if I'd even look at another man when I have Jack.* Waiting to take off, she sighed as she thought of him. *Oh God, what I wouldn't give to see him.*

Evie checked her charts and decided on impulse to take a detour past Martlesham Heath. *Maybe I'll land, just for a minute or two*, she thought. *I know I shouldn't, but I have to see him.* It was a clear day, sunlight sparkling on the breakers along the coast. Somehow just knowing she was close to him made her happy. In her mind she pictured herself walking across the runway towards him, Jack taking her in his arms and spinning her round and round. She hummed happily to herself as she banked inland, down towards the airfield. She could see people milling around the hangars, and wondered if one of the figures was Jack. Evie checked her watch. She was running late. As she circled the base, she battled with the temptation to see him. She longed to hold him, see his face, just for a moment. Evie shook her head. She knew what she had to do. 'Come on, old girl,' she said as she straightened up and set the course for Debden.

When Evie's Anson taxi landed in White Waltham that evening, she exhaled loudly, glad to be safely down. She had dozed a little on the trip back and she stretched as she got out of the plane. The light was failing now, and as everyone trooped off to the coaches and cars Evie was looking forward to meeting up with Joy and the start of her day's leave. She wandered over towards the offices and handed in her chits.

Captain Bailey opened his office door. 'Evie, can I have a word?'

'Yes, sir,' she said. *Oh God*, she thought, *what have I done this time?*

'Close the door,' he said. 'Do sit down.' He looked uncomfortable. 'I'm sorry, my dear, I have some bad news for you.'

'Who is it?' she said uneasily. She knew Stella and Megan were out ferrying planes from Prestwick and Ratcliffe.

'Your fiancé ...'

'Jack?' The breath caught in her throat.

'As you may know, he was flying a mission the other night.'

'No. I didn't know.'

'He was shot down, along with another of his squadron.'

She shook her head, numb with shock. 'Not Jack …'

'My dear, I shouldn't be telling you this. The information is classified, but I asked Captain Bradbrooke for permission, and in the circumstances he agreed. As a friend of your father's, I thought—'

'Thank you, sir,' she said briskly. 'I do appreciate you telling me.' She stumbled slightly as she stood, caught the arm of the chair to balance herself.

Evie walked blindly through the corridors; people's conversations became a white noise that merged with the blood singing in her ears. It felt as if the world was falling away around her. The floor swayed beneath her feet. She clutched her mouth, ran to the cloakroom. It was empty, and she pushed open the cubicle door just in time. She threw up, her body convulsing again and again, then slumped on the cubicle floor, her head resting against the cool wall tiles. 'No, no, no,' she whispered under her breath. The tears came and she pressed her hand to her face.

She had no idea how long she sat there. People wandered to and fro in the corridor beyond. As if at a great distance, she heard muffled voices, the sound of the last planes landing and taxiing to the edge of the airfield for the night. The cloakroom door opened, feet marched across the lino floor. Someone tried to push open the cubicle door. They knocked, tried again.

'I don't know,' a girl's voice said. 'I can't get it open.'

'Is someone in there? Maybe there's a key?' From the voices gathering in the cloakroom, there was quite a crowd. She couldn't stay there. Evie staggered to her feet, and tried desperately to tidy herself up.

'Who's in the bog?' Teddy said impatiently. 'Come on! You may have a gippy tummy but there's a queue forming.'

Evie wiped away her tears with a trembling hand, flushed the loo.

'Miss Chase?' His face contorted as she opened the door. 'It smells of vomit in here. Not pregnant are you?'

She pushed past him. 'Belt up, Teddy.'

'What? No threat of a slap this time? Are we taming our little tigress?'

He's not worth it, she thought to herself as she staggered outside. Then she remembered he had beaten up Jack. What if he was responsible? What if Jack had flown badly because of it? She walked on, the wind lifting her hair. How could she still be here, feel the breeze on her cheek, when he could not?

Beau handed in his chits for the day, and lit a cigarette as he strolled towards the mess. The atmosphere was subdued.

'Beaufort!' Teddy barked on his way past.

'What's going on?'

'Bit of a dicey-do. That Yank Miss Chase has been seeing bought it. Seems he has a few friends here.' He strode off, the metal tips of his shoes tapping on the lino. 'Good riddance to bad rubbish if you ask me,' he said under his breath.

Beau froze in his tracks. 'What did you say?'

Teddy stopped and turned slowly towards him. 'Damn Yank was half animal, as they all are from what I've seen.' He pointed to the remains of his black eye, now an unpleasant jaundiced yellow.

Beau sauntered over to him. 'Would you like the matching pair, Parker?'

'Anyone would think you had a thing for Miss Chase yourself,' Teddy leered, 'the way you're always watching out for her.'

'She was my student.'

'Of course, of course.' Teddy folded his arms and tucked his chin in. 'And she evidently likes pretty boys. What a shame you didn't meet her before this happened.' He circled Beau's face with his forefinger.

'Why you—' Beau grabbed him by the collar.

'Beaufort, Parker, that's enough.' Badger broke them apart. 'Commander Gower told me to keep my eye on you two. This is no way for officers to behave. What's this all about?'

'I was just expressing my condolences about Miss Chase's loss,' Teddy said.

Badger chewed the stem of his pipe. 'I'm not sure I like the cut of your jib, Parker. Don't you have some filing to do?'

Beau tried not to smile.

'Beaufort, perhaps you'd see that Miss Chase gets home safely? I believe she has some leave coming up. A day's rest might do her some good.'

'Is she still here?'

'Yes, I believe I just saw her heading outside. She's had something of a shock—' he began to say, but Beau was already running after her.

'Evie!' someone called, but she didn't stop. Beau ran over to her, grabbed her arm. 'I just heard.'

She was going to be sick again. He held her, took her weight as she retched.

'I'm sorry ...' she said.

'Someone once told me never apologise, never explain.' He put his arm firmly around her shoulder and guided her towards the car park. 'Let's get you home,' he said. 'It's the least I can do after the last time I saw you. I can't remember the last time I had to be put to bed.'

'I could do with a whisky or two myself right now.' She took a deep, shuddering breath.

'I'm sorry,' he said quietly.

Evie glanced at him, saw the genuine sorrow in his eyes. She nodded, unable to talk about Jack, not yet. 'I've hardly seen you lately.' She wiped her mouth with the back of her shaking hand. 'I thought you might be avoiding me.'

'I've just been busy. I asked Ops to give me as much work as they can.' He glanced around. 'Do you have your car?'

'No, it's being serviced at Hammants.'

'We'll take my bike then.'

As he guided her to his Triumph, she said, 'I heard ... I heard what Jack did, that he hit Teddy for telling lies about me.' Evie looked at him, her face full of anguish. 'Why did you tell him? He didn't need to know.'

'Yes he did.' He turned to her. 'If you were my girl and someone like Parker was spreading rumours about you, I'd want to know.'

'Maybe you're right.' Her head fell. 'How bad was it?'

'Doyle and Stent held him down while Teddy beat the living daylights out of him, from what I saw.'

She began to cry again. 'Couldn't you help him?'

'It was too late by the time I saw what was going on. Your chap said he felt fine.'

'But if he was hurt. If he had something wrong ... What if his reactions were off?'

Beau got onto the bike, kicked it off its stand. Evie clambered on behind him, wrapped her arms around him. She felt him take a deep breath and exhale slowly. 'Evie, I've seen men killed for far stupider reasons. You can't blame anyone for this – not even that cad Teddy. Jack did what he thought was right, and he died doing what he loved to do – flying.' Beau placed his hand gently over hers. 'Let that be some comfort to you.'

As they roared out of the airfield, she leant against his back, her arms tight around his waist. Nothing seemed real any more, the fields and cars whizzing past. It all seemed false, off key. After a few minutes Beau swerved into the lane and pulled up outside the girls' cottage.

'Thank you,' she said as she jumped off the bike. 'You've been very kind.'

'Would you like me to stay for a while? Make sure you're OK? I can't cook, but ...' Evie shook her head. 'Get some sleep then,' he said gently. When she didn't answer, he turned, looked full at her. 'No one is to blame,' he said. 'You made Jack very happy in his last few weeks. Hold on to that. As for the fight with Teddy, well he was just defending your honour.'

'Why are men so stupid? I'm perfectly capable of defending myself against some fool like Teddy.'

Beau folded his arms, flashed a quick, sad smile. 'I'm sure you are. But sometimes we chaps like to feel needed.'

Evie fought the tears that she felt welling in her eyes again. 'It's so unfair.'

'Who said war was fair?' Beau said bitterly. 'Innocent people, good people, babies and children who haven't even had the chance to start living – hundreds, thousands are dying every day because of this damn nightmare. Why should things be fair for us? We're nothing special.' He shook his head. 'I wish I could say something that can help, but there's nothing, no rhyme or reason that can make sense of this.' Beau took her hand and squeezed it. 'If I can do anything, anything at all, you know where I am.' He roared up the lane, dust and fumes settling in his wake as Evie stood alone and the light fell away around her.

27

That night, she cried herself to sleep on the sofa. Evie had never felt so alone. Even Stalin wanted nothing to do with her, staring balefully at her from the doorway.

At daybreak she stumbled to the bathroom, ran the bath, and crouched naked on the floor of the tub, weeping as it filled. She replayed again and again every moment she had had with him. The first time she had seen him, his dazzling smile as he helped her from the plane. She remembered his laugh, how it felt when they danced together in each other's arms. He was so alive – how could he possibly be gone? His loss was a physical pain for her; it felt as if her body was turning in on itself.

A few hours later, Stella came home to find her still in her dressing gown, curled up in a foetal position in her narrow single bed. 'Evie?' she said gently. 'I am so sorry. I got stuck out. I've been on the train all night. I just heard …'

'He's gone,' Evie managed to say, before more tears came. Stella held her for hours, rocking her like a baby in her arms, soothing her as each fresh wave of grief engulfed her. Megan arrived back in the afternoon, and ran straight upstairs.

'How is she?' she asked as she caught her breath in the doorway. Stella shook her head. 'Has she eaten? Are you hungry, Evie?'

'No,' she said. 'I never want to eat again.'

'Right, I'm going to make some soup.' Megan said firmly. Moments later they could hear her clattering around in the kitchen.

Evie pushed herself up in bed. 'It can't be true,' she said. 'Perhaps he's just hurt somewhere. Missing presumed killed can mean just missing …'

Stella shook her head. 'Beau made some calls this morning. He has friends out at Jack's base.'

'What did he find out?'

'They saw his plane go down, Evie. There was a dogfight, a Messerschmitt. They had orders to recce a convoy that was having some trouble.' She paused. 'It took out two planes over the sea. They managed to get a boat to the first pilot, but by the time they got to Jack …'

'What? Tell me everything.'

'His plane was completely burnt out. By the time they reached him, there was nothing left. The wreck sank.'

Evie felt sick as she thought of the flames. 'I hope he was dead by the time he went down. The thought of him trapped in there …'

'Beau was pretty cut up about it. You see, it's exactly what happened to him.'

'But he managed to get back and Jack didn't.'

She stroked her hair away from her face. 'We both know this could happen to any of us at anytime,' Stella said. 'This world is full of "what ifs" and "maybes". Every time we get in a plane, it could be our number is up.'

'What, so it was just Jack's turn? His luck ran out?' Her face twisted.

Stella took her hand. 'Evie, you gave Jack the happiest days of his life in the last few months. Remember that.'

'I just can't bear it. Is this what you've been living with all these months since losing Richard? How do you cope?'

Stella stood awkwardly. 'One day at a time.'

*

The girls were back at work the next day, so Evie found herself alone again in the house. She walked forlornly from room to room in her dressing gown, not able to settle anywhere. Everything reminded her of Jack – the wedding magazines the girls had been poring over, the Sinatra record on the gramophone. It felt as if her entire future had been extinguished in a heartbeat. Evie curled up in a ball on the armchair, tucked up beneath a heavy wool blanket. How on earth was she supposed to carry on?

Towards noon there was a knock, and Evie dragged herself out of her reverie to open the front door.

'Hello, Evie,' Mary said. Her face fell, full of compassion. 'My dear girl, I am so terribly sorry.' The women embraced, fresh tears coming to their eyes.

'How did you hear?'

'Captain Bailey rang your father – you know they're old friends. Lucky thought you might find it easier to talk to me than Virginia.'

'That's something of an understatement.'

'Now,' Mary said. 'I have my car here. How about I drive you into town and we have lunch at Skindles? A bit of fresh air will do you the world of good.'

'I don't think I can.'

Mary shook her head. 'Normally, my dear, I would advise you to take as long as you need, but the fact is at the moment one has no choice but to carry on.' She squeezed Evie's hand. 'You'll find there's comfort in working. It's much healthier than languishing.'

'So I'm supposed to forget all about Jack? Pretend this never happened?' Her face contorted with misery.

'No, darling,' Mary said. 'Of course not. It's just we have to be brave, to fight on ...' She took a deep breath, composed herself. 'Since Charles was killed, there have been plenty of days I've wondered how to carry on. But one must, so we may as well start today. First things first – let's get you out of your pyjamas.'

Mary picked out a dress for Evie and helped her change. As she had her hair brushed, Evie succumbed to being treated like a child. She gazed at her own pale face in the dressing-table mirror and it was like looking at a stranger.

'You're such a pretty girl, Evie, it breaks my heart to see you looking so sad and tired.' Mary handed her a tube of lipstick. 'It's a cliché but time does heal. Try and concentrate on the good times you shared with Jack. People think whirlwind romances pass quickly, but sometimes they are the most intense, glorious times of your life.'

Evie thought of the uncomplicated joy and exhilaration she'd felt barrelling along the lanes on the old motorbike with Jack. 'He made me feel so happy, so alive …'

'You're young, darling. You will find love again.' Mary fell silent. 'Your father is worried about you, you know.'

'Is he? I bet Virginia is rubbing her hands with glee.'

Mary sighed. 'I know.' Evie caught her gaze in the mirror. 'I'm not blind, Evie. I know what she can be like.'

'I thought—'

Mary squeezed her shoulders gently. 'Lucky misses you. Don't let Virginia drive you apart. That's just what she wants.'

They drove to Skindles in silence. Evie watched the fields and meadows fly by as if at a great distance. She looked up at the aircraft overhead, all the traffic passing to and fro, and wondered what it was all for.

'Here we are.' Mary pulled into the gravelled courtyard and parked her little car near the entrance. She came around to Evie's side and took her arm.

'It's awfully kind of you to do this,' Evie said. She inhaled deeply, breathed in the scent of freshly mown grass.

'Darling, it's the least I can do.' Mary led her into the foyer. 'Did Lucky tell you I'd offered to help arrange the wedding?'

'No,' she said. 'I haven't seen Daddy for a few weeks.'

Mary noticed Evie's eyes beginning to well up again as she looked around the restaurant. 'Would you like some air?'

'No, I'm perfectly fine.' Evie composed herself, took a deep breath. 'It's just I hoped the next time we had lunch together here it would be under happier circumstances. The reception ...'

'Oh Lord, how tactless of me to bring you here. Would you rather go somewhere else?' Mary took her arm as Evie shook her head. 'You dear girl, how I wish I could wave a magic wand ...'

'Well, you are my godmother.' Evie nudged her.

'I said to Lucky the other day, I'll never forget how kind you were to me when Charles was killed. I'd always hoped you and he might marry, you know. He was terribly fond of you.'

'Charles was like my brother. Peter too.' Evie said sadly. 'That's funny, though – I always hoped you and Daddy might get together.'

Mary's eyes filled with mirth. 'Lucky and me? What a hoot. I'm not nearly racy enough for your father. No, there's been no one for me since Charles' father was killed during the Great War.'

The maître d' showed them to a table overlooking the gardens. Fresh new leaves were dancing on the trees, and spring flowers peppered the borders with colour.

'How do you go on?' Evie asked her after they had ordered. 'You've lost your husband, and now your son; I can't imagine how to get through this. Does it get easier?'

'Easier? No. The loss ... well, it becomes less acute. It becomes part of you.' Mary sipped her wine. 'You will recover, darling girl. I mean, you're so terribly brave. I think you ATA girls are heroines.'

Evie shook her head. 'No, no we're not. I'm just doing my job, Mary, that's all. Flying a plane is no different to driving a car when you know how. In fact we have some girls, like Meggie, who can fly a plane but not drive a car. There's nothing glamorous about our work. It does annoy some of the chaps that we get so much attention just because we are women.'

'I can imagine. Is there ever any trouble?'

'Oh, silly things. One of the girls found she couldn't take off the other day because someone – presumably one of the chaps with a grudge – had put sugar in her petrol tank.'

'No! Really?'

'You just get on with it. Most of the men are delightful but if some idiot wants to hide a piece of equipment you need to fly the plane, you bally well go and get another one.' Evie took a sip of wine. 'I've always believed women to be capable of anything men can do, and I'm determined to do the best I can.'

Mary smiled. 'Good for you.'

'Did you hear? We're doing our conversion courses for complex single-engine planes. That means when the Spitfire comes we'll be ready.'

'Do you really think they'll let girls fly fighter planes?'

'Yes, I do. I'm sure of it.'

'There you are then, Evie. That's something to look forward to. Thank you,' she said as the waiter placed their first courses in front of them.

'Pauline Gower is an inspiration – she says we should just get in, get our heads down and quietly do a better job than the men are expecting.'

'You spend so much time alone in the air. Aren't you ever afraid?'

'Very rarely,' Evie said. 'Of course you have the odd scrape, but flying ...' She paused, twisted the sapphire ring on her finger. 'It's indescribable the joy you feel, the freedom. It's the closest you can come to heaven on earth. Sometimes it feels like you are flying with an angel on your wing.' She looked up and saw the incomprehension on Mary's face. 'It's hard to explain to someone who isn't a pilot.' She looked out at the sky. She thought of Jack, soaring out above the glittering sea in his Hurricane. In that moment she was glad for him, for the man who had stolen her heart, that he died in the air doing what he loved.

28

For the next few weeks, as Evie completed her course, she found they gave her the easiest jobs at the ferry pool. No old warhorses on their last legs, the NEAs that all the girls dreaded. The days went by in a blur of exhausting activity. She found if she kept busy, it dulled her emotions, stopped her thinking of Jack. Only in her room, alone, when she took her engagement ring out of the box on her bedside table, could she grieve in peace.

Finally there came a morning she found she could look at the ring and think of him without tears. She slipped the gleaming sapphire onto her ring finger one last time and thought of all that might have been. 'Goodbye, Jack,' she said, and threaded the ring onto the gold chain she wore around her neck.

'Evie?' Megan called through her door. 'Are you busy?'

'No, come in,' she said.

'My hands are awful from all the digging. Do you have any cream?'

Evie tossed over a tube of Dubarry's Crème Shalimar. 'Here, keep it.'

'Are you sure?'

Evie took her hands and turned them over. 'Meggie, you need it more than I do.'

Megan plonked down on the bed beside her and began to rub the cream in. 'Talking of digging, we'd better get going. I want to stop off at the market on the way over to the airfield, if that's OK.'

'Fine, there should be time. Are you after some more plants?'

Megan nodded. 'And I heard from Jean one of her lads has a stall on one of the side streets. If you tell him Jean sent you, he'll show you what's under the counter.'

'Black market?'

'Bent tins, corned beef, beans, peas, peaches ...'

Evie's mouth watered. 'Come on then, let's get a move on. Is Stella back tonight?'

'Should be if she picks up her taxi flight on time.'

'Let's see if we can't have a feast waiting.'

'Not that she deserves one,' Megan grumbled.

'What do you mean?'

'Oh, she's been a right pain in the neck lately.'

'Meggie, you have to make allowances for her. I had no idea ...' she paused. 'Until I lost Jack, I had no idea the pain she's been carrying around with her all this time.'

'But you're not a misery-guts though, are you now? I mean, you're sad, but you're still Evie, and you're still kind to people.'

'We all cope in different ways.'

As Megan haggled with the old woman on the plant stall, Evie wandered around the market. The stalls were sparse at this time of the year, and they hadn't managed to find Jean's son. Evie checked her watch. *We'd better get a move on*, she thought. She glanced down an alleyway at the sound of cursing, following the gaze of a number of people.

'You good for nothing piece of meat, I ought to—' A florid-faced man in a dirty white shirt was beating a cowering dog with a long stick. As he raised the stick above his head, Evie saw filthy yellow stains beneath his sleeve. The dog whimpered pitifully, tried to claw its way behind a dustbin. 'Come here, you!'

'I say, you!' Evie yelled, and began to race towards him. She fought her way through the crowd. 'Stop it at once!'

'Evie?' Megan called, and ran after her. By the time she caught up, Evie had wrenched the stick from the man and was beating him with it.

'How do you like that? Eh?' Evie gave him a good whack on his backside. The crowd began to cheer her on.

'Miss, I'm sorry, Miss.' The man cowered on the ground, put his hands up protectively to his face.

'You're nothing but a ghastly bully,' she said, giving him a last thwack before tossing the stick away. It rattled to the floor, splashing his face as it landed in a greasy puddle. The man scrambled to his feet and ran off down the alley to the jeers of the crowd.

Evie got down on her hands and knees. 'Come on, fella,' she said gently to the dog.

'Evie, be careful!' Megan warned her. 'Don't get any blood on your uniform.'

'Bugger my uniform,' she said as she scooped the shivering dog into her arms.

'What are you going to do with him?'

'I don't know, but he …' She checked the dog quickly. 'Yes, he isn't going to stay here and wait for that bully to come back and finish him off.'

Evie tucked the dog up on the back seat of her car in a tartan blanket from the boot. 'Do you think Stalin will put up with him?' Megan asked.

'We couldn't leave him at home all day,' Evie said as she started the Aston. 'We'll have to think of something else.'

Evie carried the dog into the offices in the blanket, holding him gently. He poked his head out, licked the back of her hand.

'Oh no you don't, Miss Chase.' Teddy stopped her. 'No animals in here, especially not some filthy fleabag like that.'

'Since when?' she challenged him.

'Hello. What have you got there?' Beau stopped and lifted back the blanket. 'Poor old chap.'

'Officer Parker was just telling me I can't bring him into the offices.'

'Poppycock,' Beau said, staring down Teddy.

'It's on your head, Beaufort,' he said, and marched off to the Ops Room.

'You should have seen it, sir! Evie was amazing!' Megan said breathlessly as she caught up with them. 'This horrible man was beating the dog, and Evie took the stick off him and whacked him with it until he ran away.'

'Now that I can believe,' Beau said. 'Here, give him to me.'

'No.' Evie pulled back protectively. 'I don't need your help.'

'Listen,' he said quietly. 'You can go on being angry at me, or Teddy, or whoever you want to blame if it makes you feel better, but it won't bring Jack back. Maybe you don't need people looking out for you, but this little chap does need help.' The dog closed his eyes as Beau stroked his head. 'Trust me. I know what I'm doing.' Evie handed over the bundle. 'Right,' he said. 'Let's get you cleaned up.' He carried the dog into the Gents, and Evie went through to the mess with Megan.

'Hello, Jean,' she said, chewing her lip. She flicked impatiently at her lighter. Beau's words had hit a nerve. 'No sign of your son at the market.'

'Oh, I hope he hasn't been picked up again.' She shook her head as she poured them both a cup of tea. 'I do worry about him. The Home Guard picked him and his mates up the other night, trying to rustle a sheep. They had it all dressed up in a mackintosh and cloth cap, squeezed in on the back seat.'

Evie smiled in spite of herself. 'Are the chitties out yet?'

'No, Miss, but there was a chap looking for you. There he is,' Jean pointed to the corner.

The man rose. 'Excuse me, Miss, may I have a word?'

Evie looked over to see the engineer from Bristol standing there, a bag at his feet.

'Hello, Taff,' she said. 'Good to see you again. What brings you up here?'

'I was just picking up some parts from the equipment section. We're heading straight back on the Anson. Actually, I came to see you as well ...'

'Oh? Do you have time for a cup of tea?'

She led him to a table away from the crowd of pilots near the counter.

'I heard about Jack,' he said. 'I'm very sorry, Miss.'

'Thank you.' She fought to compose herself. She was always fine until someone was kind to her. 'I'm rather cut up, as you can imagine,' she said briskly.

'I brought this up for you.' He pushed the bag towards her. 'Jack left it behind at Whitchurch by accident. It's a few of his things. I imagine they'll be sending on his effects to his parents, but I thought … I know how crazy he was about you. He'd have wanted you to have something.'

She laid her hand on the soft leather flight bag. 'That's terribly kind of you.'

Taff glanced out onto the runway. 'Looks like they're ready. I'd better get a move on.' He held out his hand to her. 'He was a good man, was Jack. And a good friend.' Taff's eyes filled with tears. He started to walk away and paused. 'You know that plane of yours, the one that you were bringing up from Bristol that wouldn't start?'

'The Magister?'

'Jack told us to take out the spark plugs. He said he wasn't going to let you out of there until you'd agreed to marry him.'

Evie picked up the leather bag and hugged it to her chest as she watched Taff run out to the Anson. For the first time in weeks, she laughed.

Beau walked towards her holding the dog in his arms. 'I hope I didn't speak out of line earlier?'

Evie looked into his eyes. 'No, not at all. You were right. I can't go on thinking of all the "if onlys".' She blinked, smiled sadly. 'Well, he looks better,' she said.

Beau laid the dog gently in Evie's lap. 'A few good meals inside him and he'll be right as rain. You're skin and bones, aren't you, old boy? It was nothing serious, luckily, just a few cuts and bruises.'

'Well that makes two of you then.'

Beau folded his arms. 'I'm glad to see your famous sense of humour is returning.'

She looked from him to the dog. 'Now I need to figure out what to do with you.' She rubbed its head, and he wagged his tail.

'He's a good dog,' Beau said, 'in spite of what happened to him.'

'What is he?'

'A German Shepherd.'

'What's wrong with his ears?'

'They're floppy still.' He squatted down beside Evie and held them gently up. 'You're just a puppy aren't you?'

'I don't think he's all German. You make rather a good pair.'

'Very funny. Actually, I was going to say – if you don't have a home in mind for him ...' Beau laughed as the dog licked his face.

'What are you going to call him?'

'Why don't you christen him? You rescued him.'

'How about Ace, like the Wonder Dog? He's a German Shepherd.'

'Ace, that's perfect.'

'Rather that than Target, eh?' She rubbed the dog's ears as her gaze fell.

Beau knew she was talking about his comment the night they danced together: you're either an ace or a target. He guessed from her face she was thinking of Jack. 'They're very smart, and very brave,' he said kindly.

'Chits are out!' someone called.

Evie stood and handed the dog over. She squeezed Beau's shoulder as she strolled past. 'Like I said, that makes two of you.'

29

'What was in the bag?' Megan asked, swinging her legs where she sat on the kitchen counter.

'Meggie, don't be so ruddy nosy!' Stella said as she polished her boots on a sheet of newspaper at the table.

'Alright, don't jump down my throat. What's up with you? You're so snappy.'

Stella ignored her, her face pinched and exhausted.

The girls were listening to Vera Lynn's *Sincerely Yours* on the radio and as Evie stacked tins from her shopping basket on the shelves in the pantry, she hummed along to 'We'll Meet Again'. She had traded a pair of silk stockings with Jean for a few tins of meat and fruit to stock up their supplies.

'There, that looks better, at least we won't go hungry now,' she said brightly, trying to defuse the tension. She dusted off her hands and sat down opposite Stella.

'There was nothing much in Jack's bag,' she said to Megan. She thought sadly of the crumpled shirts, a pair of socks with a hole in one toe, his well-worn toothbrush. When she held the shirts to her face, they smelt of Jack, faintly. She remembered how if felt to bury her head in his neck, the warm, clean scent of him. There was a comb, with a few strands of his dark wavy hair that she had pulled out slowly, one by one. She had hoped for something – a photograph, a fragment of his handwriting, but there was nothing. Just the abandoned remains of a life that had run its course. Evie had built a bonfire in the garden and burnt the bag, watching the sparks fly up to the sky. 'In a funny way it helped me say goodbye, seeing his things. Jack was real – not just a whirlwind that blew in and out of my life. He lived, made holes in socks.' She lowered her eyes sadly. 'He loved me.'

Stella reached across the table and took her hand. 'Try and keep your chin up, darling.'

Evie forced a smile. 'This song is making me feel frightfully sad.'

'I'll turn it off.' Stella walked through to the living room.

'Oh, I'm tired of moping around here on leave days. Come on, instead of getting on one another's nerves, let's get out of here.' Evie pushed her chair away from the table. 'Mary told me Daddy and the stepmonster are away today – why don't we go and have a little fun at the house?'

As they drove through the lanes towards Maidenhead with the roof down, a warm May breeze caressed their hair. 'What a blissful day,' Stella said. 'I thought Virginia tried to make you give the Aston back?'

'She did. Frankly, she can take all the diamonds she likes, but she'll have to fight me for my car keys.'

'My lord,' Megan said as the car rolled up the long gravel driveway. 'Is this your father's place?' The beautiful stone house lay before them, its tall windows and elegant proportions still handsome beneath the camouflage paint. The grounds stretched out as far as the eye could see, allotments now occupying the rolling lawns.

Evie laughed, which felt strange. Laughter had always come so easily to her, but lately she had felt so sad, even her face had grown tighter, older, she thought. 'Not bad is it?'

'Why on earth are you slumming it in the cottage when you could be here?'

'What, with my ghastly stepmonster? I'd rather take my chances with the mice than live another moment with Virginia.'

'I'll take my chances with her if you'd put a word in,' Stella said drily as they parked by the main door.

'Where's your father?' Megan asked.

'They're at some party or other, and it's the staff's day off.' Evie jumped out of the car and shrugged off her blue jacket. 'Come on, who fancies a swim?'

'I don't have a costume,' Stella said as she did the same.

'You don't need one!' Evie called over her shoulder. 'There's no one here, all the cars have gone.'

'What?' Megan looked uncertain. 'You mean ... Won't it be cold?'

'Daddy keeps it lovely and warm all year. Live a little!'

The girls ran after her along the terrace, shedding their uniforms as they went. Evie slipped confidently out of her silk camisole and knickers. The water looked inviting.

'Come on!' she called as she dived in, breaking the water smoothly. Stella dived in after her, and the girls laughed, splashing water at one another.

'Come on, Megan, it's glorious!' Stella floated on her back, the warm water eddying across her body.

Megan stood uncertainly on the side in her underwear, but it looked too good to miss. 'Oh, what the heck?' she said. She pulled her vest over her head, and dived in still wearing her thick white cotton pants. As she swam a length underwater, silence flooded her ears. She felt weightless, free.

'Hello?' A male voice called from the side of the house. Evie's eyes opened wide in horror and she beckoned to Stella. They pulled themselves out of the water and ran giggling towards the pool house, hiding behind a bush. Megan surfaced at the edge of the pool nearest the terrace.

'Evie? Stella?' She lifted herself easily out of the water, just as Peter appeared. He was in uniform, his arm in a sling. Megan shrieked, covered her breasts.

Peter stopped in his tracks. He had never seen anyone so beautiful in his entire life. Megan looked like the Venus de Milo to him, her slender pale limbs modestly curled in on themselves, her dark hair running rivulets of water over her smooth shoulders. 'I say, I'm awfully sorry,' he stammered, aware he had been staring, transfixed. He turned away from her. 'I'm Peter, Peter Taylor, a friend of Evie's.'

'Megan Jones,' she said, blushing violently. 'I would shake your hand, but ...'

'I take it Evie's around here somewhere?' Peter laughed.

'Over here, Peter.' Evie waved an arm from the bushes. 'Could you be a darling and fetch three towels for us?'

As Peter strode over to the pool house, Megan followed him with her eyes. He was tall, broad-shouldered, and his uniform accentuated his slender hips. She found she was a little breathless. He brought a towel to her first.

'Here you are.' He held it at arms length, smiling wickedly. Once Megan had covered up, he turned to her. 'You have the most beautiful eyes,' he said, captivated by their bright green, the frame of dark, wet lashes.

'Gosh.' She lowered her gaze.

'You certainly know how to make a first impression.' Peter held out his hand. 'Delighted to meet you.'

'Peter? Where are you? It's freezing!' Evie called. Reluctantly he let Megan's hand fall.

'Sorry, old girl.' He strode around to the bushes and tossed a couple of towels over. Stella and Evie soon appeared.

'You rotter.' Evie pushed the hair from her face, and gave him a hug. 'What are you doing here?'

'Out of action.' He gingerly lifted his arm in its sling. 'Thought I'd see if anyone was at home, and I spotted your car turning in.' Peter put his good arm around her. 'I'm sorry about your fiancé,' he said quietly.

Evie nodded, squeezed his hand. 'As you can see, we thought no one was at home,' she said briskly, and linked her arm through his. 'This is Stella Grainger, and I can see you've already met our lovely Megan!' She dug him playfully in the ribs. For the first time she could see Peter had eyes for someone else. 'Why don't we go and see what Daddy has in the fridge? I'm ravenous.'

As Peter smoked on the terrace, the girls changed. Evie lent them a couple of dresses – Stella picked out an elegant red shift, and Megan a crisp white summer dress.

'You have such beautiful things.' Megan ran her fingers over the silver dressing-table set, looking at herself in the large triple mirror. 'Where I'm from, well, it's lovely but it's nothing like this.'

Evie looked around her room as if for the first time. She pulled on a simple black dress with a sweetheart neckline and a full skirt. 'You know, things, money, they don't count for an awful lot do they?'

'Mummy always said it's better to be miserable with money than without it,' Stella said as she pulled a brush through her hair. She glanced at Evie, saw the sorrow on her face. 'Are you alright, darling?'

'Me?' Evie blinked away tears. 'I'm fine. I just realised ... he never had a chance to see where I grew up, or to meet Daddy. It's funny how it catches you at the oddest moments.'

'I know.'

Megan sat beside her on the bed and put her arm around her shoulders. Evie leant into her. 'What would I do without you two?'

'Right,' Megan said, 'I've already scandalised your friend, let's see what other mischief we can get up to.'

The kitchen was soon full of laughter and the smell of sausages cooking. Evie tossed the sizzling pan as Stella carved thick doorsteps of bread from the loaf, spreading them with golden butter and mustard.

'I haven't seen so much food for a long time,' she said. 'I thought cheese was rationed now?'

'Daddy has contacts. I think for some people the war has changed very little.' Evie looked up. 'Peter, why don't you go and get the little gramophone from the study?'

'Good idea!' In a few moments he reappeared, and cranked up the machine. Megan watched him shyly as he slipped out the record from its brown paper sleeve. There was a crackle, and a hiss as the needle hit the groove, then 'Tuxedo Junction' filled the air.

Peter walked over to her. 'Shall we, Miss Jones?' He offered her his good hand, and swung her, laughing, around the long kitchen table. Stella sat in the old velvet armchair by the Aga, where Evie was cooking, watching them indulgently. The chemistry between them was palpable.

'I think love is in the air,' she whispered to Evie.

She glanced over her shoulder and smiled. 'I do hope so. Peter's a doll. Practically like an older brother.'

'Have you and he ...?'

'Peter?' Evie said. 'No. He had a bit of a pash on me. We have a silly joke that if I'm still single by my twenty-first he'll make an honest woman of me, but no ...' She smiled. 'He's adorable, but not my type. Though he's perfect for Megan. Why don't we help things along a bit? If you go through that door over there, you'll see the steps to the cellar. Bring a couple of bottles of champagne up.'

'Champagne? What a treat. Does it matter which bottles?'

Evie shook her head. 'Go for the dustiest ones. They're normally the most expensive and Virginia's the only one who regularly drinks champagne around here.'

That evening, as the last golden rays of the sun streamed through the terrace doors, it was hard to believe there was a war on at all. They were just a group of young friends, listening to records, smoking, talking. As it grew darker Evie lit candles on the table, and Peter sat in his shirtsleeves, telling the girls the story of how he had been shot down in combat and forced to land on a remote Norfolk beach. He was modest, evasive. *Just like Beau*, Evie thought as she remembered Jack bragging at the Riviera. She forced the thought from her head, and went to pour more champagne, but the bottle was empty.

'Golly, we whizzed through those quickly.' She stood, and placed them on the draining board. 'Would you care to dance, Mrs Grainger?'

'Why, I'd be delighted!' Stella took her arm and they danced off outside, drifting happily around the terrace.

In silence, Peter and Megan watched them, painfully aware that they were alone.

'I ...' they both said at once.

'Please, after you.' Peter smiled.

'I was just going to say I think you're awfully brave.' Megan looked up at him hesitantly. In the candlelight his face looked like a young boy's, his fair hair touched with gold.

'I think you girls are the brave ones.' As he settled back in his chair, the cotton of his shirt brushed gently against her bare skin. She could feel the warmth of his arm. 'At least they give us guns, so we have a fighting chance. I've heard all about the Jerries targeting you ATA chaps.'

'So it is true! It's almost as if there's someone on the inside telling them when we're taking off,' Megan said.

'Who knows? People think there are Boche spies everywhere, but I wouldn't be surprised.' Peter was looking at her as she raised her eyes.

'What's it like, being shot down?'

He thought for a moment. 'You don't really have a chance to be frightened,' he said. 'You're too busy trying to out-manoeuvre the other chap. Afterwards, that's when it hits you.' He flinched slightly as he shifted in his chair to be a little closer to her.

'Does it hurt?' Megan gently touched his arm.

'This?' He was very close to her now. 'I was supposed to get it checked and cleaned up today. Just couldn't bear the thought of it. I'll be glad if I never see another hospital.'

'I could have a look if you wanted me to?'

'Are you a nurse as well as a crack pilot?' He wanted to kiss her. He had never wanted anything so much in his entire life.

'I take care of the animals at home,' she said seriously.

Peter laughed, and the tension lifted. 'Then I'm in good hands.

You really are the most extraordinary girl I've ever met.' As he leant in to kiss her, the kitchen lights flicked on.

'What on earth …?' Virginia strode into the room.

'Virginia!' Peter leapt to his feet. 'Hello, sir,' he said as Leo appeared at her side.

'Looks like you're having more fun here than we had in town,' Leo said grumpily as he shook Peter's hand.

'And who are you?' Virginia eyed Megan suspiciously.

'I'm a friend of Evie's. I'm awfully sorry …'

'Oh, hello. What are you doing back so soon?' Evie sauntered in from the terrace. 'Hello, Daddy.' She pecked him on the cheek, deliberately ignoring Virginia.

'How are you, darling?' His face was etched with concern.

Evie forced a tight smile. She couldn't possibly break down in front of Virginia.

'I've been wanting to talk to you,' he said as he took Evie's arm. 'I received a surprising letter a couple of days ago at the office.' Leo sorted through the papers in his briefcase on the dresser.

Virginia tossed her hat onto the side with her white gloves. 'Such a shame we didn't get to meet your fiancé.'

Evie bit her lip. She was determined not to let Virginia get to her.

'Ah, here it is.' Leo handed her a slim envelope.

Her hand shook slightly as she ran her fingertips over the address. She recognised Jack's handwriting. She slipped out the letter. It was formal, polite, so unlike the Jack she knew. *Dear Mr Chase, I am writing to ask for your daughter's hand in marriage. We are very much in love …*

She blinked away the tears, folded the letter back into its envelope. 'May I keep this?'

'Of course, darling.' Leo patted her arm. 'I'm so sorry. Do you know what happened?'

She nodded. 'He was shot down.' As she thought of the flames again, it was like a visceral, empty pain clutching at her stomach. 'Gosh, look at the time,' she said briskly, 'we must get going.' She began to clear away the plates and glasses, taking them to the sink.

'What are you doing?' Virginia said. 'Leave that for the housekeeper.'

Leo sat down with Peter at the table, while Virginia took a clean glass from the dresser and sauntered over to Evie. She lifted the champagne bottle hopefully. When she found it was empty, she sighed. 'Still, I imagine if you'd married this chap you'd have had to clean up after yourself. I can just picture you barefoot and pregnant on some farm.' She frowned as Evie refused to rise to the bait. 'It's just as well,' she whispered. 'Imagine getting engaged after only a couple of weeks. And to an American.'

'He was a good man,' Evie said steadily. 'We loved one another.'

As Stella walked in, she saw the expression on Evie's face. She strode over, put her hand on her arm.

'Love? What has love to do with it?' Virginia muttered. 'You need to consider your position.'

'That's what my mother said to me.' Stella glared at her. 'She was wrong too.'

'Have we been introduced?' Virginia challenged her. She didn't like the look on Leo's face when the slim blonde walked in from the terrace.

'Stella Grainger,' she said coolly. 'I fly with Evie.'

'Goodness, pilots are a lot prettier than when I was flying in the last war,' Leo called from the table.

'I'll second that, sir.' Peter laughed.

'Well, you're safely behind a desk these days. I'm glad that's one less thing we have to worry about.' Virginia smiled at him. 'I was just saying to Evie, it's such a shame about the wedding. I'm sure this Jack was perfectly charming.' She put her glass down. 'Not that I was looking forward to being a grandmother quite yet,' she said under her breath.

Evie rounded on her. 'You think that's why we wanted to get married so quickly? We were in love, and we realised we might not have much time together.' Her throat constricted as she fought back tears. 'As if I'd be foolish enough to get pregnant.'

'You wouldn't be the first,' Virginia said.

Evie's temper flared. 'My fiancé died, is that all you can say?'

'Evie ...' Peter said calmly, walking over.

'No! Not this time Peter. I've put up with this for years. That's it, I'm done with both of you,' she said to Leo. 'As long as you're married to this harpy I want nothing to do with you, Daddy.'

'Sweetheart,' he said, reaching out to her. 'I know you're hurting, but you mustn't call Virginia—'

'Let her go, Leo.' Virginia held the back of her hand to her forehead. 'She'll be back when this little tantrum blows over.'

Stella held Evie firmly by the arm. 'Come on, darling, let's go home.'

'Tantrum?' Evie was shaking with anger. 'I loved him, how dare you ...'

'How dare I? I wasn't the one slinging names, was I, Evie?' Virginia murmured, inspecting her nails as the girls filed out of the kitchen with Peter. 'If you're so certain you want to cut us out of your life, you won't be needing your house keys.'

'That's not necessary.' Leo frowned at his wife.

'No, Daddy. That's fine by me.' Evie rooted through her bag, and threw her keys onto the dresser.

'It's been lovely seeing you all.' Virginia scooped the keys up, twirled them on her finger as everyone filed out of the kitchen.

'Go to hell, Virginia.' Evie pushed past her.

'Do be careful, darling,' she called, waving from the door. Her eyes hardened as she murmured, 'The rate at which you pilots are getting bumped off, we don't want you beating me to it.'

SUMMER

30

'Where are we going?' Stella called over her shoulder. 'We've gone miles.' The warm breeze lifted the hem of her flowered dress as they cycled out into the countryside. June rain overnight had washed the countryside clean, and as Stella freewheeled along the lanes, her tyres humming and splashing through shallow puddles, she felt alive.

'It's a surprise,' Michael said as he caught up with her. 'Come on!' He raced ahead.

They had strapped sketchbooks and a picnic hamper to the back of his bicycle. 'Are we going to the river?' she asked as they reached Cookham.

'No, I'm taking you to church.'

'Church? On your day off?' Stella leant her bike against a white picket fence. As she turned to Michael she thought he looked so different in a white, open-necked shirt – freer somehow, younger.

He offered her his hand. 'It's a surprise. You'll see.' As they walked to the church door, he said, 'Does this look familiar?'

'The churchyard?' Stella looked around. A monument of a kneeling angel caught her eye. 'No, it looks just like every other English churchyard to me.'

They passed an old pram by the porch. As he pushed the door

open, he said, 'Wait a minute,' and stepped behind her, gently covering her eyes with his hands.

'You're mad!' Stella laughed. It felt good to have his arms around her, to be held after so long. As he guided her forward, his body was close to her; she felt the warmth of his skin through the thin cotton against her bare arms.

'Almost there,' he said softly. Stella sensed the change in light from the darkness of the church porch as they walked forward, a golden halo around his fingers. Her hand reached out blindly, felt smooth, warm wood, rough stone beneath her fingertips. 'There, open your eyes,' he said.

The interior was smaller than she had expected, intimate and warm. As her eyes adjusted to the light she saw on the front pew a man with a thatch of silver grey hair contemplating the altar.

'It's lovely, Mike, but I don't understand why—'

'Is that you, young Michael?' The little man rose and strode down the aisle towards them, swinging a black umbrella. 'Well, well.' He peered up at Stella through his thick glasses. 'This must be your pilot, eh? What a beauty.' He gestured towards her, his palms open. 'Ah, Ruskin's Athena, the Queen of the Air. I am sure the great man had just such a face in mind.'

'Stella, I'd like you to meet a friend of mine, Stanley Spencer,' Michael said proudly.

'*The* Stanley Spencer?'

'Yes.' He kissed her hand. 'Do call me Stanley.'

'Stella's an artist,' Michael said.

'Oh no, I just dabble.' She blushed. 'I've seen photographs of your work, it's marvellous.'

'Only photographs? Well, we shall have tea at the studio later. Shall we go?' By the porch he tucked the umbrella into the old pram and wheeled it up the path. 'Have you been to Cookham before, Stella?' he asked. In spite of his height, Stella had difficulty keeping up with his quick, sprightly steps.

'No I haven't, it's lovely isn't it?'

'Cookham is Heaven on Earth,' he said authoritatively.

'How did you meet him?' she whispered to Michael as they picked up the bicycles.

'Through the vicar, he's a very devout man.'

'So the little painting in your living room is—'

'Yes, it's an original,' Michael laughed.

'I thought it was a cheap copy!'

'Stanley has been helping me with my painting, and I've sat for him once or twice. He gave me the painting for my birthday.'

As they followed his little pin-stripe-suited figure up the high street, every single person stopped to say good morning to him.

'Here we are,' Stanley said finally, as they cut through towards the river. 'Isn't there a wonderful something in the air on a day like today?' he said as he chose a grassy spot for them to work. Michael leant the bikes against a tree, and spread a blanket on the warm grass for Stella. He handed her a sketch pad.

'Oh, no, I couldn't, not with—'

'Go on,' Michael said. 'Stanley is one of the most generous artists I have ever met. He won't bite.'

From the pram Stanley pulled a folding easel and a fresh canvas. 'I do envy you flying,' he said to Stella. 'How marvellous to be up there in the sacred spirit of the air. I have always maintained I am on the side of the angels and dirt.'

Stella laughed. 'You should talk to my friend Evie. She's certain she has a guardian angel flying with her.'

'Really? Fascinating,' he said as he took up his palette and selected a brush from the pram. 'Why not? I am quite sure angels go among us.' He fell silent for a moment. 'Heaven knows they are busy at the moment.' He began to paint. 'I was in Macedonia during the last war, you know. The things you see on the front line.' He sighed. 'Our poor boys.'

'I can't make any sense of it,' Michael said. He stretched out on the grass next to Stella and began to sketch her as she worked. 'Sometimes I wonder what kind of God allows these ghastly wars.'

'Man makes war, not God,' Stanley said. 'Never lose faith in Him.'

'It's hard,' Michael said. 'How am I supposed to comfort and help the parishioners when I don't know the answers to their questions myself? What do you say to a woman whose only son has been killed when she asks how God can allow such carnage, such evil as Nazism in this world?'

'Sometimes there are no simple answers,' Stanley said. 'It is a question of feeling. I know when I came back from the last war, I lost that lovely early morning feeling I had as a boy, but I've never lost my faith.' He turned to Michael. 'You have the potential to be a very good artist, but your vocation is the Church.'

'I don't know.' He looked at Stella. Her head was bent in concentration over her painting, the breeze lifting her blonde hair.

'I've told you before, my young friend,' Stanley said. 'There's an illustrious history of clergymen artists – there's no reason you cannot be both.' He looked up at Michael. 'An artist's only duty is to paint that which moves him. As a clergyman you care for people's souls. As an artist, you move their hearts.' He followed Michael's gaze to Stella, and smiled. 'What do you think, my dear?'

'About Mike?' As she looked up, she felt Michael watching her. 'I agree,' she said, holding his gaze. 'Follow your heart.'

They sketched and picnicked by the river for a couple of hours, as barges drifted past with the bobbing coots and ducks. People stopped to chat and look at Stanley's painting.

'Shall we go back to the studio for a spot of tea?' Stanley asked. 'I'm about done for today. Let me see what you have been doing.' Michael handed the sketchbooks to him. 'Very pretty, Stella,' he said. 'You have a lovely sense of form.' He flipped over to Michael's portrait of her. 'Ah.' His eyes softened. 'The work of a man who sees true beauty.' Michael got awkwardly to his feet. 'No, don't be embarrassed, dear boy. There's nothing like it. You have given Stella the luminous face of an angel. All she needs is wings.' He traced their pattern in the empty space.

Back at the house, Stanley's daily help was just finishing up and putting her mop away. 'Hello, Mrs Price,' Michael said. 'How are you?'

'Very well thank you, my dear.' She slipped off her floral housecoat and pulled on a summer jacket. 'Now, Stanley ...'

'Yes, Mrs Price?' He looked up like a naughty schoolboy.

'There's a bunch of lads hanging around by the back gate asking if they can watch you work this afternoon. I told them not to bother you again.'

'They're no bother. Let them in will you, Stella?'

She walked through the comfy, chaotic rooms and opened the back door.

'I'll be off then.' Mrs Price pursed her lips as the boys rushed in. 'And Michael, tell Stanley he needs to get his hair cut, will you? I've been on at him all week.'

'Thank you, Mrs Price,' Stanley said as he closed the front door behind her. 'Lovely lady, but she does boss me around. Half the time she's more like a mother than a housekeeper.' He clapped his hands. 'Right, let's all go through, shall we?'

'Shall I make some tea?' Stella asked.

'No, let me.' Michael ushered her through after Stanley and the children. 'I know where everything is and you must see the new paintings.'

Stella walked through to the bright studio. 'What a marvellous place to work, I'd love ...' she said, her words trailing away as she saw the huge canvases stacked against the walls.

'I've been working up at Lithgows in Glasgow,' Stanley explained. 'The War Artists Advisory Committee asked me to record the shipbuilding up there.' He pulled out the canvas he was working on to show her. 'There are going to be eight of these altogether. It's a marvellous place. I can hardly tear myself away. In fact, I may just sneak in a little self-portrait somewhere.' His eyes twinkled. 'This is "Welders", the second panel. It was finished in February. I had to paint it in sections in a tiny pub bedroom,' he laughed.

'It's huge ... epic,' Stella said as she stepped back to look at the nineteen-foot-long canvas.

'Oh good, I'm so glad you think so. It's the subject matter, you know, it has to be on a grand scale. Did you know they have women

243

doing this work?' Stella nodded. 'I've made some marvellous sketches of them working, but I don't know whether they will make it to the final piece ...' Stanley rifled through some pencil drawings.

'That's beautiful.' Stella pointed at a small pencil sketch of a nude.

'Ah, Eve,' he said. 'What are you doing in there, you naughty girl?'

'That's my friend's name, Evie.'

'The friend with the guardian angel? Then you must take it as a gift for her, a kindred spirit.'

'I couldn't possibly ...'

'Nonsense.' He shuffled through some loose pages. 'Here we are. A little memento for you too, lovely Athena.' He handed her a sketch of the angel in Cookham churchyard.

'I don't know what to say. Thank you.'

'My pleasure. I've had a delightful afternoon. Do come again.' He turned to the children. 'Right, my little friends. Settle down now, boys, find a seat. The show will begin in a minute or two.'

Michael handed them both a cup of tea. Stanley sipped his quickly as they discussed the commission. 'I know that look in your eyes.' Michael laughed.

'Yes, I do rather want to get going,' Stanley said. 'I am enjoying this piece.'

'We should head home too,' Stella said. 'Early start in the morning.'

'What time do you begin?'

'You have to sign in by nine or there's hell to pay.'

'Well, we wouldn't want to make you late. It was a delight to meet you, my Queen of the Air.' Stanley kissed her hand again. 'Pop in any time, I'm always around the village somewhere.'

Stella and Michael rinsed their cups in the cramped kitchen. Stanley's muffled voice drifted through to them; he was laughing and joking around with the boys as he worked.

'This has been such a treat.' Stella leant against the draining board as she dried her hands.

'Stanley enjoyed meeting you too.' Michael turned to her, his hip brushing against her waist. 'Athena, Queen of the Air ...'

Stella laughed uncomfortably. Her breathing seemed to grow louder to her, her heart began to beat fast. She looked up at him. She saw the desire in his eyes, the unguarded longing.

Gently, he stroked her cheek. 'Stanley was right, what he said. Though you are more beautiful to me.' He kissed her then.

Warm light filled Stella's eyes as they closed. She put her hand against his chest, gently pushed him away. 'Mike, we can't,' she whispered, aware of the voices next door in the studio.

'Why not?' He kissed her again. 'I'm alone, so are you.'

She fought it, the desire to be with him overwhelming her. 'But you're a vicar, and I'm—'

'I'm a curate,' he corrected. 'There's nothing to say I'll be one forever.' He cupped her face in his hands. 'If you were with me, you wouldn't have to be just a vicar's wife, serving up tea and sympathy. I know you wouldn't be happy with that life.'

'It's not that.' Stella leant in to his hand. 'Mike, I'm—'

'Widowed? Is that it?'

'No.' She couldn't look at him. She knew if she looked into his eyes again she would be lost.

'If it's your baby, David, I've always wanted a family. We could be so happy together, Stella, I know it.'

'Mike, I never wanted to lead you on, to make you think ...'

'Do you want to be with me?'

'Yes, I ...' she paused. He kissed her passionately. She fell back against the counter, her hands in his hair, his weight against her.

'Stella, let me make you happy,' he murmured, his kisses brushing her neck.

'No.' She struggled out of his arms, breathing hard. 'All I really want is never to feel anything again.'

He caught her waist, pulled her to him, his lips close to hers. 'You don't mean that.'

'I can't be with you. We should stop seeing each other.'

'Could you really bear never to see me again?'

'Yes, if you let me.'

Michael released her, and she picked up the pencil sketches from the counter. He sensed her anguish. 'I won't push you,' he said gently. 'Perhaps it's too soon after you lost your husband?' He took her hand. 'I just wanted you to know how I feel.'

'Mike ...'

'I love you, Stella.'

'I can't.' Her voice shook. 'I'm so glad, so terribly glad to have met you. You're a very special friend, Mike—'

'Friend?' he said angrily. 'I just told you that I'm in love with you.'

'I'm sorry, it's impossible. I can never give you more.' She ran from the studio, pulled her bike from the railings with shaking hands.

As she cycled home, the wind lashed her face, caught in her throat as the angry tears came at last. She skidded to a halt, threw the bike down beside a gate, and walked away across the cornfields, tears streaming down her face. 'It's not fair,' she cried to the sky, her arms flung out, fists clenched. Everything she had kept hidden – the raw pain of her loss, the longing to be with Michael – swept through her. She walked until there was no breath left in her, and collapsed, sobbing, at the foot of an oak tree. As the canopy of leaves shifted over her, she lay back on the hard earth. Her ribs heaved in and out, her heart pounding in her chest as the breeze whispered through the long grass around her. 'It's not fair,' she said, broken sobs rasping her throat as she pressed the heels of her hands against her eyes.

31

As the men adjourned from the dining room, Beau stepped out into the hall, Leo's voice carrying after him. He glanced back to where Pickard and Fielding were settling into armchairs by the fire with their port and cigars. A third man sat with his back towards Beau.

'May I be of assistance, sir?' Ross asked him.

'Yes, the bathroom please.'

'Certainly, sir. The ground floor is occupied. Perhaps you would care to use the guest suite upstairs? The second door on the right.'

Beau jogged upstairs, his footsteps soundless on the rich cream carpet. The great staircase swept around the marble-tiled hall, light glinting in the huge chandelier that hung at its heart. Beau paused on the landing and looked down through the tall arched window to the steaming pool below. *It's not what I'm used to*, he remembered Evie saying of the cottage. As he turned and took in the vast, echoing hall, he heard Ross's footsteps echoing up from the floor below. He was impressed that she had stuck with the cottage. The temptation to return to this easy luxury would have been too much for most people.

He strode across the landing and opened the second door. Soft lamplight illuminated the room. It was decorated beautifully –

understated elegant dark wood and neutral colours, warm creams and tans. He thought of his mother's draughty château in France, Olivia's freezing family house in Norfolk, his austere boarding school, the countless barracks that had concertinaed into one in his mind. *I seem to have spent my entire life feeling cold*, he thought.

In the bathroom, he exhaled with relief. His head was killing him as usual, the sharp pain spreading from his left temple to his jaw. Beau reached for the mirrored cabinet and opened the door. *Aspirin*, he thought. *Thank God*. He gulped down two tablets and replaced the medicine bottle. As it chinked on the glass shelf, he paused, and lifted down a bottle of Cuir de Russie perfume. Carefully, he removed the stopper and inhaled its familiar rich scent of jasmine and leather. It seemed strange that Evie's things were being stored in the guest suite. He felt self-conscious suddenly, and closed the cabinet. 'Bally fool,' he said to his reflection. In the clear light of the triple mirror, it was impossible to avoid himself. Slowly, he lifted his hand to his face and inspected the scars. Where his fingertips touched his cheek it felt numb still. The doctors had told him it would take months for the nerves to regenerate. Perhaps they never would.

Beau straightened his tie, composed his face into the tough mask he wore at all times. He paused in the doorway to the dressing room, looked longingly at the high, wide bed, golden pools of lamplight spilling across the soft cotton sheets and plump pillows. Beau imagined Evie sleeping there, her rich dark hair on the pillow, her naked arm reaching out across the warm bed to—

'Alex, there you are!' Beau turned, surprised to find Leo standing in silhouette in the doorway. 'Are you off?'

'Yes, sir. Early start in the morning. I just wanted to freshen up.'

'Of course.' Leo flicked on a lamp on top of the chest of drawers. Beau saw riding trophies gleaming on top of the wardrobe, and beside Leo's hand a doll. Leo followed his gaze. 'I see you've met Muv?' He picked the doll up. 'She was Evie's favourite.'

'What happened to it?' Beau walked over and took it from

Leo. The doll's face was bandaged; a single beautiful grey eye gazed back at him.

'There was an accident,' Leo said carefully. 'But Evie loved her more than any other doll, in spite of the damage.' He paused. 'For months she refused to believe the doll wouldn't heal itself. When she finally accepted the face would always be broken, she made these for Muv ...' Leo held up a selection of tiny masks. 'You could always tell what mood Evie was in by which mask she chose for the doll. It was beautiful originally – a Jumeau I believe.'

Beau put the doll back on the chest. 'It's a shame when toys break.'

'Better to enjoy them than leave them on a shelf unplayed with.' Leo paused. 'Muv was a gift from Ingrid, her real mother – it belonged to *her* mother I believe. I was rather cross with Evie for breaking it.' Leo's gaze fell. 'Ingrid paid us a last visit to bring the doll to her. It was ...' He sighed. 'It was hard saying goodbye, knowing I would probably never see her again.' Leo blinked. 'I'm afraid I took my anger out on Evie. Virginia convinced me that she should learn her lesson, that the doll shouldn't be mended.'

'She seems to have loved it anyway.'

'Oh yes, absolutely. When I offered to have it repaired later, she refused.' Leo stroked the doll's hair. 'I should have been kinder. I'm afraid I'm one of those fools who is blinded by love, or this ...' he waved vaguely at his groin.

Beau looked at a photograph beside the doll. 'Are these her brothers?'

'Hmm?' Leo peered closer. 'No, that's Charles and Peter. They were all about eight or nine when that was taken. Charles ...' He cleared his throat as he took down the photo. 'Charles was killed at Christmas.' He ran his thumb tenderly across their young faces. 'Evie was an only child, but they were like brothers to her. We used to call them the three musketeers. They spent every day together during the holidays, out riding or messing about on the river. She could always give them a run for their money, always keep up.'

'That I can believe.' Beau smiled at the picture of her, moved by Evie's joyful, trusting face.

'I can see why they are interested in recruiting her too,' Leo said steadily as he put the photograph back. 'Evie would be an asset to the organisation. I know they are keeping an eye on her.'

'How would you feel about that?'

'I've resisted so far. She'd be perfect of course. She looks European. She only has schoolgirl German, but she speaks French fluently ... Well, you know her well by now.'

Beau held his gaze. 'The perfect spy,' he said quietly. Already he was afraid for her.

Leo looked at the doll. 'I couldn't bear the thought of ... When you hear what some of the agents endure. It was different in my time.'

'You saw active service?'

Leo nodded. 'I wouldn't be happy sending men and women out if I hadn't been through this myself.' As he flicked off the light, he turned to Beau. 'But this is our darkest hour, they are saying. Churchill wants us to set Europe ablaze.'

'I'll do it,' Beau said. 'Tell them I'm in.'

Leo shook his hand. 'I'm glad. You're one of the finest pilots I've ever known, and you know the region well. This will make best use of your skills, and of course your languages will come in useful, should you need them.'

'Let's hope not. Françoise, my mother, will help. From the little I've managed to find out, she's already working with the Maquis.'

'Yes, your mother is a remarkable woman.'

Beau glanced at the doll. 'So is your daughter, sir.'

Leo clapped him on the back. 'Now, it goes without saying you can tell no one about your new position. Not even your fiancée. Perhaps, especially her.'

'Because of the Shusters?'

'Yes, they're being watched. Anyone with links to Mosley and the Blackshirts is under surveillance. Their allegiances are well known.'

Beau shook his head. 'Olivia doesn't share their beliefs. She's always loathed fascism, as I do.'

'Will you marry her?'

Beau was caught off guard. 'No,' he said instinctively. 'I have to break things off gently, for the sake of our families.'

In the shadows, Leo turned to him. 'Sometimes a clean break is best for everyone.'

'Perhaps you are right.'

As they stepped out onto the landing, Beau closed the door to Evie's room behind him, the latch slipping easily into the lock. 'Good luck, Alex. You'll receive orders for your new squadron in the next few days. From what I hear you chaps will be based up at Tempsford.'

'Tempsford?'

'Yes, it's a new base. No one knows about it, and we'd like to keep it that way.' They shook hands. 'Remember, trust no one.'

'Even you?' Beau smiled.

'Especially me.'

Leo leant against the banister and watched Beau leave. Ross appeared silently at his side. 'Is everything in order, sir?'

'Yes, well done, Ross. Worked like a charm.' He strode back into Evie's room and flicked on the light. As he passed the doll carefully to the butler, he stroked its bandaged face. 'It's about time I stood up for Evie and undid some of the damage we have done, eh Muv? And who knows, if I've played Cupid, well … that would be a bonus.' He scooped up the little masks and tipped them into Ross's white-gloved hand. 'Right, we'd better get these tucked away safely in Evie's trunk in the attic again before my dear wife gets home.' He looked at his watch. 'If she gets home tonight.'

'Yes, sir.'

'I have some business to take care of downstairs, Ross. I can lock up later. Why don't you and the staff take an early night? It's Cullen's birthday today – you could open a couple of bottles from the cellar and have a bit of a celebration.'

'Thank you, sir. Are you sure I can't do anything else?'

'Quite sure. I can take care of myself.'

32

Every bone in Evie's body ached after spending the night on the train down from Prestwick, sitting on her parachute in the stifling pitch-black corridor as it lumbered across the country. She had dozed fitfully, a dark forest of legs before her, a thick soup of cigarette smoke, stale bodies and greasy food scenting the air.

It was mid-afternoon by the time she made it back to White Waltham to hand in her chits. She slumped on a Windsor chair near the Ops Room, summoning the energy to cycle home. Luckily there was nothing for her until the next day.

'Still moping, Miss Chase?' Teddy looked up from the programme book. He was leaning on the counter copying in the planes that still needed ferrying, Doyle and Stent at his side. 'Thought you would have bounced back by now.'

'Go to hell,' she whispered under her breath.

'Sorry? Didn't quite catch that?' He paused, glared down at her.

'Not feeling very well.' She forced herself to her feet.

'Oh dear, I am sorry,' he said. Evie hooked her bag onto her shoulder and marched out of the offices. 'Feminine problems no doubt,' he said with distaste to Doyle. 'Women aren't tough enough for war. They have no right being here.' Teddy folded his arms. 'These gals aren't doing it for their country. They should do jobs more befitting to their sex rather than take work from our men.'

'Still there are some benefits to having them round the place.' Doyle eyed the interviewees waiting outside the Recruitment Office. 'The stooges seem to get prettier every time.'

'It's like shooting fish in a barrel, eh boys?' Teddy nudged him.

'I heard these Yanks that are joining us will go with anything in a uniform.' Stent grinned gummily, small teeth glittering. 'They say one of the girls slept with every man on the boat on the way over.'

Teddy rubbed his hands. 'Happy days, boys. Happy days.' He looked down at his book. 'Right, we've got a big delivery of Hurricanes coming in from Langley today, so I need you chaps to hang around.' Doyle groaned. 'I know, I know. But we need to get them shifted as soon as possible.'

Teddy glanced up as Stella strode down the corridor, a chit in her hand, her parachute slung over one shoulder. He ducked out of the Ops Room and caught up with her. 'Are you off again, Mrs Grainger? We do keep you busy.'

'Yes, sir,' she said without turning to him. He followed her out onto the airfield as she walked on.

'Did you see what turned up here yesterday?' Teddy pointed across the airfield to a huge four-engined monoplane. 'Focke Condor. One Captain Hansen of Denmark piloted it in. He and the plane were on their last legs.'

'I wondered who that was in the mess.'

'Dicey landing. He skidded and collided with a farm vehicle on the field. Almost took out Bradbrooke's Folly.'

'Sorry?'

'The armoured car m'dear.' Teddy reached over and took her chit, his fingers brushing her wrist. Stella winced. 'So what have we got you dicing with today?'

'Lysander to Tangmere,' she said, fastening her Sidcot suit as they walked.

'I do like the old Lizzies.'

'What did you fly exactly, Officer Parker?'

'Oh this and that, all sorts really,' he said vaguely. 'Listen, I wondered if you might fancy a bite to eat later, or a trip to the cinema?'

'Me?' Stella stopped in her tracks.

Teddy smoothed his moustache. 'Yes, my dear, you. I saw *Ferry Pilot* the other night. Jolly good to see old Bradbrooke again. Damn shame he went down. Couple of the girls are in it too, Joan and Audrey—'

Stella cut him off. 'Thank you, but I have a prior engagement.'

'Another time then?' He put his hands on his hips as she moved away. 'What's the matter, eh? Ground staff not good enough for you?'

Stella clenched her fist and walked back to him. 'No sir, if you must know you're just not my type.'

'Of all the impertinent—'

'You did ask, sir.'

Teddy watched her stride away and join the queue of pilots filing into the waiting Anson. 'Not your type, eh? Stuck-up Ice Queen. I'll show you, my girl.'

Arsehole, Evie thought to herself as she cycled through the village, past St Mary's. *I'm going to get Teddy back somehow for what he did to Jack, I just don't know how yet.* As she passed the Coach and Horses she thought of the happy hours she had spent with Jack in the bar in Bristol, and impulsively she swung a loop on the bike and went in, thirsty for a cool glass of beer. The July sun beat down on her as she leant her bike against the wall. She waved at a couple of off-duty ATA pilots in the beer garden, and a few of the locals looked up, surprised to see a woman in uniform and alone.

'A half of Guinness,' she said, and counted out 6d.

'Isn't it rather tragic, drinking alone?' a voice said. She looked up into the shadows of the snug, and saw a familiar silhouette, the glow of a cigarette. 'That's what someone told me once.'

'Hello, sir,' she said. 'Haven't seen you for a while.'

'Allow me.' Beau tossed a few coins onto the counter. 'I'll have the same again,' he said to the landlord.

'You look very smart,' she said. Beau looked tanned and relaxed, off duty in a midnight blue double-breasted suit.

'I was at the Gold Cup this afternoon.'

'Were they racing?'

'At Newmarket, yes. In fact I saw your father up there.'

'Did you? How is he?'

'Lucky as ever,' Beau laughed. 'He cleaned up in fact – he had a big wager on Finis to win.'

'Typical Daddy.' She sipped gratefully at her drink. 'I didn't know you liked racing.'

Beau shrugged. 'It's something of a family tradition. I went with Olivia's parents.'

'Oh. I thought you and Olivia ...' She hesitated. 'I'm glad if you've sorted everything out.' She felt Beau watching her.

'It's not that simple. Her father and Hans were like brothers. He was very good to me after my parents split up, I can't just cut them off. And Olivia is rather fragile at the moment.'

Fragile like an iceberg, Evie thought.

'I'd arranged to go with them ages ago. It would have seemed rude to ...' Beau laughed and shook his head. 'I don't know why I'm trying to explain. What is it you said to me? Never apologise, never explain?'

'Hello, sir.' A young ATA cadet walked in with Ace at his side.

'Thanks for looking after him for me, Archie.' Beau handed him some coins. 'Now, what will it be?'

'Beer please, sir.'

'Hello, Archie,' Evie said. 'Oh look at this dog!' She sank to her knees and ran her hands through Ace's glossy fur. He panted happily, ears pricked. 'Don't you look well? Yes, you do.' The dog rolled over and put all four paws in the air.

'Miss Chase has quite an effect on men, as you can see,' Beau said.

Evie looked up at the boy. 'Are you old enough to drink, Archie?'

'I'm sixteen, Miss.' He puffed his chest out. All the young cadets were immensely proud of their blue RAF uniforms. 'It's my birthday today, and the Wing Commander wanted to buy me a pint.'

'Do you want to be a pilot when you're older?'

'Yes, Miss. I'm doing bits and pieces round here, delivering post and so on.'

'How are you finding it?'

'Most of the chaps are friendly enough, but Wing Commander Beaufort is the tops.'

'Really?' She eyed Beau curiously.

'He's lent me all sorts of books, and he's let me go up and do his winding gear loads of times.'

'Steady on, old boy,' Beau said. 'We don't want to destroy my severe image entirely.'

Evie laughed. 'Aren't you full of surprises, Wing Commander?'

Beau handed Archie a glass and the boy clung to it as if he was afraid someone might take it away.

'There you go. Happy birthday,' Beau said. 'Why don't you take Ace outside? I'll be along in a moment.' He turned to Evie. 'How's your week been?'

'Non-stop. I've had the most awful day.' Evie shook a cigarette from the packet in her pocket. 'Took a Harvard up to Prestwick, train back last night.'

'Those trips are always fun. No wonder you look tired.'

Evie frowned. She was just about to challenge him when she saw Beau was smiling. 'Tired?' she laughed. 'Sometimes I feel like I've aged ten years in ten months.'

'I think we all feel like that at the moment.' Beau leant against the bar at her side, his shoulder resting close to hers.

Evie's head was swimming with tiredness, and the nearness of him. 'God, those Harvards make a racket on the ground,' she said quickly. 'I don't know what the Americans put in them. Then when I made it back, Teddy was winding me up.'

'He winds everyone up. Don't take it personally.'

'I'll never forgive him for what he did to Jack.' Evie stared quickly down at her drink. 'And for what he said about you. I wish he were dead.' She paused. 'No I don't, that's silly of me.'

'There's not much chance he'll cop any flak in the chairborne division.' Beau exhaled a plume of smoke. 'I'd keep an eye on him if I were you though. It strikes me Parker has it in for you.'

Evie thought of Olivia. 'It seems everyone does.'

'What do you mean?'

'Oh, nothing. All those stupid lies he told about me. Even to my face he always behaves like I'm some spoilt brat who has led a charmed life.'

'You have.'

Evie folded her arms as she turned to him. 'I've changed.'

'I know you have. It's what happens when you're facing danger every day. You soon realise what is important.' Beau reached over and adjusted the wings on her jacket. Evie's skin prickled, made goosebumps at his touch. 'How many times do I have to tell you to keep your wings level?'

'You're not my teacher any more.'

'I know.' He looked at her. 'I could tell on your first flight what an excellent pilot you would become.'

'Thank you.' Evie felt awkward suddenly. 'Listen, why don't you take Montgomery out for a ride this weekend? Do you more good than being holed up in here.'

'I'd love to, but I won't be here.'

'Why?'

'I've been given the all clear.'

'You're going back to your squadron?' Evie was surprised how the news hit her.

'I can't wait,' he said. 'As much as I love teaching you girls how not to break your necks flying, I want to be back in action.'

She tried to hide her disappointment. 'Of course you want to get out of here.'

'You will too, soon. I'm sure Pauline will have you all sent off to other bases.'

'I hope not, White Waltham is by far the best.'

'All the ferry pilots say that about their home pool. I think because you go through so much hardship together – the freezing cold, the lack of furniture ...'

'Don't forget the mice.'

'It's the little things that help to unite you, don't you think?'

257

Evie laughed. 'Where are you based now?' she asked casually. 'Perhaps I could—'

'East Anglia.'

'Not Martlesham? That's where Jack ...' Her voice trailed off. 'You will be careful, won't you, sir?' She hesitated. 'Perhaps now you're not my instructor any more I can call you Beau?'

He gazed at her, smiled sadly. 'I do wish people would stop calling me that.'

Evie touched his wounded arm, the tanned skin warm to her touch. 'Why? Because of this?' She hesitated, wary of touching his face. Gently she touched her own cheek. 'And this? They haven't changed you.'

He looked away. 'Thank you, Miss Chase.'

'Good luck, sir. Thank you. For everything.' She waited. Finally he raised his eyes to hers. In the silence it felt to her as if the air between them contracted, shifted. She felt light-headed, uncertain.

'Evie ...'

'I should get going,' she said quickly. 'Take care,' she said. As she walked out into the sunlight and the pub door closed behind her, she wondered whether she would ever see him again.

33

'Stay still!' Stella laughed.

'I can't, you're tickling!' Megan giggled as Stella drew a line along the back of her leg with a kohl pencil. 'And I smell like gravy!' Evie was putting the finishing touches to her other leg with a bowl of gravy browning.

'I'm sorry I don't have any stockings left for your big night.' Evie dabbed at Megan's ankle with a cloth. 'I gave my last pair to Jean.'

'There.' Stella stood back to get the full effect. 'Give us a twirl!' Megan pirouetted in her slip and the high heels that had been a birthday present from Evie. Her room was decked out with cards and a bouquet of yellow roses from Peter.

'I'm so excited!' Megan squealed. 'My first dinner date, I can't believe it!'

'And Peter is a perfect gentleman, so you have nothing to worry about.' Evie took the emerald green cocktail dress Megan was borrowing off its hanger, and helped her in. 'This suits you far more than me with your lovely colouring,' she said as she pulled up the zip. 'Why don't you keep it?'

Megan gasped, turned this way and that in front of the mirror. 'Thank you!' She hugged Evie. 'I don't know what to say.'

'Don't say anything, just have a marvellous time and tell us all about it when you get home.' Evie sprayed some perfume in the air, and beckoned her forwards into the mist. 'Perfect. You don't want it to be too heavy.'

'It's lovely.' Megan checked the bottle. 'Lily of the Valley.'

'That's you.' Evie hugged her. 'Our lily from the valleys.'

'There's something missing …' Stella mused, looking Megan up and down. 'I know!' She ran to her room, and returned with a diamanté brooch, clipping it carefully in Megan's hair.

'Oh, I look like a film star,' Megan sighed. There was a knock on the door and they heard Peter call hello. 'Thank you both so much, this has been my best birthday ever!' She ran downstairs, and the girls listened to their excited voices. Stella and Evie stood by the bedroom window and watched Peter open the door of his car and help Megan into her seat.

'They make a lovely couple, don't they, Evie?'

'I'm over the moon they've been getting along so well. I hope he asks her to marry him.' She linked her arm through Stella's as they walked downstairs. 'We could do with some good news for a change.'

'Talking of good news, have you heard? I bumped into Rosemary in the Jolly Farmer at Hockett's Hill. You know Pauline convinced Pop to let the girls have a go at operational planes?'

'Yes, they were at some party weren't they? Clever old her to catch him off guard.'

'Well, Winnie, Margie, Joan and Rosemary checked out on Hurricanes today at Cowley.'

'No!' Evie clapped her hands excitedly.

'Apparently Winnie jumped out of the Hurricane cockpit and said "It's lovely darlings!"'

Evie grinned. 'Teddy owes me ten bob. That should sort him and his goons out. I heard him grumbling to Doyle yesterday that we Third Officers get the same rate of pay as a Squadron Leader. We damn well deserve it too.' She put her hands on her hips. 'It looks like we've all finished our Class 2+ conversion at just the right time.'

Stella flopped into an armchair. 'Oh, the Spitfire. Just imagine. Top speed of 400 mph and the power of six racing Bentleys.'

'It doesn't matter how much you've flown, it's always nice to go faster,' Evie said. 'I can't wait. When you see them quivering on the runway ready for take-off, it always reminds me of a racehorse waiting for the gates to open.' She hugged herself with excitement. 'They say the cockpit fits you like a well-tailored dress.'

'You'd know, darling.'

Evie poked her tongue out, and straightened the Spencer drawings over the fireplace.

'Those frames are lovely,' Stella said.

Evie stepped back to admire the pictures. 'It was the least I could do to say thank you. When this bally war is over and we go our separate ways, whenever I look at my little Eve I shall think of you.' She smiled at her friend. 'You haven't seen Michael for a while have you?'

'No.' Stella looked at her hand, pushed back the cuticles on her fingers. 'God, I made a mess of my nails tying up the tomato plants with Meggie.'

'Are you going to? I thought you two were close.'

'I don't know,' Stella snapped. 'Can we just drop it?'

'There's no need to bite my head off.'

Stella chewed at the side of her thumb. 'Sorry,' she said finally. 'It's all a bit of a mess. He was so kind, and understanding. Somehow, talking to him really helped.'

Evie perched on the arm of her chair. 'You know you can always talk to me?'

'I know.' Stella smiled sadly. *What would someone like Evie know about how she was feeling? Someone who sailed easily through a charmed life.* 'I just don't find it easy to open up to people. The code at home was always "stiff upper lip".'

'It was the opposite with me growing up. Some of my earliest memories are my parents having humdingers of rows. Ingrid, my mother, was a big thrower. One night I swear she went through an entire dinner service when she found out my father had been playing around.'

'Lord, how ghastly.' Stella screwed up her nose. The thought of all that unbridled passion made her blanche. 'Is that why she left?' She paused. 'I wish ... I wish I could be a bit more like that. I wish I could let it out more often, instead of this, this ...'

'I'm sorry, darling. I didn't mean to upset you.' Evie took her hand, her face full of concern. 'What's going on?'

Stella took a deep breath. 'Christ, I don't know. After Richard, well, I thought I'd never feel anything again. It's like the world turned grey overnight.'

'I can imagine how you must be feeling.'

No you can't, Stella thought. *No one can.*

'You must miss him, and your baby, a great deal,' Evie said kindly.

'Yes, I do.' Stella pressed her fingers to her temple and closed her eyes. 'And now Mike, poor Mike. He's been such a good friend, but when he kissed me, I just panicked.'

'He kissed you?' Evie cried. 'But that's wonderful! I knew he liked you.'

Stella winced. 'No, I've made the most frightful mess of it all. I can't ... I mean, I can't give him anything more than friendship.' She glanced towards the kitchen. The back door was open and she could see through to the vegetable garden. 'What are we having for dinner? There's lettuce ready, and beans, broccoli ...'

Evie could see Stella wanted to change the subject, and she went through to the pantry. 'How do you like rabbit?'

'I can't say I've ever—'

She reappeared holding a rabbit by its ears. 'I had a little accident on the way home.'

'You killed a rabbit, on a bicycle?' Stella laughed. 'How fast were you going?'

'Poor thing never stood a chance.' Evie eyed it doubtfully. 'I haven't a clue how to prepare it, but it seemed a shame to waste it.'

'It's been the most wonderful evening.' Megan turned her face to Peter's as they walked by the Thames. Dog-rose petals floated downstream like confetti, the full moon reflected on the water as crickets sang in the long grass. 'I did enjoy *Hudson's Bay*.'

'I haven't been to the cinema for so long. The Rialto is rather nice.'

Megan slipped her arm into his. 'And the meal ... That restaurant was far too expensive.'

'Nothing is too good for you.' Peter kissed the top of her head as they paused by the lock. 'I do like you an awful lot, Megan, you know.'

'Do you? Do you really?'

'Yes. These last few weeks, well, they've been wonderful.' He kissed her. Megan closed her eyes, waited for that special feeling she had read about in books, when your knees melt and your heart sings. She waited to feel how she'd felt when Bill had kissed her.

They walked on along the towpath to Peter's car. An RAF bus was collecting a group of WAAFs to take them back to their billet at Hockett's, and Megan watched as they waved goodbye to their sweethearts through the back window. 'I don't want this day to end,' she said as Peter opened the door for her.

He sat beside her. 'It doesn't have to,' he said quietly. 'I don't have to be back at my base until tomorrow morning.'

Megan's heart was beating fast. Perhaps that was it. If she let him make love to her, then it would feel right. When she didn't answer, Peter started the car. 'I'm sorry, it was silly of me to suggest ...' he said.

'No.' She touched his hand. 'I want to,' she said.

'Oh, Megan ...' He pulled her into his arms.

They drove back to the cottage in silence, Peter wishing the miles would fly away faster, Megan hoping she had made the right decision.

'Here we are,' she said brightly as they walked hand in hand up the path. The blacked-out windows of the cottage seemed dark from outside. 'I do hope the girls are asleep.' She opened the door, dim lamplight spilling onto the grass. 'Perhaps we can sneak in and—' the words died on her lips as they came face to face with Bill.

'Megan.' His eyes lit up as he saw her. Then as Peter stepped into the room, they hardened.

'Bill?' Her cheeks coloured. 'What a wonderful surprise, to see you I mean ... How did you—'

'He's been here for hours,' Evie said, her eyes widening in warning. 'I told him my brother had taken you out dancing.'

'Brother?' Peter cut in. 'I say that's a bit—'

'So this isn't her brother?' Bill clenched his fist.

'Bill, no, don't ...' But it was too late, he flew at Peter.

'Stop it! Please stop it!' Megan cried, dragging Bill away from him, stepping between the two men. 'Leave him alone!'

'I should have known it.' He pulled his old tweed jacket from the back of the chair. 'I should have known you wouldn't wait for me.' He pushed past Peter, who was nursing a split lip. He paused at the door and turned to Evie. 'Thank you for supper, Miss.'

'It was a pleasure, Bill. Thank you for doing the rabbit ...' Her words tailed off as he stormed out.

'I'm so sorry.' Megan touched Peter's arm, but he pulled away.

'You might have told me you have a boyfriend,' he said.

'I had no idea he'd come here.'

'Come on,' Evie took him by the arm. 'Let's get you sorted out.' She glanced at Megan. 'Why don't you go and take care of lover-boy?'

Megan ran out into the dark night. She could see Bill striding up the lane ahead. 'Bill!' she raced after him. 'Please let me explain!'

He stopped and turned to her. 'What is there to explain? You'd forgotten all about me. Carrying on with some toffee-nosed English—' Her kiss caught him off guard. She fell against him, panting, then his hands were in her hair, holding her fast. 'Megan, my Megan,' he murmured, his voice hoarse with longing. They stumbled into the woods hand in hand, lay down in a clearing in the moonlight.

'I've missed you,' she said again and again as he held her. Her senses swam, the taste of clean crushed leaves on their skin as they kissed.

'The thought of you with another man ...' He pulled away from her.

'No. There's only you. I only want you, Bill.' Her head fell back against the ground, her hair spread around her, dark curls against the leaves, silver in the moonlight. She reached up to him as he leant over her, felt the curve of his shoulders, the powerful muscles beneath his cotton shirt. 'I want you, Bill.'

The blood surged in her veins, his hands on her, slipping on the satin as he pulled up her skirt. 'I love you,' she said, showering his face with kisses as he loosened his belt. 'I will always love you.' He pushed aside the thin silk of her French knickers; her back arched as she felt him. His skin was pale against the night sky, against the dark canopy of whispering leaves that hid them from the stars.

'I love you, Megan.' He murmured her name as they moved together, crushing the fresh, long grass, cool against her back.

They lay together until dawn, limbs entwined, stiff with cold, but not wanting to leave their secret place, to go back and explain. She heard Peter's car leave after a couple of hours, the note of the engine cutting through her fitful sleep.

'Who is he?' Bill murmured, kissing her neck. His black hair flopped forward over his eyes.

'A friend,' she said as she gazed up at the shifting branches above them. 'Just a friend.'

'I'm sorry I hit him.' Bill plucked a white dog rose, threaded it through her hair.

'You have nothing to be worried about.' She wondered if she would have gone through with it with Peter. If she would have felt like this. 'I've just been lonely, that's all, and it's nice to go out dancing ... What about you anyway? I bet you've had half the girls in the valley chasing after you now I'm out the way.'

Bill shook his head. 'I don't see them. All I want is you, Megan. Come home with me.' He kissed her.

'I can't. I belong here, for now. The work I'm doing, it's important. It's hard, I'm not as good as Evie and Stella, but I'm trying my best. They're going to let us fly fighter planes, Bill.'

'But what if you forget me?' He stroked her cheek, his hard, strong fingers gentle now. 'What if I hadn't been there? I saw the look in that fellow's eyes. You were going to sleep with him weren't you?'

'No!' she protested. 'I ... I don't know. It gets so lonely, Bill.'

'I knew it.' He jumped up, tucked his shirt into his trousers.

'Wait!' Megan scrambled after him, a bramble catching at the hem of her dress. 'I wanted it to be you. I waited. Bill, you're the first, I promise you.' She buried her face against his back as he turned from her. 'I'm sorry ...' She began to cry. 'Please don't go.'

'Well I'm not going back to that house with those two la-di-da girls. You're changing, Megan.'

'I'm not!' she cried. She forced him to look at her, thumped his chest softly with her fist. 'I'm not changing.'

'Yes you are,' he said, his voice muffled as he pressed his lips to her head. 'I'll wait for you. I told you that. You know where I'll be.'

'After this is all over, it will be you and me.' She raised her face to his. 'Just us. We'll run the farm, and the airfield.'

'Maybe your parents would just hand it over to your cousins if they saw how you were living here, out all night with men.'

'No!' She shook her head. 'You can't tell them. It would break Ma's heart, and Da ...' A sob caught in her throat, she swallowed hard. 'Besides, I've got nothing to be ashamed of.'

'Carrying on with some fancy man, dressed like this ...'

'Like what?' she said.

'Come home, Megan,' he begged her. 'It only took me a couple of days to hitchhike down here. We could be back in Pembrokeshire the day after tomorrow.'

'No. I'll be back when our work is done.'

Bill stepped away from her, pulled his jacket on. He felt in the pocket, handed her something wrapped in tissue paper. 'I made this for you.' Megan was shivering with cold and emotion as she tore the paper away. 'It's a love spoon,' he said. 'I carved it myself.'

Megan turned the wood in her hand, her fingers tracing the smooth barley-sugar twist, the delicate bowl and heart. 'These are for weddings,' she said.

'I was going to ask you to marry me. I waited for your birthday.'

'What do you mean, was?'

'I don't want anyone else, Megan.' His face was anguished. He pulled her to him, crushed her lips beneath his one last time. 'I love you. You need to decide whether you love me enough to come home.'

'Bill, please ...' she begged, but he walked away, and in silence she watched him leave, dawn light dancing in rays through the leaves above her.

34

'This was a good idea,' Evie said as she strolled across Henley Bridge with Joy and a couple of the girls from the base. 'It's been rather tense at the cottage since all that business with Peter and the Welsh chap. Stella spends her days off moping around in her dressing gown, and I don't know what has got into Meggie. They're both as miserable as sin.' Evie swung the wicker picnic hamper into her other hand.

'How are you bearing up?' Joy asked as the other girls walked on ahead towards the riverbank.

Evie shrugged. 'I'm fine. You know how it is – good days, bad days,' she said quietly. 'I just miss Jack still.'

'We'll have to find some lovely chap to take your mind off things.'

Evie shook her head. 'It's too soon.' *I don't want to forget him,* she thought. As she watched young couples strolling by, Evie tried to remember how it felt to be with Jack, how it felt to have his arms around her, the sound of his laugh. His smile, she could recall clearly – disembodied, radiant, like the Cheshire Cat. A soldier walked along the grass nearby, arm in arm with a pretty young redhead. She caught a snatch of their conversation: '… when we get home, I'll cook a nice pie for your tea.' *Home,* Evie thought. Where was home? She looked at the happy, carefree faces around her and wondered whether everyone felt this lonely at heart. She wished there was someone waiting for her, somewhere.

Evie slipped on a pair of tortoiseshell sunglasses and looked out across the river as a rowing crew sculled silently past, the wake sparkling across the water like molten silver. 'This is glorious.'

'It's not the same without the Boat Race or the Royal Regatta, but the Leander Club's always fun.'

'Are you sure Beau won't mind us all pitching up?' Evie walked on.

'No! It's just a friendly thing. All the proper competitions have been suspended while the war's on – so many of the chaps are away fighting. The boys just like to get together when they can. In fact, a couple of my brothers are around somewhere ...' she nudged Evie.

'I told you, Joy,' Evie laughed. 'It's too soon.' They walked on in silence. 'I thought Beau was based in East Anglia now? Olivia must be pleased.'

'When I bumped into him in Maidenhead he mentioned he was rowing today, and I said a few of us might come along. He didn't say anything about Olivia. I don't know if it's on or off, frankly.' Joy waved at a friend. 'He asked after you,' she said lightly.

'Did he?'

'By the way, have you seen that scrappy little dog you rescued lately?'

'Ace? No, not for ages. How is he?'

'He's huge! I don't know what Beau is feeding him, but he's the picture of health. Ah, here we are.' Joy indicated an attractive red-brick building with white-painted woodwork. The girls filed into the Club. It was cool and shadowy after the bright sun. Evie slipped her sunglasses back on her head and signed in after Joy.

'This is lovely,' she said.

'I've been coming here for years. My family adores rowing, but I'm more of a spectator myself.' Joy caught the eye of a steward carrying a tray of cocktails. 'Mm, bliss,' she said as she sipped at a cold glass of Pimms.

'Thank you.' Evie took a drink from the silver platter.

'Shall we find a spot on the terrace?' Joy slipped a pair of opera glasses from her handbag.

'You came prepared!'

'Well,' she confided, 'I do like to get a good look at all these gorgeous chaps.' She scanned the river, where a handful of boats were lining up for the races. 'Look, there's Beau,' she said, pointing downriver to a coxless pair near the far bank. She handed Evie the opera glasses.

As Evie focused on the crew, the starting pistol rang out and she saw Beau flex, pull back on the oars, his powerful shoulders and thighs working in smooth motion. As the first boats neared the Club, they were neck and neck.

'Come on, boys!' Joy yelled. The crowd on the terrace cheered as Beau's team streaked in just ahead.

'They've done it,' Evie said. She lowered the glasses, feeling self-conscious, as if she were spying on Beau. She sipped her drink, the ice chinking in the glass as she crushed a mint leaf between her lips, relishing its fragrant, clear taste on her tongue.

'Let's go down and see them,' Joy said. Evie followed her, pushing through the crowd of men in blazers and panamas, and women in light summer dresses. By the time they reached the riverbank, the Club chairman was shaking Beau's hand.

'Beau!' Joy called and waved. 'I say, well done.'

He caught Evie's eye and smiled. 'Thank you.'

'Don't you get a trophy or something?' Joy looked disappointed.

'No, it's just a bit of fun,' he said. 'Hello, Miss Chase. I didn't know you were a fan.'

She caught the hot, fresh scent of him, the sweat glistening on his brow as the crowd pushed them together. 'Of rowing? I'm not really. Does this make you the King of the River or something?'

'In his dreams!' Joy laughed. 'Not a little race like this. It's the Head of the River anyway darling, for the winning team.'

'I'm sorry,' Evie said, 'I don't know much about ...' She felt

Beau watching her, and she was suddenly uncomfortable. 'I didn't know you rowed.'

'I don't get much of a chance these days.' Beau dried his face and hands on a white towel. 'I did a bit at university.'

'He's being modest,' Joy interrupted. 'Beau was an Oxford Blue. If it wasn't for this war I'm quite sure he'd be in the Olympics by now.'

'I don't know about that.' He glanced down.

'I hear Ace is doing well,' Evie said, painfully aware of the tension between them. 'I—'

'Alex! Alex!' a woman's voice interrupted. Evie looked up and saw Olivia bustling towards them, trailing a diaphanous white scarf. 'I've been searching everywhere for you … Oh.' She scowled as she spotted Evie. 'Who invited you?'

'Evie came with me, Olivia. A few of the girls are here,' Joy said. 'Didn't they do well?'

As Beau fell into conversation with the other team, the girls strolled along the riverbank. Evie tuned out Joy and Olivia's conversation, and glanced back at Beau. *What does he see in her?* she thought as she turned to the river. *Can you imagine putting up with that non-stop talking and that dreadful fake laugh every single day of your life* – The next thing she knew, someone had bumped into her, hard.

'No!' she cried, arms flailing for something to hold on to, but it was too late. Evie lost her footing and plunged into the chilly river.

'Evie!' Joy raced over.

'Oh dear,' Olivia said as Evie went under. 'Shouldn't someone do something?' She strolled away from the bank, twirling her scarf.

One of the stewards ran towards them with a boat hook. 'I've got you, Miss!' he called out as Evie surfaced, hair and pond weed plastered to her face. Evie spluttered, caught her breath as a crowd gathered on the riverbank. As a duck flapped away quacking with annoyance, she burst out laughing, and soon everyone joined in.

'Darling, you do look a fright!' Joy giggled as they hauled her out. Evie's thin summer dress clung to her. 'Someone get some towels!' She leant in to Evie and whispered, 'I saw her, Olivia pushed you deliberately.'

'Olivia? I'm bally well going to chuck her in too,' Evie murmured.

'Let's not make a scene, it's exactly what she wants. Be a good sport,' Joy said. 'She's clearly jealous of you.' She eyed Evie's dress. 'Heavens, do cover up, dear heart. You might as well be in your birthday suit!'

Evie glanced down, and modestly covered her chest. Soon she, and the crowd, were helpless with laughter.

'Well, Miss Chase.' Beau draped a soft white towel over her shoulders. 'It's normally the cox that gets a dunking.'

'Thank you.' She dried her face, looked up at him as he picked a strand of weed from her hair. 'Actually I was pu—'

'Oh!' Olivia held her hand to her forehead and swayed on her feet. Beau turned to her, and caught her just as she collapsed into his arms.

'Are you alright?'

'No. It's the heat, and this crowd ...' Her eyes flickered. 'Take me home, Alex.'

'Can't your parents?'

Olivia opened her eyes. 'I'm not well. Don't be a beast.'

Beau shot an apologetic look at the girls and led Olivia away.

'Come on.' Joy put her arm around Evie. 'Let's get you a stiff drink and some dry clothes.'

'Hateful girl.' Evie pulled the towel around her. 'What on earth has she got to be jealous about?'

'You mean you don't know? Oh Evie, you can be awfully dense sometimes.' When she saw the blank look on Evie's face, Joy laughed. 'It's Beau, darling. Olivia is jealous of you and Beau.'

35

Leaving the wide, elegant street, Beau and Olivia turned down a narrow alleyway and stopped in front of a run-down mansion block. Olivia collected her mail and flicked through the letters as they walked along a dark, umber-painted corridor that smelt of cabbage and cat's piss. 'Bills, bills, bills,' she sighed, unlocking her door.

'I can't stay,' Beau said as he looked with distaste around Olivia's flat. 'What happened to the place you were sharing in Kensington?'

'Oh, it was a silly little argument. You know how girls can be. I'm quite happy on my tod.' She walked past the tiny, cluttered bedroom to the living room, and knocked a sleeping white Persian cat from the only chair. It glared malevolently at her and paced towards the kitchenette, twitching its tail. Weak sun filtered through the grimy barred windows with crosses of tape on the panes as she tossed the letters into an overflowing wastepaper basket.

'How on earth can you live like this?'

'What do you mean?'

'This … mess.' He picked up an abandoned stocking and draped it over the chair.

'Darling, you know how it is. I can barely afford the rent let alone a maid.'

'You could get a job.'

'You are funny.'

'It wasn't a joke,' he said under his breath as she walked to the bedroom.

'At least stay for a glass of wine,' she called. 'For me? I get so lonely here by myself.'

Beau glanced impatiently at his watch. 'Alright, just one.'

'There's a bottle of red in the kitchen.'

Her unwashed coffee cup from the morning lay beside the sink, a congealed film of grease floating below the lipstick mark. Beau pushed aside the dirty plates and pulled out a bottle from behind the tea caddy. He took down a couple of glasses and looked dubiously at them before rinsing them under the gurgling, spurting tap. 'Where's the corkscrew?'

'It's in the drawer.' He looked around and, spotting the drawer by the telephone, reached over and pulled it open.

Olivia padded into the room wearing only a sheer, white dressing gown. 'That feels better,' she said. She wrapped her arms around his waist and laid her head against his back. 'It was so lovely spending the afternoon with you, and Mummy and Daddy ... Just like the old times, like a proper family again.' Her fingers pushed aside his tie, snaked between the buttons of his shirt.

'Like this you mean?' Beau put the bottle down.

'Oh yes, darling, just like this ...' She reached for his belt.

'No.' He was shaking.

'Shh ... Don't say anything. I know you're still cross with me, but I adore you, Alex, I always have, and I'll do anything to show you.' Her hand dropped below his belt. 'Anything.'

'Olivia.' His voice was low. 'What the bloody hell is this?' He pulled a heavy silver frame engraved with a swastika and laurel wreath from the drawer and turned on her, his eyes blazing.

'Alex, I ...' Her eyes flickered frantically.

Beau shook his head in disgust. 'I know your parents' politics ... But this?'

'It's just a family picture!'

He looked at the happy smiling faces in the photograph, the two cousins so alike. *And so like me*, he thought, a sour taste in his throat. Beside them, his aunt was smiling adoringly at the short, dark man with the clipped moustache standing next to her. She was arm in arm with Adolf Hitler. 'It's not just a picture!' Beau yelled. 'If I'd had any idea ...' He flung it face down on the floor. 'You're bloody lucky I don't report the whole lot of you. You'd be banged up along with all the other fascist aristos.' He glared at her as if he were seeing her for the first time. 'Why? How could you? You always told me you hated Nazism.'

'I told you a lot of things to make you happy,' she said calmly.

'Olivia.' He fought to control his anger. 'I have tried to forgive you for walking out on me, I truly have.'

'Alex, darling ...' she pleaded.

'No! I shall always be grateful for how your family cared for me as a child, but this is too much.'

'You can't leave me.' She shook her head, eyes wide, staring blankly. 'You can't leave me.'

'The thought that you ...' His face contorted. 'I trusted you. I believed you when you told me you had nothing to do with Mosley and the rest of them. It's over.' She clung to his arm, but he pushed past her.

'It's never over!' she screamed after him, a vein pulsing in her forehead as he flung the front door open. The cat seized its chance and raced after him, escaping into the dark corridor. Olivia crumpled to the carpet, her gown floating around her in a cloud of white as she thumped her fists on the floor. 'I'll never let you go, Alex,' she raged. 'We are meant for one another.' She heard the sound of his footsteps echoing down the corridor, the door hanging open, the thrum of the traffic outside. Then as it slammed closed, silence. She waited for him to return, to apologise, but the silence stretched on. As her breathing slowed, she reached over and picked up the photograph. She ran her fingers over the faces of her parents. Olivia thought of the wedding dress that hung expectantly in the wardrobe of her childhood bedroom, imagined walking down the aisle on her father's arm towards Beau. She pictured her mother's proud, triumphant face as she watched her daughter fulfil her destiny. 'I promise you, I'll never let him go,' she said under her breath. 'If *I* can't have you, no one can.'

36

Michael had started visiting the airfield a couple of times a week. The vicar approved of the idea of going out into the community and encouraged him to go and talk to the pilots and crew.

'The daily dangers they face,' he said reflectively to Michael as they took off their robes in the vestry after evensong. 'These brave men and women face death every day for us. The least we can do is offer a sympathetic ear, let them talk. If the sheep won't come to us, then the shepherd shall go out into his flock!' He laughed at his own joke.

For Michael, it was a chance to see Stella. She had been avoiding him since their trip to Cookham, and he longed to talk to her again. On his first few visits she had been out ferrying planes and he had returned home to his cosy flat disappointed. Today, as he strode into the mess, he spotted her immediately. The air was thick with pipe and cigarette smoke, Jean and her girls fighting to keep on top of the orders for tea and coffee. The weather was bad, and pilots were waiting impatiently for their chance to get airborne, playing darts and listening to the radio.

'Oh look, it's that dishy vicar...' Margie nudged Stella.

'Hello, Michael.' Stella stood as he walked towards her, her cheeks flushed. 'How are you?'

'I'm well. How are you?'

'Fine, I'm fine.' The conversation foundered. Stella felt as if all eyes were on them. 'Can I get you a tea?'

'That would be lovely.'

At the counter as they waited in awkward silence, she eyed the Bible in his hand. 'I heard you'd been visiting.'

'This?' He glanced at the book, so caught up in her that for a moment he had to think what it was he was carrying. 'Oh, yes, it seemed like a good idea. The vicar suggested ...' He saw she was smiling quietly to herself. 'You always can see through me.' Stella picked up their cups and chose a quiet table away from the crush. 'I was hoping to run into you,' he said as they sat down. 'You've stopped coming to church, and you haven't answered any of my letters.'

'I ... I've been very busy.'

'Stella.' He reached for her hand, hesitated, picked up a teaspoon and stirred his tea. 'I wanted to apologise. Clearly I've offended you. I feel a complete fool. If I've ruined our friendship...'

'No.' She looked quickly up at him, her eyes scanning his kind, handsome face. 'Please don't think that. You ...' She blinked quickly, raised her eyes to his. 'You mean a great deal to me, Mike.'

'Then don't hide away from me.' His eyes softened, lost their nervousness. 'Surely we can start again? As friends if nothing else.'

'Do you really think we could?' Stella ran her hands through her hair. 'I wish I could explain ...'

'You don't have to explain anything to me.' He took her hand, he didn't care who saw now. 'You've lost your husband, you're separated from your child, of course you don't want to rush into anything.'

A voice came over the tannoy: 'Hello, hello. Anson 9799. Will pilots Hughes, Moggridge, Ellis and Baxter-Jones please go to the waiting plane.'

The first group of pilots filed out of the mess, and Michael and Stella were alone in their corner now. He pulled out the chair next to hers, sat closer. 'Stella, I don't mean to pry, but I've seen it before with some girls when they've had a baby. Everyone gets blue for a while, but for some it just goes on and gets worse.'

Tears pricked her eyes, and she screwed them shut, trying to compose herself. 'I haven't told anyone. How did you know?'

Michael exhaled. He was right. 'I guessed.' He took her hand. 'I just want to help you get well. I'll wait for you, Stella, and if it's this,' he pointed at his collar, 'I'd give up the Church for you.'

'No, please, it's not that ...'

The loudspeaker crackled again. 'Hello, hello. Will pilots Keith-Jopp, Francis, Curtis and Grainger make ready, the next Anson is on its way.'

'I must go.' She gathered up her maps and ferry notes. They were alone now, only Jean behind the counter, busy with the girls doing the washing up.

'I do like that Tommy Handley,' Jean said to one of them.

'Go on Jean, do it!' The girls giggled. 'When you do that old-fashioned look and say—'

'Can I do you now, sir?' Jean mimicked.

'I don't mind if you do.'

Michael smiled as they roared with laughter. He turned Stella's hand over in his. 'Have you been to see a doctor?'

'No.' She shook her head. 'I was afraid they might take David away from me, and then, once he was safe,' she paused. 'I thought they might not let me fly. I'm fine.' She smiled bravely. 'All this fresh air, being so busy, it's given me a new purpose.'

'It's nothing to be ashamed of. It breaks my heart to think you have been going through this alone.' He leant closer to her. 'I've missed you so much, Stella. Let me help you,' he murmured, resting his head against hers.

As the mess door swung open they flew apart.

'Not interrupting anything am I?' Teddy asked as he marched towards them. 'Telegram from Singapore for you, Mrs Grainger.' He thrust a piece of paper towards her. 'As I imagine it's important I brought it myself rather than send Mikki.' He glared at the back of Michael's head, putting two and two together, then turned on his heel.

'Telegram?' she said vaguely, her heart still racing. She

unfolded it with trembling fingers. She scanned the lines, a look of horror growing on her face.

'What is it? Not bad news I hope?' Michael took the telegram from her, and read quickly. 'Wait a minute.' His brow furrowed in confusion. 'This is from Richard.'

Stella went very pale. 'My husband.'

'You said he was dead. I don't understand.' He looked down, read the telegram aloud. 'I miss you. I need you. Come home.' Michael twisted the piece of paper in his fist. He threw it onto the table and gathered up his coat and Bible.

'Michael, please,' she begged him. 'I never said he was dead, people just assumed. It was easier that way. No awkward questions.'

'Easier?' His voice shook with anger. 'How can it be easier to lie to people who love and trust you?'

She reached out to him, tried to take his hand but he snatched it away. 'Please, I can explain.'

'Go on then.' His eyes were cold now, his face set hard.

'Not here. I know this is a dreadful shock.' Stella was shaking, unable to look at him. 'I wanted to tell you a hundred times. When I started to feel—'

'No. Don't say it,' he said angrily. 'It all makes perfect sense now. How could you? How could you let me fall in love with you when you are still married to another man?'

'Please, Mike, I can explain everything.'

'No. I don't think anything you say can make this right.' He looked out towards the airfield, a stream of aircraft taking off. 'Go on. They're waiting for you.'

37

'Are you feeling any better?' Evie stuck her head around Stella's bedroom door. In the half light, Stella lay huddled under her blankets.

'No,' she said hoarsely.

Evie put a tray with a bowl of soup and a little vase of sweet peas on her bedside table. 'You must eat something eventually. The soup's fresh, Meggie picked the peas last night. Do have a little, you look washed out, darling.'

'I just want to die,' she said, her voice muffled by her pillow. Stella forced herself to look up at Evie. 'Why are you home? Is it lunchtime?'

'Yes, I had a half hour between flights so I thought I'd pop back and see how you are. Some of the girls were ferrying Spits this morning. It will be our turn soon – that's something to look forward to.' Evie sat down on the bed beside her. 'Do you want to talk about it? It was very brave of you to do your flight yesterday after that. You must be shattered.'

'I've been such a fool. Poor Mike, his face ... He was so angry with me he just stormed off.' She began to cry again.

'Why didn't you tell us Richard was still alive?'

'He's dead as far as I'm concerned,' she said, her voice breaking. 'It was easier to pretend. But ...' She took a deep breath. 'When

I got to know you all better, when we became friends …' She looked at Evie, her eyes full of tears. 'I wanted to tell you the truth but it was too late. When you lost Jack, and I saw you grieving, I felt like such a fraud.'

'Shh.' Evie stroked her hair. 'It doesn't matter. We all knew something was wrong. Why didn't you tell us?'

'How could I? Tell you that I'd lied to your faces, tell you that Richard was still alive.' Her heart twisted with pain. 'Our marriage died a long time ago. It died the day he started having an affair.'

'Affair? Oh God, Stella, you poor thing. Who was she?'

'The daughter of our housekeeper, if you can believe it.' Stella laughed bitterly. 'She can only have been sixteen, if that. All the time I was in bed, ill with my pregnancy, he was having it off with some slip of a girl.' She wiped away an angry tear. 'It wasn't so easy for him once I had the baby. But he'd still sneak out when he thought I was asleep.' Stella closed her eyes, tried to stop the angry tears from falling. 'I saw him one night, when I was feeding David.' She remembered the warm tropical night breeze on her skin, the light muslin of the nursery curtain as she brushed it aside. She saw him striding silently across the white tiled courtyard to the servants' quarters. The girl was waiting for him at the door, pulled him silently into the dark shadows. 'Can you imagine how the servants must have laughed at the stupid white woman, too blind to see that her husband was going from her bed straight to that little whore's.'

'You poor thing. Couldn't you have gone back to your mother's?'

'What and give her the satisfaction? No,' she shook her head. 'She was hardly sympathetic, and when I heard the ATA were recruiting women I applied straight away. As soon as I got the letter I booked a passage for me and David. I told Richard if he tried to stop me he'd never see his child again.' She sat up in bed, pulled her knees up to her chest. 'He wouldn't give me a divorce, but I'll get one, just as soon as the war's over. He made me promise to take David to his parents so that he would be safe at least.'

'Do you think you can trust them? They wouldn't try and take the baby?'

'No, they know what happened. When I confronted him, Richard said it meant nothing – he said all the men he knew were having it off with local girls. But my parents-in-law are decent people – I think they're thoroughly ashamed of how Richard has behaved. They're still hoping we'll get back together again after the war.'

'Will you?'

Stella hesitated. The anger and hurt she had carried inside her for months wavered. 'No,' she said firmly. 'I loved Richard very, very much, but he betrayed me when I needed him most. I'll never forgive him for that.'

'What about Mike?' Evie stroked her hair. 'Do you think he'll forgive you?'

Stella hung her head. 'Why should he? I'm a liar at best, and soon to be a divorcee. No vicar would marry a divorcee.'

'He asked you to marry him?'

Stella shook her head. 'He talked about a future together,' she said. 'He told me he's in love with me. But that was before he knew I am still married.' She screwed up her eyes, bunched her fists against them. 'It's all such a horrible, horrible mess.'

'Could I talk to him for you? I'm sure once he knew the whole story ...'

Stella shook her head. 'No, I have to sort this out for myself.' She hesitated. 'Mike said something. He thinks perhaps, well, I've been a little down since having David. He thinks I should see a doctor. What do you think?'

'I wouldn't go to Doc Barbour.' Evie instinctively folded her arms.

'He'd have me in my birthday suit again just to take my temperature,' Stella laughed through her tears.

Evie thought for a moment. 'I'll give Mary a call. I know she saw a super chap in Maidenhead after Charles was killed. He was very kind and I think he helped her a great deal.'

'Would you?'

They heard the sound of frantic knocking at the front door.

'Who on earth can that be?' Evie ran downstairs and flung the door open.

'Sorry, Miss,' Archie panted. 'Ops Room sent me to fetch you both. Parker said unless Mrs Grainger is on her death bed she has to fly. There's an emergency P1 job on – a load of planes are coming in from the factories and they're reassigning some of the flights. They need everyone.'

'Thank you. I'll see what I can do.' Evie thought quickly as Archie kick-started his motorbike and shot off up the lane. She ran upstairs to Stella, who was already dragging herself out of bed.

'Did you hear all that?'

'Yes. Oh God, I can't possibly fly like this. Can't you tell them I'm "femininely unwell"? That's usually enough to put the wind up Teddy.'

'It's a Priority 1, he won't be happy. I'd do it for you but my chit is full this afternoon.' She glanced at her watch. 'In fact I need to get back to the base. Where's Megan? Is she in town?'

'No, she's up at the farm.'

'Maybe she'll do it? I'll stop and pick her up.' Evie kissed Stella quickly. 'Get some rest. We'll sort all this out, don't worry.'

Evie raced downstairs. Outside, she yanked the covers off her car and threw them to the ground. The Aston started first time, and she roared up the lane. It was sweltering. The steering wheel was hot to her touch and heat seeped from the leather seat through the thin cotton of her shirt. She had been saving her petrol rations for a trip to London, but this was an emergency.

38

The lamb suckled hungrily at its bottle as Megan held it in her arms, its bony legs flailing.

'Steady on.' She laughed, settling down on a hay bale. The lamb wriggled urgently as it lay in her lap, and she stroked its soft, springy fleece. 'There's no hurry.' She rested her head back against an old wooden beam and closed her eyes, inhaling the sweet scent of the animals and the hay. In the distance she could hear the sound of the tractor coming in from the fields, the farmer heading home for lunch. Coming to the farm was a comfort to her. It reminded her of where she belonged. Here, she didn't have to worry all the time that she wasn't good enough. She wished she could see her parents, feel the comforting embrace of her mother. The lamb tossed his head impatiently. Megan glanced down. 'You finished that quickly,' she said, and put the glass bottle down.

'Fancy a bite of lunch, Megan?' the farmer asked, poking his head into the barn.

'Thanks, I'll be along in a minute.'

'You're doing a grand job with that little chap,' he said. 'Didn't think he'd make it when his mother went.'

Megan shifted the lamb under the crook of her arm and carried him over to the little pen she had made in the corner of the barn. She let him down gently into the bed of hay and he gambolled in, tossed his head and bleated. 'Now, you be good,' she said. 'I'll see you later.'

As she walked across the yard with the farmer, a car swung into view.

'Meggie!' Evie called. 'Come quickly! They need us at the airfield – there's a bunch of P1s coming in. Stella can't do it.'

Megan groaned. 'Evie, I flew all day yesterday and that ruddy night-train ...' She took a deep breath. 'Don't worry, I'll do it for her.'

'Good girl!'

As Evie sped along the lanes she glanced over at Megan. 'You do look tired. If we make it back to base tonight, do you fancy going out for a drink later? A few of the girls are going up to the Riviera and I could do with a dance. I should think it would do you good to get out after all that drama with Peter and Bill.'

'That would be nice.' Megan gazed out across the golden summer fields as they whizzed past. 'How's Stella? I can't believe she lied about her husband.'

'She had her reasons,' Evie said. 'I'm sure she'll tell you about it.'

'What a glorious day. It's such a shame we haven't had a chance to swim in the river yet. Well, of course, some of us have! I wish I'd seen you, Evie. Joy said you looked like a mermaid!' Megan giggled as Evie poked out her tongue. 'We could take a picnic. Maybe we could hire a boat for the day?'

'That would be fun. I don't know where the time is going these days, we're so busy.' Evie turned the car into Cherry Orchard Lane. 'Talking of which, you're late aren't you? We're always exactly the same time, you and me ...'

Megan blushed. 'Late? You mean my monthly ... Oh, I'm fine.' As the weeks had come and gone she had frantically checked the calendar. 'I was just a bit late. I wasn't worried.'

Evie pulled up outside the offices. Pilots were streaming through the office doors. 'So you did it?' Evie said, her eyes wide. 'Peter?'

Megan shook her head. 'Bill.' She blushed. 'I did wonder … I even wrote to Ma, but it's fine.' She stared at her hands. 'Part of me even hoped I was pregnant. I love him, Evie. When this is all over, I just want to go home and run the farm with him. When I thought I might be having his baby … It made me realise what I really want.'

'Well,' Evie said as she jumped out of the car, 'at least that's one less thing to worry about at the moment.' She hugged Megan. 'I'm happy for you. Peter will be disappointed of course.'

'Could you tell him for me? I haven't had the heart to call him. Tell him I think he's wonderful, but—'

'You're in love, and you're going home?'

'Not straight away. I mean, I hope Bill and I will get married soon, but everything we're doing here matters so much.'

'I do envy you, you know.' Evie took her arm as they walked to the offices.

'You? You envy me?' Megan laughed.

'Well, you're so lucky. You know where you want to be, and the way you talk about your family, and Bill …' Evie smiled at her. 'I envy you your certainty. Sometimes I wonder if I'll ever find a place that feels like home.' She raised her voice above the hubbub as they reached the offices. Pilots were racing out onto the field, grabbing their chits from the corridor on the way.

'Right,' Teddy shouted above the noise. 'Our boys need a fresh lot of Hurricanes and Spits at their squadrons. There's a big P1 delivery coming in from the factories through the other pools, so we need to clear today's planes. Half of you will be ferrying the factory planes on to their squadrons. The rest of you I need to clear the field on the double.'

The girls changed quickly in the cloakroom, and Megan pulled on her Sidcot suit. 'Do you think it matters that I'm in mufti?' she asked Evie.

'No, you'll be fine. Here, you can borrow one of my shirts and a tie. As long as you keep your suit fastened they won't know you've got muddy old dungarees on underneath.'

Megan tugged the zip closed. 'Right, let's go and see what we're dicing with.' She followed Evie out to the busy corridor. As she slung her flight bag onto her shoulder, her ferry notes dropped to the floor unnoticed.

Evie checked her chit. 'Mine's stayed the same. I've got a Harvard to Aston Down. Ruddy noisy things.'

Megan picked up Stella's chit and read it quickly. 'Oh! My first fighter. A P40 Tomahawk I.' Her face fell. 'It's an NEA on the way to the scrapyard. I hate those NEAs,' she said. 'Why they don't just tow them to the yard I don't know. They reckon there's one more flight left in them but I've heard of girls having canopies blow off, floors drop out ...'

'You'll be fine. It's no more of a hot potato than any of the planes we fly. I wonder what's wrong with it? I heard No. 112 Squadron were taking all the Tomahawks they could get their hands on.' She glanced at Megan. 'Come here a sec.' Evie brushed a speck of dirt from Megan's face. 'There are some advantages to farm work – free mudpacks.'

'Oh, get on with you.' Megan giggled and hoisted her parachute over her shoulder.

Evie read Stella's chit. 'You've not flown a Tomahawk before? Frightful things. Don't forget about the French throttle.'

'Thanks. I haven't got time to read the handling notes, but don't worry I'll figure it out.'

As soon as they had finished checking with the Meteorological Office, the Ops Room called the numbers of several planes over the tannoy, including Megan's Tomahawk. The girls walked out into the sunshine.

'I've got to go. Will you let Teddy know it's me not Stella?'

'Sure.'

Megan grimaced. 'Eugh, look at it.' The Tomahawk's fuselage was painted with a gaping shark's mouth. 'Well, they'll certainly see me coming.'

'See you tonight,' Evie called.

'Cheerio!' Megan waved as she walked across the airfield to the waiting plane.

Evie leant against her car and lit a cigarette as she waited for her Harvard to be called. There was something about the way Megan walked, a slight skip and spring to her step that always made her seem like a little girl.

'You're still here, Miss Chase? Run along now.' Teddy shooed her towards the field.

'I was waiting to give you a message, sir.' Evie turned towards him. 'Mrs Grainger is femininely unwell.' Teddy's face went grey as he looked at the Tomahawk. She loved the reaction that choice phrase caused.

'Which pilot is that?'

'Megan Jones. Why?'

'Oh dear. The unfortunate Jones.' He paused. 'I ...'

'Yes?'

'Nothing. Tomahawks are damn tricky, that's all.'

Evie ground her cigarette under her heel. 'Megan will be fine.'

'Your plane is ready, Miss,' one of the engineers called over to her. By the time she turned back, Teddy was marching back towards the offices at high speed.

'I say!' Joy ran out onto the field towards Evie. 'Where's Megan? I just found this on the cloakroom floor. Miss Gold was going to put it up on the lost property board but they'd have Megan's guts for garters if they knew she'd lost her ferry notes.'

'Thanks, darling.' Evie grabbed the book. 'Meggie can't have noticed.' Evie raced across the field, waving to Megan to hold on. She jumped up onto the wing of the Tomahawk and found her rummaging in her flight bag. 'Lost something?' She smiled as she handed over the ferry notes.

Relief flooded Megan's face. 'Thanks, you're a star.'

Evie jumped down. 'Have fun!'

Megan flicked through the book until she found the page for the Tomahawk. She quickly scanned the instructions and settled back in the cockpit. She cranked the lever on the right of her seat, adjusting it until she was comfortable. A lever on the left shifted her harness. *Right*, she said to herself, fastening the straps. *Here we go.* As she waited for the signal to start up the engine, she looked around the cockpit. She noticed the pilot's relief tube suspended from the bottom of her seat. *Won't be needing that,* she thought, and giggled. *Only a short hop, then you're off to the scrapyard old girl.*

The circuit was full of aircraft, someone landing or taking off every second it seemed. As Megan waited for her turn she made sure her landing gear was locked, and that the fuel selector was set to the reserve tank. She drummed her fingers on the control panel, eager now to be in the air. She ran through the drill as she waited: *Ignition switches checked ... Flaps neutral ...* Finally, they gave her the signal. As the engine had been standing, she turned it over by hand. *Right, carburettor to cold ... Radiator shut.* The 1360 hp engine roared into life as she started it, and she frowned as she increased the throttle to 800 rpm. *That feels horrible,* she thought as she pulled back on the lever and the Tomahawk lumbered forward.

As she taxied over, joining the queue of aircraft waiting to take off, Megan couldn't wait to put the plane through its paces. When it was her turn, as the Tomahawk had been ticking over for a while, she ran the engine up against the brakes to clear it. She remembered the girls talking about this aircraft, swapping tips in the mess, and as it surged forward along the runway and into the wind she opened the throttle slowly. She felt a slight swing as she took off, used a little right rudder. As the ground dropped away and the aircraft climbed at 150 mph, she thought as she always did of flying out over Barafundle Bay. She found it always calmed her to think about flying the old Moth, with her brother Huw behind her. She had never managed to convince Bill to come up with her. *But I will,* she thought, smiling to herself. She checked her instruments systematically as she climbed into the clear blue sky. The Tomahawk felt a little unstable to her, but as she cranked the sliding glass canopy closed, it steadied. In her mind, she was skimming out over the Pembrokeshire coast, above the glittering sea, her nerves forgotten. Safely in the air, she retracted the landing gear, the wheels locking flush with the wings. The Tomahawk rose, and White Waltham fell away beneath her. *There we go*, she thought, settling back for the flight. Then she heard the engine sputter.

Megan's stomach tightened, a chill coursed down her spine as she waited for it to catch again. It flared, and she exhaled. But something was wrong. She was up too high now to land easily, the plane banking over the fields. She shielded her eyes from the glaring light. She was pointing directly at the sun and she was completely blinded.

'No,' she whispered under her breath as the engine cut out again. Below her, everyone on the field had stopped and was watching Megan fight hopelessly with the stricken plane.

Think, Megan told herself. She couldn't understand what was wrong with the aircraft. She checked the instruments. Nothing made sense. In her panic as the engine began to cut out again, she pushed forward on the throttle, and it cut out entirely.

'Oh God, no!' she cried out as the Tomahawk shuddered. The right wing dropped, then the nose. The aircraft was buffeting, tumbling towards the earth, five tons of armoured metal screaming downwards, like a boulder pitching out of the sky. Megan tried frantically to pull it out of the vicious stall. She felt as if she was watching herself, her hands clutching at the stick as the ground came up to meet her. All the stories about this plane came back to her in a flash. She remembered someone describing how they had seen one tumble 'arse over tea-kettle' out of the sky. She could hear herself shouting, straining to get the aircraft level. 'God!' she yelled, 'please, I don't want to die!'

Megan glanced quickly at the red emergency hood release on the forward frame of the cabin roof, imagined bailing out and parachuting to safety. She checked her height. She was too low. She looked blindly at the panel, at the whirling dials, pictured them smashing, splintering. She thought of the flames.

Her mouth was dry as she bit her top lip. She checked her speed. At 95 mph she could chance a steep glide back into the airfield. *Or any field*, she thought desperately. She was so low now, she would have to land with her undercarriage up. She stared, transfixed, as the golden summer fields came into focus, came close enough for her to make out the cars on the roads.

Snap out of it, a voice in her head told her. *You can do this.* Megan summoned all her strength, and pulled back on the stick. She tried to get the heavy nose of the plane under control as the Tomahawk banked around. She remembered to lower her flaps, but in her panic she forgot to shut off the fuel as she readied herself for the crash landing. 'Ma!' she cried out, choking down a desperate sob as the earth hurtled towards her, the wind screeching across the canopy. 'Ma!'

The wingtips brushed the treetops as she came down. That was the last thing she noticed, seeing the leaves in all their dazzling beauty, so close to her now, the sunlight catching on them like the waves on the sea. She heard the sounds of the trees rushing by, the shuddering crash as the wings came away, the fuselage ploughing into the copse, the roar as it plunged into the earth and she was thrown forward, glass and metal fracturing, exploding in slow motion.

The silence flooded in as she lay slumped, her head against the instrument panel. She blinked, something dark and wet clouding her eye as she looked across the fields through the broken window. She tried to move, but couldn't. She could see her arm, limp at her side. She blinked again. She could hear something dripping. The smell of petrol burnt her throat as she gasped, her lungs forcing a last, desperate breath into her body. 'Ma, help! Ma!'

The smoke wisped up through the cockpit floor, and Megan closed her eyes.

39

The 400 Club was packed, the dance floor overflowing as couples moved to Fat Tim's Band. For once neither the music nor the glamorous London crowd did anything to lift Evie's spirits. In the last sleepless days her thoughts had returned again and again to Megan's crash.

'Get the blood wagon!' Commander Francis had yelled. Evie had watched the ambulance racing across the airfield in the direction Megan had taken. She had prayed silently as the cars and motorbikes tore after it, cutting across the lanes and rutted fields. She had jumped on the back of one of the bikes, clinging to the driver. Then, suddenly, an explosion. A pall of dark smoke and vivid flames leapt up from behind the hedge as they drew alongside. She screamed Megan's name, and ran, stumbling across the cornfield to the crash site. The Tomahawk had ploughed straight into a copse of trees, its wings broken and scattered. Teddy was ahead of her, his arms shielding his face as he tried to reach the plane. Evie could see Megan's body silhouetted against the orange flames licking ferociously around the fuselage. She was slumped forward, her head resting against the control panel.

'Get back!' Teddy had yelled, pushing Evie clear. Evie fought him, punched him hard and struggled free. She sprinted towards the burning plane, crying out Megan's name. Teddy ran after her, and wrestled her to the ground as the petrol tank exploded.

Evie tasted earth in her mouth, the leaping flames scorching her skin even from that distance. Teddy scrambled to his feet, dragged her with him as Baldwin's fire crew aimed their jets at the wreckage.

'What would you like to drink?' Peter pulled her chair out for her as she sat down.

'Sorry?' Evie looked vaguely at him.

'How about a brandy?' He gently squeezed her shoulder. 'It looks like you could do with one, old girl.' Peter's concern was written across his face. 'I am glad to see you.'

'I just had to get away. Bert gave me a lift up in the ATA van. He had some spares to drop at Paddington.' She hung her head. 'I wanted to tell you myself. I'm so sorry, Peter.' She took his hand over their table. 'Megan was awfully fond of you.'

'I don't know, Evie.' He shrugged. 'I think she would have gone with that chap who looked like Errol Flynn. Don't have much luck with love, do I?'

What was the point in telling Peter the truth? Evie thought. 'You and me both.' She smiled bravely as she looked around the club. It was as busy as ever and she recognised several old friends. The maître d' had told her that her father was there too, entertaining friends somewhere in among all the mirrored pillars. She longed to see him, but she was too proud. *He could have called me,* she thought.

'We all feel awful,' she said finally. 'Stella's blaming herself, I'm blaming myself ...'

'It's nobody's fault. Accidents happen, especially with those old NEAs. The ATA has the most marvellous record if you think of how many planes you chaps are handling every day. From what I hear you girls have a better safety rate than the men.'

'Still ...' Evie shook her head. 'I just can't make any sense of it. I know it was an old plane ... Perhaps she forgot the backwards throttle?'

'They are tricky. It can happen, you know. All it takes is a split second. Chaps have lost their lives for much sillier reasons.' He sipped his drink. 'You're going to the funeral?' he asked, and took out his wallet. 'Can you get some flowers for me? Something fresh, and pretty – like her.'

Evie pushed his money away. 'Don't worry, I'll get some from all of us.'

Peter thought he had never seen her look so heartbroken. 'How are you, old girl?' When she said nothing, he chattered on. 'I thought someone had beaten me to it, when you got engaged, but there's still a chance ...' A tear trickled down Evie's cheek and Peter pulled a clean handkerchief from his breast pocket and handed it to her.

'It's too much, Peter,' she said quietly. 'I can't bear it. Charlie, Jack, now Megan. All these people I love, and all so young, with such hopeful lives ahead of them.' She took a deep sip of her drink. 'Being here, I keep thinking of the first time we took her to the Riviera. She was dancing with some fellow. I remember looking at her as he threw her up into the air. Her face ...' She stifled a sob. 'She was so happy. So full of joy. It's not fair.' Her voice shook with anger. 'Why her?'

Peter took her hands, kissed her fingers gently.

'Miss Chase?' someone cut in.

Evie looked up to see Beau in a tuxedo, an elegant blonde on his arm.

'Hello, sir,' she said, composing herself. She coolly returned the blonde's curious gaze.

'Glad to see you've dried off.'

Evie glared at him. How could he be so flippant when she had just lost Megan?

Peter stood and shook his hand. 'Good to see you, sir.'

'How's the arm, Peter?'

'I'll be back in action soon.'

'Jolly good.'

'Congratulations by the way, I heard they gave you the DFC.'

'Yes.' Beau looked at Evie. 'That's why we're here. I have a couple of days' leave and we thought we'd celebrate. Enjoy your evening.'

'How do you know Beau?' Peter asked Evie.

'He was my instructor.'

'I'd forgotten he was seconded to your lot for a bit.'

'Why? How do you know him?'

Peter lit a cigarette. 'Everyone knows Beau. Haven't you heard of his reputation? He's one of the best fighter pilots we have. Absolutely fearless, and more kills than anyone.'

'He's certainly ruthless.' Evie stared at him as he put his arm around the blonde's waist at the bar. 'What happened to good old Olivia? Looks like he's already moved on.' She knocked back the rest of her brandy.

'I know what would cheer you up,' Peter said. 'Why don't you ask Tim if you can sing with the band?'

Evie frowned. 'I'm not in the mood.'

'Oh, ha! Good joke, Evie – "In the Mood"!'

Peter was beginning to irritate her. 'I'm just going to powder my nose,' she said, and gathered up her black velvet evening bag.

Peter sat alone, watching the dancers, lost in his thoughts. Someone tapped him on the shoulder, and he turned. 'Leo? Hello, sir, have you seen Evie?'

'No, no I haven't, Peter. I have a feeling she might not want to see me,' he said. 'I just wanted to check how she is.'

'Not so good. She ...' He hesitated. 'We lost a good friend, one of the girls she's been billeted with. Megan.'

'Oh dear, I am sorry. The lovely Welsh girl?'

'Evie's rather cut up about it. I said she should sing a couple of songs, cheer us all up.'

'Good idea. I haven't heard her sing for ages.' Leo beckoned to the maître d' and whispered something in his ear. 'I'm just over there with a party of friends,' Leo said to Peter, indicating the best seats in the house. 'If Evie ... Well, if she wants to see me, you know where I am.'

The maître d' took Evie to one side as she walked to her table.

'Miss Chase, your father thought you might like to sing.'

'He did, did he?' Evie raised an eyebrow. 'Is my stepmother with him?'

'No. Mr Chase has a friend with him tonight.' The band played the closing bars of 'Stardust'. Peter saw her shaking her head, but before the dancers had time to leave the floor, Fat Tim turned to the microphone.

'Tonight, ladies and gentlemen, I'd like to welcome a young lady we always love to play with, Miss Evelyn Chase!'

'Oh, very well,' Evie said reluctantly. The maître d' guided her to the bandstand. As she stepped in front of the chrome microphone, she looked out across the dark room, the spotlight dazzling her.

'Thank you, Tim,' she said. 'I'd like to sing one of my favourite songs from *Right This Way*.' She caught Leo's eye. They had often listened to the tune together. He raised his glass to her and smiled sadly. He knew she must be thinking of Megan as the band launched into the tune, and Evie began to sing:

> *'I'll be seeing you*
> *In all the old familiar places ...'*

'Well I never.' Beau looked up from the bar and turned to see her perform. Her rich, clear voice soared with the opening melody. It made the hairs rise on Beau's neck like a caress.

'How do you know her?' The blonde eyed Evie curiously.

'She's the one I was telling you about.' He leant back against the bar.

'Marvellous voice.'

'Yes.' A smile twitched on his lips. 'It's what I love about her. Full of surprises.'

> *'I'll find you in the morning sun ...'*

Evie sang her heart out, her voice rich with emotion and loss. Beau felt like she was looking directly at him.

> *'And when the night is new.*
> *I'll be looking at the moon,*
> *But I'll be seeing you.'*

As the song ended, she bowed, and left the stage to cheers and clapping.

'Excuse me for a moment,' Beau said to his companion.

'You won't be long will you?' The blonde touched his arm.

'Would I abandon you in a place like this?' Beau kissed her on the cheek.

She raised her glass to him. 'Tally ho, Alex.'

The club was packed, and Beau searched in vain for Evie. Finally he went to her table. Peter was just putting on his overcoat and leaving a tip for the waiter.

'Where's Evie?' Beau asked.

'She said she had to leave, she's rather cut up.' Peter said. 'I asked her if she wanted a lift but she said she had a train to catch. She's going to Wales for Megan's funeral tomorrow afternoon.'

'Funeral? Christ, I had no idea.' His face fell. After Peter had filled him in on the details he shook his head. 'Bad business. Poor Evie, they were very close.' Beau looked at Peter. 'Tell me, are you and she ...?'

'Evie? We do have a little bet. If she's not engaged by the time she turns twenty-one in November then we'll get married.'

'November,' Beau said quietly. 'Listen, Peter, could you do me a favour? You see that delightful blonde girl at the bar?'

'I'll say.'

'Would you mind escorting her home to Eaton Terrace? I have to sort out a couple of things.'

Peter straightened his bow tie. 'Not at all. Won't she mind? I mean she came with you, sir.'

'I think you'll find my sister delightful company.' Beau patted him on the back, and made his way out of the club.

40

The birds did not know that they should not be singing so joyfully. They did not know that the world was at war, and that Megan was being buried that day.

'It should have been me,' Stella said tearfully as they stood before the plain pine coffin in the little chapel in Wales. 'It was my flight. It should have been me.'

Evie slipped her arm around her friend. 'No. You must never think that,' she said. When she looked at her friend's red-rimmed eyes, she saw her own grief and guilt reflected there. Organ music played softly, and the chapel smelt of chrysanthemums. It was full to the gallery, people talking in low voices as they waited for the service to begin. Evie reached out, touched the warm wood of the casket with her hand. She laid down a simple arrangement of white flowers and placed a pair of gold ATA wings beneath them. 'Goodbye, Megan,' she whispered, tears brimming in her eyes. The girls turned and walked down the aisle to their seats. Evie saw Bill in the front pew, his head bent in sorrow next to a grey-haired couple she guessed must be Megan's parents. The man had his arm firmly around his wife's shoulders, his head held resolutely high.

As they waited for the service to begin, Evie heard the metallic tap of military shoes on the chapel's tiled floor. *One of ours,* she thought.

'May I?' Beau stopped at their pew, and the girls squeezed up to let him in.

He looked at them both. 'I'm so sorry.'

'Sir? I didn't expect you to be here,' Evie whispered. Her hand was close to his, his hip pressed against hers. As he leant to talk to her, her hair brushed his cheek.

'Peter told me last night, I had no idea. I'm so sorry. It was the least I could do to come and pay my respects. I helped train her.' He gazed up at the coffin. 'She was a lovely girl.'

The organ fired up, and the congregation stood. 'Where's your friend?' Evie asked.

'Friend?' Beau whispered.

'From the 400.'

Beau's face relaxed. 'I left her in London.' Evie glanced up at him as they began to sing, her clear voice joining the powerful male voices of the choir, soaring to the rafters. The Methodist priest walked out in front of the altar, the vicar of White Waltham and Michael at his side.

'Look!' Evie nudged Stella. Above the heads of the congregation, Stella's eyes met Michael's.

As the coffin was lowered into the ground, Megan's mother wept quietly. Evie couldn't believe that was their friend, lovely irrepressible Megan, in the coffin. Her throat constricted as she thought of her on her birthday night, Megan's laughter as they had helped her get ready. She remembered her face when she unwrapped Evie's present, her excitement at having her first pair of beautiful evening shoes for her date with Peter. *Our lily of the valley*, Evie thought as she hung her head, unable to stop the tears rolling down her cheeks now. She glanced up at Bill, his face contorted with grief, and wondered if she should tell him that Megan had loved him, that she had talked of coming home to him. *No, it would just make it harder*, she thought.

The congregation filed out of the churchyard past Megan's parents. 'You must be Evelyn and Stella.' Rhodri shook their hands. 'Megan told us so much about you. Your room is all ready for you.'

'Are you sure it's no trouble? We could stay in the village.'

'Wouldn't hear of it.' Rhodri squeezed her arm.

'You will come back to the house, won't you?' Nia said to Beau.

'Of course.' Beau shook her hand. 'I am sorry for your loss. Megan was a brave girl, and an excellent pilot.'

'Thank you.' Her grief-stricken face lifted and shone with pride.

As Beau, Evie and Stella worked their way down the line of mourners, Stella came face to face with Michael. 'Hello, Stella,' he said awkwardly.

'Michael. I'm so glad you're here.'

'Are you?' He held her gaze as they shook hands.

'Yes, Megan was awfully fond of you.'

He took his hand away, a hurt look in his eyes.

'It was the least we could do,' the vicar cut in. 'Such a tragic loss. We're keen to support our brave men and women at White Waltham any way we can,' he explained to the minister.

'It's always a pleasure to welcome other faiths to our chapel on occasions like this.' The young minister patted him on the back. They turned and walked towards the cars. 'You'll be coming up to the house won't you now?'

'I don't know.' Michael looked across at Stella. 'It's a long drive back …'

'You're not going back tonight, I won't hear of it!' The minister stopped him. 'There's a bed for you both at my house. Drive back in the morning.'

Evie found Beau talking to Pauline. 'Hello, Commander Gower,' she said.

'What a tragedy,' Pauline shook her head. 'Poor Megan.'

'Do they know yet what caused the crash?' Stella asked.

'Mechanical failure. Nothing Megan or anyone could have done about it.' Pauline pulled on her gloves. 'I must be getting back I'm afraid. Hatfield called just before the funeral, there's some flap on as usual.' She looked at the girls, the dark shadows under their red-rimmed eyes. 'Look, why don't you take a day off tomorrow rather than taking the train first thing? Get some rest. You're no good to me in this state,' she said gently. 'Beau, you have a car don't you?'

'Yes, Commander.' He indicated a black Jaguar SS. Ace was lolling in the passenger seat, his head hanging out of the window.

'Could you drop the girls at the airfield on the way back to your squadron?'

'It would be a pleasure,' he said. He took Evie's arm as Stella trailed behind, talking to Pauline. 'Well done,' he said. 'That must have been ghastly for you.'

Evie nodded mutely. 'It was very decent of you to come all this way, sir.'

'As I said, it was the least I could do for Megan.' He paused as he opened the car door. 'And for you.'

Evie sat next to Beau as they drove along the coast road, sunlight dancing on the surf below them. 'It's beautiful here,' she said. 'It reminds me of the Med. I can just imagine Megan as a little girl, running wild ...' She blinked away fresh tears. 'What happened to your motorbike?'

'It's at the base. I must be getting old,' he said. 'Didn't fancy racing halfway across the country on it with a German Shepherd riding pillion, so I borrowed this from my sister.'

Ace reached over from the back seat and licked Evie's face. She turned and stroked the dog. 'You have a sister?'

'My "friend" at the 400.' He glanced at her, a smile playing on his lips.

'She's very beautiful.' Evie tried not to show her relief. 'When I saw you at the club, I thought ...'

'If I didn't know any better I would have said you were jealous, Miss Chase. That was quite a performance last night.'

'It wasn't for your benefit, if that's what you're thinking,' she said coolly. A warm sea breeze lifted Evie's hair as they drove. 'I thought perhaps you'd finally tired of Olivia.'

'I have. I ended things with her after that scene in Henley. I heard from one of the chaps that he saw her deliberately push you in—'

'So you broke up with her?'

'Not only because of that. It made me realise how immature she still is.' He turned to Evie. 'She never did like sharing her toys.'

'I'm sorry,' Evie said, as her heart skipped in her chest.

'Don't be. I should have broken it off months ago. Olivia is still refusing to accept it's over, but as far as I'm concerned, it is.' He glanced at Evie's profile. 'I'm a free man.'

Stella sat in the back next to Ace, pretending to take in the scenery, one eye fixed on the minister's car bumping along behind them. She could make out Michael's silhouette, his square jaw as he turned and spoke to the minister. The cars parked in the farmyard.

'Oh, this is lovely,' Stella said as she clambered out of the back seat. 'It reminds me of my in-laws' place in Ireland.'

'Really?' Michael said coldly. She turned to him.

'Not that I remember much, I only went there once—' she started to say, but it was too late, he had already walked on into the house.

The farmhouse was subdued but bustling with visitors, cups of tea on every surface, sandwiches and cakes piled high. Staffordshire pottery crowded the mantelpiece above the range, with red geraniums spilling down over lace doilies. A gentle hum of voices, Welsh mingling with English, filled the air. Evie spotted Bill sitting in a corner, a pint of beer in his hand. From his ruddy cheeks she guessed he had been drinking steadily all day.

'Hello again,' she said. 'I'm so sorry. Megan loved you very much.'

Bill glared up at her, glassy eyed. 'Love? What would someone like you know about love?' He rose unsteadily and pushed past her.

'What did she see in him?' she muttered crossly.

'The man's grieving,' Beau said, reaching for a beef sandwich.

She followed Bill's path outside. He stopped in front of two men – one short and fat, the other tall and scrawny with wire-framed spectacles. Within moments, an argument started. Bill pushed the fat one, and the scrawny one laid into him. Rhodri stormed outside.

'Do you have no respect?' he roared. 'This is my little girl's funeral!' His voice broke. Nia ran out to him, put her arms around him. 'No, no it's alright.' He composed himself and turned to the men. The scrawny one let go of Bill's collar and dusted himself down. Bill whistled for the dogs and set off across the fields alone.

'I am sorry,' Rhodri said to the gathering, and the murmur of conversation resumed.

'Imagine,' a woman nearby said in a low voice. 'Now Megan's gone, surely he's not going to leave the farm to Bill?'

'No,' another woman gossiped, 'it'll go to the cousins for certain.'

'So that's who they are,' Evie whispered to Stella. 'Remember those creeps Megan was always talking about? The ones trying to get the farm away from her after her brother was killed?' She looked over at Megan's mother, her lovely sorrowful face, and wondered what on earth it was like to lose both your children. 'I could do with some air,' she said. 'How about you? We could take Ace for a walk.'

As they stepped into the yard, she saw Beau deep in conversation with Michael, the dog sitting obediently at his side. She slipped her arm through Stella's. 'Hello boys,' she said. 'Fancy a walk? Megan told us there's an airstrip around here somewhere on the farm. Why don't we give her a proper send off?' She flashed them a bottle of champagne she had brought from home to toast Megan. Michael glanced uncertainly at Stella but fell in step as Beau walked with the girls.

'Cigarette?' Beau asked Evie.

'Yes please.' Her arm slipped from Stella's. 'It was a lovely service, wasn't it?'

Beau took two Player's from his silver case, lit them and passed

her one. 'That's the kind of thing people always say at funerals.'
He exhaled as they walked on. 'A lovely service. It's like "you
must be very proud" at weddings and christenings.'

'I was only trying to make small talk.' Evie blew smoke
sharply away.

'Well don't,' he said. 'It's one thing I like about you. You don't
chatter on like most women.'

Evie looked up to where Stella and Michael were talking as
they walked across the field ahead.

'Is that a compliment, sir?'

'Perhaps.' He slipped his hand into his pocket. 'And for God's
sake call me Alex. I'm not your instructor any more and you're
not in the Service.'

The wind lifted her hair as she turned to him. He had grown
more tanned since she saw him last, his hair bleached golden
white in the sun. 'Mmm ... no.'

'What do you mean, no?'

'It reminds me of Olivia.' Evie thought of her flickering eyes,
the thin, insistent whine of her voice: *Aaaalex*. 'I shall call you
Beau whether you like it or not, because that is what you will
always be to me.'

He laughed and shook his head. 'Very well.'

'And no more Miss Chase ever again, thank you. It always
makes me feel like you're about to tell me off.'

'Someone has to keep you in line.'

Evie put her hand on her hip. 'Maybe I don't like being kept
in line.'

'Maybe you do.' Beau half smiled. 'I shall call you Eve. It suits
you better than Evie.'

'Oh really?'

He stepped closer to her. 'Or possibly Evelyn if you're
very naughty.'

She nudged him playfully, and walked on. 'It is good to see
you, you know.'

'And you.' He fell into step easily beside her. 'When I heard
one of the girls had come down, I thought ...'

'You assumed it was me?'

'I must admit it was a relief to see you at the 400. You do fly like a maniac.'

'I learnt from the best.' She glanced at him out of the corner of her eye.

'I realised ...' He paused. 'I realised how I would have felt if it was you. How much I would have missed you.'

'I've missed you too.' Evie found the words escaping her lips before she could stop herself.

He turned to her, began to say something.

'It's over here!' Stella interrupted, waving her arm in the direction of the hangar. They walked faster to catch them up.

Beau and Michael heaved open the hangar doors. Ace rushed in, chasing something that scuttled into the shadows.

'Rhodri said the RAF has taken their old Moth,' Stella said. She stepped into the half light, looking around the empty hangar. She turned, gazed out across the sea. 'This really is the most glorious place in the world,' she said as she joined Michael in the sun outside.

Evie took the champagne from her inside coat pocket.

'You could always be a poacher after the war with a coat like that,' Beau said as she handed him the bottle to open. 'I don't suppose you have any glasses hidden in there?' He eased the cork out, sending it flying into the sky. 'To Megan,' he said, and passed it to Evie.

Evie lowered her eyes. 'We'll never forget you, Meggie.' Her voice broke as she remembered watching Megan walking towards the Tomahawk, the sun shining down on her lovely dark hair as she turned and waved. *Cheerio*, she thought. She remembered how Megan's face had lit up with relief when she jumped up on the wing and handed her the notes. *You're a star.* Evie laughed sadly as a tear rolled down her cheek. She could picture her here, soaring out across the sea in her old Tiger Moth. The thought of all Megan's plans – the airfield, marriage – broke her heart. 'I can't believe she's gone. Everywhere I look, I'm reminded of her. The garden at home, all her flowers ...'

'Her precious chickens,' Stella smiled, her breath shuddering as she broke down. 'Oh, Meggie,' she said. 'I am going to miss you.' Michael put his arm around her, and she buried her head in his shoulder.

'What are we going to do? She made all of it bearable somehow. Even on the toughest days, she kept us all going,' Evie said as she wept. 'How can she be gone? I keep on expecting her to come breezing through the door, full of news. It's so terribly quiet without her.' She looked up at Beau, saw the compassion in his face. She wondered how many friends he had lost. Gently, he reached out and dried the tears on her cheeks with his thumb. Evie took a deep breath. 'To Megan.' Her hand shook as she raised the champagne to the sky. 'To our beautiful Meggie.' She took a sip, then handed it to Stella.

'To Megan,' they toasted in turn. When Michael passed the bottle to Beau, he looked out to sea.

'The beauty chorus has lost a true beauty,' Beau said quietly. He felt in his pocket and handed Evie a clean handkerchief.

'Thank you,' she said, and blew her nose.

'Do keep it,' he said.

'I didn't imagine for a moment you would want it back after that.' Evie laughed through her tears. She looked out across Barafundle Bay. 'Oh, Meggie, what a damn shame. She so wanted to come back to all this, to make a life for her and Bill.'

'I can see why. It's beautiful,' Beau said. 'Shall we go down to the beach? There must be a path here somewhere.'

They strolled through the long grass to the cliff edge, only the sound of keening gulls and the surf breaking the silence. Ace bounded ahead as they followed an old sheep trail that led to a steep path down to the bay. Michael went first, nimbly picking out a way down. His feet skidded on loose earth. 'Here, let me help you.' He reached up, took Stella in his arms and swung her down safely.

'Thank you,' she said, her hand resting against his chest.

'Well, aren't you going to help me?' Evie called as Beau jumped down ahead.

'Since when did you need help, Miss Chase ... Eve?' he corrected, flashing a smile back at her. She stood, hands on hips, until he returned and offered her his hand.

'You told me once a chap likes to feel needed,' she said as she leapt easily down into his arms. The sun beat down on them, warming her hair and skin, bringing the colour to her cheeks. Stella and Michael walked on ahead, an awkward distance between them again. She felt light-headed suddenly. 'Beau ...' she said, her lips close to his.

'Not here.' His breath was shallow, like hers. They walked on, hands drifting reluctantly apart.

They sat together on the deserted beach, watching the birds wheeling and turning overhead. The view to Caldey Island was dazzling, only faint mare's tail wisps of cloud in the sky.

'This is wonderful,' Michael said as he tugged off his dog collar and slipped it into his pocket. His black shirt fell open, blowing like the sails of a ship in the breeze. Stella glimpsed the smooth muscles of his chest, longed to touch the indentation of his collar bone. He kicked off his shoes, rolled up his dark wool trousers. 'Anyone coming in?'

'Why not?' Stella said. Discreetly she slipped out of her stockings, and tucked up her skirt.

Evie caught Beau eyeing her legs as she walked out to sea. 'Hey,' she kicked sand at him.

'Sorry,' he said, smiling. 'Bet yours are better.'

'You think so do you?' Evie rolled onto her stomach, took another swig of champagne.

Beau brushed a strand of hair from her eyes. 'I'd like to find out.' He checked Stella and Michael were looking out to sea. As he leant forward and kissed her, cupping her jaw in his hand, Evie closed her eyes. Sunlight danced through her eyelids, red and gold, luminous and hot like the touch of his lips. The sound of the surf washed over her. It felt as if she was disintegrating into the warm air.

'I've wanted you to do that for a long time,' she said. 'I liked it. Do it again.'

'Do your men generally follow orders?'

'Yes.' She smiled. 'Normally I get away with it.'

'You could have kissed me, you know,' Beau said. 'You strike me as the emancipated sort.'

'I thought you loathed me.'

'I do, can't you tell.'

'You told me I reminded you of Olivia.'

'You did, at first. I loathed her too, once.' He kissed her again. 'But I loathe you more, if that means you drive me crazy. I can't stop thinking about you.'

Evie dipped her head as she laughed, looked up at him through her lashes. 'I loathe you too.' She ran her index finger along his wrist, looping a slow figure eight. 'How long have you loathed me?'

He shifted closer to her, their legs resting gently against one another. 'Since you turned up in that ridiculous fur coat and got your heels stuck in the mud. I've never seen anyone attempt to fly a Moth barefoot before.'

Evie bit her lip. 'That long?'

'It annoyed me at first, that I was so attracted to you. I thought you were everything I didn't need.'

'You thought I was too like Olivia?'

'Yes.' He ran his hand through her hair, pulled her closer to him. 'But you're not at all.'

'You told me I was spoilt, headstrong ...' She placed the palm of her hand flat against his chest, felt the lean, hard rise of his ribs as he breathed, the beat of his heart.

'You're still headstrong.' He gazed deeply into her eyes. 'But you've surprised me time and time again. I never want that to change.' Beau kissed her, gently. 'When you became engaged to the American chap, I thought I'd lost my chance.'

'You could have fought for me. I had no idea how you felt.'

'Perhaps I didn't, until I thought I'd lost you. Then when I saw you holding hands with Peter in the club the other night—'

'Peter? Is that why you were so off with me?' Evie slid her hand upwards, her thumb arcing out to caress his neck, his jaw, as she kissed him. 'No one has ever made me feel the way you do,' she said quietly. She thought of her doubts, the dreadful things Olivia had said. When he looked into her eyes, she could not believe it of him.

Beau settled back on his elbows, smiled at her. 'So what are we going to do about it?'

'We could get married,' she said recklessly.

'With our track record? I don't fancy our chances much as fiancées.'

Evie tried to hide her disappointment. 'Well, I agree never to marry you,' she shot back.

'I didn't mean—'

'Come on you two!' Stella called. 'This is wonderful!'

Evie scrambled to her feet, and pulled her dress over her head. The breeze lifted the thin silk of her camisole. 'What are you waiting for?' she said over her shoulder.

Beau stood up and kicked off his shoes, loosened his belt. 'I was right,' he said, holding her gaze as he stripped off his shirt. 'You do have good legs.'

'Well, if you want a closer look, you'll have to catch me first,' Evie called as she ran down the golden sand to the sea, gasping as she dived into the surf.

Michael watched as Beau purposefully stripped off to his boxer shorts and strode down the beach into the water. The shore fell away steeply, and Beau plunged in after Evie, his powerful crawl stroke cutting through the surf.

Michael shielded his eyes and stared out to sea. He spotted Evie doing an elegant backstroke, some way out towards Stackpole Head, but Beau was gaining on her fast. 'What's the story with those two?' he asked Stella as they walked in the surf.

'I saw it coming months ago.' Stella brushed her windswept hair from her face. 'They've been fighting like cats and dogs ever since they laid eyes on one another.'

'Is that how it is with your husband?' Michael asked.

'Richard? No.' She didn't want to think of him now, didn't want the moment to be spoilt. 'Michael, I …'

'It's alright,' he said. 'I understand now why you said we couldn't be together. I've, well, I've talked it all through with my vicar. He helped me see things from your point of view. I've come to accept things the way they are.' His face gave away his true emotions. 'I forgive you.'

'No, you don't understand,' she stepped closer to him, the cool water eddying around her feet, sand trickling away between her toes. 'Richard was having an affair.'

Michael looked at her. 'He must be a fool.'

'No,' she shook her head. 'I was the fool. A stupid, trusting, naïve fool.'

'How any man could …' He reached out to touch her, his fingers close to her cheek. His hand dropped. 'You're married. I can't …'

'I know. I knew we could never be together. That's what's been tearing me apart. It's so unfair. Megan, you, this damn war …' she said helplessly. He took her in his arms. 'I love you,' she said, her voice muffled as her head lay against his chest. They clung to one another as the wind and surf danced around them.

'I love you too.'

'But it's impossible.'

He kissed her hair, turned her face to his. 'Now that I know you love me, nothing is impossible.'

'Are you planning to swim to Ireland?' Beau called, fighting to keep up with Evie as she swam ahead. Once they were around the headland and out of sight, she swam towards the coast, trod water in the shallows, waiting for him to catch up with her. Her hair fanned out around her, undulating in the water. Beau didn't hesitate, pulled her to him. In the cool water, there was nothing between them. He ran his hand over her breast, brushed his thumb over her hard nipple. She gasped, wrapped her legs around his waist as he kissed her, his tongue in her mouth. The sea lifted them, saltwater washing their kisses. 'Where are you staying tonight?' he asked.

'With Megan's parents.'

'Can't you get away? I have a room at the hotel in town.'

Evie shook her head. 'I want to, Beau.' Her lips brushed his, tasted salt water on his skin. 'But I can't, not tonight. The least we can do is spend some time with them. We both feel responsible.'

'No. Every pilot is responsible for him ...'

'Or her ...'

'... self.' Beau groaned as Evie's fingers splayed out at the base of his spine. He kissed her neck, her chest, hungrily as a wave lifted them in one another's arms. 'When am I going to get you alone?'

'Soon.' She released him, arching gracefully back in the water. He ran his hand down the slender, strong curve of her ribcage, across her stomach. Time stood still for them as they floated in the cool water together, the hot sun caressing their skin. All the weeks and months of longing contracted to a single point in time. As they kissed, a huge breaker washed over them. Evie held fast to Beau, laughing.

'We may drown if we make love here,' he said, sluicing the seawater from his hair.

'It would be worth it.' She stroked his face. 'Anyway, what makes you think I want to make love with you quite yet?'

He pulled her to him, and Beau's hand drifted underwater. 'This.' Evie's head fell slowly back in the lapping water, sunlight blinding her eyes, the breath catching in her throat.

'Beau ...'

He was breathing hard as he took her in his arms. 'There's no hurry. I've waited months for you. I can wait a while longer if that's what you want.'

She shook her head. 'This feels right, for the first time, with you. Unlike most people we may not have all the time in the world.'

'I have a feeling the angels are on our side.'

'Do you think so?'

'I hope so. I don't want to lose you, Eve.' The way he said her name it was like a sigh full of longing.

'The tide is turning, we should swim back.'

As he held her close, she wrapped her arms around his neck, kissed him one last time. He groaned softly as she released her hold. 'You're killing me.' He smiled slowly. 'You go ahead. There's no way I'm walking out of the water like this.'

By the time Beau reached the shore, the girls had dressed, and they sat finishing off the champagne as the sunset washed the beach.

'Good swim?' Michael asked.

'Invigorating,' he said, shaking the water from his hair. He lay on the warm sand next to Evie to dry off. He was weary, his strong muscles aching. All he wanted to do was be with her somewhere far away from the world. He thought of the night at Leo's house, of Evie's bed, imagined making love to her there.

'We've been hatching a plan while you were having fun,' Evie said. Her skin was flushed and radiant from the sun.

'Really?' He casually brushed some sand from her ankle.

'You know Megan's parents were counting on her to run this place after the war?'

'No, I didn't. Doesn't she have any brothers or sisters?'

Stella shook her head. 'Her elder brother was killed at Dunkirk.'

'I'm sorry. Her parents seem like good people.'

'That's why I'd like to do something for them, for Megan,' Evie said. 'Daddy may have stopped my allowance, but I'm twenty-one in November, and there's nothing Virginia can do to deny me my trust fund.'

'You're going to buy this place?' Beau's face softened. 'I can't picture you as a farmer.'

'Neither can I. That's where Stella comes in.'

'Stella?'

'And me.' Michael took Stella's hand. 'Hopefully.'

'I'm sorry, how long was I out there swimming?' Beau took a swig of the warm champagne.

'We're going to run this place for Evie, if Megan's parents agree to sell. Hopefully Bill will stay on.'

'It's too early to talk about it with Rhodri and Nia, I'll wait a while, but Megan always said she couldn't bear to let the farm go to the horrible cousins,' Evie said. 'This way I get to make two of my dearest friends happy.'

'Sorry to be a wet blanket, but how can you practise your ministry from here?' Beau asked Michael.

'I've just decided I'm leaving the Church,' he said. 'Not because of that. Because they wouldn't let me marry a divorcée.'

Beau shook his head. 'Divorcée? I thought you were a widow.'

'No ... For various reasons it was easier to pretend Richard was dead. I'm going to divorce him, and we can be together.' She settled back into Michael's arms. 'You always wanted to be an artist, didn't you? There are few better places than this to paint,' she said, looking out across the luminous sky. 'This is how I always imagined Britain to be – whitewashed cottages, green fields. I want to bring David up here, far away from everything.'

'Happily ever after?' Michael kissed the top of her head. He smiled but there was an uncertainty there.

'I hope so.'

Beau built a fire from scrub and driftwood as the sky darkened. 'Do you believe in all that?'

Evie leant on her elbow, watching the flames cast shadows on his face. 'The fairytale? I'd like to. I haven't really had the best role models.'

'Your parents?'

'Leo is a romantic. He's like a big child, really, all the horses, the cars and pretty girls.'

'What about your mother?'

'She was a ski champion. She rescued Leo when they were stuck on a black ski run. I think it was the first time he'd ever met a woman who was a match for him.'

'Now I see where you get it from.' He settled down beside her.

'I should have smuggled out two bottles.' Evie stuck the neck of the champagne bottle down in the sand.

'No, that was perfect. I want to remember everything about tonight.' Beau took off his jacket, draped it over her shoulders. 'Here, it's getting chilly.'

'Thank you.' She nestled into his side as they watched Stella and Michael walking along the shoreline. 'So what do you think of our grand plan?'

'It seems like a good investment,' he said. 'And there's the airfield.'

'That's where I come in,' she said. 'It could be a thriving little business after the war.' She traced her finger in the sand. 'Though of course it's a lot of work for one woman. I'd need a partner ...'

Beau turned his face to hers, firelight illuminating his eyes. 'You think I'd go into business with a pilot like you?'

'Have you got any better ideas?'

'Commercial flying is very different, you know. Not so many risks, rather dull in some ways.' He stroked her cheek. 'Though I can't imagine ever being bored with you around.'

'I'm a damn good pilot, and you know it.' Her eyes were heavy with desire and tiredness. 'We could have a string of airfields, from Britain to France ...'

'You have a lot to learn.'

'So teach me.' She leant forward, kissed him softly.

Beau fought the overwhelming desire to make love to her there and then. He tried to push his thoughts to the back of his mind. 'Instruments,' he said suddenly. 'What do you know about flying blind?' She closed her eyes, her hand running across his hip bone, pulling him closer to her.

'I can do most things with my eyes closed.'

Beau glanced at Stella and Michael. They were too close. 'I'm serious.' He caught Evie's hand. 'I don't want you slamming into some hillside now.' Beau rolled onto his stomach and sketched out a rough instrument panel in the sand. She sighed and rested her chin on her hand as he explained the basics.

'I know all this,' she said. 'I was just about to take my instrument rating when I had to stop my lessons. I did all the theory and had several hours' practice. I'm bored. Kiss me.'

'It never hurts to refresh your memory.' As he went to take her in his arms, he noticed Stella and Michael approaching, and he moved away.

'What are you two up to?' Stella asked as she sat down by the fire.

'Instrument flying 101,' Evie yawned.

'Wake up,' Beau said. 'This could save both your lives.'

41

At first light, Evie woke. Her dreams had been full of fire and water. She saw the faces of Baldwin's fire and crash team, black with soot as they battled to save Megan. She saw the grim expressions of the engineers and staff back at the base when they returned. She dreamt of sea water eddying around her ankles, rushing through the ferry pool offices, rising higher and higher until the place was like an aquarium, fish swimming from room to room as everyone went about their work. Only she could see there was something wrong, and as she fought, trying to swim her way out of there, she woke. She lay tangled in the hot sheets, thinking about Megan. Evie sat up in the bed and looked around her friend's childhood room – the old stuffed bear with his fur worn from cuddling, the faded rosettes from farm shows and peeling posters of Clark Gable and Gary Cooper. 'Oh, Meggie ...' she whispered. She nudged Stella as she glanced at the clock. 'Are you awake?'

'Hmm?' Stella rubbed her eyes. 'What time is it?'

Evie swung her bare feet down to the floor. 'We have to go.' She picked up an old Enid Blyton from the bedside table, thumbed through it. Inside the front cover, she saw 'Megan Jones, Age 12' written in neat, girlish handwriting. 'I can't believe we're going home without her.'

'I know what you mean. Some part of me hopes she'll be there, waiting for us …'

Evie thought again of the last time she had seen Megan. She had seemed like a doll, dwarfed by the huge old warplane. 'Do you really believe that was a mechanical failure? Surely someone would have noticed something was wrong.'

'You think someone did that deliberately?' Stella propped herself up. 'If they did, it was meant for me.'

'I think we need to keep our eyes and ears open,' Evie said as she dressed. 'Not everyone thinks we're the queens of the air like your artist friend. To a lot of the men we're just a pain in the neck and have no right to be there.' Evie chewed her lip. 'We owe Megan the truth.'

'Don't make any waves, Evie,' Stella warned her.

'I won't!' she held up her hands.

'Morning, girls,' Nia said as they appeared downstairs, carrying their overnight bags. 'I hope you slept well?'

'Thank you, Mrs Jones.' Evie said. 'And yourself?'

'Oh, you know …' Her eyes were red and swollen from lack of sleep. 'You will have some breakfast before you go?'

'I'm afraid we have to be on our way, the car is waiting,' Stella said.

'You girls, no wonder you're all skin and bones.' Nia reached for a basket at her side. 'I've packed you a little something for the journey, and there's a bone in there to keep your friend's dog happy.'

'You're very kind.' Evie took it from her.

'I wanted you to have this as well.' She took a letter from her pocket. 'Megan wrote to me last week. I know,' she said, tears pooling her eyes, 'I know she thought she might be having a baby …'

Evie took her hand. 'She wasn't pregnant,' she said gently. 'But she had decided to come home, she wanted to be closer to you, and to marry Bill.'

'Oh, thank God.' Nia wiped at the corner of her eye with a hand pink and soft from washing up. 'The thought of her … She

317

was so young, and if there had been a baby too.' She squeezed Evie's hand. 'I won't tell Bill. He's heartbroken as it is.'

'I'll keep in touch with you, if I may?' Evie said. 'Megan told me about her plans to run the farm and airfield, and I'd like to help if I can.'

'Megan and her plans …' Nia shook her head. 'First Huw, now my little girl.' Tears welled in her eyes. 'No, Rhodri will give it all to the cousins now I'm sure.'

'Don't rush into anything,' Evie said. 'I mean it, if you can persuade Bill to stay on, I'd like to help.' Nia raised her eyes to Evie's, and understood.

'You're a good girl, Evie,' she said as the women embraced.

'I'll leave you my address. When you're ready, let's see if we can't keep Megan's dream alive.'

As Nia waved them off, Evie looked around at the farm. 'We can make a go of this.' She linked her arm through Stella's. 'We can do it, for Megan. It may be the first sensible thing I've ever done in my life, deciding to go into business with you.'

'What's in the letter?' Stella asked as they walked down the misty farm track towards the main road.

Evie pulled the envelope from her pocket and quickly read the note. 'I can't … You read it.' She choked up as she handed the piece of paper over, filled with Megan's familiar looping handwriting.

> Dear Ma,
> I don't know how to tell you this but I think I am having a baby. Bill is the father. Please don't tell him until I have a chance to find out for sure. It sounds crazy but I hope I am. I am so happy, Ma, please don't be angry. I love Bill, and if we have a son Da will have his boy to pass the farm on to. I am just so sorry to be leaving the ATA. I hope they'll let me stay as long as possible. This has been the best time of my life. I always wanted an adventure, and it has been that. Evie and Stella are like

the big sisters I never had, and I shall miss them so very much.

Stella's vision blurred. 'She thought she was pregnant?' As she looked up, she saw Evie running on down the hill towards Beau. He stood smoking a cigarette against the bonnet of the Jaguar, and Evie flung her arms around him.

'That's what I call a welcome,' he said.

'Miss me?' she whispered, burying her head in his neck.

'Worst night's sleep I've ever had.'

There was no time to be together. Beau drove against the clock, and dropped the girls at the cottage before midday.

'Take care, Stella,' he said as he carried their bags inside.

Evie stood stroking Ace's head, waiting for Beau.

'I'll ferry down on my next leave, I promise,' he said as he took her in his arms. 'I must go now.'

'Is it soon? I have a couple of days off in two weeks.'

'I don't know.'

'Now is not the time to play hard to get.' Her eyes fell. 'I don't even know where your squadron is based.'

He raised her chin. 'Trust me. If I could tell you, I would.'

'You're so evasive it's easy to believe you really are a bally spy,' Evie said, frowning.

'You always did have a vivid imagination.'

She felt him slipping away from her already. She saw the old, closed look in his eyes. 'Take care won't you, Beau?'

He winked at her. 'Same back at you.'

As Evie walked inside, the cottage felt cold and damp, even on such a beautiful summer's day. It was empty without Megan. Everywhere she looked she saw reminders – the sticker albums on the coffee table, the jam jars on the draining board in the kitchen, washed and ready for Megan to make pickles and chutneys for the winter.

Stalin wound himself around her legs chirruping a greeting before sulking under the stairs, punishing them for leaving him alone. As Evie dragged a brush through her hair, she called up to Stella. 'I'm just going to check on Monty and the chickens.'

Stella poked her head over the banister. 'OK, but be quick. There was a note on the mat when I came in – we're needed at the airfield.'

'So much for a day off,' Evie muttered as she unlocked the back door. She pushed through the swaying branches of the apple trees lining the path to the back garden. Wasps muzzed around the fallen fruit in the grass. Montgomery trotted over in the paddock, tossing his head. 'Hello, old boy,' she said. 'Has the farmer taken good care of you?' She suddenly realised how quiet it was, and turned her head slowly towards the chicken coop. 'Oh no, the fox,' she said under her breath. 'Stella!' she cried.

'What is it?' She ran outside, and froze with horror beside Evie. The chickens had gone. All that was left was a tangled mess of blood and white feathers, and in the centre of the coop a single broken wing.

AUTUMN

42

The fields around White Waltham were a pale gold now against the sky. Horses and carts loaded down with hay trundled along as Evie drove to the airfield. They passed an orchard where land girls in their brown dungarees were picking the last of the plums.

'It's such a shame Meggie's not here to see the harvest,' she said sadly. 'We mustn't let all her lovely fruit and veg go to waste. She was so proud of that garden.'

'Michael's going to come over and give us a hand later. I said he could have some of the spare veg for the retirement home.'

'Good idea.' Evie turned the car into the airfield. 'Any idea why Frankie wants to see us?'

Stella shook her head. 'Nope, but I'm sure we'll find out.'

Commander Francis sat behind the desk toying with a pencil, Doc Whitehurst at his side. Evie and Stella stood to attention in front of him, uniforms immaculate, arms clasped behind their backs. 'Miss Chase, you're a girl with imagination. What do you think about using elephants instead of tractors to pull the planes?'

'Elephants, sir?'

'Yes. A local circus is closing up shop, and they have a couple of elephants for sale. One's OK, the other one is a bit green.'

'Green elephants, sir?'

'Untrained. I thought we could recruit the mahout, give him an ATA uniform.'

Whitehurst shook his head. 'They won't let us do it, Frankie. They'll come up with some lame excuse like the elephants will be dangerous if there's a raid and they get loose.'

'We'll see.' His dark blue eyes twinkled. 'Now, you girls recently lost a dear friend, Third Officer Jones. My condolences,' he said. 'It's bad enough losing a pilot in combat, but when it comes down to mechanical failure ...'

'Sir, I wanted to ask you about that,' Evie said. Stella shot her a warning glance.

'Yes, Miss Chase?'

'There have been rumours of foul play on the base, that a person – or persons – are targeting the female pilots.'

Whitehurst leant forward on the desk. 'Do you have proof?'

'No, sir.'

'Well until you do I'd suggest you pay more attention to your job than to gossip, Miss Chase.'

Commander Francis folded his arms. 'In my experience the male and female members of the ATA get along exceptionally well together, with a great deal of mutual respect. We are, I would dare to say, a model example of modern thinking.'

'Yes, sir.'

He sorted through a stack of papers. 'In fact ... Yes, here we are.'

He passed Evie a sheet of paper headed *ATA Headquarters Accidents Committee – Finding*. She read on: *T/O Megan Jones. Aircraft crash landed in field. Complete engine failure of NEA P40 Tomahawk I. Pilot not responsible.* It was signed by the Chairman of the Accidents Committee.

'It wasn't her fault,' she said quietly.

'Certainly not,' he said. 'And in the circumstances we have chosen to overlook the fact that she was not allocated the plane.' Stella's eyes fell as he turned his attention to her. 'As civilians, ATA pilots have ultimate responsibility to choose when they fly. It was Third Officer Jones' decision. No one else is to blame. Now, the reason I asked to see you today ...' He shuffled through some papers. 'Here we are. You did exceptionally well on your conversion courses. You are both to be promoted to Second Officers.'

Stella nudged Evie. 'Does that mean we will be able to fly Spitfires like Winnie and Joan, sir?'

'Yes, Mrs Grainger.' He passed them both letters of confirmation. 'Spitfires, Hurricanes and all the complex single-engine planes. You are both jolly good pilots. I have no doubt in due course you will proceed to twin- and even four-engine planes. I have high hopes that Lettice and Joan will lead the way with those.'

Evie scanned her letter quickly. *On the satisfactory completion of your conversion course you are hereby promoted to Second Officer.* She noted a small pay rise and thought immediately of a pair of shoes she had been coveting in Maidenhead.

As he walked them to the door he shook their hands. 'Congratulations. Make Miss Jones proud.'

Evie was impatient to get in the air. After all those weeks of work in the classroom, today was the day. As the flight instructor wrote a series of figures on the blackboard she leant over to Stella's desk. 'When are they going to let us loose on the bally Spits?' she whispered.

'Don't be so impatient, Evie.' Stella passed her a mint. 'Not everyone picks things up as easily as you. It's good to run over things one last time.'

Evie sat back in her chair and folded her arms. *Hydraulics, retractable undercarriages, braking systems, superchargers, speed propellers – we've been over this a thousand times,* she thought.

The instructor turned to the class. 'I know some of you chaps have already been flying Class 2s and Class 2+, but the Spitfire is a different ball game. When you get up in your first Spit, we want you to do a simple climb, straight and level flight, then a series of climbs and descents with increasing rates of turn.'

'I saw a fellow flying one upside down the other day, sir,' one of the pilots cut in.

'Yeees.' The instructor sucked his teeth. 'Let's leave that to the test pilots shall we? What's wanted from a fighter pilot and an ATA pilot are two different things. No aerobatics from you chaps. Remember what you're dealing with here – 1600 hp Rolls Royce Merlin engines in one of the most sensitive, responsive planes you will ever fly. All we want you to do is get the planes safely from A to B.' The instructor perched on the front desk. 'To start with people often overcompensate, end up slinging the kite all over the place. Now then ...' He checked his watch. 'If you'd all like to go and get suited up, your aircraft are waiting for you.'

Evie did a little dance for joy in the cloakroom as she changed into her Sidcot suit. 'Finally,' she said. 'Aren't you excited?'

Stella laced up her boots. 'Yes, a little nervous though.'

'You'll be fine.' Evie dabbed Chanel behind each ear. 'I bet you and Lettice will be flying Lancs by next spring.'

They heard their names called over the tannoy and raced out to the field. Evie's heart was thundering in her chest as she walked towards her Spitfire. The early fog had cleared and the air was crisp. It was a glorious autumn day with a clear blue sky, and the camouflage paintwork on her plane gleamed.

'Your kite's ready, Miss,' the engineer said. 'If you want to start her up, a couple of us will perch on the tail until you're ready to take off. Mind you, give us the signal though, I had a couple of chaps airborne last week because they didn't jump off in time.'

'Thanks, I'll bear that in mind.' Evie ran her hand along the curve of the wing and thought of the day with Jack. The voice of the instructor came back to her: *No aerobatics*. 'Yes sir,' she said under her breath, and she fastened her flying helmet. Evie climbed up on the wing and leant against the canopy to slide herself into the cockpit.

The Merlin engines roared at first touch. Black smoke and a flash of flame shot from the exhausts near the propeller. Evie coughed, but the smoke soon cleared and the engine settled. It felt as if the plane was as impatient to be in the air as her. She glanced behind her, waved the ground crew clear. They jumped from the tail. The Spitfire quivered, and she taxied forwards, getting a feel for the stick, swinging the nose side to side so that she could see where she was going.

They're right, she thought. *You can't see a damn thing on the ground with that cowling blocking your view.* She knew once the engine was running she had to get going quickly. Spits overheated notoriously fast. As she took her place at the end of the runway for take-off, she eased the brakes. *Gosh, they are sharp*, she thought, and remembered the warnings about how easy it is to pitch a Spitfire on its nose. *Easy does it*, she said under her breath.

Evie turned the Spitfire into the wind. *OK, here we go.* She ran through her checks: *hydraulics, throttle, fuel boosters on ...* She felt the deep surge of energy as the engine roared and the plane gathered speed. With a thrust she was airborne, the urgent acceleration of the plane matching the rush of adrenalin she felt. Once she was clear of the airfield she let out a great whoop of delight, and pulled her canopy closed. Evie pumped up the undercarriage, and turned her full attention to the controls. 'Right, let's see what you can do little Spitty,' she said.

Flying felt effortless to her; it was as if her thoughts transmitted directly to the aircraft through her light touch on the stick. Evie soared above the countryside. She performed the requested manoeuvres, aware that the instructor was watching from the ground. 'Oh God, I could stay up here forever,' she murmured as she brought the plane back into the circuit. *Right, landing*, she thought, and ran through the drill. *Wheels down and pump. Green light on panel ... down. Final approach speed 140 mph ... There, that does it, spot on. Flaps down ... 80 mph, and we're down. Not quite a three-pointer but we're down.* Evie taxied over to her crew. *Throttle off, flaps up, radiator shutter open.* As she switched off the engines the blood hummed in her ears.

Evie jumped out of her cockpit and ran to find Stella.

'Well done, Miss Chase,' her instructor called.

'Thank you, sir,' she said.

Stella was checking the noticeboard, chatting to Miss Gold when Evie walked in.

'How was it?'

'Amazing. It was better than—'

Stella smiled broadly. 'I know. But then it depends who's flying, if you catch my drift.'

As the girls laughed, Teddy walked over. 'Just the people I'm looking for. You're cleared on complex singles now aren't you?'

'Yes, sir,' they both said.

'In fact,' Evie said, putting her hands on her hips, 'you still owe me ten bob, Teddy.'

He patted his pocket. 'Wallet's in my jacket. Remind me another time, eh?' Teddy checked his clipboard. 'Now, I need a pilot to deliver a Typhoon to Duxford for me. Rush job. Would you like to toss for it, or shall I toss for you?' He licked his lips.

Evie frowned. 'That won't be necessary, Teddy. I've nothing on and Stella has a date, so I'll take it.'

'Jolly good.'

As Evie took the chit from his hand, she turned to Stella. 'I should be back later, but it will give you a bit of time with Michael.'

Teddy folded his arms as Evie walked away. 'Is that your vicar, Mrs Grainger?'

'He's not a vicar, he's a curate.'

Teddy stepped uncomfortably close to her. 'I haven't met the chap, but I would have thought a red-blooded woman like you would have enjoyed the company of a real man.' Teddy shrugged as Stella held her ground. 'Oh well, perhaps not.' He began to walk away. 'You are awfully clever, you know,' he said over his shoulder. 'I don't know how you do it, getting the other girls to do your flights. Let's hope Miss Chase is luckier than the unfortunate Miss Jones.'

43

Stella could not rest. She cleaned the cottage from top to bottom, frantically counting away the hours while Evie was out on her mission. Finally, at nightfall, as she sat in the kitchen labelling jars of jam, she heard Evie's voice, singing as she walked in through the door.

'Am I glad to see you back.'

Stella was listening to Lord Haw Haw on the radio: 'This is Jairmany calling ...'

Evie smiled wearily. 'I managed to get the last Anson back. I'll tell you what, those Typhoons aren't nearly as much fun as the Spits. God, I'm dead on my feet. Is everything alright?'

'Yes. It was just something that hateful Teddy said.'

Evie dumped her bag by the door. 'Ignore him, he's a bully, that's all.' Evie raised her nose and sniffed. 'Something smells delicious. Have you made a crumble?' She unfolded her handkerchief. 'Look, I picked some blackberries on the way home. We could have put those in.'

Stella laughed and shook her head. 'It's not for us, unfortunately. You have a visitor.'

'Beau?'

'Poor thing has been hanging around all afternoon for you. He decided to take Monty out for a ride, and then he cooked something for him.'

'Bran mash?' Evie quickly raked her hands through her hair and checked her face in the mirror. She scooped up some of the blackberries and ate one, staining her lips with the juice.

'Go on.' Stella shooed her through the back door. 'He's not going to care what you look like. I'll make myself scarce. I'm meeting Michael at the cinema – you've got the place to yourselves.'

Evie ran down the garden path towards the paddock. The last rosy rays of sunset washed the glass of the old greenhouse, and golden light spilled from the open stable door. 'Beau?' she called.

'There you are.' He turned to her. He was stripped to the waist, rubbing the horse down.

Evie noticed he was wearing a thick leather strap over the burn on his arm. 'You look like a blacksmith,' she said.

'This?' He flexed his arm. 'I find it helps.'

As she walked into the stable, the warm smell of bran, molasses and apple perfumed the air. Both Monty and Beau were slicked with fresh sweat. 'I think I'm jealous. Monty gets dinner and a massage. What about me?'

Beau tossed the towel to the ground. 'Come here,' he said as he took her in his arms.

'I've missed you.'

He glanced down at her hand. 'What have you got there?'

She pushed one of the berries between his lips. 'I've been foraging.'

When he kissed her, their lips tasted of sweet juice. 'Eve, Eve, Eve …' He whispered her name like a sigh. 'God, I've missed you too. How have you been?'

'Busy.' Her gaze fell. 'It's the best way.'

'It is. Though it still doesn't stop me thinking about you day and night.'

'Why didn't you let me know you were coming?'

'I didn't know myself. I only had a few hours between flights.'

'You mean you have to go?' She stepped back.

'I'll come again as soon as I can. This is just a bonus. At least I've seen you, and we had a good ride.' He ran his hand over the smooth, firm flank of the horse.

'That makes one of us.'

'Don't sulk. I hear you flew your first Spit today. How was it?'

Evie leant back against the manger. 'It was incredible. I said to Stella it was better than sex.'

Beau leant in to her, trapping her with his arms. 'Really? And how would you know?' He kissed her, nudged her legs open with his knee, pulled her to him hard and insistent.

'Do you have to go?' she asked breathlessly.

'I do, I'm late already. You always were distracting.'

Evie bit her lip. 'I don't want to rush this, do you?'

He shook his head as he pulled on his shirt. 'I promise, I'll be back soon.' He kissed her one last time, crushing her lips beneath his.

She leant against the door of the stable, watching him disappear into the darkness. It was a full moon, and the stars carpeted the heavens. 'Where do you go, Beau? Where do you go?' she murmured as she raised her eyes to the clear sky.

44

Evie landed the Lysander Mk III at Tangmere, and as the ground crew waved her in she taxied to a halt near the hangar. While the engine stilled, she took some deep breaths and released her Sutton harness.

'Have a good flight, Miss?' the engineer asked as he jumped up into the cockpit.

'Yes thank you, but I'm glad to be here. These black Lizzies give me the spooks. What are they for anyway?'

'Can't say I know, Miss. They go out at night, must be something hush-hush.' He tapped the side of his nose.

After gathering up her maps and flight bag, Evie slung her parachute over her shoulder and strolled into the Watch Office. 'Hello,' she said, 'are you the Duty Pilot?' A harassed, pale man looked up from a stack of paperwork, his pipe clenched between his teeth.

'For my sins. Would you like your chit signed?'

'Yes please.'

'Are you the pilot picking up a Spitfire for No. 6 Pool?'

'Yes.' Evie glanced at her papers. 'I've got a Spit to Ratcliffe and an Airspeed Courier back to No. 1. Do you think I have time for a cup of tea?'

'I'd get a move on if I was you.' He handed back her slip of paper. 'Sir Lindsay is very hospitable. If you get there in time for lunch I don't doubt he'll ask you in for a bite to eat.'

Evie was parched. She stopped off in the mess for a glass of water, and as she walked in, a dog bounded over to her.

'Ace? Is that you?' She went down on one knee to fuss him. 'Where's your master?'

'Are you looking for Beau?' One of the officers looked up.

'Yes, is he here?'

'Afraid not. I'm dog-sitting for him. We were expecting him back hours ago but still no sign of him.'

A chill ran through Evie. She hadn't heard from Beau for weeks, and had no idea about the work he was doing. When the officer saw the expression on her face, he sauntered over.

'I shouldn't worry,' he said kindly. 'He is one of the finest pilots I've flown with.' He offered Evie his hand as she stood and shifted the weight of her parachute. 'Are you with the ATA?'

'Yes I am.'

'One of the Spitfire girls,' he said, smiling. 'Can I give Beau a message when he shows his face?'

'Would you mind telling him Evie sends her regards?'

'Not at all. How do you find the old Spits?'

'Tremendous fun. I haven't had one for a while. The last one had to go for repairs at Vickers in Castle Bromwich, so I'm looking forward to today.'

'Well, there's nothing wrong with the kite out there as far as I know.'

The tannoy crackled into life: 'Spitfire ready for Second Officer Chase'.

'I must go,' she said. 'Good to meet you.'

'Oh, I say, your pocket is undone.'

Evie looked down to see her silver compact sticking out of the top pocket of her Sidcot suit.

'I'd keep an eye on that. We had one of your girls deliver a

Spit the other day and the whole bally cockpit was full of powder. Turns out she'd tried a few aerobatics on the way over and her compact slipped out, went shooting round the canopy. Lovely girl, she looked just like a clown when she stepped out.'

As Evie waited for take-off, the slipstream from the Spitfire's exhausts flattened the grass on the airfield, rivulets of moisture coursing down the wing. *'Remember, girls'*, Pauline's words came back to her, *'neatness and precision, safety and punctuality. No stunts or gallantry.'*

'We'll see about that,' Evie said under her breath as she thundered up the runway. The Spitfire was doing 200 mph by the time Evie cleared the hedge, and she put it into a steep climb, the cowling blanking out the horizon.

She exhaled as the plane soared into the clear skies. It was an azure blue photo-reconnaissance Spitfire, and as she looked out of the canopy the sheen of the wings against the sky thrilled her. It was hard to tell where the sky began and the plane ended. The roar of the engine reverberated around her heart, and as she steered the plane onto course, her blood sang.

You can't do a damn thing to help Beau, she told herself. *There's no point worrying. Buck up.* As she levelled out, the Merlin engine thrummed. To distract herself from thinking about him, she began to sing 'Blue Skies' at the top of her voice as she tooled along.

Evie's Spitfire roared across the open skies towards Leicestershire. She checked her maps for balloon barrages and gun placements, then as she relaxed a familiar feeling of unreality settled on her. The warm sun through the canopy and the white-noise rush of the air lulled her into a state of calmness. 'No dawdling in the sky,' she mimicked the flight instructor's voice. 'Keep a good speed.' She checked her instruments and bearings occasionally, in a contented daze. Suddenly, glancing in her rear-view mirror, she spotted something dark not far behind. Her heart raced. It was following her.

'Oh God,' she whispered. All the stories about the Luftwaffe targeting the ATA came back to her. Her mouth went dry. 'Right, you bastard,' she said. 'Let's see if you can keep up with this ...'

Evie threw the plane into a steep climb. She looked behind her. Was it a Messerschmitt? She screwed up her eyes trying to make it out. *Whatever the hell it is, it's on my tail.* First she tried to outrun the other plane, but it kept up with her every move. She accidentally put the Spit into a high-speed stall. With a half flick, she kicked it out of the spin. She did a loop-the-loop, zooming along upside down for as long as she could bear it. Still it followed. *'No aerobatics ...' Sorry, Pauline,* she thought. Evie began to taste real fear. 'Come on, guardian angel,' she said under her breath as she righted herself, powering closer to No. 6 Pool. She craned around to get a better look at the aircraft following her. It was still exactly the same distance away, close behind her. 'What the ...?' Evie squinted.

As she realised what had happened, she began to laugh. She reached back and wiped a speck of dirt from inside the canopy. *You stooge,* she thought. *Fancy mistaking a spot of mud for a Messerschmitt. This isn't one I'll be shooting a line about.*

As she entered the Ratcliffe circuit, she checked her instruments. *Right,* she said to herself, trying to calm her racing heart. *Slow up, propeller in fine pitch, over the fence at 70 ... There, perfect three-pointer.* Within a few hundred feet she rolled to a stop, and taxied over to the waiting crew.

Evie threw back the canopy and pulled off her helmet.

'Nice landing, Miss,' the Duty Pilot said as she handed him her chit.

'Thank you. There's your new toy. Careful how you handle her.' Evie took her slip of paper. 'You might want to get the erks to clean the canopy.'

Evie lit a cigarette as she walked out onto the airfield.

'I say.' A smartly dressed man in tweeds waved at her. 'Super landing.' He shook her hand. 'I'm Lindsay Everard. Do you fancy a spot of lunch before your next flight? Your VIP passengers aren't quite ready.'

'Who am I taking?'

He tapped the side of his nose. 'Wait and see my dear.'

45

Ratcliffe Hall was a hive of activity, and the genial atmosphere felt to Evie more like a pre-war aeronautical club than a ferry pool. ATA and RAF pilots sat together at a long table for lunch with the Everard family. Evie found a spare seat next to some American pilots.

'What's all this?' she asked, looking at the pumpkins in the centre of the table and the paintings of skeletons and bats hanging from the walls.

'Halloween, ma'am,' the young pilot said. 'We're having a little party tonight, shame you can't stay.'

'Gosh, I've never heard of it.'

'It's big back in the States,' he said as he handed her a plate with a generous slice of game pie. 'Sir Lindsay and his family are really neat, they've made us feel right at home. They're even fattening up a turkey for Thanksgiving.'

Evie glanced up the table to where Sir Lindsay sat. There were a couple of empty spaces at his side and she guessed they must be for her VIP passengers.

'This seems like a good pool,' she said.

'It's a blast.' He laughed. 'One of your guys from White Waltham was down here the other day. Stewart? Nice guy. We had Lady Astor and George Bernard Shaw for dinner that night too.' He helped himself to a spoonful of mashed potatoes. 'Yeah, they're a nice family. We help out around the place too. A few of us have been picking apples and pears, helping store them for the winter ...'

The butler, Smart, opened the door as the young pilot talked on, and Evie looked up. A senior RAF officer strode in and joined Sir Lindsay at the head of the table. As he turned to usher the final guest to the table, her mouth fell open.

'That's not ...' Her eyes widened as a portly man with thinning grey hair settled down next to Sir Lindsay and tucked into his pie.

'Sure looks like Churchill, don't it?' the young pilot said. 'Who knows. He's got plenty of doubles around the place.'

'I know, but that's uncanny.' Evie finished her pie. 'We've got at chap at White Waltham, Norman Shelley. He's an actor, and he's always dashing off to do Churchill's broadcasts for him. Honestly, when he puts on that voice, you wouldn't know the difference.'

As the lunch party broke up, Evie shook Sir Lindsay's hand. 'Thank you very much. That was delicious.'

'Good show. You must come again.' He glanced over to the RAF officer, who nodded. 'Looks like your passengers are ready now, Miss Chase. Hope you have an uneventful journey.'

'One of the girls, I see,' Churchill said to the RAF official. His voice was unmistakable. 'Hope we're in for a smooth flight.'

As Evie piloted the Airspeed Courier back to White Waltham, she tried not to swivel her head around to get a better look at her passengers. *It can't be him, can it?* she thought.

The light was beginning to fade and the weather was closing in by the time she spotted familiar scenery beneath her. Just as she was beginning to relax, she caught sight of something on her starboard side. She glanced up. The RAF officer had spotted it too, but Churchill was deep in thought with his eyes closed. Evie's stomach lurched as the distinctive silver spiral of a tracer bullet shot past them. She craned her neck and looked up. 'Damn, a Messerschmitt, and it's tracking us,' she whispered. It was so close she could see the dark cross on the fuselage and the swastika on the tail.

That's no speck on the canopy this time. Think, Evie, think, she told herself calmly. *There's no way I can outrun or outmanoeuvre him in this old thing.* She took a deep breath as another tracer whizzed past. *What's he doing all the way over here? Hopefully he's low on fuel and won't hang around too long.* She looked up. There was a thick bank of cloud above. *It's our only chance.* She swallowed hard and pulled the Courier up into a steep climb. As she glanced behind, the Me110 was following.

They entered the clouds, candyfloss wisps flying past the cockpit window.

'You may want to strap yourselves in, gentlemen,' she said to her passengers. As they flew into dense cloud, the plane shuddered and the world went white. Evie checked her instruments and maps and calculated their position.

The RAF officer leant forward. 'Is everything alright?'

'Yes sir, I know we're not supposed to fly in cloud, but I think it's our best chance, don't you?'

'Do you have an instrument rating?'

'Yes, sir.' *Well, as good as,* she thought.

'Jolly good. Carry on.' He leant back in his seat and looked at Churchill, who still had his eyes closed.

Please, God, let this work, Evie thought as she levelled out in the cloud. As she calmed down and the familiar sense of having someone flying at her side came upon her, she recalled Beau's words from the afternoon on the beach: '*Straighten up. Pilots almost never fly straight into cloud. Remember the last spot on the map and your height, add a bit, turn 180 degrees and descend slowly.*' She started to turn around, praying she wouldn't come face to face with the Me110. As she descended, she remembered Beau's final words on the subject: '*Think. Everything will be telling you that it's wrong, that your instruments are off, but trust the facts, not your instinct.*'

She guided the Airspeed Courier out of the cloud, and exhaled with relief as she spotted Shottesbrooke Church below her. There was no sign of the German plane. 'Thank you,' she whispered. Evie entered the circuit, and landed the plane safely just as dusk was falling.

Churchill stepped out onto the runway. 'Thank you, Miss Chase, an excellent landing.' He shook her hand and was escorted to the waiting car.

The RAF official paused to pull on his gloves. 'Good bit of flying there, my dear. He almost had us. I couldn't have done better myself.'

46

'How can you be sure it was him?' Stella asked Evie as they washed up the tea things a few days later. 'Apparently they have Churchill lookalikes all over the place to keep Jerry guessing.' She piled the last plate on the drainer. 'Even that chap Norman keeps going off to do voice-overs for Churchill.'

'That's what I said to one of the Americans. I suppose he's like Father Christmas – he can't be everywhere, but it certainly looked like him.'

'It is good to see you. We've been so busy I've hardly had a chance to catch up with you.'

'Are you going out with Michael tonight?'

'Yes, just to the cinema.'

'Again?' Evie nudged her. 'I am glad you two have made up.'

Stella smiled. 'We're just taking it one step at a time as friends, for now.' She glanced at Evie. 'You know, we must decide what we're going to do for your birthday – that's coming up soon isn't it?'

'It *is* my birthday, today,' Evie said quietly.

'No? Why didn't you tell me?'

Evie shrugged. 'I know it's my twenty-first, but I didn't feel like there was much to celebrate this year.'

'Well, happy birthday. We must do something to celebrate the next leave day we have off together. Have you heard from Beau?'

Evie shook her head. 'Peter sent a card.' She couldn't hide her disappointment. 'Beau promised he'd come and see me, but I haven't heard anything from him for weeks. It's like he's disappeared off the face of the earth. I haven't even been able to find out if he made it back to Tangmere safely. No one will tell me a thing.'

'People are disappearing all over the place. Have you noticed Jim Mollison hasn't been around for a while? I heard in the mess today he's piloting some hush-hush new plane overseas.'

'Is that what he's doing? I did wonder.'

Stella tossed aside the tea towel. 'Listen, why don't you come to the cinema? You can't sit around here by yourself on your birthday.'

'You don't need a gooseberry. Go and have fun.' Evie yawned. 'All I want is an early night.'

Evie hummed a Gershwin tune to herself, bumping the cupboard door closed with her hip. 'They can't take that away from me ...' the record sang on. She had a turban wound around her hair, and a blue face pack on that clashed violently with her red silk kimono. 'Nice to have the house to ourselves for a while, eh, cat?' She whisked Stalin into her arms as she danced around the kitchen. He yowled at her, and she plonked him down. 'Now ...' She scanned the kitchen cupboard, thinking longingly of ice cream and chocolate. 'Pickled cucumbers?' She dusted off the jar and unscrewed the lid, took a doubtful sniff. Her stomach growled with hunger. 'Oh well, that will have to do,' she said to him. 'I just don't feel like cooking a thing tonight.'

Something scurried across the kitchen floor, and Evie jumped. 'Not you again.' She got down on her hands and knees and looked under the table. A small brown mouse stared back at her, its dark eyes gleaming. 'Stalin,' she called, and looked over. The cat slinked away to his favourite armchair by the fire and jumped up. He stuck his back leg in the air like a hambone and leisurely started to lick himself. 'Thanks for nothing.' Evie rolled up her sleeves and fetched a pail from the laundry and a sheet of card from the salvage bags by the back door. 'If I can handle Jerry, I can handle you, matey,' she said as she gingerly crept towards the mouse. She popped the bucket over the top and slid the card underneath, holding the whole thing at arm's length.

Evie hooked open the back door and put the trap on the ground in the middle of the garden. The grass was already cold and frosty, and her breath hung in a heavy cloud. She kicked the bucket over and jumped back. The mouse looked at her for a moment. 'Go on then.' She shooed it away, and it scampered off into the night. She looked up at the dark sky. *No fireworks this year*, she thought, and hugged herself.

Evie slammed the kitchen door and bolted it. 'Good-for-nothing cat,' she said affectionately as she turned up the record player so she could hear it in the bath.

Outside, the wind lashed the cottage. Draughts rattled the bathroom door on the latch. Evie slipped out of her kimono and into the steaming bubble bath, exhaling with pleasure. The candlelight flickered and she closed her eyes, her body relaxing in the warm water. She'd had a near miss with another Spitfire today. It had seemed like a good idea to try flying upside down again, but then she had found she couldn't right the thing until the last ragged moment.

Twenty-one, she thought. For a moment she allowed herself to imagine another time when there would have been a glorious party, a night of friends and laughter, the attention of handsome suitors. She thought back to the last summer before the war, the endless parties and beautiful weather. It had felt like it would all go on forever. It seemed like a lifetime ago. *Still, I had my chance. Daddy did offer to throw a party tonight in spite of everything. Perhaps it was unkind of me to ignore his note, but I can't bear the thought of being in the same room as Virginia any more.*

A bump in the kitchen made her jump, and she sat up in the bath, senses alert. 'Must be Stalin,' she said to herself. The wind shook the window, the low branches of the tree scratching against the glass. She settled back in the water, soaking up to her chin. As the record played on, Evie didn't hear the front door handle turn. She didn't see the candles gutter as a dark figure walked by, or hear the soft tread of footsteps on the creaking floorboards. It wasn't until the bathroom door slowly opened that she sensed she wasn't alone in the house.

Evie screamed as a hand crept across the doorjamb. She leapt forward and slammed the door down hard.

'Ow! Jesus!' a male voice said. 'Evie is that you?'

'Beau?' Her hand flew to her face, stuck in the blue goo she had spread all over it. 'Just a minute!' She quickly sank underwater and washed her face clean, then jumped out and wrapped a white towel around herself. She pulled open the door to find Beau nursing his hand.

'I thought you might have been pleased to see me ...'

'I don't like surprises.' She took his hand. 'Does that hurt?'

'Ow! Yes it does,' he said, flinching as she examined it.

'You should knock first when someone's in the bath.'

He pulled her towards him, kissed her lips, still warm and fresh from the bath. 'I bumped into Stella in town as I was getting you some flowers. She said you were home alone.'

'You remembered?' Evie broke into a broad smile.

'Of course. November 5th.' He leant down, handed her a bouquet of scented white lilies and roses. 'I remember when I saw it on your application form I knew you'd be trouble.' He kissed her again, his hand at the base of her spine.

'As you can see, no party, no fireworks.'

'I'm not much in the mood for a party, but I thought you might like some company. Let's see what we can do about the fireworks.'

Evie turned away from him, placed the flowers in the basin. The rich, powdery incense-like perfume of the lilies was intoxicating. She glanced over her shoulder at him as she dropped her towel and said 'Come on then ...'

Beau kicked off his boots as he pulled his sheepskin flying jacket off. His eyes were fixed on hers as Evie sank into the warm water. 'How long have you been back?' she asked.

'I came down yesterday,' he said as he slipped out of his clothes.

'And you've only just come to see me?' Her eyes flickered over his body as he sank into the bath, facing her.

'I've been busy.' His hands ran along her smooth legs under the water.

'Too busy to see me? Where have you been?'

'Here and there.'

She splashed him. 'Beau, I've been worried about you. I took a plane down to Tangmere the other day and they said you were late back.'

'Did you see Ace? He's turned into a marvellous dog, best I've ever had.'

'Don't change the subject.'

'I'm flying out of Tangmere regularly, that's all I can tell you.'

'With Douglas Bader's lot?'

'It's not the same down there since he's gone.'

'But are you—'

Beau silenced her with a kiss. He saw the jar of pickles beside the bath. 'Late-night snack?' he laughed. 'I would have thought you had more sophisticated tastes. Is there something you need to tell me?' His hand moved to the gentle swell of her stomach.

'It would have to be an immaculate conception if that's what you're getting at.'

'Oh good, I thought you might have become bored waiting for me.'

'Bored?' She raised an eyebrow. 'With you, never.'

He pulled her towards him, her legs encircling his waist. 'I missed you,' he said as Evie wrapped her arms around his neck. 'Why do we always seem to end up in water when we spend most of our life in the air?'

They learnt one another's bodies by heart that night. As the hands of the clock on her bedside table ticked away the precious hours, and the fire in the hearth burnt low, they lost themselves in one another.

'I love you,' he said, staring deep into her eyes. 'I love you, my darling, my Eve.'

Evie sighed, arcing her spine as she pulled him closer, deeper. 'Beau!' she cried out at the sudden pain, digging her nails into his flesh. He buried his head next to hers, his breath against her cheek.

'There,' he whispered, moving gently, waiting for her.

Lights danced as Evie closed her eyes, the pain washed away by the pleasure that was radiating into every nerve, every cell of her body.

'Look at me,' he murmured as she called his name. He kissed her temple as she caught her breath.

'Oh God, I didn't know it could be like that,' Evie said, laughing with the sheer joy and newness of loving him. She reached up to him, ran her hand through his golden hair.

'I told you Spitfires are good but not that good.' He laughed softly as they began to move again. 'We're not done yet.'

Evie rolled him over, straddled his hips, rocking rhythmically. She fell forward, her lips close to his ear. 'I love you,' she murmured as she felt his body tense, his hands on her hips holding her fast to him. 'I want you.' Her fingers contracted, clenched the white sheet in her hand as he cried out her name.

Evie lay sated in his arms, listening to his thundering heartbeat slow, then pulse steadily. 'Have you had many lovers?' she asked.

'No. Why do you ask?'

'Well, you're very ... I never ...'

Beau laughed, and kissed the top of her head. 'Thank you. You're wonderful. It's never felt like this for me either.'

'Really?' She looked up into his eyes.

'Really.' He stroked her cheek. 'How about you?'

'Lovers?' She shook her head. 'No. There was Jack, and one other chap – a summer romance, it was nothing really. But I never wanted to do "it" just to get it out of the way. You know how some girls do go on so about their virginity.' She stretched her arm across his chest and sighed happily.

'I'm glad. I can't tell you what it means that ...'

'You're the first?'

'Yes.' He kissed her tenderly. 'Are you thirsty? I brought some champagne with me.'

'Champagne?'

'It is your birthday.'

'I'll go and get some glasses.' Evie slipped out of bed and pulled over her kimono. She leant down to smell the lilies on the bedside table, and Beau traced her spine with his index finger, kissed the indentations at its base.

'Don't be long,' he said, as he pulled the bottle of Moët from his flight bag. Glancing into the bag as she passed, Evie spotted the corner of a pink envelope; the looping pale blue handwriting was unmistakably a woman's.

She ran downstairs, the floor cold beneath her bare feet. The letter troubled her. *Don't be a ninny*, she told herself. *It could be his sister.* Just as she was returning from the kitchen, Stella let herself in at the front door.

'Hello, darling,' she said. 'Did you have a miserable night?' She glanced down at the two glasses in Evie's hand. 'Or perhaps not?'

Evie hugged her. 'He's here.'

'I'm so happy for you.'

'Did you have a nice time?'

'Yes. Dropped home with a chaste kiss on the cheek, unfortunately, unlike you.' Stella smiled. 'Go on, you'll catch your death running around this place in your birthday suit. I'll be as quiet as a mouse, you won't know I'm here.'

'Is that Stella?' Beau asked as Evie slipped back into bed.

'Yes, she's home safely.'

He eased the cork out with a muffled pop, and Evie handed him the glasses.

'Happy birthday, Miss Chase,' he toasted her.

'I told you not to call me that.'

Beau kissed her, cold champagne flowing from his hot mouth to hers. 'Eve,' he said.

'I'm not sure I'm ready to be called Eve.'

'Yes you are. Evie is a girl's name. Look at you,' he rolled on to his side, ran his hand over the smooth curve of her waist.

'You're beautiful. Eve herself couldn't have been more lovely.' He reached over onto the bedside cabinet. 'I have something for you.' He handed her a red leather box.

'Cartier?' Her eyes sparkled. 'You shouldn't have.'

'Well, this is a special birthday.'

Evie eased back the lid. 'Oh, Beau, it's beautiful.' She ran her finger over the heart-shaped brooch, diamonds glittering on the filigree wings.

'It's to bring you luck. You've been keeping your guardian angel rather busy lately, so I asked them to make you a spare set of wings.'

At dawn, Evie crept out of bed and pulled on her uniform. She couldn't help smiling to herself as she looked at Beau stretched out in her bed. She picked up her brooch from its red box on the dressing table and pinned it to the underside of her jacket collar, smoothing it flat. As she turned to him, her eyes fell to the flight bag. Evie checked he was still sleeping, and crept silently forwards.

Her hand trembled as she pulled the letter out, her eyes on Beau. Quickly she flipped it over. There was an address on the back. 'Olivia Shuster, 2 Mansion—' She had no time to read further.

'Evelyn …' Beau's voice was low.

She jumped. 'My God, I thought you were asleep.'

'So you thought you'd have a poke through my private papers?'

Evie blushed. 'I'm sorry. I noticed the letter last night and I—'

'You couldn't resist the temptation?' He beckoned for her to come over. 'Where are you going anyway?' he mumbled sleepily as he pulled the letter from the envelope. 'Come back to bed.'

'I have to get to work,' she said, kissing his cheek as she reached across for her watch on the nightstand.

'Look.' He handed the letter to her. 'I have nothing to hide from you.'

Evie leafed through the pages of frantic scrawl. 'Oh dear, she's not taking this very well.'

Beau sighed wearily. 'She's never been easy. I dread to think what she'll do when she finds out about us.'

'Will you tell her?'

'Yes. I think having received this it's better if I do it face to face.' He caught Evie's hand, kissed it. 'You never have to doubt me, you know.'

'I know.'

'I could get used to this.' He yawned, rubbing at his eyes. 'It's quite a novelty being the one left in the bed in the morning.'

'If you want to make yourself useful, there's a load of wood in the back that needs chopping, and Monty could do with a good ride ...'

'So could I.' He pulled her into the bed, pinning her down as she laughed.

'Later.' She kissed him. 'You will be here won't you?' Evie turned as she ran to the door.

'Yes.' He settled back on the pillow, one arm behind his head.

'There's no food in the house.'

'I'd noticed. If I don't fancy the pickles I'll get a bite at the Bell. I thought I might take you out dancing tonight – Sunny's perhaps?'

'Sounds fun.'

Beau reached over to her bedside table and picked up a book. 'Instrument flying? Evelyn ...'

'Yes, I know it's naughty but I want to be prepared.'

'Don't tell me you were a Girl Guide?'

'Actually I was.'

'You're adorable. Fly safely, Miss Chase,' he said in his instructor's voice, 'and remember the four C's—'

'Compass, chart, clock, common sense.' She mock saluted him, then blew him a kiss.

WINTER

47

The Christmas lights on the tree cast pools of coloured light on the wall beside the fireplace. The girls had strung holly and ivy around the framed sketches of Eve and the angel that hung above the hearth.

'Have you heard from Beau?' Stella looked up from her knitting.

Evie yawned as she shook her head, and covered her mouth. 'Sorry. Gosh, I am sleepy. That wine with supper has knocked me out.' She was reading her instrument manuals, curled up in an armchair as they listened to the radio. It was bitterly cold and she was wrapped up in cashmere socks and a ruby scarf. Snow fell steadily from the dark sky outside, drifting on the windowsill, and Stalin lay sleeping as close as he could get to the fire, a faint smell of singeing fur in the air.

'That was a smashing meal,' Michael said. 'I didn't think I liked pheasant.'

'Ross delivered them. I think Daddy is trying to win me over. Ross said he hoped he'd see me for Christmas.'

'What about Beau, Evie?' Stella insisted. She cupped her cheek on her palm. Her face was rosy from the fire and wine, her words slightly slurred.

'He's not terribly big on letters.' Evie tried to hide her disappointment. Since her birthday there had only been a couple of stilted phone calls. The thought that he might be seeing Olivia to tell her about them bothered her. *They have so much history together, she thought. What if she manages to talk him round?* She forced the doubts from her mind, and laid down her book. 'I'm just glad we've been so busy, I haven't had a moment to think about him,' she lied.

Michael was sitting on the floor, sketching Stella, and he looked up at Evie. 'Why don't you go up and see him? You've got a day off coming up.'

She frowned. 'I would if I knew where he was based. He knows where I am,' she said stubbornly.

'No one really knows what those boys are up against. If he's flying out of Tangmere on missions, Lord knows what he's doing.' Stella said. She glanced up as the nine o'clock news programme came on the radio, and turned up the volume.

'Singapore has come under heavy attack by the Japanese,' the newscaster said gravely. 'HMS *Prince of Wales* and HMS *Repulse* have gone down with all souls on board—'

'Oh no.' Her hand flew to her mouth. 'That was where Richard flew. His squadron patrols the South China Sea.'

As Evie watched her, she saw Stella's face change.

'You know what that means?' Stella said. 'If he's been killed in action, there's no need for a divorce. We can get married straight away, and you can stay in the Church,' she said to Michael.

'Stella!' Evie was shocked. 'What about everyone else out there – your family and friends?'

'Yes, I suppose so ...' Stella coloured. 'I'm sorry. I don't feel quite myself. I opened my mouth without thinking.'

'I should jolly well think so,' Evie said.

'No, no, I'm sure they are fine.' Stella tried to make a joke of it. 'I don't know about Richard but I'm quite sure my mother will give the Japanese a run for their money.'

'Don't you care what happens to them?' Michael was looking at her in a strange way.

'Of course I care.' Stella threw down her knitting, blue wool spilling onto the floor. Stalin slunk under the chair and batted it away from her. 'Get off, you damn cat!' She whacked him, and he retaliated, scratching her hand. Stella sucked at the cut, tasting iron. 'Now look what you made me do.'

'I have to get going.' Michael stood and slowly folded over his sketchbook.

'Already?' Stella followed him to the door. 'Mike ...' she reached out for his arm but he pulled away. 'What is it?' Evie diplomatically headed out to the kitchen.

'I'm not sure I know you at all,' he said finally. 'If you can wish innocent people dead just so we—'

'I don't! I'm sorry, it was a stupid thing to say. I'm tired and a little shot up from the wine.' She rubbed her eyes, her fingertips smoothing the grey circles. 'Besides, who says Richard is innocent?' Her face darkened. 'How can you call him innocent after what he did to me?'

'He betrayed you, but does that mean he deserves to die?'

'Of course you're right.' She scowled. 'I'm always wrong. Just ask my mother. Poor old Stella – disappointing daughter, frigid wife, hopeless mother.'

'What brought this on?' Michael frowned. 'All this bitterness, I don't know that it's the best way to start our relationship.'

'What relationship? It's a friendship. One day, I hope it will be more.' She looked at him unsteadily. 'Michael, every time I go up in a plane, it could be my last flight. I don't want to waste any more time, can't you see?' She laid her hand against his chest, touched his face. 'I love you, and I want to be with you.'

He shook his head. 'I don't know any more.'

'What do you mean you don't know?'

'You ...' He shook his head. 'Sometimes you can be very cold.'

Stella saw the look of sadness in his eyes. She kissed him, desperately, her lips searching his, her arms pulling him to her.

'Stop, please.' He turned away from her. 'I can't do this, your husband ...'

'I want to be with you, Michael, really be with you.' She ran her hand along his broad back, felt the dip of the muscles at the base of his spine. Gently he pushed her away. 'I don't understand,' she said angrily. 'In Wales you said all those things ...'

'It was a wonderful night,' he said. 'But we got carried away, Stella. Right now, you are still a married woman.'

'Just go,' she said angrily, swinging the door open wide. 'Why don't you go and marry yourself one of those doe-eyed little imbeciles who queue up to touch your hand after every service? Get yourself a good little virgin ...'

He stepped out into the snow. 'Do you mean that?'

In answer she slammed the door in his face. She rested her head against the wood, waiting for his knock, for his voice to call her. In the silence she turned to face Evie.

'Are you alright, Stella? What happened?'

'I don't know,' she said hoarsely. 'I think we just broke up.'

'You shouldn't have said that, about Richard.' Evie leant against the kitchen door. 'God knows we all wish people were dead sometimes but to actually say it ...' She walked over and put her arm around her. 'Michael hasn't broken up with you. He has some big decisions to make, that's all.' She gave Stella's shoulder a squeeze. 'What do you say we finish off the wine, old girl? You look like you could do with another drink.'

The girls settled back on the sofa, the dancing flames of the fire illuminating the glass of red wine in Evie's hand. 'Why don't you tell me what's really going on? Have you been in touch with Richard since his telegram?'

'Do you know what I sent back? "You need me? I need a divorce."'

'Have you heard anything back?'

Stella shook her head. 'You know, he thought the Japanese would invade. He wanted David to be safe. Not once did he say he wanted me to be safe. It suited him, me coming to England. I thought it was a grand gesture, leaving, that he'd come running after us when he realised how much we meant to him, but no, he's probably been carrying on with that little whore all this time until he got bored.' Tears came to her eyes. 'Oh God, I hope they are all alright. Mummy couldn't bear to be in some ghastly POW camp, and my stepfather Reggie ... Lord knows what the Japs will do with the men if the island falls.'

'They want blood, for sure,' Evie said.

'The thing is, I don't know how to start again.' Stella's tears fell freely now. 'Everything ... the future was all bound up with Richard.' She thought of their friends, the nights spent laughing in the Grill Bar at Raffles. She wondered if she would ever feel that young and carefree again. Where were her friends now, dead or alive? 'And now, meeting Michael, I'm so confused.'

'Was it any help talking to the doctor?'

Stella shook her head. 'He was very kind, gave me some tablets for anxiety, but they're no use. They just make me drowsy – I mean look at the state of me tonight, and I can't fly like that.'

'Pills and wine? No wonder you're behaving oddly,' Evie said gently. 'Perhaps you should take a break? I'm sure they'd understand. Why don't you go to Ireland in January? You have some leave coming up.' She tucked her legs up on the sofa and turned to Stella. 'Think of David. You have your future there. You and your son. There's so much to look forward to.'

'I don't know. I can't think ahead. This war ... Who knows where we will be this time next year.'

Evie laid her head back against the sofa and closed her eyes. 'I don't know about you but I feel like I've aged ten years this year.'

'You're young, what are you talking about?' Stella laughed. 'I'm thirty-two, practically an old crone.'

'Thirty-two? I thought we were the same age.'

'No,' Stella shook her head. 'I was very firmly on the shelf when Richard picked me. That was half the problem, I think, I was just so grateful. I'd wanted a baby all my life, and when David came along I hoped it would all be perfect. But then Richard ...' Stella's face clouded as she remembered the moonlight, the tropical air, the soft moaning from the shuttered room. She stood watching them, chilled and nauseous, her husband's hands encircling the waist of the lithe girl, her dark hair spilling like oil over his arms as she writhed on top of him. She heard him call out, and then as she began to choke and cry, his voice uncertain, horrified, '*Stella?*'

'Stella?' Evie was looking at her. 'Are you sure you're alright?'

'Yes, absolutely,' she composed herself, blinked a couple of times. 'I think I shall take a few days off soon. It was a good idea of yours to go to Ireland and see David.'

'Good, I'm glad. You've had a horrible, horrible time. Richard's affair, Meggie, everything we've been through here. It's enough to have killed a mere mortal, Ice Queen.' Evie nudged her, and Stella laughed through her tears.

'I think I'm melting.' She sighed. 'Oh God, I wonder what will happen to them in Singapore?'

Evie drained her glass. 'Sometimes I wonder what will happen to all of us. I still can't believe the Japanese attacked Pearl Harbour. Surely the Americans will declare war on Germany now? At least united we'd stand a fighting chance.' Evie stood and wandered to the window. As she pulled aside the blackout curtain and looked out at the swirling snow, she thought of Beau, and hoped he was safe. *What will happen?* she thought. *What will happen to us all?*

48

'Aren't you coming out tonight to celebrate New Year? I heard the ATA parties are great fun.' Stella dragged a comb through her hair. She was sitting at her dressing table in a white cotton dressing gown. 'A few of the girls are going on to the Riviera afterwards.'

'No, I don't feel like celebrating. The news just seems to get worse and worse. I can't believe they've firebombed London. All those beautiful Wren churches, and the Guildhall...' Evie flopped down on the bed, still in her uniform. 'Besides, I'm shattered.'

'At least the Americans are in the war now.' Stella glanced over her shoulder. 'Come on, Evie, we can't have you moping around here.'

'I'm not moping,' she snapped back. 'I'm just tired.'

'Listen,' Stella said. 'You can't just sit around waiting to hear from Beau. Get out, have some fun with other men. He'll soon be down, you'll see.'

'Is that what you're doing? Trying to make Michael jealous?'

Stella dabbed perfume behind her ears. 'Yes, it makes me feel better if other men take an interest in me.' When she looked at Evie, her eyes were bright and defensive. 'Michael has the nerve to treat me like some temptation, something he has to resist. When I saw him at the Christmas service, it was like I was a stranger. Just another one of his parishioners.' Stella's head slumped. 'I don't know what I'm doing, Evie.'

'What you are doing,' she said calmly, 'is borrowing my silver evening bag, fixing your hair, and going out with the gang. Forget about everything else. Have fun, be young.' She pulled her car keys out of her pocket, and tossed them to Stella. 'Why don't you take my car, then at least you haven't got to rely on some drunk boy to get you home.'

At 1 a.m. Stella walked back from the Riviera towards the cars arm in arm with a young ATA pilot she knew from the base, laughing with Joy and the other girls.

'Let me drive you home, Stella, it's still early,' he murmured in her ear.

'Darling, you are sweet, but I have a car, and I'm shattered,' she lied.

He slipped his arm around her waist, pulled her closer to him. 'Come on, Stella, you know we'd have fun together.'

'No, really.' She was beginning to tire of him.

'I promise I'm not like the other chaps blathering away. You should have heard what Teddy was saying earlier, after a few pints. He's really got it in for you girls.'

Stella had seen Teddy and his cronies at the bar and had studiously ignored them. 'What was he saying?'

'That girls are only useful as bicycles not pilots.' The man swayed slightly. 'That he could think of a thing or two you could do with his joystick.'

'Did he say me, or just any of the girls?'

'Oh it's you, Stella, half the men in the base want to make love to you. He really lost his wool when you gave him the brush off. Do you know what they call you? The Ice Queen.'

'I know, but I'm not—'

'I promise you, Stella,' he slurred, 'you're pukka you are. I wouldn't do a thing to hurt you. Not like those twerps Doyle and Stent. Remember that Tomahawk?' He leant against a lamp post.

'What do you mean? What did they do?' she demanded, but he only tapped the side of his nose.

Stella felt sick. She began to run, pulled the keys from her pocket. As she drove through the dark roads towards White Waltham, she thought quickly. What if it were true? What if Teddy really did have it in for them?

The rectory was in darkness as she pulled up outside. Michael's flat was on the ground floor so at least she didn't have to risk shinning up the drainpipe. She ran around the side of the house to his bedroom window. She tapped softly and waited, shivering in the snow. The sash window slid up, and Michael poked his head out. 'Stella?' he said sleepily. She could see past him to a rumpled bed, white sheets golden in the lamplight.

'Michael, I need your help,' she said.

'Stella I can't ...'

'I haven't come here to make love to you, Michael. It's important, but there's no time to explain.'

He started to pull his clothes from the chair.

'I've got clothes in the car for you, just bring your boots,' she said.

Michael shrugged on Stella's flying jacket in the alleyway by the Riviera. 'This is madness,' he said as he bent down to the car window.

'Teddy won't recognise you. He never goes to church. You'll be perfectly safe.'

'I'm not worried about myself,' he said gently. 'I'm worried about you. You seem awfully tired, Stella. You need a break. Why don't I just take you back to the cottage?'

'Please, it's not for me,' she begged. She leant over the steering wheel towards him, her face in shadows. 'It's for Megan. I think they did something dreadful. Just find out what you can. If they ask, tell them you're down visiting family or something.'

'Where am I supposed to be based?'

'Debden, Norfolk. Tell them you're flying Spits.'

Michael slammed the door and strode towards the club. Luckily he was only slightly taller than Stella, so her Sidcot suit was a perfect fit. He pushed open the door of the club – it was quieter now, just a few couples left on the dance floor, but in a haze of smoke he saw Teddy and the other pilots still at the bar, laughing and talking. He took a stool nearby. Doyle looked up and he nodded at him.

'What'll it be?' the barman asked.

'Pint of beer.' Michael caught Teddy's eye. 'And whatever these boys are having.'

'Jolly decent of you,' Teddy said. 'Haven't seen you here before?'

Michael swivelled around on his stool to face them. 'Visiting my mother,' he said, imitating his clipped Service tone.

'Where are you based?'

'Debden, flying Spits.' Michael took a sip of his pint. 'What's this place like? Not many girls in tonight.'

'You missed most of them,' Stent said miserably. 'Bloody prick teasers every last one of them.'

'Blue balls, old boy?' Michael leant casually on the bar. His heart was racing.

'Occupational hazard now they've got the little bitches on every base,' Teddy said, his mouth twisting into a sneer.

'Don't agree with it at all, taking jobs from our boys, and as for the money they're paid ...' Michael goaded him.

'Good for you, that's just what I was saying.' Teddy slammed his palm on the bar. 'These girls take home more than our fighter pilots – it's an outrage.'

'Still, what can you do?' Michael's heart was in his mouth.

'Oh, this and that ...' Teddy took one of the pints the barman placed in front of him. 'Cheers,' he raised his glass to Michael.

'Things can go missing, or get mixed up,' Doyle leered.

'Such as?' Michael waited.

'Well, take that Tomahawk a while back,' Stent lurched unsteadily on the bar.

'You mean you ...?'

'Us?' Teddy's eyes narrowed, warning Stent. Michael realised they were all watching him. 'You ask a lot of questions, young man.'

'Just curious. Got to show these bitches who's boss.' He held his ground as Teddy leant towards him.

'Why would I get my hands dirty when there are plenty of men willing to do it for me,' he hissed. 'Of course,' Teddy went on, 'they can't prove a ruddy thing.' His face clouded for a moment. 'I didn't mean it to be that silly little girl ... Just wanted to show the Ice Queen a thing or two. She'd have been able to land the plane ... never would have flipped out ...' he rambled.

'The Ice Queen?' Michael drained his pint.

'Stella Grainger.' Stent belched as he put his empty glass on the bar.

'I'll melt her,' Teddy said under his breath, 'whether she likes it or not.'

'Excuse me.' Michael tapped him on the shoulder. As Teddy looked up he slammed his fist into his nose. 'That's my friend you're talking about.'

'Oh God, what happened?' Stella had the car running as Michael jumped in, holding the back of his hand against his mouth. In the shadows the blood looked black.

'Just drive,' he said. They pulled away just as Doyle, Stent and the others spilled onto the pavement. 'You were right,' he said, craning over his shoulder to see if the men were following.

'Michael, I'm so sorry, I had no idea they'd—'

'It was me.' Michael began to laugh. 'I threw the first punch. It felt good.' He flexed his fist. 'But the things they were saying ... It was dreadful, Stella.'

They drove back in silence. At the rectory she helped him out of the car. 'Thank you,' she said, unable to look at him.

He raised her chin. 'I had no idea what you have to put up with.'

'Most of the chaps are lovely, but I'm used to men like Teddy.' Stella's eyes fell. 'It was always the same, even in Singapore. I remember at a dance once I overheard Richard talking with some friends ... Horrible, like he was a different person. It's just men. The way they talk about women when they are alone.'

'Not all men are like that,' he said gently.

Stella raised her eyes to his. 'That's why I love you.'

'Stella—'

'No.' She put her fingers against his lips. 'I don't want you to say anything. I know you have a lot of things to think about.' She picked up her flight bag from the footwell. 'Can I come in for a moment?'

Michael sat stiffly on the bed, wincing as he lowered himself down.

'Let me take a look,' Stella said. He eased off her leather flying jacket. 'Thank God you were wearing this. It could have been a lot worse otherwise.' As Michael pulled off the flying suit, she ran a basin of cold water and soaked a couple of flannels. She turned to him. He sat in the lamplight, his white vest dazzling against his warm skin. 'Where does it hurt?' He peeled up the vest, his lean, hard stomach marked with a vivid bruise. Gently she placed the flannel there. 'Hold this,' she said, and with the other flannel began to clean his face, wiping away the blood from his swollen lip. The clock on the bedside table ticked softly. 'Why don't you lie down?' she said. She eased off his boots, and helped him into bed. 'I'm so sorry.'

'You have nothing to be sorry about.' She could hear the anger in his voice. 'It could have been you, in that plane. He said you would have landed it.'

Stella looked up. 'So it's true?'

Michael nodded. 'In the morning we're going to go and see your Commander. I'm going to tell him exactly what they said.'

'Thank you.' Stella perched on the edge of the bed. 'I let Megan down. It was my flight.'

'She was an adult, she knew what she was doing.'

'But I lost ... I lost her.' She began to shake.

'People make mistakes, Stella.' He stroked her cheek. 'Forgiveness is the greatest of all the virtues. Forgive yourself, Stella. None of this was your fault.'

'I don't want us to fight any more, Michael. I don't expect you to forgive me, or make any decisions,' she said. 'I can wait. I'm going to Ireland next weekend, to see David.' She looked at him. 'Richard's parents know what he did. They know I want to divorce him. If you were to come with me ...' When Michael didn't answer, Stella started to button her coat. 'I should go,' she said.

He caught her hand. 'No. Stay with me.'

'Are you sure?'

'Nothing's changed,' he said. 'I still can't ...'

'I know.' Stella slipped off her coat and curled up next to him fully clothed. 'I'm tired, Mike,' she said wearily. 'It's impossible. I'm just so tired of it all.'

As Stella drifted off to sleep, her head resting on his shoulder, he kissed her hairline, inhaled the warm, intoxicating scent of her. 'Nothing is impossible,' he whispered.

49

Commander Francis paced behind his desk.

'You are absolutely sure?' he said to Michael.

'Certain,' Michael said firmly. He was sitting next to Stella with his back to the door. 'Parker, Doyle, Stent – they were all in on it. The plane that Megan flew, that Stella was meant to fly, was deliberately set up.'

'Parker will deny it,' Francis said, 'and of course there's no evidence. The whole plane went up.' Stella flinched. There was a knock on the door. 'Well, let's see what he has to say for himself. Come in,' he barked.

'You wanted to see me, sir?' Teddy stood behind them. 'Mrs Grainger ...' He stared at Michael, who did not turn.

'Parker,' Commander Francis leant against the desk. 'Is there anything you want to tell me?'

'No, sir.'

'Are you sure? It would be a lot easier if—'

Teddy suddenly placed Michael. 'Whatever this girl and this young pilot have been saying ...' He floundered.

'You told me,' Michael said clearly, 'that you ordered the plane of a female pilot to be deliberately tampered with.'

'I said no such thing!' Teddy flushed purple. 'Commander, are you really going to take the word of some drunken, wet-behind-the-ears pilot over—'

Michael stood slowly and turned to him. For the first time Teddy saw his dog collar. 'What the ...?'

'Michael is the curate at St Mary's,' Francis said slowly. 'When Mrs Grainger came to him with her concerns he agreed to find out what he could.' The Commander strode around the desk and came face to face with Teddy. 'You fool, Parker. Shooting your mouth off in a public bar. Whatever you boys think in private,' he said evenly, 'you are at best an irresponsible, misogynistic fool, and at worst you are responsible for me losing a pilot.' He stepped back and cleared his throat. 'At the very least you should never have let Jones take Second Officer Grainger's flight. Consider yourself suspended until further notice.'

'Sir, I ...'

'That will be all.'

Teddy's fists clenched, white knuckled, and he marched out of the office.

Commander Francis shook Stella's hand. 'Let me assure you there will be a full investigation.'

'Do you think he's capable of sabotage, sir?'

'Capable, yes. Did he do it? Perhaps we'll never know, but an investigation will clip his wings. There have been isolated incidents of sabotage against our girls, I know.' Francis paused. 'But to actually cause another pilot's plane to fail like that? It would need to be sugar in the fuel, or water in the oil tank. Of course the evidence just disappears in an explosion. Impossible to prove one way or another.' He ushered Stella from the office. 'Enjoy your leave, Mrs Grainger. I do hope you will come back to us, in spite of all this.'

50

As Evie trudged through the drifts along White Waltham High Street with her shopping bag, she hummed softly to herself. Snow fell softly, deadening the sound of her footsteps. It was bitterly cold, and she pulled her knitted hat down over her ears. 'Afternoon, Miss Gold,' she said as she passed the secretary from the pool.

A car drew up alongside her and she glanced over.

'Need a ride?' a male voice said as the door swung open.

'Beau?' She lifted her bag into the car and jumped in beside him. Ace sniffed her hair from the back seat, licked her face.

'You look like a little pixie in that hat and with your red nose.'

'Charming.' She threw her arms around him. 'I've missed you,' she said, her words muffled in his scarf. 'Where have you been? I haven't had a word from you for weeks.'

'I'm sorry. I got caught up in something.' He stroked her cheek. 'I've been longing to see you.'

'I'm just glad you're safe.'

Beau pulled out onto the road. 'I was on my way over to your place.'

'Well you're in luck. I've just done the shopping.'

'Damn,' he said, laughing. 'I was rather looking forward to some of your pickled cucumbers ...'

'I wish we could stay like this forever,' Beau sighed contentedly. His shirt hung open, and Evie was wearing a grey silk nightgown. Night had fallen, and the remains of their meal lay on trays beside the fire.

Evie tossed another log on from the basket. She settled back in his arms on the floor, pulled the blankets closer around them. 'I think I've told you all the news from the pool. I still can't believe they've suspended Teddy,' she said. 'Good old Stella.'

'I heard they bollocked him from arsehole to breakfast time,' Beau said, 'and about time too. The man gives the rest of the chaps a bad name. I never trusted him, the way he pretended to have flown—'

'You mean he didn't?'

'It wasn't my place to call him on it, but I can't imagine he saw a great deal of action behind his mahogany Spitfire.'

'But I thought he'd been wounded.'

'His leg? That's real enough. He came off a motorbike, smashed up his hip.'

Evie stifled a giggle. 'I'm sorry, I shouldn't laugh.'

'I said to him once: "Why can't you be proud of what you are? Not everyone is cut out to be a fighter pilot, and the Ops chaps do a valuable job." But he wouldn't have it. "I don't like the cut of your jib, sir."' Beau mimicked Teddy's booming voice perfectly. 'I told him he was a jumped-up penguin.'

'I wish I had seen that.'

'Men like Teddy are dinosaurs. You girls are good, and each intake seems to be learning faster.'

'Well, the ATA training is second to none. Hadn't you heard? We have excellent instructors.' Her hand ran across his stomach, traced the hard edge of his belt. 'I always thought Stella would be a good instructor, she's so calm and methodical.'

'Unlike someone I could mention.' He kissed the top of her head and settled back, watching the leaping flames of the fire. 'Have you heard how she's getting on in Ireland?'

'She sounded so different on the phone, so light and happy. I could hear David gurgling away in the background. She said he's grown so much.'

'It must have been very hard for her, being away from her child. When's she coming back?'

'Saturday.'

'Do you think she'll stay?'

'I hope so, but losing Megan ...' Evie's brow furrowed. 'It really shook her up. I think she's still coming to terms with a lot of things.'

'Stella will survive. She's been through a lot, but she's strong.' He sighed as he looked at the fire. 'God knows, we need all the good pilots we can get.'

'Don't let's talk about the war,' Evie sighed sleepily.

'Alright.'

'Tell me what you want—'

'Right now, to get to bed. My leg's gone to sleep.'

She kissed him as he shifted towards her. 'What about later, after the war?'

'You. All I want is you, and I can't think beyond that, and this moment.'

'How about we disappear for a while soon? I have some leave coming up.'

'We could go to my place in Scotland.' He thought of the old stone house by the loch, near the little whitewashed church. He slipped his hand into his trouser pocket, felt the indentation of his mother's ring against the leather wallet. 'Evie, there's something I want to ask you.'

'Yes?'

He thought of the mission coming up. *What if I don't make it back? I couldn't bear to do that to Evie after Jack.* 'It can wait,' he said. 'We have all the time in the world, darling.'

'Do we?' Evie thought of all the people she had lost in the last few months.

'If not, we have to make the most of the time we have,' he said, pulling her into his arms. 'I've searched my whole life for you, and I'm not going to lose you now.' He kissed her neck, his words washing over her. 'I love you, Evie, and if we get through this war, I want our life, and our family to be different.'

Evie rolled over, straddled Beau as he reached up, his hands in her hair. 'Will you marry me?' she said.

'Marry you?' Beau laughed in surprise. 'Hold on a minute, I like to think I'm a fairly modern chap, but aren't I supposed to ask you?'

'You took too long. Like I said, we may not have forever.'

'But we have each other, now.'

Evie dug him in the ribs. 'So?'

'Ow! It's not fair. You can't just spring this on a man when there's no chance of escape!'

'I like it when I've got your full attention.' She gazed into his eyes.

'Evie ...' he said, serious for a moment.

'It wouldn't have to be a big wedding. We could just slip away, the two of us.'

Beau kissed her. 'Darling, I have to go away again soon,' he said.

'Away? Where?' Evie's face fell. 'Beau, I can't bear it. I never know where you are, or if you're in danger.'

He pushed a strand of hair away from her cheek. 'Trust me.'

Evie stood and stoked the fire. 'Well, you've had your chance.' She pulled a face at him and laughed, trying to hide her disappointment. 'I shan't beg you to marry me.'

'Is that the last of the wood?'

'Yes, would you mind getting some more?' As Beau pulled on his thick blue wool coat and opened the back door, a draught of cold air swept through the house. Evie flopped down on the floor and rolled over on her stomach to watch him. She could see snow falling in the light from the doorway as he trudged out to the woodshed, before the door banged shut behind him. She flicked on the radio for the news and it crackled into life. 'This is the BBC Home Service ...' The dancing flames were hypnotic, and when there was a knock at the door it took her a moment to come round. 'That's funny,' she said to Stalin. 'Maybe Beau's arms are full.' Reluctantly she heaved herself up and pulled on her dressing gown. She went to the back door, but there was no one there. Another knock, and she turned quickly, walked to the front door. 'Who on earth would be calling at this hour?' She unlatched the door, and pulled it open, snow dragging onto the mat. 'Daddy?' she said.

Leo turned to her. She was shocked at his appearance, dark circles under his eyes and a couple of days' growth on his chin.

'Evie,' he said uncertainly. As she hugged him tightly he relaxed. 'It's good to see you, darling.'

'You too, Daddy. Come in, come in.' She bustled him inside.

He picked up a crate from the doorstep. 'I thought you might like some fish. There's a couple of lobsters too.'

'Are you still going to South Ken on a Friday?'

'Yes. Funny isn't it? You can't get cheese for love or money, but you can have as many lobsters and prawns as you can carry ...' They fell into an awkward silence.

The back door blew open. 'Hello, Leo,' Beau said as he strode in with an armful of wood, dropping it into the wicker basket beside the stove. He offered him his hand.

'Alex, what a nice surprise. I hope I'm not interrupting anything?' He eyed Evie's dressing gown.

'Not at all,' Beau said. 'It's good to see you again.'

Evie looked from one man to the other, Leo dark and stocky, Beau athletic, golden. 'You two know one another? How?'

'This scoundrel?' Leo laughed. 'I've known Alex for years.' He pulled a bottle of wine from the inner pocket of his coat and handed it to Beau.

'Now I see where you get your tricks from,' Beau said to her. 'Do you have a corkscrew?'

'It should be in the dresser drawer.' She watched Leo as he settled down next to the fire. 'How do you know Beau?' she said, hands on her hips.

'I knew his mother, before the war.' He leant forward and beckoned Evie to come closer. 'Alex is a fine pilot and horseman, but not someone I'd want you to be involved with.'

'Excuse me?' she said indignantly. 'You waltz in here unannounced, after months of silence ...'

'I didn't want to intrude. I thought you needed time, and you made it clear you didn't want any fuss on your birthday. Talking of which,' he reached in his pocket and handed Evie a velvet pouch. 'These were Ingrid's, and I know she'd want you to have them. I was furious when I found out Virginia had made you hand them over.'

Evie tipped her diamond earrings out onto the palm of her hand. 'Thank you,' she said, and clipped them into her ears. 'You still can't come here and start dictating who—' Beau walked back in with a tray of glasses and she stopped herself. 'Look, Daddy brought my earrings back.' Evie showed him the large diamond studs in her ears.

Beau's face fell for a moment, but then he smiled. 'This is a treat, Leo,' he said, turning the bottle in his hand. 'Château Lafite?'

'It's a peace offering.' Leo raised his glass. 'I've come to apologise to Evie, and I noticed a few bottles had gone from the cellar so I guessed she liked it.'

'I've been busted. Sorry, Daddy, I should have asked. Anyway, what do you mean, apologise?'

'You were right, darling. Ross heard Virginia bragging to one of her bridge cronies about the bet she'd made with you. God knows I've turned a blind eye to a lot of things over the years with her, but when he told me what she was up to, that was it.' He took a sip of his wine.

'Where is the stepmonster?'

'Actually I don't know. In a funny way you being at home kept us together all this time. After you left, she turned the full beam of her dissatisfaction on me. I couldn't bear it.' He raised his glass. 'Quickie divorce, and I'm a free man.'

'Quickie?' Evie looked doubtful. 'How? I can't imagine Virginia walking away easily.'

Leo dipped his index finger in his wine and traced the lip of the glass. 'Let's just say I had my suspicions about her for a while ...' He paused. 'I have certain documents and photographs.

When I threatened her with a scandal, she went quietly enough.'
He emptied his glass. 'I just wanted to let you know the coast is
clear at the house.' He patted Evie's hand. 'I'll leave you to enjoy
your evening. Cullen must be getting cold out in the car.'

'You left him out there?' Evie said incredulously. 'Daddy.'

Leo considered her thoughtfully. 'You've changed, Evie. I'm
glad.' She helped him into his fur-collared coat, and Leo pulled
his hat on. 'I'm very proud of you, my dear,' he said. 'I wasn't sure
this was a good idea at all, but when I think of what you have
been through ...' He patted her cheek affectionately. 'Come home
anytime you want to.'

'Thank you,' she kissed him. 'But I'm perfectly happy here.'

'I'll see you out,' Beau said.

Leo closed the front door behind them and stepped out into
the snow, pulling his leather gloves on.

In the shadows, Beau's lighter flared. 'How did it go?' he asked.

'Perfect. We're all set.'

'For heaven's sake, you didn't talk me up did you?'

'No, no, exactly the opposite, just as you asked.'

Beau took a drag of his cigarette. 'If you gave me your seal of
approval she'd run a mile.'

'Do you think she's that childish?'

'No,' Beau laughed lightly as he exhaled. 'Rebellious,
headstrong ...'

'Just like you.' Leo clapped him on the back. 'Thank you for
calling. I'd wanted to come and see her for some time, but after
that dreadful falling-out when the American chap was killed ...
well, I wasn't sure she'd want to see me.'

'She loves you very much, sir,' Beau said. 'She missed you too.'

'You're a good man, Alex,' Leo said as they walked to his
steamed-up car, the silhouette of Cullen visible just above the
steering wheel. 'We older generation do appreciate doing things
the proper way. I'm so glad you asked me for Evie's hand. When
will you propose?'

'When the moment is right.' Beau laughed softly. 'Funnily
enough, Evie just asked me.'

'Did she? Good for her.'

'I was a bit taken aback.'

'You don't strike me as the traditional sort, Alex.'

'Perhaps not. I'd still like to propose properly. I was going to tonight, but this looks a bit insignificant after those earrings.' He showed Leo the solitaire diamond ring.

'Oh I say, old boy, sorry if I stole your thunder.'

'It can wait.'

'So you've cleared everything up with Olivia?'

Beau shook his head. 'She knows it's over between us. She doesn't know about Evie yet. I haven't had a chance to tell her face to face.'

'You're a braver man than me, Alex. Hell hath no fury ...'

'How are you, by the way?'

'So-so. Good days, bad days.'

'Are you in pain?'

'No, the doctors are very good. I've cheated fate many times in life, and I'm not going to let this ghastly disease get the better of me. I'm not called Lucky for nothing.'

Beau took a drag of his cigarette. 'Does Evie have any idea?'

'No. And I don't want her to. I have another round of treatment coming up. I'll only tell her if there's no hope.'

'I understand. Perhaps we both need some luck.'

'You take care of Jerry and I'll sort out this damn cancer.' They shook hands. 'When's your next mission?'

'I leave tomorrow.'

'Give my regards to your mother – if you see her.' Leo hesitated, hugged Beau tightly. 'Take care, my boy.'

51

Evie walked briskly along to the cottage, her boots skittering on the frozen, rutted track. She was fed up with the months of cold weather, and thought longingly of balmy spring days. 'I'm home,' she called. 'Managed to get back a bit early …' Her voice trailed off as she noticed the pile of suitcases by the door.

'Hello, Evie.' Michael stepped out of the shadows of the kitchen, his dark hat in his hands.

'Mike? What's going on?' Evie turned to the stairs as she heard Stella's footsteps on the bare boards. She could see her friend had been crying, her eyes red-rimmed and swollen. 'Stella?'

'I'm so glad you're back.' She ran to her, hugged her tightly. 'I felt awful just leaving a note.'

'You're leaving already? But you've only been back a couple of weeks. When are you coming b—'

'I'm not,' Stella interrupted. She pulled a crumpled telegram from her pocket and handed it to Evie. 'Richard's dead,' she said, tears streaming down her face. 'No. 232 Squadron lost some Hurricanes. He was one of the pilots that went down.' She balled up her hand, pressed it against her eyes. 'Oh God, I feel so guilty, after all those dreadful things I said.' She composed herself. 'I'm going back to Ireland, to be with David and his parents, until they … they send his remains. Though what they can possibly send home, I don't …' Her shoulders began to shake as Evie took her in her arms.

Michael stepped forward and picked up the cases. 'I'm going to take Stella to Ireland. I don't think she should be travelling alone in this condition.'

'Stella, I'm so sorry,' Evie said. 'What am I going to do without you? Megan, now you …'

'You have Beau, darling.'

Do I? Evie thought. She had heard nothing from him for weeks, and the uncertainty was killing her. 'Of course I do.' She forced a smile as she hugged Stella. 'But everyone knows chaps come and go. We girls have to stick together.'

'I don't feel like I'm much use to anyone at the moment,' Stella said as she glanced at Michael. 'I feel broken …'

'No,' he said kindly. 'You're not broken. As I said to one of my recently widowed parishioners the other day, you can't let yourself break down, you need to break open. Holding all this grief inside you all these months, that's what has made you ill, darling. To get well, to feel whole again, you need to let yourself grieve. Every loss we face and survive makes us stronger.'

'I'm sure you're right.' Stella's face was etched with sorrow.

Michael's words struck a chord with Evie. She looked at her friend. 'You have to go out there and fight for your happiness. You can do it, Stella.'

'I'm sorry, we have to go if we're going to catch the train,' Michael said as he looked at his watch. 'I'll wait outside for you.' He turned to Evie. 'See you soon.'

'You're lucky,' Evie said as she gently wiped away Stella's tears. 'It may not feel like it now, but you have so much. You have a beautiful child, and a good man who clearly loves you. Don't let him go.'

Stella hugged her. 'Thank you, Evie, I couldn't have survived this year without you. Will you be alright?'

Tears pricked Evie's eyes. She felt very tired suddenly, and very old. 'Me?' She smiled brightly. 'I'm fine. I'll be fine.' She glanced at the sketches above the fireplace, and walked over. 'Don't forget your drawing.' She handed the Spencer to Stella.

'Queen of the Air.' Stella smiled sadly.

'That's you. And don't you forget it.' Their eyes met. 'You'll get through this. It's time to let go, Stella – forgive, grieve, do whatever you need to do to get well.'

Stella nodded, unable to speak for a moment. She turned to Evie as she walked outside, a tear trickling down her cheek. 'I'll miss you.'

'I'll always be there when you need me,' Evie called from the door. She watched as the taxi drove away up the lane and disappeared into the fog. She raised her hand as the lights disappeared around the bend, and silence fell. The light was fading, and her footsteps sounded loud to her as she walked back into the dark cottage. She looked around her, remembering all the nights she had spent here with Stella and Megan, with Jack, with Beau. It didn't feel like home any more. 'I want to go home,' she said softly. Without bothering to change, she locked up the house and went out through the frozen garden, the wind biting at her raw cheeks. In the stable, she quickly saddled Monty, and flung open the door. 'Come on,' she said as she wheeled him around and dug her heels in. 'We're going home.'

The milk sky grew dark as she rode, her breath and Monty's mingling as she galloped across the countryside. The pounding of his hooves on the frozen earth, his surging body, were in rhythm with her heart. Ice-encrusted power lines cracked and hissed above her, frosted trees bowed down to the ground. Evie kicked Monty on, guided him down the driveway to her father's house, his hooves scattering the gravel as she raced home. She leapt down from the saddle by the main door and yanked the heavy iron bell-pull. Evie calmed her breath as she waited, the bell ringing distantly in the blacked-out house. Above her the moon was rising, a perfect silver orb, the first stars appearing in the sky.

The door opened and golden light spilled out. 'Miss Evelyn?'

'Hello, Ross. Is Daddy at home?'

'I'm afraid not. Mr Chase is working late in town tonight.'

Her heart sank. 'Working late?' *At the 400 more likely.* 'Never mind. I'll wait up for him.'

'Shall I ask the groom to take Montgomery round for you?'

'No, that's fine. I'll settle him in.'

Evie could see the concern on the old butler's face. 'Have you had supper yet, Miss Evelyn? I could ask the cook to lay up the dining room for you.'

'Don't go to any trouble for me. I'll make a sandwich or something.'

Ross watched Evie walk her horse around the corner of the house to the stable yard. He smiled and nodded. 'Good girl,' he said quietly. 'Welcome home.'

Evie sat on the kitchen table, swinging her legs as she ate her cheese sandwich.

'Right, I'm off to collect Mr Chase,' Cullen called from the scullery passage.

'Thank you, Cullen. Mind the roads – it's treacherous out there tonight.' Ross was polishing the silver cutlery, placing each piece carefully in a velvet-lined drawer.

'Ross, how long have you known Daddy?' Evie asked him.

'Since the Great War, Miss. I was his batman, as you know.'

'Does he seem alright to you?'

Ross paused, put down the knife he was cleaning. 'I think it would be best if you asked your father yourself, Miss Evelyn,' he said kindly.

'I'm sure you're right.'

The luxuriousness of the house was like a drug to Evie. She walked barefoot across her room, and stepped into a hot bubble bath, sighing with relief. Her eyes drooped as she sank into the warm water, and her thoughts roamed over the last weeks and months. She ran her hand across her stomach, the jutting arc of her ribcage, as she thought of Beau. *I need to see you,* she thought.

Evie wrapped herself in a heavy white towelling gown and walked to the window, pulled back the blackout blind. She stared out at the full moon, its silvery light illuminating the frosted grounds as brightly as the sun. *Where are you?*

There was a tap on the door. 'Come in,' she called.

Ross popped his head around the door. 'It's my night off, Miss Evelyn, but I've laid a fire in your father's study, if you want to wait up for him.'

'Thank you.'

After he left, Evie dressed in soft, lavender-scented pyjamas. She pulled a pair of cashmere socks from the drawer, and hopped on one foot as she slipped them on. 'I feel like a new woman,' she said to Muv. Evie picked the doll up and traced her finger across its bandaged face. 'Good to see you out and about again,' she said, carefully replacing the old doll on the polished cabinet.

In the study, Evie poured herself a cognac from the cut-glass decanter Ross had put by the fireside for her, and settled back in the leather wing-backed chair to wait for her father. She closed her eyes, her fingers stretching appreciatively over the warm, soft leather. *And she fell asleep for a hundred years*, she thought to herself. She dozed fitfully, dreamt of the moon, and Beau, his face so real she could reach out and touch it. With a jolt, she woke, and rubbed her eyes. The fire had died down, the coals glowing softly. *What time is it?* Evie looked up at the ornate gold clock above the mantelpiece. *One o'clock? It's late for a week night, even for Daddy.*

Evie yawned and stretched. She padded around to her father's desk and flicked on the brass lamp, the green glass shade glowing softly. *I wonder if he's seeing someone new?* She tapped a pencil on the leather jotter. The corner of a black-and-white photograph caught her eye, and she flipped the folder open. Lying on top of a letter Leo had been writing was a photograph of Evie in her ATA uniform. Evie's gaze travelled to the letter.

Dear Ingrid,

Evie's eyebrow arched in surprise. *He's writing to Mummy?* Evie picked up the letter and read on, trying to decipher Leo's tangled scrawl.

Thank you for your letter, my dear. It's good to know all is well with you and the children. I'm glad you liked the last photos I sent of Evie. Enclosed is the latest of her in uniform. You would be very proud of our little girl - a second Officer now, and giving the chaps a run for their money! I'm glad to report she is seeing a most suitable young man.

'Most suitable?' Evie muttered. 'Daddy told me to stay away from Beau.'

After all the heartache of losing her fiancé and her dear young friend, I haven't had the heart to tell her about my recent illness

A wave of nausea swept through Evie.

Unless things reach a critical point, I have no plan to. Our dear girl has had so much loss in her young life, I won't burden her with this. Just be aware you may need to step up to the plate, as it were.

Her hands were trembling as she read on.

Everything is in place with Evie's trust fund, you'll be glad to hear. Thanks to you, she is now an independently wealthy young woman. It will amuse you to hear she didn't rush out and blow the lot on shoes as we suspected she might. In fact she has a most interesting business idea that I shall fill you in on later. We can be proud, Ingrid. However much we, or I, to be

381

*more truthful, messed up our marriage, we
raised a truly marvellous young woman.*

My love, as always,

Lucky

Evie carefully replaced the letter and photograph just as they
were and returned to the fire. She stoked the coals, her mind
reeling, and settled back into the chair, tucking her feet beneath
her. *What illness?* She took a gulp of the cognac.

She heard the sound of the car pulling into the driveway, and
her father's voice bidding Cullen goodnight. The front door
slammed shut, and the heels of his shoes clicked across the marble
floor towards the study. Leo swept in and tossed his briefcase
and coat onto an armchair.

'Evie!' She ran to him, buried her head on his shoulder. 'Is
everything alright darling? What's wrong?' He led her to the old
Chesterfield in front of the fire. 'Come on, darling, sit down. Let
me get you a cognac.' He glanced over. 'Oh, I see you already
have one. What is it, darling? Is it Alex?'

Evie shook her head. 'No, he's fine, as far as I know.' She
looked at her father. 'Daddy, why didn't you tell me? Why didn't
you tell me you're ill?'

Leo's gaze fell. 'How did you find out?'

'I saw the letter you were writing to Mummy.'

Leo playfully smacked her hand. 'Evie. You know what they
say about curiosity ...'

'Daddy?'

'I'll be fine, don't you worry about me.' He could see she was
waiting for an explanation, and sighed. 'It's cancer, darling.'

'Cancer? Oh God!' Evie's hand flew to her mouth.

'Now look, this is exactly what I didn't want. After
everything you've been through ...' He hugged her tightly. 'I
don't want you worrying about your old man, do you hear? I
have excellent doctors, and they don't call me Lucky for no
reason.'

'Stop it, Daddy.' Evie settled back on the sofa, holding his hand. 'How long have you known?'

'A few months.'

'And?' He suddenly looked very fragile to her as he shook his head silently. 'Well, that's it. I'm moving back in.'

'You don't have to do that, darling. You have your own life now.'

'Nonsense, I want to help take care of you. First thing tomorrow I'll go and pick up my things from the cottage.' Evie touched his face gently. 'I'm here now, Daddy. It's all going to be alright.'

52

'It is good to talk to you, Stella. It's been ages. You wouldn't recognise the place. Some woman called Jackie Cochran has turned up with a bunch of Americans. It's great fun. So, have you changed your mind? Are you coming back?' Evie covered her ear, the noise of the mess cutting into the phone booth.

'I'm not, Evie, I'm sorry. Or at least not yet. I might put in for a transfer eventually,' Stella said. 'I'm feeling so much better, but seeing David again, I just can't leave him for so long next time.'

'Has there been any news of your mother?'

Stella fell silent for a moment. 'No,' she said. 'All we know is she's in a POW camp. There's been no news of Reggie at all. Richard's father has been so kind, trying to help me find out more. It's unbearable to think of what they all must be going through.'

'Keep strong, darling, for David.' Evie twisted the flex of the phone around her finger. 'What about you? What are you going to do now?'

'I'll stay here for a while. George and Sarah have been so good, I didn't feel I could just go. In a funny way it's like we've been living in a bubble. I can't believe it's March already. What's been happening with you?'

'Busy as ever. Daddy seems to be doing well.' Evie leant against the wall of the phone booth. 'Oh, and we had a visit from King George and Queen Elizabeth at the pool.'

'No! How exciting.'

'Archie was as pleased as punch – he was tasked with being an escort for the day. The Queen seems lovely. She shook everyone's hand and spent ages talking to Pauline.'

'What about you? Have you been out much? I hope you haven't just been sitting around waiting for Beau to turn up.'

'I'm fine.' Evie hoped she sounded convincing. 'When I'm not flying, I'm busy at the house taking care of Daddy.'

'I hope you're taking care of yourself too?'

'Don't worry about me. I went to a preview of *They Flew Alone* the other night with a few of the girls.'

'Was it good?'

'It was fun – Anna Neagle was good as Amy – but they made women pilots seem frightfully glamorous.'

'Did they? Isn't that hilarious.'

'If only people knew. They delivered a new top dressing for the runway, and the damn stuff was full of rusty nails. Took them a while to figure out why all the tyres were bursting on landing. We've all been crawling around on our hands and knees for the last few days.'

'Sounds *very* glamorous.'

'At least now they've found some big magnets and they've got trucks sweeping the field.'

'Do you think it was sabotage?'

'No, just a ruddy cock-up.' Evie put some more coins in. 'It's all going ahead with the farm, by the way,' she said. 'Daddy drove up to Wales to meet Rhodri and they hammered out a fair deal. It's ours, Stella, whenever you're ready.'

'You mean it?'

'Absolutely. Rhodri and Nia are so relieved about it all, and Bill will stay on in the farm cottage to run things. Apparently the dreaded cousins are livid. I keep thinking how happy Megan would be—'

'I can't believe you're doing this. It's so generous of you.'

'Nonsense. I need a tenant for the farm, and the airfield makes good business sense for me.'

'Oh, it's so exciting. I can't wait to move to the farm. Do you remember how beautiful it was, that lovely beach?'

Evie thought back, remembered the first time Beau kissed her. 'Yes, it was wonderful.'

'Perhaps if I got a transfer to Whitchurch, I could convince my Aunt Dorothy to come up from London and help me with David when I'm flying.'

'It will be good for you to have some company. I'm just looking forward to visiting you and Michael there.' When Stella didn't answer, Evie pushed more coins into the slot. 'Stella? He will be there, won't he?'

'I hope so. We had a wonderful time here, and he adored David. It was a bit strange for him, I think, meeting Richard's parents.'

'Let him get used to it.' Evie checked the coins in her hand. 'This is real life. What does he expect?'

'The fairytale, don't we all? Talking of Prince Charming, where's Beau?'

'I don't know.' Evie bit her lip. 'I don't like it, Stella. I haven't heard a peep from him for weeks.'

'Trust him, Evie.'

'What if he's seeing someone else, or Olivia has got her claws back into him?'

'No, not Beau.'

'Why not Beau? Men are all the same.'

'No, they're not,' Stella said firmly. 'There are good men out there.'

'I just can't shake this feeling there's something going on.'

'Look after yourself, Evie.' Stella's voice was strained with emotion. 'I don't know what to say, how to thank you.'

'Be happy, darling, and get to Barafundle Bay as soon as you can. That's all the thanks I need.' The pips sounded. 'I've got to go. Give David a kiss for me.' The phone cut out, and Evie pushed open the door, jumping as Stent stepped forward.

'Alright, Evie?' He stood a little too close to her. 'What you dicing with today then?'

'Hurricane from Martlesham to Tangmere, and a Spit to drop back to Debden for No. 111 squadron. Nothing very exciting.'

'Going to see your Jerry are you?'

'He's not German, and I'll thank you to mind your own business.'

Stent's eyes scanned slowly down her body. He had her trapped against the phone booth. 'Bloody shame if you ask me. Americans, Germans, why don't you give a proper Englishman a try, eh?' He brushed the back of her hand with his fingertips and she flinched. 'No?' His face contorted. 'Well I'd watch my back if I was you. Couple of our lads got shot at ferrying Spits yesterday. Messerschmitts appeared out of nowhere. It's like someone is leaking information. Maybe someone with ATA and German connections ...'

Evie pushed the door hard against his shin. As he doubled over she stepped neatly out of the booth. 'I'd be careful what you're saying, Stent. Careless talk and all that. Look what happened to Teddy.'

At the counter she ordered an orangeade.

'Everything alright, dear heart?' Diana asked her. Her lustrous dark hair was neatly brushed into an elegant roll, and she had a leopard-skin coat draped over her shoulders.

'Hello, Di.' Evie pecked her on the cheek. 'I'm so glad you're here at last. You look marvellous.'

'You'd never guess my face had been smashed up, would you?' She inclined her head. 'I've been terribly restless in hospital, just dying to get in the air again.'

'I promise you,' Evie said wearily, 'your feet won't touch the ground. We are frightfully busy.'

'Is everything OK? It looked like Stent was bothering you.'

'Him? No, he's nothing to worry about. I think the goons are vying for top position now Teddy has been suspended.'

'Do you think they'll let him back?'

'Let's hope not, or perhaps they'll just shove him to some base where there are no women for him to terrorise.' Evie sipped at her drink. 'You do look pretty. Are you going to town?'

'Yes, there's a party at the Embassy later. Would you like to come? There's room in my car.'

'Thank you, but I've got a chit.'

'Another time. Can't have you staying home when Beau's not around.' Diana picked up her gloves.

'Di, do you know Beau well?'

'Not terribly. He's a bit brusque, but I can see why you've fallen for him.'

'Do you know what he did before the war?'

'He's been in the RAF as long as I've known him. His mother has a stud in France, I think. I'd see him occasionally, skiing in Chamonix.'

'What about his father? Did he ever go to Germany to see him?'

'Why don't you ask him?' Diana nudged her. Her eyes opened wide in mock horror. 'Goodness, do you think he could be a spy?'

53

The weather had closed in at Martlesham, and Evie spent a frustrating morning waiting for the cloud to clear so she could fly her Hurricane down to Tangmere. She had some change left and decided to ring Leo to warn him she may not be home that night. There was no answer at the house, but the phone box took her money.

'Damn.' Evie thumped the handset down. She thought for a moment, then decided to ring him at work. She knocked on the Duty Pilot's door.

'Excuse me, do you have a telephone directory? I need to call the Air Ministry.'

He looked up at her through a haze of pipe smoke. 'Oh dear, I hope it wasn't something we said?'

Evie smiled as he handed over the heavy book. 'Not at all. I just need to speak with my father.' She rang the number and waited. 'Hello? Yes, I'd like to speak with Leo Chase.' She tapped a pencil on the desk as she waited. 'He's not there? Thank you.' She hung up the phone and frowned.

'Chase?' the Duty Pilot said. 'There was a call for you earlier, put through from No. 1.' He sorted through some papers and handed her a number. 'I am sorry. One of the chaps should have passed this on to you earlier. Your father was trying to get hold of you.'

'May I?'

'Help yourself.' He turned the black Bakelite phone towards her again. 'I was just going to get a cup of tea, can I bring you one?'

'Thank you.' Evie dialled the number and waited for the connection. 'Hello, is that you, Daddy?'

'Evie,' he sounded relieved. 'I am sorry to call you at work, darling.'

'Is everything alright?'

'No, not really, darling, but I don't want you to worry—'

'Daddy?'

'I'm in hospital ...' The line crackled. 'They want to operate tonight ... The cancer ...'

Evie sank back onto the chair. 'Where are you? I'm coming straight there.'

'No, no you're not. Evie, I want you to find Alex. I want you both here before—'

'Daddy, you will pull through won't you?'

'I'll be fine. I won't let them touch me until you both get here, come tomorrow if you can.'

'But why do you want to see Beau? You told me to stay away from him.'

'Evie,' he said, laughing gently. 'If I'd have told you quite how much I admire the chap you would have run a mile.'

'No I wouldn't, I—'

'Darling, I know you.'

'I don't know where he is,' she said, her heart racing. 'Daddy, all the stories I've heard about him ...'

'Don't listen to them. Alex is a good man. Trust your heart, Evie ...' The line hissed, crackled. 'Trust him, in spite of ...' The line cut off.

'Daddy?' Her heart lurched, she felt sick. 'Daddy?'

'There we are.' The Duty Pilot placed a cup of tea in front of her. 'Oh dear, not bad news I hope?'

'Thank you.' The spoon rattled in the saucer as Evie took the cup from him. 'It will be fine.' Her mind was racing. 'I just need to get out of here as soon as possible.'

Evie paced to and fro in the mess, waiting for the cloud to clear. Being in East Anglia reminded her uncomfortably of the time she had flown over Martlesham, hoping to see Jack. She flung herself down into an armchair by the stove and picked up a pack of cards. Evie skilfully shuffled the deck, her heart beating fast. *I have to get out of here*, she thought, *but how on earth am I going to find Beau?* The thought of Leo, alone and in hospital, was unbearable to her. As she flicked the cards into an empty cup, a young pilot approached her.

'Say, aren't you Evie?' the young American asked her.

She glanced up and smiled. He had sandy hair, a wide, friendly grin. 'Yes, I'm Evelyn Chase.'

'I recognised you from Whitchurch. Do you mind if I join you?'

'Please do.' Evie took her feet off the chair opposite. She felt sick, and shaky, but she tried to appear calm.

'It's great to meet you properly. My name's Jim, but everyone calls me Red.' He ruffled his sun-streaked red hair. 'Jack Whitman was my best buddy.'

'You're Red?' Evie sat up straight. She thought back to Bristol, to the man Jack had shared a room with. His face was vaguely familiar. 'Jack told me about you.'

'He was a good friend.' He turned the cup of coffee in his hand. 'There aren't many of us Yanks over here yet, but I think that'll change now.'

'Did you go home for his funeral?' Evie had forced herself not to dwell on Jack. She was surprised now to find that instead of the keen pain and anger that had haunted her for months, she felt a new peace when she thought of him.

'I couldn't get enough leave. Wish I had gone. We grew up together, you know. Same school, signed up together ...' Red paused. 'Just a couple of buddies, it all seemed like a big adventure.' He fell silent. 'Did you meet his parents?' Evie shook her head. 'They're great, straight up, just like Jack.' He stared around the mess. 'Half the time I don't know where I am with these guys. There's something going down again tonight.' He sighed. 'Jack had written his parents, you know, told them about you.'

'Really?' She smiled sadly, thinking about that other life they had dreamed of.

'In fact, I have something for you.' Red pulled out his wallet and flicked through. He slipped out a photograph and handed it to her. 'I'm guessing Jack never gave you a photograph did he? He wasn't that kind of guy.'

Evie ran her thumb across Jack's smiling face. His cap was tipped back on his head, and he had a cigarette clamped in the corner of his mouth.

'He was crazy about you,' Red said. 'Never seen him like that about a girl. Maybe he didn't show it, I don't know ...' Tears pricked Evie's eyes unexpectedly. 'Hey, I'm sorry, I didn't mean to upset you.'

'No, really, it's fine.' She wiped at her eyes with the heel of her hand. 'I've had some rather bad news, and it's just ... it's seeing his face again. You forget, don't you.' She forced a smile. 'Have you got a girl?'

'Me? Sure I have, back home.' Red flipped the photographs over, showed her a picture of a young girl sitting on a swing seat, her blonde hair tied back in a ponytail. 'I'm going to ask her to marry me next time I'm home,' he said proudly.

Evie looked at the photograph of Jack. 'I have something for you too,' she said, and pulled the long gold chain from around her neck. She unclipped it, and slid Jack's ring onto her hand. As she passed it to Red, the sapphire glinted in the winter sunlight. 'Jack would have wanted you to have it,' she said.

'No, I couldn't possibly ...'

'It seems right,' she said, 'you taking it home.'

'But don't you want it as a keepsake?'

Evie slipped the photograph into her breast pocket beside her cigarette case and laid her hand flat against where Beau's brooch was pinned on the underside of her collar. 'No, I have everything I need here.'

The tannoy crackled. 'Will Second Officer Chase go to the field. Hurricane standing ready.'

'At last,' she said, and quickly gathered up her charts and parachute.

'Fly safe,' he said.

Evie paused and glanced over her shoulder. 'I always do.'

54

As the Hurricane roared through the skies towards Tangmere, Evie thought of everyone she had lost in the last few months. It seemed like a lifetime since Peter had introduced her to Captain Bailey at the New Year's party. She thought of her father that night, in his element at the heart of the party, so vibrant and full of life. She desperately wanted to see Beau, to feel his arms around her, to feel safe. It was as if the whole world had keeled on its axis. The thought of her father gravely ill made her feel like a small, lost child.

She had flown this route so many times now, she barely had to check her maps. The only thing she had to worry about was every pilot's nightmare, the odd stray 'nomad' barrage balloon that might pop up unexpectedly. When she landed at Tangmere, she saw a black night fighter Spitfire Mk VB ready on the runway and guessed it must be hers. The clouds were still low, sleet drumming on the roof of the hangar as she raced to the Watch Office.

'How's the weather looking?'

'Well,' the Duty Pilot said, his pipe clenched at the corner of his mouth. 'It's bally cold, low cloud, apart from that it's perfect flying weather. Frankly you were lucky to get in safely.'

'Thank you,' she said as he handed her the slip of paper.

'Still, there's a full moon tonight and they say it's going to clear up later, so we mustn't grumble.'

'How are things here?'

'It's not the same since Jerry captured Bader. Morale is a bit low, but we carry on.'

'Tell me, do you know Wing Commander Beaufort?'

'Beau? Yes, he's always coming through here. Super chap, and jolly popular. You're the second gal we've had asking about him today. His fiancée was in earlier.' Evie's heart sank as he carried on scanning the roster. 'Then again she's in most days ...'

Evie gripped the back of the chair in front of her. *Fiancée?* she thought. 'Is he here today?'

He made a show of checking the roster. 'I can't say.'

'Please. It's very important. My father—'

The Duty Pilot sighed. 'Miss Chase, if I could tell you—'

'You would?'

'I really can't tell you his movements.' He waited until a couple of pilots left the office. 'All I will say is, if you hold on a minute or two before taking off, things might clear up for you.'

'Thank you,' she said, and raced out towards the airfield.

Evie stood in the shadows of the hangar, smoking nervously. *What the hell is Olivia doing down here? I was right. What a fool ...* Leo's words came back to her. *'Trust him. Trust your heart.'* Evie ran her thumbnail against her lip. *Nothing makes any sense these days.* A black cat crossed in front of her, trotting inside carrying a limp mouse in its jaws.

'Someone got lucky,' she murmured. As she watched the driving rain illuminated against the weak lights of an approaching black car, she thought of Amy Johnson, how she had been caught out on a day just like this a year ago. It made her think of the poem the girls all loved so much: *Dicing with death under leaden skies ...*

'What do you think, Miss?' An engineer appeared at her elbow.

Evie shook her head. 'The cloud's on the deck. I'm going to lie doggo a bit longer. It's not a Priority 1.' She ground out her cigarette, and hunkered down to wait out the rain.

A black car stopped at Tangmere Cottage and the driver jumped out to open the passenger door. As Evie watched, a dark figure ran from the cottage and dived into the car, holding his hat to his head, crouched down against the wind. The car sped along towards the hangar, tyres hissing through the puddles as a black Lysander Mk III circled the airfield and straightened up to land. It taxied to a halt a little way from the hangar, and a couple of engineers ran out to meet it, the mist and fumes swirling around them.

'Fill up the long-range tanks,' a voice said. Evie pricked up her ears – it was Beau. She poked her head out to wave at him, but it was raining so heavily now she pulled back. Her eyes widened as she saw him run to the dark car and signal them to drive towards the hangar. She didn't want to tell Beau about her father while there were other people around, so she quickly crouched down in the shadows behind a pile of parachutes. She heard the car pull in, and Beau ordered the engineers out. Evie's heart was racing – he was talking to someone in German.

She could hardly hear above the noise of the rain on the curved tin roof, but gradually she began to pick up the conversation.

'Yes sir, the plane is ready,' he said. 'No one knows what is going on here … They are expecting you, but we must get you out of here before anyone sees you.' Peeking through the parachutes, Evie couldn't see the other man's face. Beau looked exhausted, his hair plastered against his skull from the rain, dark circles under his eyes. All she could see of the other man was that beneath his dark overcoat he was in the unmistakable grey uniform of a German officer. Beau pulled the coat closed.

'For God's sake, keep covered up. Don't put your cap on until we're away. Someone might see you, and you know how gossip spreads.' Something warm and slimy fell against her hand and Evie jumped. The cat had dropped his half-chewed mouse on her. Shaking, she flicked it away.

'Yes, sir,' she heard Beau saying. 'The weather is bad but that should work in our favour. Once we are over the top, our route to France will be clear, it's a full moon, and the forecast is good on the other side so we can come in at treetop height as arranged.

Our first turning point will be Caen, and we will follow the River Orne down to the Argentan region. I assure you, I have successfully helped many people ...' Their voices faded away as they walked to the Lysander.

Evie was trembling as she crept out, shaking the stiffness from her limbs. *What is he up to?* For a split second, as she thought of her conversation with Olivia, doubts filled her mind. *Think*, she told herself. *There's no way on earth he'd be smuggling out Jerries from an RAF base. Daddy said I can trust him. Whatever he's up to, he's on our side.* She checked her watch. If she was going to get her Spit out of here while it was still light, she had to get moving. As the men checked over their papers, she ran to the mess to pick up her charts. *Olivia is another matter*, she thought, as she stuffed them into her flight bag. *When, if, he calls me, I'll find out what's going on with her. Right now, I'm going to deliver my Spit and get on the first train to London, without him.*

As she raced out of the offices, from the shadows someone grabbed her arm. She came face to face with Olivia, soaked to the skin and deathly pale.

'What on earth ...?' Evie snatched her arm away angrily. 'How did you get in?'

'I told them I'm Alex's fiancée. What do you think?' She flashed her opal ring. 'More to the point, what are you doing here?' Olivia challenged her.

'Excuse me? I work here.' Evie started to walk away, but couldn't resist finding out the truth. She strode back to where Olivia stood, sheltering from the rain. 'You're making a fool of yourself. The engagement is off, Olivia. Beau told me he'd broken with you once and for all.'

A smile twitched on her lips. 'Beau now is it? He doesn't get you to call him sir when you're in bed?'

'That is none of your business!' Evie clenched her fist. 'Olivia, you need to move on. Nothing happened between me and Beau while you were still engaged, that's all you need to know.'

'Oh, how decent of you. That's supposed to make me feel

better is it?' As a group of pilots in Mae Wests crowded through the door the girls stepped to one side. 'It's not over,' she hissed.

Evie heard the Lysander's engine start up out on the runway. 'Well if you're looking for Beau, you've just missed him.'

Olivia shrugged. 'I just came to say thank you. I had the most marvellous dinner with Alex last night, or perhaps he told you? We've been seeing a lot of one another.'

'I'm not his keeper. I imagine he felt sorry for you.'

'Sorry for me?' she laughed. 'Alex loves me. He'll always love me – that's what he told me last night.' She twisted the ring on her finger. 'He'll tire of you, and I will be waiting.'

'You lying bitch,' Evie said as the wind and rain lashed her face. 'Beau loves me.'

'If he loves you so much then why am I still wearing his ring?'

'Probably because you won't give it back.'

'We are meant to be together.' Her eyes flickered. 'You are nothing, he's just sowing his wild oats.'

Evie looked at her incredulously. 'Grow up, Olivia. You can't force Beau to marry you out of some sense of responsibility ...'

'He will marry me. I was made for him. Alex would never, ever pollute the family blood.'

'Is this what you've been told since you were children? That you were destined for some hideous farce of an arranged marriage to keep the money, the title, the land in the family?' She paused. 'Pollute? You disgust me. You really believe in all this Nazi bile?'

'So does Alex,' Olivia said calmly.

'I don't believe that for a moment.' Evie shook her head. She was shivering, drenched to the skin. 'My father ... he ... if he says I can trust Beau, I believe him – about this, and about you.' She glanced over to where the Lysander was taxiing towards the runway. 'Now get out of my way, you horrible, evil girl. I have a job to do.' When Olivia wouldn't move, Evie shoved her out of the way and tossed her parachute onto her back.

'Look at you!' Olivia sneered, running after Evie. 'What kind of a fool are you? As if Alex would choose someone like you over me. You do a man's job, you dress like a man—'

Evie wheeled around outside the hangar and slapped her hard on the cheek. Olivia's eyes flew open in shock. 'I may do my job as well as a man, but I am all the woman Beau will ever need.' There was a polite ripple of applause from the engineers in the hangar. 'Beau is mine, and I am his, and nothing you can do will change that.'

As Evie walked towards her Spitfire, the Lysander straightened up to take off.

'It's not over!' Olivia yelled. 'He'll tell you!'

'I don't need Beau to tell me he loves me and not you. I know it.' She walked back towards Olivia. Close to, Evie could see her slap had left a livid welt on her cheek. 'I feel it.' The wind snatched her words away. 'Anyway it's too late!' Evie was losing her temper now. 'Look, there he goes, off to France—' She regretted it the moment she opened her mouth.

'France?' Olivia said in a low voice. 'One call, that's all it takes. Daddy can get a radio message to Uncle Hans.' The look in her eyes chilled Evie. 'He loathes Alex, you know. They'll send out every spare plane in the Luftwaffe – Alex wouldn't stand a chance.'

Evie's heart was racing. 'Is that it? You love Beau so much you can't stand to see him with anyone else? If you really loved him, you'd never want to hurt him.'

Olivia sneered. 'I love my family. The very thought that some little half-Jewish whore could be the next Countess? No. One way or another I will be the Countess von Loewe ...'

Evie was shaking with anger. 'You evil, evil girl. You'd rather Beau was dead?' She could see Olivia was thinking quickly.

'... because if he is killed, the title will go to my father when Hans dies.' Olivia ran towards her car.

'Stop her!' Evie yelled to the ground crew. They were too slow, and Olivia sped out of the airfield.

One of the engineers ran over. 'Everything alright, Miss?'

'No, no it's not.' She looked up at the sky, saw the Lysander heading into the distance. 'Call the police. That girl ... She's called Olivia Shuster. She has to be stopped. Her family are Nazi sympathisers, and she's trying to sabotage that mission.' Evie shielded her eyes, straining to see the Lysander. She leapt into her Spitfire, and roared up the runway as the engineer ran into the hangar and reached for the telephone.

'She must be mad!' he said to his friend as he dialled. 'No one's taking off anywhere now.'

As the Merlin engines throbbed and the Spitfire soared into the sky, Evie's face was grim. *It's my fault. If I hadn't opened my big mouth ... I have to warn him somehow. Olivia is mad enough to betray him. Beau's flying straight into a trap.*

55

Evie tracked Beau through the broken cloud as he banked the plane, heading across the Channel. *If I can just catch up,* she thought, *I can signal him to turn back.* She checked her gauges. *There's plenty of fuel for me to get to Debden still, and from there I can go straight to the hospital.* She saw Beau rising through the cloud, and as she followed him, she climbed steadily, through to a clear sky, the first stars and the full moon rising. She could see Beau clearly up ahead, skimming along, the Lysander's exhausts flaring.

She took the photograph of Jack out of her pocket and tucked it on the control panel. *'A straight-up guy ...'* Red's words echoed in her ears. 'Not like Beau,' she said aloud. *'Trust him',* she remembered her father's words again. *All this time I've been waiting to hear from you, and you've been seeing Olivia.* She thought of the German officer she had seen in the hangar. *And what's that all about?*

Just as Evie began to catch up with him, Beau started to descend into the cloud. She decreased her speed to match the slower Lysander's. Nervously, Evie looked at her gauges. *This is taking too long,* she thought, but she followed him, and she began to fly by instruments. She checked her speed and guessed she had overshot him. She pulled up again into the darkening sky, and checked around. Sure enough, he was suddenly above her, and behind. He must have spotted her. She craned her neck around as he brought the plane down to her height. She could see him in the cockpit, his passenger in silhouette behind, studying papers by torchlight.

Evie suddenly realised how stupid she had been. She'd been following Beau and lost all track of where she was. If she lost him, she was in big trouble. She checked her compass and watch, and quickly calculated her bearings. *Right, Evie*, she thought. *Straighten up and think.* As she jotted down the co-ordinates on her chart, she bit her lip. *I am going to be in a hell of a lot of trouble if this ever gets out. The number of times they've told us that ATA pilots aren't allowed to fly to the Continent. Though there were those rumours about Amy ...*

'What the bloody hell is that Spit doing?' Beau said. He gazed out of the high, glazed cockpit of the Lysander at the plane below. 'I'm going to see what's going on. Perhaps the mission has been aborted.'

Beau dived down, brought the Lysander level with the Spitfire, wingtips almost touching. He scowled when he looked across and saw Evie's face in the other cockpit. She was waving frantically, pointing back to the English coast.

'I knew it. She's mad,' he muttered. 'She's going to get us all killed.' He signalled frantically for her to turn back. Evie shook her head and pointed for him to head back. The light was fading now. 'What on earth does she think she's doing?'

'Now where's he gone?' Evie said, as he shot ahead. The cloud was beginning to break up beneath them, patches of sea showing between. She spotted the exhaust flare and followed his path. Something streaked past her cockpit, silver bursts tracing through the sky. 'Oh God,' she said as she manoeuvred the plane to avoid them. Someone was firing at her. She looked around frantically, until she saw to her horror the unmistakable outline of a Messerschmitt. She was close enough to see the hideous gaping jaw painted on the front of the plane, and the crosses on its tail marking the number of hits the pilot had made. She counted ten before she dived down. *She did it, Olivia betrayed him.* Evie's stomach lurched as the plane plummeted downwards.

The Messerschmitt was on her tail now, and she knew she had to get away. She pushed the engine to the limit, skimming down low, hoping she was still over water as she barrelled through the cloud. 'Come on, come on,' she prayed quietly under her breath. Every sense was alert, her reactions immediate and precise. 'Guardian angel … if you're up there, give me a hand,' she said. She thought of one of the girls who had pitched up in the drink in a Barracuda. The aircraft had sunk immediately, but by some miracle she had got the hood back, and she'd managed to flag down a ship. *But if I go down here, there will be no one to help me.* The Messerschmitt was gaining ground. Bullets shot past her, missing the Spitfire by a hair's breadth. Evie spotted the coastline of France ahead, and she banked up, just as she saw Beau's plane returning. She veered out of the way. Beau and the Messerschmitt were on a direct path, head to head. Beau held the plane steady until the last moment, but as he flew by the Messerschmitt opened fire.

Evie looked around. He had been hit.

'Beau,' she said under her breath. The Messerschmitt was after him now. She made a corkscrew dive to port, and a steep climb to starboard, drawing fire. The planes danced like swallows around one another In a final burst, the Messerschmitt rained fire on Beau's Lysander, and she saw the flash as bullets tore along the fuselage and canopy. Still Beau did not give up, and she saw him turn sharply. 'Let's hope that Jerry was on his way back home and is short of fuel,' she said. Sweat was trickling in her eyes now, and her muscles ached as she threw the Spit into a steep climb to avoid the Messerschmitt. Her eyes fell to her gauges. 'Damn. He's not the only one who's short of fuel.' She had no idea where she was, or if she had enough fuel to get back to Debden now.

*

'Bugger off,' Beau swore under his breath as he brought the Lysander around on course. He looked to the port side and saw the Messerschmitt retreating to its base. 'Hey, Joe,' he called to his passenger. 'You're going to have to bail out I'm afraid. I don't know if I can get this old girl down in one piece.' The stick shuddered in his hand. He had been hit, and his shoulder was beginning to throb with pain. 'I'll give you the signal once we're over the target.'

Where the hell has Evie got to? he thought, desperately searching the sky behind him for the flare of her exhausts.

Evie reduced her speed to under 140 knots and opened her canopy, the wind rushing against her face. Her cockpit lights glowed on the big black dome of the semi-circular panel, and the glare from her roaring exhausts made night flying even more difficult. Above the note of her own engine she could hear Beau's misfiring. She swung around, followed the course he was on as his plane limped over the French coast. *Oh God, I have been so stupid*, she thought, as she slid the canopy closed again. There was no way Beau could make it back to England in the stricken Lysander. The sound of his engine cutting out brought back Megan's crash. She hadn't been able to help Megan, but maybe this time she could do something. She couldn't leave him. Perhaps together they could make it safely home.

Evie's hand shook as she tossed her British maps to one side and dug around in her flight bag. She pulled out a torch and put it in her mouth, then flipped open her diary and found a map of France. *Think clearly. 'First point is Caen. Follow the river'*, she remembered.

Up ahead it was snowing as the scarred, deserted beaches gave way to open fields. *There it is.* She spotted the silver river snaking across the dark countryside, and curved around to starboard. She could see Caen at her side. 'Oh thank God,' she said aloud when she spotted Beau's exhausts in the distance, and the faint outline of his black plane against the midnight blue sky. This time she stayed close, afraid of losing him again. They carried on along the river for some time, until he veered off, Evie on his tail. The Lysander was misfiring badly. She saw a figure leap from the back of the plane, his parachute unfurling as he drifted to the ground.

Beau sent out a Morse signal, flashing his wing light. As she circled, Evie saw someone on the ground reply, and three pinpoint lights illuminated one by one, marking out a triangle on the landing field.

'You can do it,' she whispered as she watched Beau's plane gliding in to a descent. Fear rose in her as she remembered Megan's crash, the roaring flames. Up ahead there was an open, snowy field, with a barn at one side and a dark copse of trees. Beau landed heavily, his plane ploughing along the fresh snow as he deliberately aimed it at the trees. Evie eased the Spitfire into a slow descent, and with a quick burst of throttle made a perfect short landing near the copse. She turned her engine off, and all she could hear was the sound of her hot exhaust stubs ticking.

By the time she got out of the Spitfire, there was no sign of Beau. She ran to the Lysander, fighting through the tangle of branches. There were holes in the cockpit canopy where the bullets had gouged the fuselage.

'Beau!' she called, stumbling in the snow. She clambered into the plane, saw him collapsed over the instrument panel. 'No!' she yelled, lifting him back in his seat. There was a bruise on his forehead, and his shoulder was dark with blood. She reached over, released his Sutton harness, and dragged him into the back of the plane. 'Beau?' She shook him, slapped his face until he came round.

'Evie?' he said. 'What are you doing?'

'Rescuing you.'

'You're rescuing me?'

'What the hell's going on?'

'I could ask you the same thing.' He scowled, touched his head. 'We have to get out of here.' He struggled up. 'Where's your plane?'

'Near the wood.'

'How much fuel have you got?'

'I don't know,' she said.

'Think. Where were you heading?'

'Tangmere to Debden.'

'Then there's not enough to get you back.' He winced as he tried to put pressure on his arm. 'In fact you were bloody lucky there was enough in the tank to get you here.'

Evie tore off her silk scarf and tied it tightly around the wound. 'Will you be alright?'

Beau flexed his arm. 'Yes, it's fine. Luckily the bullet just nicked my shoulder.'

'Anyway, what do you mean, get *me* back?' She leant away from him. 'Beau, whose side are you on?'

'I'll explain later,' he said as he swung his legs down to the ground. 'We have to hide your plane.'

'Is that why you aimed yours into the woods? I thought that was a duff landing, even for you.'

'Flattery will get you everywhere.' Beau dragged her down behind a pile of timber not far from the plane. 'They'll be here in a moment. Christ, Evie, this should have been a three-minute turnaround. What are you doing here?'

'I saw you, Beau. I saw you talking to that German at the base ...'

'And you just had to stick your nose in and find out what was going on?'

'No!' She paused. 'Not just that. Olivia was there. She threatened to get a message to your father. They were going to ambush you, Beau, I was trying to help,' she said miserably. 'I thought I could just get a signal to you, get you to head back ... but then I got lost, and the Messerschmitt turned up.'

'He just got lucky. Fortunately he must have been low on fuel and on the way back to his base.' Beau saw the concern on her face. 'It's nothing to do with the Shusters – there are Jerries everywhere. Olivia's father likes to think he's deeply involved with the Nazis but he's nothing. The British are on to him anyway.'

She shook her head. 'I feel like such a fool. Olivia said some horrible, horrible things.' Evie looked into his eyes. 'Did you know that she's a Nazi sympathiser?'

Beau winced. 'I knew about Hans and her parents, but no, I didn't have a clue until recently.'

'And yet you've still been seeing her?'

'God, not now, Evie.' He looked at her, saw the confusion and fear on her face. 'I told her about us, and she threatened to kill herself. I've been trying to make sure she's alright.'

'She should be locked up,' Evie said bitterly.

'Olivia is just a naïve girl.'

'You would say that.' Evie shrugged him away as Beau put his arm around her.

'Darling, everyone thinks this evil that we are fighting is some great terrifying force, but it's cleverer than that. Evil can be seductive, and tempting – all the high ideals that appeal to people like Olivia and her family, all these aristos seduced by the idea of a master race ...' He shook his head angrily. 'Well, all the opera, and art, and healthy young Aryans, it's a mask, an illusion, behind which are some of the most inhuman and barbaric ideas and actions mankind has ever known.'

Evie touched his cheek. 'I'm sorry. I knew in my heart she had to be lying about you.'

'Let me get this straight,' he said gently. 'You risked your life, your career, to try and save me?'

'Yes. Ridiculous isn't it. I felt responsible. I heard you saying you were heading to France, and it slipped out. I—'

Beau silenced her with a kiss. 'I love you. Olivia can't touch us. Trust me.'

Trust, Evie thought. 'Daddy called. Beau, he's in hospital. We have to go and see him. He has cancer—'

'I know.'

'What do you mean you know? Why didn't you tell me?'

'Evie this is no time for a domestic argument.'

'They're going to operate, but he won't let them until he sees us both. Beau, I don't understand—'

Three men in dark clothes appeared from the forest, and Beau leapt up. He spoke quickly to them in French, and they helped him heave open the doors of the empty barn.

'Right, Evie. Taxi the Spit in here, they'll push,' he called.

Once the Spitfire was hidden in the barn, he closed the doors behind her and the men slipped off into the night. 'You'll be safe here,' he said. 'I'll be back as soon as I can. The Maquis have gone to find my Joe. Once they let me know the coast is clear, I'll get help so we can transfer the fuel from the Lysander's long-range tanks to the Spit.'

'Will that work?'

'It will get you safely out of here, that's all I care about. You're bally lucky this field is firm and level. On most of them your Spit would have pitched right over on its nose.'

'Since when have you been flying Lizzies?'

'I'll tell you all about it later. Now, stay here.'

'I'm not staying here by myself!'

'This is not the time to be stubborn, Evie. Do you know where we are?'

'France … somewhere,' she said.

'This is occupied France. There are German troops everywhere, and as that Messerschmitt spotted us on the way over they will be looking for us.' Beau flinched as he pulled away some straw bales at the back of the barn. 'Help me will you?' Evie reached down and fished out two pairs of skis.

'One for you, and one for him?'

'Only for emergencies. He'll be fine, he knows what he's doing – unlike you,' Beau said as he brushed the straw from his skis. As Evie followed suit, he glanced up at her. 'What do you think you're doing?'

'I told you, I'm coming with you.'

'What am I going to do with you?'

'Frankly, I don't know. I don't know anything any more. Who are you, Beau? What's all this about?'

Beau pulled a bag from behind the bales and shook out two

dark ski suits. 'If you insist on knowing right now, the "German" you saw at Tangmere was an SOE agent. I'm with No.138 Squadron based at Tempsford—'

'Where?'

'Special Duties. It's been continual practice the last few months, learning to navigate and plot by moonlight – that's why I've been so busy.' He slipped his feet into one of the suits. 'We've been flying clandestine intelligence missions since February. Hitler and Goering know we have a secret base somewhere, but they haven't found us yet. Unlike you ATA chaps. We're always having to shoo away curious girls from the gates.'

'Special Duties? Why didn't you tell me?'

'I couldn't. That's the whole point, you can't tell anyone.' He looked at Evie. 'That's why I was so reluctant for them to recruit you.'

'Recruit me?'

'Your father is quite keen.'

'What's Daddy got to do with all this?'

'He's M19, Evie. His job at the Air Ministry is just a cover. I've been working with him and the chaps at SOE for months.'

'M19? Is there an M19? What on earth—'

'Frankly, I fought the idea. This is a tough job, and I don't want you involved with SOE.'

'Maybe that's my decision.'

'Well, you can talk to him when we get back to the hospital. I imagine that's why he wants to see us both.' Beau stepped towards the door as he zipped up his suit, looking for the Maquis.

'I think I'd make a good spy,' she said. 'Look how I managed to keep up with you.'

'I let you follow me.'

'How did you know it was me?'

'When I saw the Spit following me do that ridiculous little wiggle you do with the wings.'

'I do not wiggle my wings.'

He smiled as he turned to her. 'Haven't I always told you—'

'I know. Keep my wings level.' Evie shivered as Beau pulled the door closed again, and a cold wind swept through the barn.

'Do you really think I'd have let you see me if I didn't want you to? I guessed you were following me for some reason.' Beau shifted his shoulder, wincing at the sharp pain. 'I came back to get you. There's no way a pilot with your lack of experience could follow me at night.'

'But I did.'

'You did well, better than I expected.'

'I had a good teacher.'

'You will make a good agent, if that's what you want, but at the moment you are too impulsive. You have a lot to learn.'

'Will you teach me?'

He shook his head. 'I'm just the pilot. They won't let you fly to Europe, you know that don't you?'

Evie stepped towards him, slipped her arms around his waist. 'I'm sure I can find something useful to do, if you'll help me,' she said, her voice muffled as she buried her head against his chest.

He kissed the top of her head tenderly. Beau couldn't bear the thought of it. 'If that's what you want, I'm sure Leo will help,' he said evenly. Evie looked up at him. 'Right now, we need to get you out of here and off the hook at home so you can get to the hospital and see him.' Beau thought for a moment. 'The weather was lousy when we took off. I suggest when you get to the base at Debden, say you put down in a field somewhere overnight, and couldn't reach the phone. Hopefully they will be so relieved to see you and the Spit in one piece they won't ask too many questions.'

'Well that is the ATA motto, better late than—' Her words were cut off as he kissed her.

'Now, take off your Sidcot suit.'

'What, here? You've just been shot.'

'Not that, woman.' He tossed her the other dark suit. 'As much as I would love to ravish you on the spot, if you're coming with me, you need to get changed into this.' At the sound of a low whistle, he strapped on his skis and went to the door.

'Ready,' she said, stepping awkwardly to his side, her skis slapping against the earth floor.

He tossed her a silk square. 'Take this.'

'Oh Beau, it's lovely.'

'It's not a gift, Evie, it's a map.' She held it up in her hands. Beau checked the pistol in his belt. 'Stay close beside me,' he said. 'Look, we are here, near Argentan.' He pointed on the map. 'This is the Forest of Gouffern in the Orne. We're heading to the Château d'Or, here. If we get separated, head to the church in the village marked at the base of the valley and ask for Madame Moitessier. They'll know how to get you back here.' He pulled a button from his jacket and handed it to her. 'To be safe, here's a compass. The screw cover has a left-hand thread.' He looked at the Spit and shook his head. 'If the ATA find out you've taken a plane to the Continent you know you'll lose your wings?'

'I know, I've been very reckless,' she said. 'I just couldn't bear the thought of you being shot down.'

'That's what I risk every time I set out,' he said quietly. 'Come on.' He skied out onto the field and turned to her. 'Let's just hope we can get you back.'

56

In the moonlight they skied down into the valley, descending quickly through the silent countryside. Evie matched him at every turn. Snow fell softly around them. It was picture-perfect, impossible to imagine this was a world at war. Eventually she spotted a turreted château below them, encircled by fenced pastures. They followed a faint pathway leading up to the stables, pushing themselves along the final approach. They skied noiselessly over the bridge across the frozen moat, beneath the steeply pitched mansard roof of the château. Evie gazed upwards. The countless windows were silver in the night, reflecting the light of the moon. As they skied into the yard, Beau was gasping, his face pale. He tossed his poles to the ground and unclipped his boots. As he bent down, he keeled over.

'Beau!' Evie cried. The kitchen door flew open. A woman wearing jodhpurs and boots and holding a shotgun stood there. 'Help me! Please help me!'

'You need to remember you are in France now,' the woman said in English. She pushed her elegant dark hair behind one ear, and leant over Beau. 'Alex? Mon amour ...'

Evie took a step back. As the woman turned her face to her, she caught the look of confusion on Evie's face. 'You must be

Evie,' she said. 'I am Françoise, Alexander's mother. Help me take him inside.'

Beau sat bare-chested on a wooden chair in the kitchen, as Françoise wound a bandage around his shoulder. 'You are lucky, no? If the bullet had been a few centimetres closer ...'

'Well it wasn't,' he said.

'You take too many risks,' she muttered as she tied the bandage tightly and tucked in the ends. 'Just like Hans.'

'Maman,' he complained. In spite of herself, Evie smiled as she sipped at her hot coffee laced with cognac. Beau was so independent it was hard to imagine him belonging to anyone, being anyone's son.

'Are you warm enough?' Françoise asked Evie. 'I'm sorry it is so cold in the house. I've never known a winter like this.'

'I'm fine, thank you.'

'Now, you need to get a move on. Alex, there's a German uniform and papers ready. You need to speak to Marcel at the bar. He can get some men. If they take one of the small tankers from the farm up to the field they can transfer the fuel, then Evie can get out of here.'

'Will you be alright?' Beau took his mother's hand.

'Me? Of course.' She waved him away. 'No one would risk touching me. I am the wife of the great Count Hans von Loewe. Go on, scoot.' She led him to the library.

'Has he been to see you?' Beau asked her.

'He wouldn't dare.' Françoise placed her hand on the bookcase. 'Be careful though, I know he is nearby, waiting for his chance.' She nodded back towards the kitchen. 'It is lucky Evie looks like Ingrid, not Leo. They have been ...' She shook her head. 'A lot of Jews have been taken.' She pulled out a volume, and a secret door swung open. 'She's very beautiful, in fact she looks rather as I did when I was younger.' Her eyes twinkled mischievously.

Beau kissed her cheek. 'That's a bit too Oedipal for my tastes. You'll give me nightmares.'

413

'Now hurry!' Françoise returned to the kitchen. She pulled her cashmere cardigan tighter around her, and lit a cigarette. 'So, Evie.' Françoise sat opposite her. 'If you insist on going into town you will stick out a mile in that suit. We must find you something pretty to wear.' She took her by the hand and led her through to a suite of rooms.

From the wardrobe she pulled a beautiful silver velvet dress. 'There, I think we are the same size and height?' She handed Evie a matching pair of shoes, and sat on the bed as she dressed. 'You know, you look like your mother,' she smiled. 'The same fine features, beautiful grey eyes—'

'You knew my mother?'

'Yes, I knew Ingrid very well. And your father ... He and I, we had a little rebound fling after I left Hans and your mother left Leo.' She shrugged. 'Leo was fun, exhilarating. Alex's father, Hans, was the opposite, so brooding, masculine. You know that gut feeling you get about a man?' She clenched her fist low on her stomach.

Evie thought of Beau. 'I know.' She smoothed the dress over her hips, the silk velvet soft to her touch. 'Will I pass?'

'Perfect.' Françoise hugged her. 'I am glad that you are with my son. You are a better match for him than poor Olivia. Hans was always very keen for them to marry, for obvious reasons, but she always struck me as a little ...' Françoise twirled her index finger near her temple.

Evie's eyes fell. 'That makes two of us. I feel a perfect fool for following Beau out here. I put us both in danger. I don't know if he will forgive me for all this.'

Françoise put her hand on Evie's shoulder. 'You were trying to protect the man you love. I can tell you are a woman who follows her heart, Evie. Don't worry, Alex would forgive you anything.'

'I don't know where I am with him. I had no idea about all this.'

'That he was helping the SOE? Of course, no one would know. It's better that way. He is a very brave man, a good man. He has integrity, courage. He understands he has a duty to all men, and our freedom depends on people like him, like us.'

'What will you do now?'

'I'll carry on doing what I can for the Resistance until my luck runs out. I help the Maquis, hide agents. No one dares touch me without Hans' orders, and I have to stay for my horses.' She waved her hand at a side cabinet covered with silver-framed photographs of horses and trophies. 'Do you recognise anyone?' Evie looked closer as she quickly brushed her hair. 'That horse looks just like Montgomery,' she said.

'He is Monty's father,' Françoise said. 'When Leo wanted a present for you, there was only one place to come, naturally.'

'So we're practically family?' Evie embraced Françoise. 'I hope we'll meet again, in happier circumstances.'

'So do I. You must go now. Be safe.' She hesitated, then handed Evie a brooch from her jewellery box. 'Just in case.'

Evie flipped open the gold cover. 'A pill?'

'Cyanide. It's better than the alternative, trust me. Hans knows no mercy.'

57

'Evie, you need to listen to me,' Beau called back to her as the motorbike sped through the dark fields. She clung to him, her head resting against his shoulders. 'Try not to speak at all once we're in town. If you are addressed by anyone, say as little as possible. Your father tells me your French is fluent, yes?' She nodded. 'Good. When we get there, I will drop you off around the corner from the hotel. I will go in first. Wait five minutes, cross the main road and the hotel is immediately opposite you. Go to the bar on the left, the one with all the tables. Sit near the back and watch me. When I leave, go to the bathroom. Follow the corridor around the back of the stage, through the kitchen and out into the alley. I will be waiting for you there.'

Her heart thumped as they passed a convoy of German soldiers on the way into the town. Beau dropped her by a flower shop, and leant in to kiss her on both cheeks. 'Evie,' he whispered, 'I love you. If we get out of this, will you—'

'When.' Her gaze held his. 'When we get out of this. Ask me then.'

'Five minutes,' he whispered, and as she stepped away he rode off towards the main street.

Evie stood in front of the pavement display. Rich velvet roses gave up their perfume to the cold evening air. She reached out and touched one with her fingertips. As she looked up, she saw her reflection in the window, traffic streaming by behind her. Fear heightened every sense. Her heart missed a beat as she noticed that two German soldiers had appeared behind her.

'C'est belle, la rose,' one of them said in halting French. They were either side of her now. Evie's hand drifted away from the flower. Coquettishly she turned her face to his. He was just a boy, pale, fresh faced, younger than her probably.

'Oui, c'est belle.' She smiled, and walked away towards the main road, confidently swinging her hips, followed by their low whistles.

She stopped on the pavement. Just as a dark car pulled up outside the hotel, she looked right, stepped out, was nearly hit by a motorbike.

Count Hans von Loewe stared right at her as she leapt back onto the pavement.

'Follow her,' he said to his companion. They watched as she strode across the road, pushed open the gleaming door of the hotel. 'Well, no need.' Hans smiled slowly. 'The little bird has walked straight into the cage.'

Evie paused in the lobby for a moment. As she walked to the bar beneath the dancing light of the chandelier, her heels tapped on the wooden floor. There were groups of people already at the tables – a few locals, but mostly German soldiers and officers. She took a table at the back, in the shadows, and as she lit a Gauloises, her hand shook slightly. When the waiter came over she ordered a glass of red wine in flawless French. Beau was at the bar, talking with the bartender. She thought he looked perfectly at home among the German soldiers in a way he never did at home; strong, blonde, the Aryan ideal.

Some of the soldiers near the door stood to attention and gave the Nazi salute as a senior officer entered. He shrugged off his long leather coat and gave it to his companion.

'Leave me,' he told him as he took off his cap.

Evie gasped when she saw his face. At that moment Beau

turned and looked at him, and it was as if time stood still.

'Well, Alexander, we meet again.' Hans leant against the bar, made no attempt to shake hands with him.

Evie strained her ears, trying to follow the conversation. She was horrified – this had to be Beau's father, it was as if he was looking in a mirror.

'Hans,' Beau said steadily.

'What an unexpected pleasure.'

'Unexpected? I heard Olivia's father had alerted you.'

Hans pursed his lips. 'No, no, no. One of our pilots reported British aircraft nearby.'

'So you got lucky.'

'Luck? No. You were followed. I've had a patrol watching the château for months. I knew it was only a matter of time before you paid your mother a visit.'

'I'm flattered you'd go to such trouble.'

His eyes were cold as he turned to his son. 'How is Olivia? You will marry her soon.'

'No.' Beau clenched his fist.

'We'll see,' Hans said lightly. 'You know, I lost track of you when you left your squadron. I wondered where you would turn up. But here we are.' He smiled at his son but his ice blue eyes glittered dangerously. 'Still drinking alone, Alexander? Always alone, even as a little boy, so sad.' Hans raised his finger, beckoning the barman. 'Two cognacs, Marcel.'

'You think I would drink with you?'

Hans leant towards him and said in a low voice, 'I think you will do whatever I tell you. If you don't, I will have your little friend arrested immediately.' His eyes travelled to Evie.

'Who? I'm here alone.'

'Don't insult my intelligence. My men saw two people arrive at the château. Perhaps you are wondering how I spotted her?'

'No doubt you are going to tell me.'

'You'd think they would train these SOE girls better, it's just sloppy.' Hans sipped his cognac. 'She looked the wrong way crossing the road, silly girl.'

'I told you I don't know her. Let's not drag this out shall we? It's me you want.' He winced as he turned to the bar.

'So, you are injured?' Hans laughed, squeezed his shoulder. 'Does it hurt?'

'No.' His jaw set hard.

'No doubt you ran home to Mummy to get patched up.' Hans released him. 'My pilot thought he got a few shots in on the way home. Still, you survived. Your flying must be improving.'

'But it's not as good as yours I suppose?'

'I've had more practice. They always say there comes a moment when the son surpasses the father, but I can't see it myself. I want a rematch. There's no sport in capturing you here.' Hans lit a cigar. 'I'm going to give you a head start. No doubt you are planning to take off in the Spitfire that followed you tonight? The Lysander was too badly damaged wherever you landed it.'

'Maybe I am, maybe I'm not,' Beau said.

'You will. I know you. Efficient, like me. You've carried out your mission – delivered your package.' He tilted his head towards Evie. 'You can go. I have my entertainment for the night. Another little SOE dove. How I love it when they sing for me ...'

'I don't know her.'

'Are you sure?' Hans beckoned Marcel over again. 'Who is that?'

While Hans was looking at Evie, Beau pointed to a piece of sheet music among the newspapers on the bar.

'She is the singer. Tonight we have a cabaret.' Marcel put down the glass he was polishing and gathered up the music. 'Alphonse!' He called to an old man at the end of the bar, and handed him the music. 'Are you ready? The singer is here.' Alphonse shuffled to the piano by the small stage, and Marcel dimmed the lights, the silver-sequined curtain glimmering softly. He walked over to Evie's table. 'Mademoiselle,' he said, 'I hope you have a good voice. It is your only hope.'

'You want me to sing?' she said incredulously.

'Come with me.' Marcel took her arm. Without looking at Beau, she went over to Alphonse and checked the music. 'Smile,'

Marcel whispered. 'You need to look as if you are relaxed and enjoying yourself.' She selected a song and took to the stage to whistles and clapping from the soldiers. As she began to sing the room fell quiet.

'*Devant la caserne, quand le jour s'enfuit …*'

Her voice rose above the soldiers' conversation.

'*La vieille lanterne soudain s'allume et luit.*
C'est dans ce coin là que le soir
On s'attendait remplis d'espoir
Tous deux, Lili Marlène
Tous deux, Lili Marlène.'

'I do like that song. Lovely voice too. A shame, such a waste.' Hans tapped ash into the heavy glass ashtray.

'Why are you letting me go?' Beau said, desperately trying not to look at Evie.

'As I said, better sport if I give you a head start. Besides, Françoise would never forgive me if I took you out in cold blood.'

'You still think she would forgive you, after what you have done?' Beau said incredulously.

'She loved me once. She will again.'

Beau shook his head. 'What did I ever do for you to hate me so?'

Hans regarded him impassively. 'You don't know?' He stared at his son. 'She loved you. I saw it in her eyes. With you, the moment she held you in her arms … She loves Hélène of course. But with you it is different.'

Beau stepped closer as Evie sang on. 'That must have killed you, Hans,' he goaded him. 'You always told me you can have anything you want in life.' He was near enough to feel his father's breath on his face. 'But you can't have the one thing you want – Françoise's love.'

'Don't be ridiculous.' A vein pulsed in his temple. 'Françoise loved me. She still loves me.'

'Do you think so? She hates everything you stand for.'

Hans slammed his glass down on the bar. 'She will see sense.'

'How are you going to change her mind, Hans?' The blood sang in Beau's head. 'The same way you made me "see sense" when I was a boy?'

'I would never lay a finger on your mother, you know that.' His eyes blazed. 'But you … you drove me mad, the way you could always wrap Françoise round your little finger, the way she loved you.'

'You were jealous of me?' Beau laughed in disbelief. 'Is that really it?'

'Jealous?' Hans raged. 'Don't be ridiculous. You are inferior to me in every way.' He squared up to his son. 'In every way.' His face was pinched with hatred.

Beau watched his father transform before his eyes, the rage giving way to a familiar icy calm. 'We'll see. I'm not a child any more.'

'I adore Françoise,' Hans said quietly. 'I will do anything to have her to myself.'

'Even if it means killing your own son?'

'I wouldn't be the first. Think of the Greeks, the Romans …' Hans looked at his son, what passed for a smile twisting on his lips. 'There's something of a noble tradition.'

Hans' companion strode over and tapped him on the shoulder. 'Excuse me, Generaloberst, we have him.'

'Who?'

'The agent who parachuted in tonight. He is refusing to talk but there is no doubt he is SOE. They found him hiding in the hills with the Maquis. They escaped, but he has a broken leg. There's no sign of the pilots. Our men are searching the area for the aircraft but haven't found them yet. We have him in a car outside. The Gestapo are waiting.'

Beau's face gave nothing away, but his pulse was racing. They had captured his passenger. It was only a matter of time until they found the crash site.

'Wait for me by the door,' Hans said to him. He turned to his son. 'So, this is interesting.' He swirled his drink in his glass. 'If you were flying a male agent in tonight, then where did our little songbird appear from?' He tilted his head, watched Evie as she sang on stage. 'Unless of course she was flying the other plane?' Beau's face remained impassive. 'I heard you were flying with girls, Alex. Is she a friend of yours? That would explain the slip crossing the road. If she is ATA not SOE ...'

'I told you. I have no idea who she is.' Beau knocked back his cognac. 'Tell me something. Are your boys targeting the ATA?'

Hans blew smoke into his face. 'For our new fighters it's easy target practice. For me, it is a little dull if your enemy is unarmed.'

'Sir, I am sorry ...' The soldier waiting for Hans interrupted again.

'Very well.' He glanced at his watch. 'Go on, Alex,' he whispered. 'I'll give you quarter of an hour's head start. That will give me time to take care of this and get to my Messerschmitt.'

Beau leant casually against the bar. 'So you haven't told anyone I'm here? I imagine your superiors would be rather annoyed if they knew you'd let an enemy officer go.'

'What do I care?' Hans murmured as he pulled on his coat. 'It's so long since I had any sport.' He sneered. 'Go on then, run along, Alex. "Run, rabbit, run", as the song says.'

Beau grabbed his father's wrist. 'Run? I never ran from you, did I, Hans? I always took my punishments bravely.' He tightened his grip. 'That's why we are going to win this war. Maybe you'll kill me tonight, maybe you won't, but there are hundreds of good men to take my place who will carry on regardless. We don't like bullies, Hans. We didn't want this war, but we'll take great pleasure in shooting every last one of your ruddy kites out of the sky. We'll show you how to fly. We'll make you wish to God you'd never dreamt of war.' He released Hans' arm. 'I'll see you in the air.'

Hans gave him the Nazi salute, and turned on his heel. He paused by the door, and spoke to some soldiers as he pointed to the stage. 'Our boys are enjoying the cabaret. Let her finish, then arrest her.'

Evie's song ended just as Hans reached the street.

> *'Il me semble entendre ton pas,*
> *Et je te serre entre mes bras*
> *Lili, Lili Marlène*
> *Lili, Lili Marlène.'*

She left the stage to applause. 'Encore!' someone cried. 'Encore!' Pretending to get a glass of water from the bar, she stood beside Beau.

'That was your father, wasn't it?'

'I don't have time to explain,' Beau said. 'We must leave now.'

'No. If I go, it will be too suspicious,' she said. She wanted desperately to hold him one last time. 'You go. I'll keep everyone happy, give you a chance to get away.'

'I'm not leaving without you.'

'Beau, I'm nothing,' she said, 'just a girl, just a pilot. What you are doing here – it's saving hundreds of lives. What is one life, my life, compared to so many?' The crowd began clapping for her to return to the stage. She sipped her water, slowly patted her lips with a white napkin. 'I hope they like "Lili Marlène" because it's the only song I can remember right now.' Her voice shook as she laughed. 'I love you,' she said without looking at him.

'I love you too. I'm damned if I'm leaving you here for Hans.' Beau thought quickly. 'After your next song, go off into the wings. As they wait for an encore there will be time for you to slip out through the kitchen. I'll be waiting for you at the end of the alley.'

Evie took to the stage, the lights dazzling her. She sang with all her heart as she watched Beau walk away. She thought of when she had first seen him, walking across the airfield towards her out of the sun. *Come on, Evie*, she thought to herself. *You can do this.*

At the end of the song she bowed and walked off into the wings with her head held high. The sound of applause washed around her as she slipped through the curtains to the back of the stage.

She clambered over old paint pots and scenery, and jumped down to the kitchen passage. A young couple kissing looked up at her, their eyes glazed with desire. Her mouth was a smear of red, his pale fringe flopped into his eyes. *Oh God, he's a Jerry.* A bead of cold sweat trickled down Evie's spine as she walked past them. The young woman caught the soldier's face in her hand, pulled him down to her chest. The woman nodded her head towards the kitchen. Evie weaved her way out through the steaming prep areas, waiters carrying trays of food above their heads, all turning a blind eye to the young woman making her escape. The sound of impatient clapping drifted out to her from the bar, the shouting and whistles becoming more insistent.

Just as Evie pushed open the door to the alleyway, an argument broke out in the bar. A young woman was berating Marcel.

'What do you mean, the cabaret has already been?' she said furiously. 'I am the cabaret.'

The soldiers by the door looked at one another, and marched outside.

Evie ran into the alleyway, snow falling silently around her, her evening shoes slipping on the cobbles. She raced to the end, but Beau was not there. Fear chilled her. Any moment, soldiers would come pouring out of the back of the hotel, she knew it. At the sound of a patrol car, she ducked into the shadows. It screeched to a halt and the door flew open. 'Evie?' Beau called.

She leapt into the car. 'Thank God, I thought you'd gone.'

'You rescued me,' he said as they screeched away. 'It was the least I could do to rescue you back. They found the bike,' he explained. 'Slashed the tyres. I had to find a patrol car.' He glanced in the rear-view mirror, saw flashlights washing the street of the town behind them, soldiers running to their cars. Beau put his foot down. 'Marcel has sent some men ahead, they're refuelling the Spit, getting it ready for us. We have to hurry, Evie, we have to get you out of here.'

58

The patrol car tore through the countryside, bumping along the rough road. Beau's eyes were fixed grimly on the road ahead. 'I hope this snow doesn't get worse. You won't be able to take off,' he said.

'We'll make it,' Evie said. 'And you're coming with me.'

'No.'

'I won't take off without you.'

'You will.'

'Beau, I'd rather die with you tonight than leave without you.'

She could see the silhouette of the Spitfire up ahead, a couple of men standing ready. They passed a farm tractor dragging a tanker, and Beau saluted as the patrol car skidded up the hill. He slammed on the brakes, took Evie's hand. 'Come on,' he said, 'they won't be far behind us.'

'They're coming, Madame!' Françoise's maid banged frantically on the dressing-room door. Françoise smoothed her gleaming dark hair slowly with a silver brush. She dabbed scent on her wrists, and then from her drawer she pulled out a Beretta pistol and tucked it into the waistband of her black evening trousers, against her spine. She lifted the collar of her immaculate white shirt, and nodded.

'Where is he?' Hans' voice thundered through the hallway of the château, candles guttering in the wind as he flung the front door open. Storm troopers poured into the house behind him, searching every room.

'Hans. What a surprise,' Françoise said as she appeared on the landing. As she walked slowly down the sweeping stone staircase he couldn't take his eyes off her.

'You look captivating,' he said.

'Thank you.' She offered him her hand, and he pressed his lips to it.

'Françoise …'

'Why are you here, Hans?'

'I want them. They've given my men the slip.'

'Have they? Good.' She raised her chin. 'You don't think Alex would be crazy enough to hide here?'

'I know you are helping the Maquis, I've been protecting you.'

'You'll never rest, will you? It's too late. Alex is miles away by now.' She wavered as she heard the screams of the servants.

'I can still save you,' Hans whispered. 'It's not too late. I love you. We should never have had children. He ruined everything.'

'No, Hans. You did that all by yourself. My children are the one thing I am proud of in my life. That, and this.' Françoise pulled out the pistol.

At the sound of the gunshot, the soldiers raced back to the hall to find Hans lying on the steps in her arms. They raised their rifles.

'No!' Hans gasped. 'You will not touch her. It was an accident. Stand down.' His hand lay across his chest, a look of surprise on his face as he looked up at his wife. 'I love you, Françoise,' he whispered. 'I will always love you.'

'I am sorry,' she whispered, tears in her eyes. 'I loved you, but this has to end.'

Hans gasped, the air gurgling in his throat. His eyes rolled back in his head, flickered for a moment. 'Françoise,' he sighed, 'Françoise …'

*

426

A shot was fired in the forest as Beau spoke quickly to the Maquis. 'Once she is up, burn the Lysander.'

Evie stood by the Spitfire. 'Beau, I'm not leaving without you.'

'Yes you are,' he said as he slid back the canopy.

Evie clambered up onto the wing. 'We don't have time to argue about this. We can fly the Spit together.'

'Don't be a fool!'

Evie took his face in her hands. 'Beau, I've seen it done. You must have heard all the stories about RAF chaps taking their girlfriends up for a spin?'

'It's too dangerous, a damn stupid thing to do.'

Evie kissed him. 'We can do it. I love you,' she said, her hand on his face. 'If you won't come with me, I'm not leaving. They'll get both of us, and the Spit.'

He jumped into the cockpit. 'God damn it, Evie, you're mad. I wish you would just leave me.'

'Never.'

Beau pushed back as she squeezed in on his lap. 'Well, this is cosy.' He started up the engine. 'It's going to be very distracting having you in the cockpit with me. A fighter should always be on top, seldom on the same level, and never underneath.'

'Are you complaining?' Evie's head turned at the sound of gunshots.

'No. Under different circumstances this would be most enjoyable.' He could see cars streaming up the hillside towards them. 'Right, hold on tight.'

Two men jumped on the tail of the Spitfire as the engine roared, and the propeller began to turn. Beau ran the engine up against the brakes, one hand on the throttle, the other on the stick and brake lever. He glanced at the instrument panel, saw the photograph of Jack that Evie had stuck there.

'Did you do this before, with him?'

'Fine time to be jealous.' Evie was breathless with fear. 'No, I've never done this.'

'Reassuring.'

'But I've seen it done. I'll tell you later.' Evie looked out into the dark night, the snow eddying around them. She gripped the control panel. 'Let's go home, Beau. Take me home.'

At Beau's signal the men jumped off and ran for the Lysander in the woods. The Spitfire surged forward, the powerful exhausts blasting flurries of snow on the ground.

'Come on, Spitty,' he said under his breath, 'you can do it.' They roared down the hillside towards the cars, bullets whizzing past them. At the last moment, the Spitfire lifted, and they rocketed into the sky.

Thank God, Evie thought. As the Spitfire soared upwards and the snow-covered fields fell away beneath them, her heart beat fast, a cocktail of adrenalin and relief pulsing through her. The moment they had taken off, the Lysander had exploded, shielding them from the advancing troops, bright flames leaping into the luminous midnight blue sky as they soared away.

Evie pulled the canopy closed, and settled back in Beau's arms. She felt him rest his head against her shoulder for a moment. The noise in the cockpit made conversation impossible, but she sensed he was trying to reassure her as he squeezed her hand.

Beau glanced behind him, wincing as his arm twisted. At any moment he was expecting the tracer fire of a Messerschmitt. He knew it would come, and that they would have to outrun the plane. *We'll be fine as long as we don't come across a Focke-Wulf 190.* As they cleared the coast, his mind flashed back to the last time he had flown above the sea in a Spit. This time, there would be none of the raw, primitive exhilaration he felt with every kill – the sheer relief that the other man had bought it, not him. His heart thundered as he remembered the last, relentless dogfight, the screaming air, the flames, the searing pain. Now, he had no guns, no radio – to outfly the enemy was their only hope. He held Evie tightly as they banked up through the cloud, alone in a world of white. She had risked everything for him. There was no way on earth he would let her be hurt. He would never let her down. The cloud began to thin out, and the Spitfire broke through. A perfect full moon guided them, dazzling silver light and a blanket of stars above them.

Let's see what this old girl can do, Beau thought as he increased their speed to over 350 mph. He was banking on the fact it was a new Spitfire, far more powerful than the older Marks, and its clipped wingtips would give them increased speed and roll rates at lower altitudes. *Run, rabbit, run*, he thought. He felt Evie settle back in his lap, relax in his arms. *It's not over yet.* A tracer bullet spiralled past the cockpit. *Damn, there you are.* There was a Messerschmitt on their tail.

Have you met my father? Beau thought to himself. He felt the old, familiar sensation of tension transforming into pure concentration as the enemy pursued them. His heart skipped, and he swallowed hard as he looped around. He felt Evie brace herself as the Spitfire pitched. The planes danced like fighting kites in the sky. When he couldn't shake the German, Beau sent the Spitfire into a steep spiral dive, cutting into the cloud. 'Hold on …' he said. The Spitfire turned tighter and tighter inside the Me109's path.

'*Never fly level for more than twenty seconds or you're done for.*' The voice of Beau's instructor came back to him. They rocketed towards the earth, Beau watching the instruments closely.

'My God, Beau, the water,' Evie cried, her voice drowned out by the screaming engine. She automatically pushed back in the seat and screwed her eyes closed as they plummeted towards the sea. The g-force was so strong she felt as if she was about to pass out.

Come on, come on. Beau willed the Messerschmitt closer.

Just as it seemed they weren't going to make it, he used all his strength to pull them out of the dive. The Spitfire shot upwards, the Merlin engines screaming. The Messerschmitt was caught off guard, and plunged into the Channel. As Beau looked back he saw a great plume of water exploding in its wake.

It wasn't Hans, he thought. *He would never have fallen for that.* Beau exhaled. *Another time.* He levelled the Spitfire's course for home.

They flew on between heaven and earth, powering through the dawn. As the minutes ticked away, Evie closed her eyes, lost in the sensation of speed, the safety she felt in his arms. Her limbs felt weightless, as if she was floating, the boundaries between them and the air dissolving. *This is my home*, she thought. *Here, with Beau.*

The cloud above them was breaking up now, the rising sun a bright line on the horizon. The full moon, the guardian of the sky, lingered in the dawn like a last guest unwilling to say goodbye. Evie felt Beau squeeze her arm. He pointed ahead. As her eyes blinked open, she saw the English coast.

Evie cried out with delight as the Spitfire soared over the white cliffs. The rosy colours of sunrise washed the canopy apricot, lavender, gold. Beneath them, England was a quilt of frosted green. Beau took her left hand, pressed it to his lips. *We made it*, she thought, as the new day dawned. *We made it home.*

AUTHOR'S NOTE

Some of the events in this book are true, and some of the characters lived – but many are my invention. Some of the words spoken were said and have been reported here, but most I have imagined. I hope that in blending fact and fiction this book still honours the men and women of the ATA. The little-known true story of their bravery and 'brief glory' is the equal of any fiction.

The ATA's incredible contribution was finally recognised by Downing Street in 2008 when 59 veterans received a badge of honour. 173 men and women died ferrying over 309,000 aircraft during WW2. Amy Johnson is the only one many now recall from those remarkable pilots of 28 nations. The film of her life was dedicated to 'women who have driven through centuries of convention' – a fitting sentiment for all the modest and magnificent Spitfire girls.

When you walk among the graves at cemeteries like Arnhem, white crosses stretch as far as the eye can see. They stand as a proud memory to our lost souls. Every marker is a person who lived, and loved, and was loved. Every one of them was taken too soon. At All Saints in Maidenhead, there is a smaller plot of seventeen ATA war graves. These alone mark the loss of six different nations. Every death in war is a death too many. May we always remember, and never forget those, like Amy, who gave up their tomorrows for our freedom today.

KLB August 2010

ACKNOWLEDGEMENTS

My thanks are due to a number of people who generously helped with the research for this book. Richard Poad of the ATA archive in Maidenhead Heritage Centre gave invaluable assistance. Betty Lussier's recollections of life as an ATA girl and her work with OSS were inspirational. David Coxon of Tangmere Military Aviation Museum, Katherine Moody of the Imperial War Museum, Daniel Milford-Cottam of the V&A, Andrew Cormack of the RAF Museum Hendon, Matti Watton of Lambeth Palace Library, Tony Hill, vice-chairman of White Waltham PCC, Carolyn Grace, Leslie Danker, Raffles' historian and the Poetry Library at the Royal Festival Hall all helped get my facts straight. Sabine Walkenhorst of Cartier, Mark Gauntlett of Aston Martin, Chanel UK, Debretts and Dr Robert Treharne Jones of the Leander Club all kindly helped with period detail. Thank you also to This England Publishing Ltd, Williamson Music Inc, Redwood Music Ltd and Universal Music Publishing GmbH for their co-operation.

I am grateful to Nicholas Royle and my MA group at MMU for their help and advice with the story. My thanks go to Laura Palmer, Rina Gill, Lucy Ridout and the wonderful team at Corvus, and to the incomparable Sheila Crowley of Curtis Brown whose insights and encouragement helped enormously. Finally to my family – your patience and support can probably only be understood by the families of other writers. Thank you.

Book Club Questions

Which main character did you relate to most
– Evie, Stella or Megan – and why?

What was unique about the setting, and how
did it enhance or impair the story?

What themes did the author emphasize in the novel?

How do you think the main characters evolved throughout
the story? What events triggered these changes?

Did certain parts of the book make you uncomfortable?
If so, why did you feel that way?

Did you know about these women pilots before reading
The Beauty Chorus? Why do you think their contribution
to World War II has been overlooked?

Further Reading

Brief Glory, E. C. Cheesman (1946)
Spreading My Wings, Diana Barnato Walker (1994)
Spitfire Women of World War II, Giles Whittell (2007)

For more information about *The Beauty Chorus*,
links to online content and videos visit
http://thebeautychorus.blogspot.com

About the Author

How did you become interested in the ATA 'Spitfire Girls'?

I read a tiny obituary in an aviation magazine (I'm married to a pilot). My first thought was 'Wow, I didn't know women flew fighter planes during the war.' We have Lancaster pilots in the family, and yet I'd never heard about these incredible women. Months of research stemmed from that article.

Do you think Evie, Stella and Megan are typical of the ATA girls?

I hope so – I read as many first-hand accounts and memoirs as possible. Evie is very much one of the 'beauty chorus', the rich debutantes whose pre-war life revolved around flying clubs and parties. Stella was inspired by the women who travelled to Britain from the Colonies to 'do their bit' and have the chance to fly. Megan reflects how young some of these girls were, and perhaps those who came from less glittering backgrounds, who had their pilot's licence for one reason or another. What united all these 'types' of women was their gung-ho attitude, their bravery, and their modesty. When you hear the veterans talk now, it's still apparent they felt they were just doing their job.

How have the 'real' ATA girls reacted to the novel?

I was lucky enough to work closely with the ATA archive in Maidenhead (http://www.atamuseum.org). Through them I was able to read the wartime diaries and papers of ATA pilots, and work with the veterans. The response has been good – though apparently one of the 'girls' (now in her eighties), said something along the lines of 'nonsense, we didn't cry'. They were – as Diana Barnato Walker said – 'tough cookies', doing dangerous, skilled work in extraordinary times, side by side with the male pilots.

Stiff upper lip doesn't even begin to describe how they just got on with it. I think though, with historical fiction as opposed to non-fiction, you do need to see inside the characters and see the emotions people were buttoning down. The parts about women weeping in dark cinemas, for example, are entirely true.

Why does your work blend fact with fiction?

I'm interested in forgotten histories, and fascinated by people like Amy Johnson, and Pauline Gower whose true stories are so remarkable. I think even 'straight' history is interpretation and a partial view – there are always gaps in accounts, unnamed people in photographs. This is where I fit my fictional characters in. I think it's an interesting way to breathe life into the past, and working with a fictional framework allows you to create characters that give you an emotional hook into real events.

Life at a Glance

Born
England, 1971

Educated
Courtauld Institute of Art

Career
International art consultant, travel writer, novelist

Lives
Middle East and England with her husband and two children

A Writer's Life

How do you write?

I always have a notebook on me (or at a push, the back of an envelope) with ideas scribbled on it. There's a lot of research with my books, so this (and writing the final book), happens when my children are at school, or when they are asleep. I write the first draft longhand, then edit on the computer.

Where do you write?

Wherever I can – it's a case of 'hot desking' around the family or in cafes as I don't have a room of my own yet. I read longingly about other writers' sheds! I always write to music – Chopin's 'Nocturnes' most of all.

How do you write a book?

It's never sequential – I write key scenes first, whatever is bursting to get out of my imagination. Then I put the puzzle together.

Which living writer do you admire?

I loved William Boyd's advice to write about what interests you rather than what you know. That was very liberating, and I really admire books of his like *Any Human Heart* that weave fact and fiction together so brilliantly.

What inspires you?

I grew up in a really wild and beautiful part of the West Country, so still love the countryside, escaping to deserted landscapes and beaches that give you space to think, and travelling.

What are you writing next?

I'm completing a novel I began working on over ten years ago, when we lived in the orange groves near Valencia in Spain. It was such a beautiful place to live, but I was always aware of a hidden history, and our friends' reluctance to talk about the Spanish Civil War. I did a lot of research, and came to understand why so many people might want to forget the past. The war was a prelude to World War II, and I was moved by the bravery and idealism of the men and women who joined the International Brigades to fight for democracy. *The Perfume Garden* is set mainly in Valencia, and charts the story of a family caught up in the war. At the heart of both the contemporary and wartime stories is an old house, surrounded by a garden holding secrets.

The Perfume Garden will be published by Corvus in June 2013.

Favourite Books

Light Years, James Salter
By Grand Central Station, Elizabeth Smart
The Republic of Love, Carol Shields
Brother of the More Famous Jack, Barbara Trapido
The Sheltering Sky, Paul Bowles
The Leopard, Giuseppe Lampedusa
Le Grand Meaulnes, Alain-Fournier
Bonjour Tristesse, Françoise Sagan
The Poetics of Space, Gaston Bachelard
The Little Prince, Antoine de St Exupéry

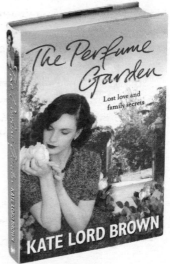